To Sara

- from one 'Poor Cow'
to another!

love
Adèle
24th April
1998.

ANOTHER POOR COW

Catherine Hall

MINERVA PRESS

LONDON

MONTREUX   LOS ANGELES   SYDNEY

ISBN 1 86106 731 3

First Published 1996 by
MINERVA PRESS
195 Knightsbridge
London SW7 1RE

2nd Impression 1997

Printed in Great Britain by
Antony Rowe Ltd, Chippenham, Wiltshire

ANOTHER POOR COW

For David, Maggie A and Maggie R
and a special thank you to John and Kath.

Part One

Anne sat in the back of the large, comfortable car; cushioned, windows up, doors shut, protected, cut off from the streets that passed her. She watched, expressionless, as she was propelled through the streets of Wimbledon, through all the mean and merging shop rows of South London.

It was 7 a.m., it was going to be a beautiful summer day, shops were opening, and people were standing at the bus stops, men in casual clothes, leaning against a post or shop façade, some with *The Sun* tucked under one arm. Snapshots of life, like a succession of still frames, were passing her; sometimes she let it all pass by, hardly taking it in. Other times she focused on a person, a building, and watched it until the car had passed by, seeing one, two or three seconds of some other life, and thinking, how can it all be so normal, how can it still be carrying on? The screaming in my head, the horror of this life, bubbling just below the surface, does no one else see it?

She looked at the people in the front of the car. The driver, a man, large, affable, with thick, greying hair, straight-faced as he glanced at the rear-view mirror, then back to the road. The front passenger, a woman, fair, young, deferred to the driver as he spoke, her face turning from the road ahead, watching him. She wore a police uniform.

"You'll feel better once you're home, seen your boyfriend and had a bath in your own house," he said, glancing over his shoulder at her.

"It seems so long ago since I was there, I can't imagine it'll still be the same," replied Anne, her voice level, controlled, but quieter than usual: lacking the animation that was so crucial to her nature, had these people, these strangers, known it.

'Surely this will change it all,' she thought as she started to recognise the streets around her. 'It hasn't hit me yet. I know that it has happened and that it is waiting, in some part of my brain, or perhaps totally externally to me, waiting, yes, waiting to become part of my life: to become my life. Is this what it will have taken to change things? For it will have changed everything totally and irrevocably.'

When they drew up at the large, grey house, set back from the road in what had probably been a nice area once, her heart started to pound. I am going to go back in there – the flat I left seven hours ago – it will look the same, he will look the same. If I just walk back in will it all fall from me? Will it not have happened? Be the same as before? How else can I go back into that flat, if not as the person I left it? She said none of this, she did not know these people. She felt nothing towards the woman, neither like nor dislike. Towards the man she felt a trust, which even now she could see objectively, realising it was incongruous. He stepped out of the car, after pulling in at the mouth of the driveway. She followed him, easing herself out of the back seat. He turned to look straight at her, pain across his features, "Just don't let that bastard ruin your life, remember that. Don't let him, then he hasn't won."

She felt his words, felt the raw nerve that made him say it. He knows. She felt her eyes fill up with gratitude. Earlier she'd thanked him for his understanding.

She could not say it again.

She turned away from him and walked stiffly towards the side door, where two bells down she pressed the button thinking, let him just come down, don't please, don't look out of the window first. They lived in a large, low-ceilinged, attic flat and, often, through habit, looked out of the window before coming down the three flights of stairs to the main door.

The sound of the window moving; he looked out as she looked up and she saw herself, the reflection of herself, in the expression in his eyes. She was covered from neck to toe in a white, stiff paper that had a zip from neck to groin, with sleeves and legs that were much too long and wide. The legs finished in enormous feet. He came rushing down the stairs, opened the door, face crumpling, "My God, you poor, poor thing." Anne looked him straight in the eye then walked past. "I'm okay." She preceded him up the stairs, conscious of him being directly behind her, of her ridiculous clothes, her awkward walk, her hair scraped back, eyes swollen. She passed straight through the open flat door and through the living room, not looking at anything. She wanted to take nothing in until she was in a fit state to look around her and be looked at.

In the bedroom, Neil hovered in the doorway as he watched – and tried not to watch – Anne as she practically ripped the garment from her. She felt stifled, being watched, and hesitated just before she stepped out of it. He was confused, not knowing whether to walk away or stay. The silence surrounded and separated them.

"That horrible thing," she burst out. "God, how could they put me in that, I look like the bloody Michelin man, as if I don't feel bad enough." She could feel the sob, rising hysteria in her voice – it was coming closer now, close but not quite with her yet. She grabbed the white material from the floor and rolled it into a ball, in a quick burst of temper, yet all the while feeling that she was doing these things, saying these words, as a part of a script. It was as if she felt compelled to do what she thought was expected of her.

"Throw it out, will you? Right out, in the outside bin, out of my sight."

His dark head was bent over, his normally furtive look now appeared guilty. He was verging on tears. He turned, grabbing the clothing, and walked from the room.

As soon as he went out Anne felt that she could breathe again. She looked around the bedroom, bed not slept in, dressing table with all her bottles and cotton wool on it, still as she had left it. She looked at the wardrobe and full-length mirror. She instinctively moved away from that, she did not want to see her reflected body in it: naked, open, wounded. All through the night as she was examined and as she showered, she had kept her face averted from her body. She didn't know how to see it, how to feel about it; she felt she had to come up with an attitude to it before she could let her eyes stray there. Her head and body were separate – she thought this all through as she stepped into a loose, green, summer cotton dress. I can look at my situation, the whole situation objectively, she thought. What is wrong with me? I'm watching myself and my actions as if I were someone else, like I'm thinking through some kind of cause and effect.

Neil came back, walking up to her at the dressing table. "Anne, Anne, I'm so sorry." She let her head rest on his chest and then guided him silently by the hand, back into the living room. She lifted a packet from the floor, took out and lit a cigarette. "Can I have a cup of coffee, please?"

Neil was in the process of sitting down, then abruptly made a jerky movement and walked, with apparent relief at knowing what he was doing, into the kitchen.

What do I say, she thought. Can I tell him it all, will he be able to take it? The horror, the blame. She didn't feel any of the resentment, rage and hurt she normally felt when he stayed out drinking half the night, forgetting her. No calling, just ignoring her. This time, this time it had happened: the worst fear, the worst that could happen. She'd gone looking for him, as she had done many times before, and got caught. Caught, she thought, drawing deeply on her cigarette, by the sewer vermin that daily, nightly, crawl around the streets, looking for women to rape.

As he walked back, she watched him, trying to work out whether she resented or pitied him. He'll change now, he'll have to, now I need him more than he needs me. Though even as she thought this, she questioned the certainty of it. He sat down in the seat opposite her.

"What time is it?"

"Half past seven," Neil replied quickly, then immediately said, "Tell me how it happened, but don't tell me it all, not all at once, I can't handle that."

She looked at him, level-eyed, expressionless. "You can't take it," she said slowly; then as she exhaled, putting out a cigarette and immediately lifting another to light, said resignedly, "No, I'm sorry, I know you can't."

She sat back in the chair and started, "You were supposed to come home at eleven thirty. You said, last orders for meals were ten, so the latest you'd leave was eleven. Well I was on edge, you don't know what it's like, waiting and waiting, watching every minute. Some shitty, sexist film was on and I'd run out of cigarettes. So at eleven minutes past twelve – I know exactly you see, I'd watched every minute for over an hour – I left the house. Isn't it strange; as I walked out the front door I was scared, you know the way the bulb has gone in the hall? I thought, what am I doing, but I went on. I just thought, at least if I'm walking I'm doing something, not just sitting and waiting."

Neil's head was in his hands, his fingers going backwards and forwards through his hair, "Don't, please don't," he pleaded.

"It's true," she answered, calmly, noting her control, amazed. Then she thought, none of it matters now because this is as low as I can possibly go. His drinking isn't the centre of my life any more, everything has stopped now, there's only what's happened, nothing else.

She carried on, "I walked down the road towards Miguel's, and when I came out from under the bridge I saw a man on the other side of the road. He saw me and that was it. His whole body became alert when he saw me and he started and stared at me, then I knew, I knew." She could hear her voice rising, she heard it as if she were listening to someone else. The wall, it's coming, coming towards me now. She stopped, looked at Neil opposite. He was still leaning forward but he'd raised his head and was staring at her, wide-eyed and horrified.

"Don't, don't go on; I can't listen."

"I won't tell you everything, but I need you to know how it happened. It happened to me and I will have to cope with it and I need you to know." Her voice, insistent and rising, had the beginnings of a bitter ring. She recognised it and stopped talking, then started again, more quietly, "He ran at me across the street." No, she thought, I'm losing it again, don't break, just say it, she told herself, don't let go, you can't afford to. But the cry in her voice was mounting, "He was coming straight for me. Then I held my arms out from my sides and dropped my bag on the ground. I thought, 'Oh God, I'm going to die, no, please, please, no.' He was coming for me and I saw him reach into his jacket and then I saw a flash of silver and I knew, I just knew, this is it..."

Her voice had risen; the last few words, punctuated by sobs, distorted her face. She lowered her head, covering the two halves of her face with both hands and felt the tears forcing their way out, painfully, slowly. Relief now, she thought. But almost immediately they stopped. There were no more tears to come. She looked up at Neil. He was struggling to keep the movement of his face under control. His eyes were glassy, brimming, but he couldn't cry either.

"He made me go into his flat, the dirty, disgusting bastard," Anne blurted out; she wanted to speed up, missing out the step by step and get to what he did to her. She was already feeling that this was a story she told: she'd told it to the police and the doctor during the night, sometimes starting at the point when she went into the flat, sometimes at the beginning when he ran for her. She wanted to get the worst parts said and finished, but found she couldn't bring herself to say it to him, as much as he couldn't bring himself to listen to her. She stopped again, stubbed out her cigarette and stood up.

"I'm going for a bath." She turned round as she reached the door, "My third one, actually, in about eight hours."

"Third?"

"Well yes, if you'd come home you'd have known. I had a bath at ten last night and put my dressing gown on, waiting up for you, watching this crap film and then do you know what? When he got me into the flat and he pushed me in before him, the first thing I saw was the television, because the screen was facing the door. Big surprise, the same thing was on the television in there as had been on in our flat. I saw some tart standing on a bar thrusting her hips out, in nothing but a suspender belt and stockings. And people wonder why it happens? It happens because perverts are given permission by what they see on the bloody box."

The venom was mounting in her. She felt hot and sore, her back ached where it was torn and bruised. It seemed to her that she had been taught a terrible lesson; the truth of which she had already known for years. She was vehemently anti-pornography, anti-sexism, anti-everything that showed women degraded, ridiculous, defined in men's terms. She had known and preached this to all her friends for so many years: now she felt angry and beaten that she had had it proved to her in such brutal, physical ways that she would never be able to forget.

*

In the bath, she told him how her back had ended up in this state. The four scratches around her neck needed no explanation.

"I jumped out of the window," she explained flatly. Her narrative seemed to swing constantly from what she described mentally as the 'dum-de-dum-de-dum' recitation: the flat, expressionless storytelling; and her bitter, acrimonious half-cry of accusation. In answer to Neil's prompts and questions, she went on.

"He was going to make me watch films. He was looking for a video recorder or a film, I don't know which. He had the scissors shoved into my neck, pushing me along beside him, naked. Then I saw the window, it was pulled up and open. Outside was the world, do you understand that? I saw the normal place I'd been in before and I just ran and leapt. Two or three paces and I was there. I pushed myself out head first but he caught me, first by the thighs, then he lost his grasp and he caught me by the knees."

Neil's face was contorting again. He was standing next to the sink, looking down on Anne, one hand passing over his face, again and again, pulling at the flesh of his face. Anne speeded up, her voice getting louder.

"Then he had me by the ankles and I was yelling, 'Help, help me!' I kicked to get away from him, to fall. I knew now that I could get away, he wasn't going to kill me. I didn't look down, I know that sounds funny, but that didn't matter. I could see stars, the sky, St John's church tower and houses and people at their windows in their bedrooms; I was getting away, that was enough. Can you imagine what that was like?"

Anne, knees drawn to her chest in the bath in a self-protecting pose, stared wide-eyed at Neil. He stood still, silent, eyes downcast.

"I feel like it is all my doing, I feel like it was me that's done this to you."

Again she felt torn in her feelings towards him: between pity and anger. How could he not see that this was totally separate from him, completely separate from their lives and their relationship?

Suddenly weary of it all, all explanation, she fell silent and stretched out in the bath, facing the ceiling. She saw his glance drop from her face to the top of her legs.

"I don't look any different there," she snapped, although she had kept her own eyes away from that place since she'd first found herself in front of the doctor, naked again.

"The pain is all in here." She tapped her temple with her forefinger.

*

As she was getting dressed again the doorbell rang. Two men were shown into the living room by Neil, who hung back apologetically then immediately escaped to the kitchen to make coffee after he introduced them.

"This is a police inspector from Croydon CID and his sergeant, come straight from that flat to see you," he announced.

As Anne walked over to them from where she stood in the doorway to the bedroom, it occurred to her for the first time that a whole drama would now be being played out at the flat where it had happened – she imagined tape across doorways, and men measuring distances with their paces – all in the safe light of day where they couldn't be touched.

She shook hands with both men, who introduced themselves, and allowed herself to be amused by their slightly shocked expressions at her offered hand.

"Pleased to meet you," she stated, catching sight of herself in the long, horizontal mirror that ran the length of the dining table behind them. Her features were composed and set; she barely recognised herself and became conscious of the lines and con tours of her face as she supposed she would have done a mask. Her face felt like it was an addition to herself, as if it were painted on top. Yet she was at her most natural, as she had been last night: no make up and her shoulder-length hair tied back in a band, straight off her face.

The older man spoke. He was sympathetic in his attitude, hesitant, looking down as he spoke. She supposed him to be about fifty. She wouldn't have thought him to be a policeman, though she couldn't have said why. "We'd like to go through the contents of this bag, which we believe to be yours, found in the bathroom of the flat," he said.

The other man, in his early thirties, watched Anne, his expression judgmental, his eyes shrewd, taking everything in. They sat down at the table and Anne went through each item, one by one, that he laid in front of her in rows on the table. Cheque book, purse, comb, hankies, keys, address book, and diary. It seemed to her that all these ordinary items had taken on a significance because of what had happened. She suspected that they would ask her why she had a cheque book with her when she was only planning a ten minute walk to where her boyfriend worked: but they asked nothing.

Neil came in with coffees and sat down after giving them out, away from them, on the sofa. The younger policeman, DS Small, switched his attentions from Anne and watched Neil's reactions intently to anything that was said. The other, who introduced himself again as DI Munro, as if knowing she had not retained their names, asked her how she felt about giving a statement that day.

"The details you remember now, which could be vital for the case, might slip your mind after another twenty-four hours."

"It'll all be with me for ever," Anne protested. "I certainly don't mind giving a statement today, but I will never forget any of it, I can tell you."

Neil started to protest, too loudly, that she should be let be for the day, but his words were broken by the ringing of the phone. It was Liz, the stalwart of Anne's life when things got bad with Neil. He answered the phone and half-covered the handset for a second to say, "It's Liz. She wants to speak to you."

Anne looked confused. Why was she ringing first thing in the morning? She knew from Neil's face that Liz knew. How, when? She couldn't speak to anyone. She shook her head at Neil, irritated.

He covered the mouthpiece again. "She wants to know if she can come over."

"How does she know?"

"I phoned her last night, when I got home," he answered, "before I knew from that policemen's call what had happened."

He sounds guilty, she thought, and he will do to these policemen too, they can hear it.

"Yes, tell her to come over; isn't she going to work?" She answered the question for herself, "No, I don't suppose she is." Turning back to the two men she said, "She can keep Neil company when I go to the station to give this statement."

She focused her attention as she realised DS Small was speaking, "Could you tell us how you ended up in the bathroom and what you saw and touched, Miss Elliot?"

Anne tensed at the question, conscious of the fact that they were about to enter a part of the 'story' that Neil had not yet heard. He visibly flinched, Anne saw from the corner of her eye. Small saw too; she saw it register on his face: He doesn't know what happened yet, he doesn't know.

Anne dragged heavily on her cigarette and, closing her eyes momentarily in pain, said, "He told me to go into the bathroom and steered me off left, when I first went in through the flat door. It was very small; the loo was to the left, the bath on the right, and the wash basin was in front of me. The basin was below a window that was open a bit, that looked over the train station." She paused and looked at them both.

Munro nodded, quickly, but encouragingly, Small prompted her, "Go on."

"He pushed me forward so I stopped at the basin. He stood behind me and kept saying, 'Don't turn round' and 'Don't look at me, and you'll be all right.' He also kept saying that it was someone else's flat," Anne added, remembering the incongruity of what he'd said. "He said he had to find something that was his. Then he went out of the bathroom, turning the light off as he went. He came back a few seconds later and turned the light on again. I hadn't moved, but I suppose I may have touched the rim of the sink to steady myself. Yes, actually I'm sure I did."

Anne paused to steady her hand that, shakily, had just put out a cigarette and immediately lit another, offering the men one. Small took one, Munro shook his head, then carried on with the spidery notes he'd been making as she spoke.

"Carry on if you can, Miss Elliot."

"It's Anne, please."

He nodded his acknowledgement of what she said.

"When he came back in, he put cigarette papers in a pack and what looked like a piece of dope in clingfilmy stuff on the window ledge in front of me. He said, 'Roll one up.'"

Anne paused, dragged on the cigarette and looked at the men across the table from her, weighing it up, wondering if she would lose sympathy with them when she told them that she tried to roll it and knew how to roll one because she'd seen it done scores of times. They'd read her mind.

"So you rolled it then, yes? You didn't have much choice, did you?" His tone was kind. He wasn't against her, she knew that much.

"I tried. I know how to, from years back," she assured them, slightly defensively, "only I couldn't do it, because I couldn't keep my hands steady. I've only done it a couple of times, ages ago, anyway."

"That's all right, we aren't going to have a go at you for knowing how to roll a joint. Most people have come across it at some time, and set against this kind of offence it, well, it rather pales into insignificance." Small had leaned over the table, towards her, as he spoke. He smiled.

"So when you weren't able to roll the joint, what did he do then?" Munro pushed on.

"Um, he went out of the room and turned the light off again, I think." Anne's voice was rising, getting higher and louder; her face was still expressionless and felt heavy, as if it were cast in clay.

"Then he came back in, and you know he'd said so much when he first caught me and then when he'd forced me across the road, and up the steps to that stinking flat that I almost believed him. Over and over again he kept saying, 'They're after me, they're all after me, the police and all the rest of them. I need you to do something for me', and 'You won't get hurt as long as you do what I say and don't look at me.' Over and over he'd said that it was someone else's flat and they had something that belonged to him, and then," Anne had been speeding up through this whole speech until this point, when, elbows on the table, she lowered her head to her hands and stopped. "Then he came up behind me and said, 'Take your clothes off,' just like that, really slowly and deliberately." She said the words in a drawn out monotone, hearing them echo in her head. "Then I knew that the tiny, tiny part of me that was starting to believe him had been fooled."

She scraped her chair backwards and, not looking towards Neil, who she knew had been stock-still for minutes, made for the bedroom.

"Excuse me," she managed to get out.

In the bedroom, she went to the dressing table and stood in front of it, her hands covering the lower part of her face; she stared at her own watchful face, as her breathing gradually came back to normal. She heard them next door; Small was talking.

"So you work late then, do you?" His voice was slightly hostile, certainly not the way he'd spoken to her, she knew. She imagined Neil's paranoia increasing, his expression becoming blacker.

"Does she often come to meet you?"

Anne came back into the room where the men waited expectantly for Neil's response. He looked cornered.

"No, not often, but I was late, so..." he trailed off, defensive, untrusting.

"Still, you didn't get home until nearly three, did you?" interrupted Munro.

"Detective Inspector Davies was with your girlfriend last night at the Wimbledon Centre and didn't get an answer when he phoned until then. Anne told him you finished at eleven."

"Yeah, okay, I stopped on last night. I thought she'd be in bed when I got home. I just had a few drinks with the guys who work there."

"Just guys, Turner?" demanded Small.

Anne, sitting down again at the table, looked from one to the other, saying nothing. She knew Neil was suffering and being shown up, and she also knew that she was acting well in these police officers' eyes. This feeling of 'acting well' that had been with her all morning had started last night in the police station. She had been taken in, in the nightgown passed to her by a neighbour. She'd then started to cry in great gasping sobs when a young, uniformed policewoman said all the perfunctory things, "It's all over now", and "It's okay, you're safe now." She'd let go then, crying hard and making broken, disjointed statements. "He made me suck that thing." "He said, 'Take your clothes off' like that, just like that. I knew this was going to happen", she'd cried, the whole consciousness of being a woman and the probability of being 'caught' rising up before her, so that now it seemed like a foregone conclusion. The policewoman became guarded now and suspicious. Anne could practically hear the cogs of her mind turn round. Anne sensed her shifting attitude, thinking the 'victim' wouldn't notice, "What do you mean you 'knew it was going to happen'?" Anne had known she was going to say that. She rejoined quickly, aiming to kill all suspicion immediately, "Not what you're thinking. I mean what every woman risks each time she walks down the road. I've always known it would happen, that's how it feels now." She looked at the woman, hating her for her patronising attitude and lack of trust in her.

The policewoman left the room shortly afterwards, after a few more mundane and ineffectual comments. The great breaths of sobs changed almost immediately after the door was shut behind the woman. Her unrestricted surge of emotion subsided as she let herself realise and take in the knowledge that she was somewhere safe. The tears stopped in her relief. She stopped crying totally as she looked round the yellow, thickly plastered walls. She thought that there was nothing to cry about any more while thinking that if they had a camera in this room they would think that she'd been putting on the tears, so complete was their cessation. Then the same words kept going through her mind: 'It's happened but it's stopped happening now, it's over,' as a dead calm filled her whole body. It felt as if the thought, which had started demanding to be heard in her mind, was ebbing down through her body and along her limbs until the calm reached her fingertips and feet. Then she sat immobile, conscious only that she had to be careful: she'd met three police officers now and none of them had given her any cause to think that they believed her. She told herself that she must act well and be logical and make them see what happened, mustn't alienate them. Her evolving thought processes were interrupted by the door opening abruptly and the large form of a middle-aged, greying policeman entered the room. He rushed straight towards her, looked intently into her eyes for a moment, and slamming his fist down on the table in front of her, shouted out, "The bastard, the fucking bastard. We've got him now and he won't get out again, don't worry about that. Tell me, did he come?" The first person to trust her: the importance of that immeasurable.

The doorbell rang shrilly and, as Anne looked to Neil, the telephone rang also. She knew she was going to have to 'react' again to the person at the door, probably Liz, and perhaps to the person at the other end of the phone. Who was that going to be? Oh God, she thought, it's like all of life is on hold because someone's died and I'm going to have to carry on bearing up and acting well. Small pushed back his chair after a moment's hesitation.

"I'll get the door," he said. "You get the phone," he looked at Neil.

Neil sprang up immediately to answer the phone, thankfully stopping the urgent ringing. Anne remained staring in front of her.

"Stella, hello, she's here now, yes."

Anne again thought, how do people know? It's only morning, the next day. Already her sister in Chester knew. Neil struggled to speak naturally to Stella, looking over enquiringly, pleadingly at Anne.

"No, no way. I can't speak to anyone. Tell her I'm all right, just tell her what's happened, will you?"

She felt annoyed that he was trying to draw her into conversation with others. I've got to find out what my own reaction to this is first, she thought, before I start presenting it to other people, even Stella. She loved her and was close to her, but it seemed impossible to speak to her now, as if they spoke different languages or as if there was solid glass, impenetrable, separating them.

As Neil carried on talking, self-consciously turning his back on Anne and Munro, saying, "Yes, about seven this morning... some bruising, oh God, Stella, she jumped out the window, I don't know any more," the door opened again. A tall woman in a serge suit, with well-cut, short red hair, shiny and straight, walked into the room, followed by Small.

"This is Woman Detective Constable Rook, Anne," Small announced.

Anne, feeling herself to be hovering some few feet above her own head, removed, disconnected, objective in some strange, calm way, watching these strangers come into her flat, her life, thought, yes, I can see she's a woman. That, unlike everything else, does not need explaining.

DC Rook came forward; her voice, softly Scottish and deep, was kind and melodic. "Anne, whenever you are ready I would like to sit down with you and you to tell me everything, step by step, all that you can remember. I know it's going to be difficult and you're tired, but if you could do it today it would really help us a lot. We've got him, he's not going to get off, but we really need all the help you can give us to make sure that he's put away for a long time."

"Where is he?" Anne asked, "Is he at Croydon Police Station?" "No, don't worry, we didn't take him there. We wouldn't have taken him to the same place as you last night. He's at Brixton and that's where he'll stay."

Anne felt her mind racing. Until last night she knew nothing of the existence of this person. Now, though she didn't even know his name, his presence, his whereabouts were totally enmeshed with her own existence.

"What's his name?" Again the direct, blunt questions, again the expressionless face.

Small replied, "What do you want to know that for? He's scum and you want to forget him now."

"Well I won't be able to even if I tried, will I? What does he do?" She paused. "What's his job?"

Small, looking over to DC Rook, sat down again, opposite Anne. "You'll know it soon enough. That isn't important now, forget it."

Suddenly the image of the crucifix shot into her mind; it jumped, gold glowing, before her eyes, as she saw it resting on a hairy chest, shirt open, as she sat between his legs on the floor, gagging, and crying, "Please don't, let me go, please." The bile rose again from her stomach upwards, towards her throat. The wall was in front of her, she was rushing towards it.

"He was wearing a crucifix, he made me do those things to him when he was wearing a crucifix. God, I've always hated those." She shuddered, and Rook, leaning towards her, said quietly, "That's a part of all the details I need to know. First off, can you tell me what clothes you were wearing and where your clothes were left in the flat, and do you remember what he was wearing?"

Anne described her peach T-shirt, sleeveless, loose jeans and sandals. "I wasn't wearing a bra, I suppose that will go against me," she proclaimed, only half in sarcasm. DC Rook retorted that details like that, when walking down the road in the pitch dark, wouldn't come into it. Anne thought back to the rapist. She saw a shirt, plain, breast pockets, a light colour. She knew there were breast pockets because when he told her, as they were just beyond the steps of the station car park, to take the keys out of his pocket, she had gone first to the pocket facing her: his shirt pocket, at eye level. "No, the trouser pocket," he had snapped. "No, other side," when she, thinking she was going to feel his erect prick, had gone first into the right-hand side, then the left.

"We'll leave you now and I'll come back later and then you can come to the station with me, if you feel up to it."

Anne, wanting suddenly to tell the whole story to someone, wanting to give it a start, middle and end, to contain it somehow, making it in some way manageable, palatable, said she'd be okay to give the statement in the afternoon. Rook looked relieved, Anne thought, proud of her in some way. She sensed an ally in this woman; she was proud and strong and she believed her – that much she knew. She had said nothing of believing her, yet it was like the premise from which she started: it didn't need to be said, it was fact.

Anne showed them all out. Neil remained in the room. Once again, she felt the buzz of pleasure and pride at being able to be polite, shake hands, say the right thing – somehow surprised at even being able to walk properly, upright, one foot in front of the other, after what she had been through. Then she saw it reflected in their faces: mild, watching surprise at the way she was acting, the way she was able to carry on looking normal and calm, so calm.

*

When Liz arrived later in the morning, tear-stained, unable to go to work, Anne was able to be open, unguardedly, for the first time. Liz, shocked firstly by the normality of Anne's appearance – in a loose green dress, hair tied back, a little eye make-up on now, looking pretty, groomed, was then shocked for a second time by the expressionless mask that Anne's mobile and animated features had become.

Neil went out, his "I'm going out" was always a euphemism for going to the pub or, sometimes, going to buy cans of lager. It was as if he could no longer openly admit what he was doing. His alcoholism, known to everyone around them, made it not necessary to say where he was going anyway, because there was only one place to go and everyone knew it.

The last attempt to stop drinking had fallen through last night, after five days of not touching it. Each of these fights to stop raised Anne's spirits to a height where all was possible and happiness lay before them. Each time it failed (how many times now? five, ten, she didn't know) another piece of her optimism and trust in life died, the hard core at her very centre strengthened, became more bitter.

This latest failure had paled now so that it barely mattered, so eclipsed was it by the nightmare that Anne had been through that it hadn't seemed important enough for either Anne or Neil to mention it that morning, except obliquely. Yet somewhere inside, she had not believed that he would "go out" that lunchtime, though she knew that once he started it had to carry on.

Liz had only just arrived when Neil disappeared into the bedroom and returned, shoes on, and sheepishly announced that he was going out. Anne saw it all, the passing over of the responsibility to Liz, because of course she couldn't be left on her own, not after what she'd been through. His sigh of relief must be great, she thought, now that he could put her in someone else's hands.

"How could you? I don't believe it, you're going out?"

Liz went to the bathroom, embarrassed that she had come to see her friend who had been raped, and yet the focus of the situation was changing to become the same old pattern of Neil's drinking.

"Anne, when something like this happens you don't all of a sudden become stronger than you were before, you know. Don't you understand that if I needed a drink before I need it twice as much now? It's my prop for Christ's sake; I need it!"

The bitterness inside her welled up, and she leaned forward, her legs parting, her clasped hands between them as she hissed at him, her voice still controlled, echoing in her mind as if it were someone else's, "Where's my prop then, where's mine? I don't have that! Well lucky you, you just lose yourself in drink and all I've got is you!"

His face crumpled and she relented. She stood up and went towards him, placing her hand on his arm and, thinking how little they had touched that morning, said, "I know you don't want to be like this, but now, now it's got to change, because I won't be strong enough to take it any more. Now I will need you." She emphasised the last words and he nodded like a child, listening, understanding, accepting it and taking it in. She thought for the hundredth time that he was too soft for the world, too weak; where would it end?

With Liz she could say it all. When Neil went out it became calm all around them, unsaid at the moment, but able to be said, open, secure. Anne had seen Liz two days before, they had drunk together on the Sunday night; all evening, Liz, Steve and Anne in the pub across the railway track from their flat. The same railway track that two miles down the line, in the flat that overlooked the station, Anne had been removed from the logic of life, its time, place and meaning.

"Isn't it strange Liz, of all the people you know, who is the most hung up about rape, about what women come across in everyday life, all the filth, the sexism? Who Liz, who has now been taught the biggest lesson ever, eh?"

She tried to adopt a cynical smile, but it wouldn't come. "I've been taught it good and proper, haven't I? Lesson number one: don't try to beat the bastards, because they'll come at you with knives, scissors and pricks to show you that they can make you do whatever they want you to. It didn't matter last night that I'm outspoken and stand up for myself, did it?"

She recounted what had happened when the man came for her: arms out from her sides, her bag falling to the ground. Again she started to cry, but again, as the feeling of release that the tears brought started, they immediately stopped. The wall was still there, but she wasn't going to crash into it yet.

Liz had driven past the walkway under the bridge when she came to the flat. She hadn't been sure about where it had happened from Neil's call at four in the morning. He'd been drunk, muddled and upset, having only just put the phone down on the CID policeman, Davies. Then when she'd come up to the bridge she'd seen the luminous tape mapping out the pavement on both sides. It was still in the heat of the morning as it wound up the steep metal steps towards the train station. Then she'd known: it was here.

As she told Anne this, her soft, brown eyes filled, brimming over almost immediately. Anne wanted to tell her, to unburden it all. She wanted to spell out what happened, so that having said it once it would then become a thing separate from herself, not just in her and in her mind, but external as well, with an identity of its own. She couldn't explain the 'story' of what happened, starting at the beginning and carrying on through the horror as it happened, she didn't want it to have the build-up of a drama.

"He made me open the flat door; I went up flights of stairs, until the top. There was light under one door and I didn't know which one he wanted me to go through. It was weird – I didn't think of screaming, the scissors were in my neck and I was going where I didn't want to go, obediently. It all happened in the bathroom; dirty, disgusting place, I swear I'll never see them properly again. He'd been ranting on and on about people wanting to get him, and this being someone else's flat where he was going to get something that belonged to him, all this shit, like he was on some TV programme. Isn't it funny, I knew that, even though I thought I was going to die, I could hear it all sounding hollow and melodramatic? Then he tried to get me to roll a joint. I was gasping for a cigarette; all my senses were alert, and, from the bathroom where he'd made me go, I could see the station entrance, dark and empty. I had this idea that someone would come out of it and I could shout to them. Then he came back in and he said, 'Take your clothes off.'" Anne's voice started to crack. Liz's hand had risen instinctively to cover her mouth, her eyes wide and brimming with tears. Anne wondered could Liz bear to hear it? Could she even get the words out to tell her?

They'd been friends for two years, since Anne had moved from Manchester to South London. They'd worked together in an insurance company; a job Anne had taken simply because it was the first she'd been offered. They'd become close, confiding friends within weeks. Theirs had been a relationship where lovers and sex had been discussed openly. There was no reserve between them, they could say anything to each other, yet now, in these circumstances, the words they'd used before seemed almost taboo to Anne.

"He told me to play with his dick and he was sitting on the toilet. Oh Christ, Liz, how can I tell you? But I want to." She realised that Liz was holding her hand tightly. I must keep in control, I must, she chanted in her head. I can't let go, tell her, say it. "Then he made me suck it." Liz let out a squeal, a gasp that once more made her clamp her hand over her mouth. Anne's free hand was clutching the front of her neck, pulling the skin. "I just kept saying, 'Please just don't kill me, please, please, don't.' I saw this cross around his neck, I couldn't believe it. And his thing, it was so big, God, it was horrible. But I did it, I couldn't do anything else, but do it. You won't believe this, but I was thinking, you don't have to do this, surely you can get it without forcing someone. And all the time those scissors stuck into my neck, scratching." She was crying now, sitting upright on the settee, talking through the tears flowing unchecked down her cheeks. She looked at Liz's face, the expression of horror and shock had gone now, replaced by sorrow, her face soaked too. Anne's voice rose and fell as the tears obstructed and distorted her speech and she fought to overcome them. Through the tears she carried on.

"Then he made me stand up and face the sink. He told me to put it in. Christ, you can't do that to yourself, I tried and tried and I wailed and pleaded and all he said was, 'Over the bath,' and then he shoved it in. I kept thinking he's doing it, he's raping me and it can't be giving him any pleasure because I'm standing here, shaking, my leg was shaking, really quickly and I couldn't stop it. Oh shit, Liz, I was just standing there. I could hardly even feel it, it was really weird, but my head and my body seemed totally separate from each other. What he was doing to me was behind me, you know, and it felt like it was a long way away and I felt like I was hovering somewhere above myself."

Anne stopped, unsure whether she was making any sense now. She passed her hands over her face, wiping the wetness away. "He didn't come and obviously needed more, the dirty, fucking rat." Liz lit a cigarette for Anne and one for herself, silent, concentrating on what she was doing. "He said, 'Okay, now it's time for films, the worst kind of propaganda I know, but it has to be done.' Again it sounded like something from a bad film, and that word 'propaganda' didn't seem to make any sense. I thought maybe he meant pornography and had said the wrong word, and then I thought about how much I overuse that word myself, and the way he said it was all chirpy like he was talking about having to go and do the dishes or something. Then I was also thinking, what the fuck is next? My mind was going mad. Did he mean take a film of me or make me watch films; what was I in for? He led me out of the bathroom, I saw then that it was scissors that he had, because up to then I'd presumed it was a knife, but it was those pointy, hairdressing scissors. He walked me across the room. It was covered in litter, clothes, Kentucky Fried Chicken boxes and God knows what else; I don't know how I noticed all this, but I did, and he was searching like this." Anne made a sweeping movement with her head, slowly scanning the floor around them, from right to left. Her eyes were wide, she felt totally caught up in what she was saying. Then she saw that Liz was sobbing, her face contorted, her head shaking. "Come on Liz," Anne commanded, fired by what she was about to say, by the fact that she was here and able to say it. Wanting to buoy her friend up, she again put on her cynical, joker voice, "I'm just getting to the good bit. I got away, didn't I?" Liz smiled through her tears; for an instant they had reverted to the normality of rallying banter that made up so much of Anne's conversation. She told her how she'd seen the window and freedom and how she had not feared the fall. The fall that could've killed or paralysed her, she was just beginning to realise. Twelve feet, Munro had told her that morning, a twelve foot drop, to land on someone else's roof. From the other window it would've been a three-storey drop. For ever after, when she heard people flippantly exclaim about 'jumping out the window' and when she heard about fatal falling accidents on the news, sometimes a few feet more or less than twelve, she would shudder, recalling the total, consuming fear and hysteria that had made her, without hesitation, leap out of a window, not considering for even a split second what was on the other side, because anything – life or death – was better than what she was going through and what may have been to come.

*

Neil came back in the mid-afternoon, subdued and sluggish. Surprisingly to Anne, though it mattered so much less than it normally did, he was not drunk. She could tell by the opening and closing of the flat door and the sound of his foot on the stairs, whether he was drunk or not.

He sat down in the chair opposite Liz and Anne, looking as though he felt he were an outsider. Anne sighed inwardly; two pints she reckoned, three at the most. If this didn't stop him, what would?

The conversation between them was awkward at first, the situation false. The day already seemed interminably long, though it was only half past two. Time had lost all sense for Anne, she was in the closed, separate world that disaster or death dictates. Bed, sleep or food seemed alien concepts to her. She couldn't imagine ever being relaxed enough for sleep and couldn't imagine ever being able to swallow and keep down food again. Her mind and her body still seemed to be two separate, independent entities.

DC Rook came back. When the bell rang, all three of them acknowledged it with relief. The shame of Neil's drinking, now an uncommented on criticism, and the fact that Liz now knew what had happened and Neil didn't, added to the strain and strangeness of the situation. The rape was too awful, Anne felt, to be discussed with more than one person at a time – too horrifying and too personal to become a discussion. If not talking about that though, what else was there to say?

With the policewoman came a photographer, whose appearance baffled Anne to begin with. She stood up as Neil showed them into the room, the man following DC Rook with a camera case over his shoulder and tripod in his hands. Rook introduced them, saying he needed to take shots of Anne's back to show the scratches from the wall and the incisions from the scissors round her neck. These were small and would probably fade the next day, she said. As she mentioned her neck, Anne's hand involuntarily clutched her throat, feeling the fear welling up again. Liz left then, sensing that the four people with Anne were too many and too diverse, making different demands on her frayed nerves.

The photographer was in his forties, businesslike and seemingly unaware of the reason why he was taking the photographs. As Anne got undressed and wrapped a towel around her body as instructed, she again averted her eyes from the cheval mirror that stood next to her in the bedroom. She wondered about the police photographer's job – she, with her superficial cuts and bruises, must be one of the most petty subjects he'd taken. She hoped this wasn't going to be a large part of the evidence as, other than the scissor marks around her neck, the other marks were those she'd made herself in trying to get away. God, if only they were all the marks on her, the only changes, she thought as she caught sight of her reflected face in the mirror; I'm not the same person and I will never be as I was again.

She stood on a chair as, being only five foot two, she was too small to be shot with the camera secured to the tripod. She faced the wall, as he told her, dropping the back of the towel down over her shoulder blades. He asked her if the ripped skin was sore, she answered with a disinterested, "No." She sensed his lack of empathy or interest in her. She would not see him again; he was here for a particular function and that was all. She remained silent.

He left as soon as he'd taken pictures of her legs, back and head from all angles. DC Rook looked at her enquiringly, "Tired yet?"

"No, not at all, actually. Sorry, I wasn't very communicative there, was I?"

"Well no, but it's hardly surprising as he's not exactly the most interesting person in the world, now is he?" She'd spoken with a completely straight face and then flashed a brilliant white smile that made her face alight and kind. Anne wondered what age she was; she looked younger when her face broke into the smile. Early thirties, she supposed. Yes, thought Anne, this is the kind of person I need, it's almost too much luck but we seem to speak the same language. She can help, please let her be able to help.

"What's your first name?"

"Jackie, Jack, whatever you like. Are you fit to come down to the station, do you think? Oh yes, and we'll have to take your fingerprints as well, only so that we can sort out which are yours in the flat. Okay?"

Anne nodded. Yes, she felt that the responsibility was going to be taken out of her hands and all she would have to do was what she was told to do. Thank God, she thought, to have someone else take control, and sort it all out, yes that was what she needed.

They left Neil, and Anne felt the usual panic she always felt when she left him. What would he do while she was away? Would he be there when she got back? Would he disappear for a day or two? As Jackie Rook and Anne made to leave the flat, Anne said, "Wait just a second, sorry," and ran back up the short flight of stairs from the front door and back into the living room. Neil, still sitting, turned round to face her quickly, guiltily.

"If you're going to do it, please stay in and drink, will you? I don't know how long I'll be, but I can't bear to come back to an empty flat. You know that, don't you?"

"Christ, Anne, I wouldn't do that to you." His expression was one of hurt.

She nodded, as if reassured. "Yes, I know you wouldn't. I'm sorry." But she didn't, she just hoped.

As the two women walked across the driveway towards the car, Anne registered, for the first time since the drive that morning, that life was going on all around her as normal. There were eight flats in their house in Cadogan Road, and in seven of them life would be a continuation of the pattern of yesterday and last week. Only in hers had that pattern, that ongoing life, been hacked, hacked to pieces.

As Jackie pulled away from the kerb and they moved down the road, Anne realised that they would pass underneath the bridge on the way to the station, passing the station steps. The way to anywhere at all is going to be past that place, she thought. Unable to stop herself, she had a brief glance upward as they passed the bottom of the steps; the tape had been removed now, it was all back to normal. She glimpsed the bathroom window, at a right angle to the road, where she'd stared intently at the station below for any sign of life.

"I've got to move away from here."

"Because it's so close to where it happened?"

"Yes, I mean you just can't go anywhere from our flat without passing here, can you? It's only five minutes' walk down the road."

"Oh yes, I know what you're saying, but don't do anything rash. It's only the day after and you've had no sleep. Give yourself plenty of time before you make any decisions about what you want to do. You'll probably find that you go through lots of different feelings about everything in the next few weeks."

Anne nodded and leaned back in the seat, closing her eyes, head spinning. As they passed the end of the road where the bank was she thought about work for the first time. In there, they would all be thankfully coming up to the end of the day. Looking at their watches or thinking about what they were doing that evening or worrying about some petty drama that had taken place that day – some assumed slight in a long list of the actions that formed the ongoing, shifting office politics. She looked out of the car window; and if they think of me, what do they imagine? It's Tuesday, the second day of my holiday, they'll be thinking, lucky thing, it's good weather. The holiday hadn't promised to be much in the first place, as Neil's drinking and his quick succession of jobs had made it impossible to go away anywhere. She had, with resentment, resigned herself to a week off at home. She now thought how moody she had been a few weeks ago, when she'd finally admitted the impossibility of them going away anywhere. My God, if only I'd cancelled the holiday, I wouldn't have gone out after twelve at night if I'd known that I'd have to get up for work the next morning. It suddenly hit her how totally circumstantial the whole situation was. It was all down to chance and timing. One 'if', one 'but' different, and the future of her whole life would be changed, because from now on, no matter how well she coped or how much she refused to let this unknown person ruin her life, she would always be a woman who'd been raped.

*

In total, she was in the police station for six hours. She came home worn out, yet her eyes were alert, taking everything in, her mind still active. Like the buzz after exercising, she thought, it's the same in a way – you don't want to do it in the first place but, once done, you feel you've achieved something. Another hurdle that she'd overcome, another test she'd passed and still she had not allowed herself to smash into the brick wall. Going step by step through the whole ordeal, being taken back over it, "I need more detail here," Jackie had pushed, "You've got to say exactly how you took your clothes off, at what point you stopped, did you say anything then, where was he standing in relation to you when he pulled down your pants. I need every second, every movement, you can do it. Come on." At times, she felt she couldn't carry on saying it, she felt worn out by it all, how strange that every movement of hers should suddenly become so important.

The kind of person she was, was becoming all important; she could see that by the way the police treated her. They were counting on her to be the person they needed, in fact, the person they needed it to have happened to in order to get this man. Anne could see, with cynical accuracy, the truth of this. Sitting in the CID room – not much light, everything around them slightly shabby, like an old school room – she asked Jackie, "Are you glad that I'm not the girl who works in the fish and chip shop, the one who maybe couldn't express herself and maybe just wanted to put her head under the pillow and forget it?"

"Of course I am, Anne. God, I'd be lying if I said anything else. You're smart, you can express yourself properly and you've got a mind for detail; what more could I want?" she ended, holding her hands out, palms upward, a smile crossing her face.

"Seriously though, it's true, we take him to court, we prosecute and perhaps if you couldn't give evidence we might have enough to put him away, but it's doubtful. We need you, you to stand up, you to convince the jury. It's a shit system I know, but all we can do is work within it and stop that bastard from ever doing it again."

"What's he done before? The same, worse?"

"I can't tell you the details. I'm not even sure how much of it would be good for you to know. But he's done it before, the same virtually, with a similar outcome." She paused. "At least once, possibly up to four times now, the other three are incidents that happened close to where you, and he, live. We suspected him, but we had nothing to go on really, no forensic, same old story."

"You've got that this time, haven't you?"

"Oh this is different, totally different, we've got him now. For God's sake, he walked out of the house, you were on the roof next door, what more do we need?"

"Okay, that's as far as I got, wasn't it? Shall I carry on?"

Jackie nodded, already writing again.

"I didn't think about where I was going to fall to until I got free from his grip round my ankles or that there wasn't anything to hold on to. I know that sounds stupid but it's true. When I'd kicked him off and I felt his hands slipping, I just thought, yes, I'm getting away. Anyway, I'd got this idea as I dropped that I could hold on to the drainpipe. I don't know why this seemed sensible, but anyway that's what I tried to do." She stopped, remembering his shout of, "Stop, you stupid bitch, you'll kill yourself."

Dragging heavily on a cigarette as she thought this, she committed it to memory, she wouldn't say it. Maybe someone else in the street, at their open bedroom windows, heard it; she'd agree to it if they did, but she wasn't going to offer it herself. It might sound as if he were concerned. No, I'll leave that out. She had thought of leaving something out earlier, had hesitated when, in the midst of detailing the actual violation between her legs, she'd started to cry. She was saying all the details, not as she'd told it to Liz earlier, but minutely. Saying, "Then he pushed it into me," then correcting herself, "I'm sorry, into my vagina."

"How did you know what he'd put into you, Anne?"

She looked up, uncomprehending.

"How do you know exactly what he shoved into you if you couldn't see it?"

"Oh God, you know," she burst out. "I know what it was. It was big, and I, I don't know what you want me to say."

"What I'm asking is, was there any way you knew exactly what it was? For instance, how do you know that it wasn't his hand or a bottle? I'm just asking you this now because in six or eight months time when the trial comes around you'll need the details."

Anne nodded wearily, but vehemently, understanding, her hands dragging back through her hair which was rumpled now, tucked behind one ear.

"Yes, yes, I see. I could feel him, feel his pelvis and the tops of his legs hitting against my backside, you know pushing, backwards and forwards," she continued.

Jackie said nothing, not looking up from where she was writing. "That's it, that's what I need." Jackie wrote furiously.

During the interview, Anne had hesitated over recounting what had happened and thought of leaving out some of the insults he came out with, but in the end she'd said it all. Jackie fired her up, made her feel she was doing better and better, each time she said the next grotesque sentence.

"The next thing was I'd hit the roof of the next house. I don't know what I thought really. I hadn't known it was there but it didn't come as a surprise. I suppose I didn't pay much attention to where I'd landed. I just remember standing up and shouting the same things over and over, "He's going to kill me, help, he's raped me, help!" I just kept yelling and yelling those things and I was crying and thinking, get them all out, out of their bedrooms and doorways and out on to the street. The more people who look and see, I thought, the more I know I'll live. I saw the church spire then too, you know, St John's that's next to that street and I thought, I want to climb up there, right to the top, as close to the sky as I can get and as far away as I can from the earth, the street, the houses, the surface of this horrible, stinking world.

"Then he yelled out at me again. I looked up to the window I'd jumped from and he was leaning out, shouting, 'You stupid, stupid bitch, what did you do that for? You're mad.' His voice was controlled, you know the way I'd told you when he was saying, 'They're all after me,' and 'This guy's got something of mine and I've got to get it back'? It all sounded like it was false, like some drama on television; well that's the same voice he said it in. When I saw him I realised how close I was to him still and thought that he might jump down too. So then I went right to the edge of the roof and there were people on the street now too, I don't know, maybe fifteen or twenty of them. I walked over to the edge and sat down with my hands clasped around my knees. Then my shouts weren't to attract attention so much but because I could feel myself becoming hysterical, letting go. I couldn't stop myself crying. Someone shouted up, "It's all right, we've phoned the police, they're on their way." Someone else said that they had too, an oldish man, sixty or so, I suppose. There was a woman there too. She was about thirty, dark hair, quite plump. She was good, she was the one that kept talking to me; she said, 'It's okay, you'll be all right now, he can't touch you now.' She kept saying things like that to me, and then someone appeared at the window below me. I yelled, I nearly jumped out of my skin because I didn't know who it was; I thought it was him for a second. But it was a man with a woman's dressing gown and he passed it to me. It was only when I was putting it on and had to half-stand up to do it that I felt embarrassed, conscious of the fact that I had nothing on. On the scale of things that hadn't mattered at all up until then. I hadn't even thought of it."

Anne stopped, unsure of whether she was saying it too fast or not saying it exactly as Jackie wanted to hear it, but Jackie only glanced up, still writing, so she carried on.

"Then I heard a door bang and I saw him walk out of the house; well I saw someone, a man, walk out of the house, on to the street where all the people were. He was walking slowly, in a measured way. I knew it must be him, it couldn't be anyone else. I looked down at the people. There were two men, youngish, I'm not sure what age, at the edge of the group, nearest where he was walking by. I shouted to them, 'That's him, please, please get him, stop him.' The bastard just carried on walking, slowly, looking over his shoulder every couple of paces, calm as you like. I was practically pleading with these men now, 'Catch him, stop him, please.' Then he turned round and shouted at me, 'Fuck off, you stupid cow,' or 'bitch', I can't remember which. I saw one of the guys move to go after him, then he hesitated and looked back up to me. You know what's strange though is that through all this no one had actually spoken to me, except that one woman, and the old man at the beginning. Then, after a second or two's hesitation, the man started to run after him, and, after a look again over his shoulder, he broke into a run as well. He just bolted as soon as he knew someone else was moving, and disappeared.

"The police pulled up then, and by the time I looked from the police van back to the direction of the station, where he'd run, the young guy was walking back, alone. I yelled to the police that he'd just run away. They looked up at me and do you know what one of them said? 'Calm down, miss. Calm down.'

"I couldn't believe that. They were all down there talking and no one was listening to me. To tell the truth here, Jackie, I made the decision then to be very careful with the police. I know what they can be like and I knew that if I alienated them at the start I'd have a fight on my hands. The police I met all last night – until the big Welshman, Davies – were all stupid. You know, they just assumed what had gone on, they made instant assumptions, based on their preconceptions, and didn't look at what was in front of them, at what was actually going on." Anne leaned forward in her chair, her left hand once again wrapped around her neck, pulling at the skin. Her eyes were wide, her face intense, lit up in a strange way through the tiredness.

Jackie nodded. "I know, the ones last night weren't any good for you at all. They were young and totally inexperienced; it's one of the problems we're trying to get over. They're normally the first to arrive and they can muck it up completely by the time we get on the scene. Just carry on from there. So, after they said that did they say anything else to you?"

"No, it just all got confusing then. I felt completely out of it, I was completely out of it, I was what, thirty or forty feet up in the air? Anyway, two men then came over to the police. I was just sitting holding myself around the knees then, perched like a bloody bird on the edge, trying to keep a head on my shoulders. Then it seemed like everyone below started arguing, or disagreeing, at any rate. I didn't say another word, like I've said, I knew I'd have to be careful and I wasn't quite sure what was going on. So I just sat there and waited. Now I realise that it must've been him who came back, with the man who caught him, I presume that's who it was. But I didn't know that then."

"So you were just sitting there then, huddled up?"

"Yes, I suppose so, I know I had my hand over my mouth, I think I was crying, but I don't think much sound was coming out." Anne lit another cigarette, Jackie shook her head when offered one and finished writing. Anne's hand moved rhythmically from her chin, down her small neck to the base, in quick repetitive movements.

"Then one of the policemen looked up to me and said something like, 'Miss, we'll have to call the fire brigade for you. Don't be alarmed. A cabin will come up the side of the building and then you can get in and be lowered to the ground.' I just didn't want that, I wanted down and away as quickly as possible. I didn't want another major event happening, where even more people would get involved, so I said I could get back in the way I'd come out."

"What did the policeman say to that?"

"Well, I don't think that he answered. I couldn't be totally sure, but I don't think so. Certainly the other one was talking to the people in the street in that extremely 'police' voice: 'Now everybody just calm down, one at a time please.'" Anne had lowered her tone and spaced out her words, lowering her chin towards her chest as she pronounced the last sentence.

Jackie smiled. "You've got him right, I'll say that. That's just the way he speaks."

Anne paused, sighing, the bones in her arms and legs felt heavy, and in her back a numb pain was starting.

"The next thing I heard was a noise behind me on the roof and then the crackle and then the sound of a radio transmitter. It really startled me and I thought, he could've told me he was there! I heard him say into the radio, as I scrambled to my feet and went over to him, 'I am now on the roof with the young woman and will ascertain whether she will be able to descend to the street.' Everything inside me just boiled up; not only had he not told me that he was there in the first place, but now he was talking about me as if I were an awkward piece of baggage. I was in front of him now and I said, shouted, I suppose, 'He's got away. You've let him get away and he made me suck that thing. Do you understand what he's done to me, do you?' I'd grabbed him by the sleeve by then and he said – I've not got the words exactly right but this is the gist of it – 'Okay miss, we'll take a full statement at the station, just calm down. Do you think you can get back in through this window?' I hadn't really looked around until then, although I knew I was further back on the roof than the place I'd fallen to. Now I saw that there was a wall just before me that was maybe six foot high. It ran along from the wall of the house with the window in it that I'd jumped from. It looked as if there was some kind of balcony at the top. The other policeman was peering out through a lit window just above the wall. He spoke directly to the one with me, 'Can you get her up this far and I'll pull her in from here?' I spoke then. I'd had my hand over my mouth again before that, but I butted in on them and said that all I needed was a hand up and then I could get to the top of the wall. We did that and I got up quite easily. The other policeman was leaning out of the window, offering his hand to me. I could see behind him from the light in the room. It must've been the kitchen because I could see open wall cupboards, with pans and tins of food inside. I thought then, God, how normal and messy it looks: a flat lived in by a man. The balcony of the flat, or whatever it was that I was now standing on, was about the same distance again from the window this other policeman was leaning out of. It was more difficult to get in there than it had been to get up the first part of the wall. I managed to get one foot squarely on the vertical wall in front of me, then he leaned down and took my hand, pulling me up. I was crying again, in gasps, and couldn't quite do it. The first policeman then appeared behind me and hoisted me up and I got through like that."

"Okay, what did you see when you got in through the window. Can you remember what you touched?"

"Yes, strangely enough I can remember all this next bit quite clearly, almost as if everything was in slow motion. I was on all fours when I came through the window on top of a steel draining board. It was creaking under my weight and the ridges were digging into my knees. I got to the edge of that and the policeman, who seemed to fill the whole room up, was standing next to me. Everything seemed to be lit up in really strong light and I remember thinking how ungainly I must look, scrambling down from the draining board. As soon as my feet touched the floor, all I wanted was to be out of that place and I couldn't even wait to tell the policeman that. He hadn't spoken as I was getting down, and I just ran. I felt suffocated. I don't know if that makes any sense to you, but I had to get out, right away.

"You see I'd got out once and now I was back inside there again. I flew past him and out the kitchen door and then I was back in the room he'd made me walk through, the room I'd jumped out of. I saw a bed to my right and a door open next to it. The bed had a blue and white, small checked mattress on it. It was messy and unmade, the sheet half on, half off. That's what I mean when I say it was all like slow motion. I only hesitated a moment at the kitchen door, but I saw that in detail, like a picture I was looking at. I could see that almost every inch of the floor was covered in clothes, newspapers, cartons; it was disgusting. The next thing I was out the door; it was the same door I came in with him behind me, the scissors at my neck. The stairs were in front of me. The policeman had shouted as I ran off; I heard his voice from a distance, but I haven't a clue what he said. I ran down two, maybe three, flights of stairs, holding on to the banister and swinging round the landings on it. Then I heard the policeman shout again. I could hear him running behind me; he shouted, 'Stop, stay there, don't go any further,' or words to that effect. That really made me cross, because I felt like I couldn't breathe and that I had to get to the fresh air before I could breathe again. Couldn't he see that, Jackie? Anyway, I just stopped dead where I was. Like I've said, I didn't want to antagonise them. I shouted back up the stairs, 'I just want to get out of here, as soon as I get out the front door I'll stop. I won't run away, I promise you.' Once I'd said that, I ran on: I didn't wait for an answer. I came out the front door to the street. Was it open? Yes, it must've been because I know I didn't stop again until I was out. Yes, yes, definitely, the front door was open. Then all of a sudden I was outside, in the night, right in front of the crowd. All those people I'd seen from a height were now right in front of me. I didn't need to be told to stop then, because I didn't know what to do anyway. They were all in a group a little distance in front of me and all of them had turned and were looking at me. I stopped, very still then, and just waited for the policeman to catch up with me. It was probably only a couple of seconds, but it seemed much longer, and then he was with me. The other one was just behind him. I don't really think they knew what to do either. There was a police van on the road, just to the right of the group of people that hadn't been there before, I'm sure, and two other policemen stood at the front of it. The two with me had gone either side of me, then one walked off to the van, leaving the other guy standing on my right-hand side. He spoke to the crowd and said something like, 'If you wouldn't mind just waiting for a few more minutes then my colleague will take your details, in case we need to come back to you at a further date.' Then the first policeman came back from talking at the front of the van and asked me to follow him. I still hadn't spoken. I walked past all the people and it felt really weird, because I'd been yelling and screaming at them and now I'd nothing to say. I felt very small and was conscious of the fact that I'd only got a dressing gown on, nothing else, no shoes, nothing."

Jackie interrupted, "You didn't have shoes on. Did you take them off when he told you to take your clothes off? You didn't mention it before; can you remember the order?"

"That's easy. I can't get my jeans off without taking my shoes off. They're quite baggy jeans but they're tight around the ankle."

"Right, good answer; okay, so the policeman asked you to follow him through the crowd?"

"Yes, then we reached the front of the police van. I could see in there that there were two men inside in ordinary clothes and one policeman in uniform. When we reached the front of the van, the policeman said, 'Look into the van and tell me if there is anyone in there that you recognise.' Those were his exact words; that is firmly in my memory. I looked in like he said, though I didn't know why and I didn't understand why they weren't explaining things to me or asking me anything at all. When I looked in, one of the men in the back half stood up and, lifting his hands, shrugged his shoulders, you know, like this," Anne made the well-known gesture, Jackie glanced up and nodded briefly, "and he mouthed the words, 'come on'. I didn't hear the words, I couldn't have, he was behind metal and glass, but the expression on his face and the way he'd shrugged like that made me able to lip-read it perfectly. I didn't know who it was; I know now that it was him, DI Davies told me that later, but at the time I was totally confused. I didn't know they'd caught him and anyway I didn't know what he looked like. I just couldn't understand why someone I didn't know was motioning to me like he knew me."

Anne's voice was shaking. It had been rising throughout her last speech, as much from confusion and outrage as upset. Jackie opened Anne's cigarette packet, lit one for her and passed it over. Anne closed her eyes, nodded in thanks, taking it from her.

"I know, I'm nearly there now, there's no point in cracking now, I've said the worst of it, God knows." She paused, "I can tell you now, I honestly didn't know it was him, I just couldn't understand someone acting as if they knew me when they didn't. The policeman said to me when I was looking in the window, wondering what I was supposed to be looking at, 'Is that him?' Those were his exact words. Sometimes I remember the exact words, sometimes just the gist of it, you know the meaning, but not exactly what was said. I turned to him and said, 'I don't know, you tell me. I didn't see his face. I don't know.' He then looked at the other policeman and they moved off a little to one side and left me standing there. I didn't know what to do. I heard their murmuring and then one of them came back to me and asked me to come over to the police car and asked me if I would mind getting in. He opened the back door and sort of guided me in and then he got into the front. We sat in silence for a few seconds and then the other one came over and got into the driving seat. The one in the passenger seat turned round as the driver started the car and – I'd not noticed before that he was so young, he only looked about twenty – he said in that horrible South London accent I hate so much, he actually said, 'Did he rip your clothes off?' I said, 'No, I took them off.' I saw them look at one another, Jackie, I saw it all in that one glance they thought I was too stupid to notice. I could see what went through their minds, and, do you know what, they didn't say another word to me after that, didn't even tell me where we were going, and then I recognised that we were turning into Croydon Police Station.

*

In the living room, she sat staring in front of her; Neil was on the telephone again, talking to her other sister, Valerie, who'd obviously been told by Stella what had happened, Anne surmised. Anne sat, dazed, and thought how this must be what it is like when someone dies. Time had no meaning or significance, the outside world had no longer any connection with what happened inside this flat, and the phone rang, and rang.

She looked at Neil. He'd run his fingers through his short dark hair so many times that it stood on end. She watched him as he spoke, he was conscious of her presence, listening to him relaying the story – as much of the story as he knew.

She'd been with him now for four years. How much he'd changed! She'd been attracted to him initially because she'd sensed his weakness, his vulnerability. She loved his looks, his swarthy skin and deep-set eyes, looking injured and resentful by turns. His eyebrows were dark and thick, and furrows formed above them on his brow now, where when she first knew him it had been smooth and shiny with health and youth. He's twenty-seven now, she thought, and half-way down the drain already. She watched him and felt suddenly detached wondering, is he strong enough to see this through? Is he strong enough to help me?

She'd thought about leaving him many times in the last two years. She'd gone as far as leaving him for one night, a few times two, going to Valerie's house in Epsom; seeing the normality of family life, suburbia, two kids, responsible, capable husband and tea on the table at six. Did she want it, resent it or despise it? She wasn't sure. But she knew that as time went on her 'want' became stronger: she wanted security, she wanted happiness, most of all she wanted something, someone, reliable and safe, not this shifting, changing life with its disruptions and moods always dictated by someone else. She increasingly recognised that Neil's power over her was in his weakness; his drinking was so overwhelming and all-consuming that it controlled and subjugated everything else. Looking at him now she thought, there's him and me, but more important and stronger than us both – there's drink.

No, she thought, more than that, more important than that, was what had happened to her. That, too, was in a way separate from them. It had everything and nothing to do with her, although it was now a definite part of her, it had not come from her but had been thrust upon her. Like everything else, she thought. If he can't see that I need his help now then I can't stay with him.

Neil put down the receiver. He smiled, quickly, sadly at her and walked toward the settee where she sat, glancing at the clock on the fireplace. It was nine o'clock. Jackie had left Anne back at the flat half an hour ago. She'd washed her face, put some make-up on and made coffee. She read his mind now as he sat down beside her. She said nothing.

"I need a drink." This statement was more direct, more blatantly honest, than he normally was. What had happened to Anne had allowed him to be like this; it was no longer their biggest problem. She'd barely noticed what he'd drunk today.

Normally she knew of every sip, but today all she knew was that he couldn't have had much because of the expression in his eyes; he hadn't lost control, he was still there, with her, in the room.

'Have one," she retorted.

"Oh, come on Anne, don't make me feel any worse than I already do."

He stood before her, looking thin and nervous, his green T-shirt shapeless now as it hung over his jeans, his arms hanging limply by his sides. The look in his eyes was the childlike, hurt expression he so frequently had, the one that Anne could never decide whether natural or assumed, knowing the effect it had on her. She felt a sweep of anger – how can he go on about drink, as if him and drinking were the only important things? Then quickly on the back of that she thought – I can't change anything, not even through this, evidently. She'd given in time and time again and, like with an undisciplined child, she no longer had any control over him. Like the parent who'd said 'yes' after saying 'no' ten times over, she could only do as he did or be left behind alone, again. Finally, she felt pity, pity for him and self-pity, for what she was about to do.

"What do you want to do then, go out and buy some more?" she asked wearily, trying to keep the sarcasm out of her voice.

"Let's go to the pub, just for one. The pub on the old back road to Purley... in the opposite direction. I think it's a good idea, don't you?"

She couldn't think where he meant, at first, then she remembered – a small, shabby pub next to the railway line, further down the track from South Croydon Station. The other pubs in the area, any off-licences or the small, dingy newsagents and general stores were all beyond that bridge and after passing South Croydon railway station.

"Just don't try to make out you only want to go there to protect my feelings and get me out of myself this evening. Just be honest," she countered as she rose and walked out of the room into the bedroom. He didn't answer and she imagined his expression behind her; chastised, hurt, repentant. Deservedly told off, she thought. I may act like a fool, but I don't want him thinking that I am one.

They walked down the road, hand in hand, Anne wanting to press every part of the left-hand side of her body against him. The inch or two between them felt like a gulf, she felt as if she could be pulled away from him entirely by an unseen current, by anything, anyone. He was reassuring in his body movements. He seemed to know how she was feeling, she thought. He kept a tight hold of her hand.

A car pulled up. It had been driving slowly behind them for a little while, then it pulled up opposite them on the other side of the road. The driver turned round to face them. Anne, who reached only just below Neil's shoulder, half-hid her face in his sleeve, her whole body pushing towards his side, wanting to lose herself in him, her heart pounding. He's going to get out and grab me, she thought, her mind and heart racing. I must hold on: he's going to pull me into the car with him. Oh God! She was rooted to the spot; she'd come to such an immediate standstill before Neil realised what the problem was that he almost tripped.

"Excuse me, mate. Do you know where London Road is from here?" Neil disentangled himself from Anne's grasp, his attention already with the man in the car. He walked over to the open car window. Anne, marooned, stood where she was. Blackness surrounded her, she felt isolated, exposed. She told herself he was only asking for directions, and looking over she saw Neil gesturing down the road. He walked the few paces back to where she stood, and the man in the car, with one backward glance towards her, drove off.

"Do you have to walk off on me like that? Don't you know it's bad enough being outside at all? He could've been anyone, he could've grabbed you or punched you, or me. Think how I feel, for God's sake."

Neil, his shoulders hunched over, turned to face her, "I'm sorry, I didn't think. I mean he looked okay and I knew that he wanted directions."

"My whole world is totally cock-eyed now, with nothing logical in it. Do you understand? So there's no point in telling me that he looked okay, because you can't tell. They all look the same, therefore no one's exempt, okay?"

They walked on to the pub. Neil walked in first. They'd been there twice before; it was a locals' pub, a few old men, working class South Londoners, who'd lived in the area all their lives and seen it changed from the edges of rural Surrey, as it had once been, to the vast, sprawling metropolis it now formed a part of. There were ten or twelve people there, two women, Anne noted; middle-aged, thick-set, coarse-featured but kindly-looking. One woman and four men were sitting around a table playing dominoes. They looked up as Anne and Neil came in, registered them without much interest and carried on playing. They both went to the bar, and Neil ordered from the barman; he had a pint, she a half.

As they sat down on the poorly covered seats, Neil spoke, "I'm sorry for bringing you out, but we haven't slept for nearly two days now and if we're to get any rest tonight I had to have another drink."

Anne, taking in all that was going on around her, her back pressed against the seat, said, "It doesn't matter now we're here. It was getting here that was the problem. It isn't threatening once we're in here." She looked around her, at the shabby wall lights covered in faded red satiny shades and the pictures, dull, smoke-darkened, scenes of horses, country views.

"In a room I'm all right. It's hard to explain but the street, the sky, everything outside is like a gauntlet that I have to walk through. Outside there, I felt like the street was lined with a firing squad or something like that, that I had to get past."

Neil sat close to her, listening, nodding, his drink untouched. She looked at it and thought how strange it was that he could have the drink in front of him and not touch it for maybe five minutes. She knew why: it was the assurance it was there when he wanted it that was important. She, sipping her own drink, thought, not for the first time, how they understood each other's minds and how, in a setting like this, and not at home, in front of the television, they often got on better, spoke more.

"Tell me, it's only right that I should know, what happened to you?" he blurted out, his dark brow furrowed. "For God's sake, all I have to do is to hear it, I don't have to go through it like you did. So what right have I got to say I can't cope with hearing it?"

She reached for his hand where it lay on the table and covered it with her own, squeezing it. She began to tell him the parts she had left out earlier. His face became contorted and then, with visible effort, smoothed out, several times.

"The strange thing is, disgusting though all of it was, and it was vile and horrible, the absolutely worst part was knowing that I was going to die, do you understand that, can you imagine it?"

She was leaning towards him, her face incensed, as she tried to rid her mind of the images she'd just described. Her voice speeded up though the volume was unusually low for her.

"Yes, I know what you're thinking: what could be worse than what he did to me. I can see it in your face. But even during all that I kept thinking, when he's finished he's going to kill me, he has to, I'm in his flat, there's nothing else he can do with me. So in one hour or six hours, when he's finished with me, he's going to have to kill me. It's going to happen."

"Stop, please stop, for Christ's sake please stop." Neil pleaded, "Enough, enough now."

She answered him in a soft, coaxing manner, "I've said it all now, I'm not going to say anything worse. It's just I wanted to explain to you that knowing I was going to die was the worst bit. It's important for you to know that." She lifted her glass again from the table, holding it in front of her. "There is nothing that is worse than that, believe me."

She looked at him to see that he was taking it all in, understanding what she meant, and carried on, "The whole thing didn't come to an end; he didn't do that to me and then finish. I finished it, do you see what I mean? I brought it to an early end by jumping out the window."

When they got back to the flat, the hall was in darkness. "We've got to get a new bulb for in here, this is awful," Anne said as she followed Neil up the first flight of stairs, towards their own front door. The five minute walk back had been worse than the one going to the pub. She'd felt as if she'd held her breath from leaving the pub until they got in the main flat door. Still, even now, she felt tense, as if she needed the security of her own living room to make her feel safe.

As she followed Neil up the stairs, she thought how alike all these converted houses were around here. Rows and streets of identical houses. We've got to move, she thought suddenly, get me away from this cesspit, this overcrowded, anonymous place. At the top of the stairs, Neil handed her the flat keys.

"Can you open the door? With my eyesight I can't see anyway, light or not."

Anne took the keys, her heart pounding, thinking that less than twenty-four hours ago she'd had to do this at his door, and he'd stood behind her as she tried to push the key in the lock. Her hand was shaking. She span round to face Neil fully, thrusting the keys at him, starting to cry in rage, "You'll have to do it, for God's sake, how can you make me do it?"

He took the keys from her quickly, his one thought to get them inside the flat and turn the light on. He pushed the door shut quickly behind them, then stood still at the bottom of the flight of stairs that lead to the living room and kitchen of the flat, next to Anne. His voice was high and strained.

"I didn't know, I didn't know he made you open the doors, I'm so sorry. I didn't know."

She sank against his chest. "I'm sorry too. How were you supposed to know? It's just I don't know myself what is going to remind me, what is going to scare me, until it happens."

They went up the stairs, into the living room, Neil switching on the lights as he went in front of her.

"Can we keep all the lights on when it is dark? I don't want to go into a black room and I can't bear to go into the bathroom and see the toilet when it's in darkness. I just won't be able to stand that, I know I won't."

Neil nodded, head downwards, "And tomorrow I'll get some bulbs for the hallway."

"We've got to leave here. I can't live here any more, I can't work in Croydon, live in Croydon, especially I can't live where I'll go past that place every day. That is, if I can ever go out on my own again. I'll tell you something, I can't imagine it, I really can't. How can I ever do it? How can I risk it happening again?"

"Let's leave decisions for a while yet. Yes, we should move, but can we let things go on for a few days before we decide what to do? Do you want anything to eat?" She shook her head. "You should have something, let's go and see what you could have."

He spoke coaxingly, as if to a child. To encourage and not to offend his new solicitousness, she followed him through to the kitchen, watching as he opened all the cupboards to see what there was for them to eat. He started to slice some bread, "Do you want some?"

She shook her head, quickly, dismissively, not wanting to be questioned further.

He put the bread under the grill and Anne moved behind where he stood to fill the kettle with water. Such ordinary jobs, she thought, here we are doing normal things for a couple of minutes and it makes me want to scream, I can't believe it. She felt something cold move down her backbone. Her heart stopped, the blood pounded in her ears and she swung round on him. "What the hell do you think you are doing. Are you trying to crack me up totally?"

Neil stood, speechless with the teaspoon in his left hand, which he'd idly passed down her back as he passed.

"That's what he did with the scissors, up and down, up and down." She imitated the movements on his chest with her forefinger. He placed both hands over the two sides of his face, slowly, his eyes filling.

"You've got to know," she cried, her voice rising. "Don't ever do that to me again, don't stand behind me and don't put your hand on my breast from behind me either: he did that too."

The whole sexual minefield stood between them; the enormity of it was dawning on them slowly. They faced each other, Anne accusing, angry, "I'm sorry but you've got to know."

Hours later, in the dead of night, they went to bed. All the lights in the flat had been left on. They undressed and lay on top of the bedclothes. The night was warm and heat came beating down from the ceiling, where the sun, unnoticed by them, had been beating all day. They lay side by side, unsure, nervous, like children. Neil began to kiss her face. First her forehead and then all over her cheeks and chin, finally her mouth, smothering her face with kisses, his eyes open all the time. They stared into each other's eyes, both too scared to close them. He moved from her face to her arms and legs, kissing and watching her. She lay, inert, watching him, watching her own feelings. She felt him move on top of her, slowly, hesitantly, and remembered what happened last night. She let herself remember it, she knew there was no point in trying to blank it out. If she tried to clear it completely from her mind she knew it would return, immediately with a heart-stopping thud, then all this would be spoiled. She knew why Neil was doing this now, and she wanted it. She wanted her body to be his and hers again, she wanted the last mark on her body not to be last night's. This had nothing to do with last night, there was no connection.

She let it happen as tears filled her eyes. He touched her all over, giving with each touch that part of her body back to herself. She could not touch him, she could not look at him except for his face. They both cried silent tears together. Hers were mixed with relief.

That taboo had been overcome, it had been faced. It wouldn't be a problem. As she drifted into a light sleep that was at once asleep and awake she knew that her body was her own again and that she could look at herself once more in the mirror.

Part Two

Anne had always had vivid dreams. Her mind, always active when awake, questioning, analysing the inadequacies and insecurities which vied for supremacy during the day, which came out in dreams littered with people and situations that demanded decision and action from her and were fraught with her frustrations at her inability to solve the problems the dreams threw up.

Now she feared her dreams; she feared sleep where she would no longer have control over her own mind. Over the weeks that followed, she felt a control over her waking mind, as tight as the reins on a nervous and unpredictable horse. During sleep the reins loosened, she was afraid of other hands controlling them, hands that would let the horse go where it wanted, as it wanted: her mind in control, able to dominate and lead Anne into the mental situations she could not bear to face.

Sleep. So difficult to attain: lying still in the bed, eyes to the ceiling, she willed herself to get to sleep and when she eventually achieved the deep, trance-like sleep from which she awoke sharply, with a sense of panic and urgency, eyes wide, mind racing, she realised, surprised, that she had not dreamt at all. Rather she went into an unconscious state, as if she were dead, a state that was so different from ordinary sleep as to be impossible to conceive of ever dreaming in.

*

The second day after it happened, Jackie and Adam Small came, early in the morning, to the flat. Anne looked at them, from where she sat, as they came into the room, Neil behind. Already they looked familiar. Jackie smiled as she walked towards Anne.

"Get any sleep then? You're certainly looking better."

Anne felt better. She'd washed her hair that morning and had it falling around her face and neck in loose curls. The severity of yesterday when she couldn't bear to have her hair around her face as normal was gone. She'd put on the little make-up she usually wore: lipstick and some mascara. Even with the toll of the last couple of days her tanned face looked healthy. Only the expression of vacancy in her eyes and the set expression round her mouth were clues to the trauma that went through her mind, round and round, a mouse on a wheel. But she didn't feel that she was the mouse itself, rather it seemed as if she were watching the whole scene. The realisation that it was her in the scene was close, very close, but it wasn't her, not yet, it was coming.

She wore jeans and a T-shirt, and felt small next to Jackie, as the other woman sat down beside her, tall and elegant in a navy suit. An aura of control and intelligence emanated from her. Anne looked to her as she answered her question, gratitude rising up through her. Thank God, she thought, thank God she is here and will help, will guide me through it all, tell me what to do, how to act, what to say.

Jackie opened the briefcase beside her and took out a newspaper and, opening it, passed it across to Anne.

"I take it you haven't seen this yet? We thought it a good idea to bring it round, so that you don't come across it unexpectedly."

Anne held the paper open in front of her. It was the local paper, *The Croydon Post*.

"We do get it delivered here, yes, in the evening I think. Is it in here?"

She scanned the front page eagerly now, her reactions quickening, her mind speeding up.

"It is mentioned, Anne," Jackie continued. "It's difficult to explain. You probably expect to see it splashed over the front page and that's understandable. But we wanted to keep it low key. To a certain extent you see it is up to us. We have a press office that releases only the amount of information that we want let out. So, because he has been caught and there is no need to alarm people around here, we just released the bare minimum. Also, we don't want to jeopardise the trial and that's always a possibility if it becomes over-reported."

Anne had been looking from Jackie's face to the paper as she'd been speaking, flicking over the first few pages and scanning the headlines, COUNCIL MOVES FORWARD WITH ONE-WAY SYSTEM and TODDLER HURT. END TO MID-SUMMER REVELRY made no sense to her. What was this? It was being totally ignored.

As her resentment mounted, Small came over to where she sat and knelt down on one knee next to her.

"Here, I'll get it for you. It's on page six. As Jackie says it's in our favour that as little as possible is said at this stage. I know how you are feeling though, seeing the kind of stories that make the headlines in this rag." As he spoke he pointed to a small column-width heading, one of many running down the left-hand side of the page. She stared at it, barely taking it in at first, then words jumped out at her: the name, of course he had a name, he was a person, with a mother and father, a childhood, friends? Rapidly these thoughts shot across her mind. Thirty-one, he was thirty-one, the same age as Stella. He was a lorry operative; what the hell was a lorry operative? A lorry driver? Leering at women he passed, pathetic, insulting pictures inside the cab of the lorry? Yes, it all fitted. Trying to control and concentrate her mind on the rest of the article, she read, 'Detained by Croydon CID, until his appearance at Croydon Crown Court on 3 August, for allegedly raping a woman, 24, at his home in Park Street on Monday 24 July.'

"Is that it? 'Allegedly raping', how can what happened to me be described like that? It's so bloody insulting. I don't know what I expected but it wasn't this."

The muscles in her jaw tightened as she fought back the tears.

"I know what you're feeling, I can understand it, believe me." Jackie reached over and took her hand, covering it with her own. As she looked up from the paper, Anne saw Jackie's face close by, her flecked brown eyes widened, concerned and sympathetic. Anne would have found it difficult to explain at that moment why she felt so angry and hurt and to have articulated what she would have wanted the report to say exactly, but with this woman she didn't need to explain; she understood. She heard a door shut, looked up and saw that Small and Neil had left the room.

"Where are they going?"

"Adam wants to talk to Neil on his own for a minute or two and I need to go over some things with you."

She took a clipboard and a number of papers from her case. Anne watched silently. She saw they were the statements that Jackie and she had signed yesterday, the printed name of the police station at the top of each one. Her eyes picked out words and sentences from the page. She looked away.

"I need to take a further statement. I need to know about you personally."

Anne rolled her eyes. "The 'Is this the kind of girl who deserves to be raped' scenario?"

"I know it's wrong, 'cause it shouldn't matter a damn what you are like as a person but, believe me, we need to do all we possibly can to make sure that there aren't any loopholes for the defence to catch on to. We need to make the case as airtight as we can. Listen, things have improved a lot since I first came into the Force, honestly, but it still stands that you have to come across as a respectable girl to get the full sympathy of the jury."

Jackie asked questions about Anne's early life, her schooling (private, girls) and her family: parents dead, mother in her early teens from an asthma attack, an unnecessary, preventable death that made light of life and any meaning in it; thoughts that had only occurred to Anne in the last few years, since her father had died from a stroke the year she graduated. She couldn't talk about either easily, her feelings, a mixture of anger and guilt: she'd loved them, but not enough and now their whole existence was made meaningless by the fact that they no longer lived. Jackie said she only needed an outline, of her family, education and jobs. Anne felt a brief stirring of the growing interest one feels when oneself and one's life is discussed as a matter of importance.

Then they went through what Anne had done earlier in the day of that Monday night. How Neil and she had gone to Miguel's at lunchtime, to pick up his pay, how they'd stayed there for lunch, and talked to the waitresses and the other chef, John. Neil had a drink there, Anne only a mineral water. In the afternoon, back at the flat, Anne had sat out in the communal back garden and read a book while Neil had spent most of the afternoon in the flat, then had come out to sit with her a while before he went to work. She'd expected him back at eleven thirty.

"The weak link in all this is Neil, you know that, don't you?" Jackie said after she'd finished writing, looking at Anne intently. Anne nodded. "Put it this way, he's the weak link in two ways. One, it's difficult to understand why you went out of the house after midnight; he's not a child. If he had to work late, he could find his own way home, couldn't he? The second thing is that he's not taking it as well as you. It's obvious," she continued, seeing Anne's expression as she prepared to interrupt, "That's why Adam has taken him into the other room; he wants to fire him up a bit, make sure he'll support you."

Anne nodded. "I know it doesn't seem as if he's taking it that well, but then it's difficult for him. For a start he's not getting the attention that I am, is he? He's a good person, really he is, it's just that he isn't that tough. He's really sensitive and he takes everything to heart." She could hear her own voice echoing in her head, sounding lame, making excuses for him, as she had done so often and she hated herself for it. "I need him, now, God knows, I really need him, Jackie. He can be strong at times and he is good to me. In a way I couldn't have any other man; especially now, how could I ever? I trust him. In that way I trust him totally. I'm sure you've noticed that he's got a problem, a big problem."

She stopped.

"Go on."

Anne had only spoken to Liz about this, no one else, and Liz hadn't needed to be told much as she saw so much of them both. It just gradually came to be discussed between them, first by saying that he drank too much (didn't they all? – then relieved laughter) and then again when Anne had a swollen eye, the faint yellow tinge still visible on the Monday at work, three days after he'd hit her. They'd both been drunk; Anne had niggled him – her discontent and frustration rising – and after all it hadn't been that bad, had it? He wasn't bad, they'd both agreed that, it was that he was too soft to cope with life; he lived in the wrong place, he should've stayed in Wales. He was disorientated here – there were too many people, the life was too fast and money-grabbing – and because of that he'd started to drink too much. That's what they'd said to each other. It sounded almost poetic.

But now, now she would have to admit it to herself properly, by telling someone she'd met only yesterday, whose respect she desperately wanted to earn and keep. She would have to admit the enormity of the problem, it couldn't be a secret between her and Neil now, which had rarely even been called by its correct name, rather referred to obliquely.

"He's an alcoholic." She said it. She told Jackie he'd been one for a few years now; it was hard to put a date on it, but he hadn't been when she'd first known him, when she'd been at the polytechnic in her home town, Manchester. He'd been working for a few years already by then and seemed older than her friends on the course or the guys she met in the Union or at The Hacienda. Everyone in the group of flats where she lived liked him. He was good fun, liked good music, knew lots about geography and nature and, like the rest of them, liked a drink. He knew the good places to go, knew lots of people and was well liked. In his oversized dark jumpers and jeans that never quite seemed to fit right he looked as though he didn't care a damn about his appearance, while his moody-looking expression, deep-set eyes and dark skin, above which his short dark hair always looked as if he'd just run his fingers through it, meant that he didn't have to try too hard. Those eyes hadn't had that look of frightened hatred then. That look had come gradually, over the last year. But when? Anne didn't know, she just knew that they'd both changed because of it. She'd become harder, and more resentful (he won't allow me to be happy, why?) and his resentment was turning increasingly towards her. She knew that but didn't know how to stop it. Perhaps this could stop it.

"Only you can decide what you want from your life Anne, but don't let him hold you back; you can get over this. You're strong enough, but the question is whether he is too. But thanks for telling me. I'd guessed it really, but we need to know everything so that we can try to lead the trial in such a way as to avoid the pitfalls. Now, getting back to your description of this bastard, you got it nearly right with his age, as you saw in the paper."

Anne had forgotten the paper. It lay at her feet; COUNCIL MOVES FORWARD emblazoned on the half she could see.

"You put his age at twenty-eight or twenty-nine, with short, mousy hair, curly perhaps, wearing jeans or dark trousers and a checked lumberjack shirt, pocket at the left breast, at your eye-level. Can you think of anything to add to this, any other physical description? I know you didn't see him properly, but anything at all?"

"Yes, there is one thing I thought of last night when I was talking to Neil. I think he had finely shaped eyebrows, almost like pencilled eyebrows. I can't think when I saw them to remember that, maybe when I glanced at him the one time at the beginning, when he kept saying, 'Don't look at me.'" Jackie wrote it all down as Anne spoke, "I suppose, thinking about it, the reason I noticed is because Neil has such thick eyebrows – it was the difference I noticed, just like I noticed that he'd got a disgusting, podgy stomach."

Anne stopped, shocked at the vivid memory of her face looking upwards, seeing his stomach, the full force of the memory hitting her, of her crouching between his legs, sobbing. She felt at that moment as if her face had been slapped; she hadn't meant to think of that. More and more of these snap shots of memories were happening, unseen and unasked for, each one more horribly real than the last.

Jackie signed the last sheet of paper and, passing the clipboard over, motioned to Anne to sign the box marked 'witness.'

"One last thing, which Adam has been talking to Neil about as well, is that the tests have shown a certain amount of sperm in your samples but it must be Neil's. He'll have to give a blood sample to clarify it, because it doesn't match up to you know who, unfortunately."

Anne flinched briefly with revulsion, then raced on to worry and fear for Neil.

Her mind seemed continually to oscillate between her preoccupations with Neil and being haunted by the memories of what had happened to her, which she constantly tried to contain and control. She knew Neil would not be able to cope with going to a hospital or the police station. He'd not been able to travel even the shortest journeys without having a drink, for months now (how many? She couldn't remember).

*

As Anne had guessed, Neil wasn't able to go to the station without having two cans of beer first. She watched him drink them with a mixture of disgust and embarrassment. He knew it – he didn't meet her eye – as, lacing his shoes, he downed the last of the can and prepared to go.

She watched him leave, filled with this new sense of calm which made her feel as if she were watching everything on a film and not actually involved herself. Normally if Neil were leaving, having been drinking, not saying when he was coming back, not reassuring her that he would return, she would be panicking and at the last minute would break and run after him, demanding to hear the promises which he nearly always broke. This time she watched him go, silence between them, his actions helping neither of them as far as she could see, and she said nothing. What good would it do?

When she was alone, she walked aimlessly over to the long landscape mirror across the wall above the dining table and blankly stared at her reflection. Two images of herself met in that look: the one that fought to get to the surface, from her mind outwards, the one that had come into contact with the lowest, most depraved person, where she'd been forced to see life at its worst and come into contact with the seedy, pornographic existence she'd always imagined herself so raised above. The other image was the one easily visible: the one that looked back at her. A smooth-skinned young woman with regular, pretty features, with only her eyes showing any incongruity as they stared blankly back at her.

She thought how many decisions there were in front of her and wondered how she was ever going to face them. As she walked over to the window and looked out, she couldn't imagine ever walking down that road alone again. All the logic in the world won't help me now, she thought. I know how vulnerable I am, it could happen again. My God, I think I would die from the fright of it, how can I put myself in the situation where it could happen? How am I going to get through this when I can't rely on Neil? She knew that he would swing between understanding and helping her and then dash all hope completely. She felt the awful hopelessness of wanting to be at the bottom, right at the very bottom, so that nothing and no one could damn her further. She'd had the succession of raised and dashed hopes that is life with an alcoholic and doubted whether she could carry on facing it now. Bitterly, she thought that these two men combined were ruining her and unfortunately she loved one of them.

Alone now, she sat down and cried. Her tears were those of pity, the awful pity of seeing her life like this and not knowing how to escape. Her mind started to race again as she started to wipe her cheeks with the palm of her hand. She would have to move – they would have to move now – where? This flat they rented was the best one they'd had yet, the only one they'd been happy with, with its good, solid furniture, space, character. In a way she'd be sorry to leave; they would not find one as good as this again for the price, as owners of rented houses were normally a lot more money-grabbing and tight-fisted than Mrs Lord. Work. She was due to go back to work in less than a fortnight's time; how could she ever sit there again, at her desk, overlooking the roundabout and flyover, and work her way through the mundane administration, ordering reprints of brochures and caring about booking exhibition halls? How could she sit amongst those people when she was so different now? She felt raw and naked, as if a protective covering, a layer of skin, had been peeled back in the last few days. The conversations in the office, the jokes, the discussion of television the night before – she couldn't handle all that any more. Not that she'd ever handled all that particularly well as she always had been too sensitive, too easily wound up by what others said and too intolerant of others' views. In her defensiveness she was a mystery to most of the people she worked with, who looked at her in confusion over her obstinacy at rejecting and dismissing the whole mass of 'popular culture' that others took up and swallowed whole. They often saw her as a contradiction: she was attractive and confident, swore, smoked and liked a drink, was neither shy nor innocent, yet when an invisible mark was overstepped she would become instantly offended and either wouldn't laugh at the joke or froze and bluntly told the person to remove their hand from where it was slung across her shoulder. She fought for feminism from her corner, which was more intuitive and instinctive than it was informed. She felt what was right and knew what was wrong.

When Neil returned, he was full of self-pity at the treatment he'd received from the police doctor. He'd had a few more drinks by now, two, maybe three, Anne guessed, as she listened to him.

"He was practically accusing me!"

Anne watched him silently, wondering how much of the dramatics were put on to excuse his further drinking.

"The important thing is whether the drink you had will ruin the blood test. Forget the rest of it. You knew it wouldn't go down well, going in reeking of drink. Think of all the scum he deals with, day in, day out. You can hardly blame him."

Neil left the room and she heard the creaks as he lay down on the bed. She moved her mind on to think of Stella. She could help and she was coming down to see her. It seemed strange to think of Stella in these surroundings, Anne had always gone to visit her; her life was stable, she was settled. Seven years older, she'd always been a sister/mother to Anne, someone over the years she'd relied on and confided in. Stella and Valerie, even before their mother's death, had helped to bring Anne up. She'd lived with Valerie for a couple of years when they were not long married – after pleading from Anne who could no longer bear the overbearing dominance of her old and overly strict father. At the time, Anne had not considered the strain the presence of a sixteen year old might put on them, and only lately had she appreciated that they had tried to give her some discipline and guidance, had felt themselves responsible for her upbringing, rather than just the providers of her home, which is how she'd seen them then.

Thinking back now, her life seemed made up of several diverse areas, with a total break between each. She didn't carry the baggage of many people from one era of her life to another. Only her sisters and one friend had come with her through each stage. In recent years there had been so much in her life that she didn't want people to see, it was often easier to stop contacting them, which meant she could stop making the excuses she was so often forced to; wriggling out of this or that invite as Neil couldn't go and she couldn't leave him, knowing what she'd come back to if she left him when he felt threatened or abandoned.

He'd always, motivated by his subconscious she believed, gone to pieces if she left him for any length of time. Gradually he had tied her to him more surely than if he'd done it physically.

*

Stella and Anne were walking towards the bridge together. Anne had wanted to do this but Stella had been unsure.

"Don't feel you have to force yourself to do things; however you act, no one will criticise you. We're all concerned about you, you know that, don't you?"

Anne had smiled her thanks. The situation seemed less charged since Stella had arrived. She'd come alone, leaving her husband and two girls at home. She'd been daunted by the five hour journey, never having had to negotiate London traffic before, but she couldn't bear to think of Anne with no family around her, dependent only on Neil's support. She'd introduced them, as he once, briefly, worked at a hotel in Chester where Stella was manager. She'd liked him instantly, charmed by his smile and innocently flirting manner. But she'd also sensed his stubbornness, seen the expression in his eyes change quickly to sullenness, and feared for her sister. She'd noticed from early on that he needed to bend people to his will, would only do as he wanted, and noticed too that he took no responsibility for himself. She'd seen her sister's loyalty before; she remembered it from when Anne was a child – when she committed herself to someone, something, they were everything to her, for she had a desperate need to belong and also to own. Once decided, her loyalties didn't shift.

As they neared the bridge, Anne's fear began to mount. Suddenly she couldn't bear to walk underneath it, along the same footpath, to see the same scene she'd seen as she came around the pillar a few nights earlier. She touched Stella's arm.

"Can we cross over?"

Stella protectively put her arm around Anne's waist, conscious only of the need to reassure her sister that she was there, that she understood. Anne felt exposed and frightened as they crossed the road together. Stella was a couple of inches taller than Anne, small, but not extremely so. She was thinner, very thin, her exposed arms frail. Anne felt the complete difference from when she was walking along with Neil. He had felt like protection, although he was none in so many ways. Now, Anne felt scared walking under the bridge on the opposite side of the road. There was more light here than on the opposite side as the pathway was straight; you could see the daylight in front of you all the time.

It was seven in the evening, and they were going to a pizza restaurant near where Neil worked. He was at home, but he hadn't wanted to come and they'd both been glad. He had been subdued since Stella had arrived the previous day. Anne knew that he'd had a few drinks although nothing had been said and she'd seen no evidence of it. She'd said nothing to Stella either, out of some loyalty to Neil and a desire for these few days of Stella's visit to be stable and as happy as possible.

"How do you feel now?" Stella asked. Anne felt her face tightening and said nothing until they had passed a bus stop with some ten people gathered loosely around it. They had to negotiate their way through them, Stella propelling Anne in front of her. When they'd passed through, Anne replied, "I feel that everyone we pass knows. They must see something in my face. Christ, I feel like a scared rabbit and I just can't imagine feeling any different Stella. How can I? I'm not going to be able to forget this ever, am I? It's always going to be there so I'm always going to look and feel like this."

"You don't look bad, honestly. You're an attractive girl and you're smart. For God's sake, you are able to analyse exactly why you feel like you do and it's only been a few days. Being able to understand why you feel as you do will help you, really. Things won't stay like this forever, they won't. They can't. Gradually you'll get back to normal. Don't push yourself too much; you're doing well."

In the restaurant Anne ate. She'd had nothing other than some pieces of toast and cheese for days now. The previous night Neil had made sausages and mashed potatoes in an effort to encourage her to eat. It had been a standing joke between them that her favourite meal had always stayed the same since she was a child, when she'd eaten it almost exclusively. But when he'd put the plate in front of her, her appetite had started to wane. It seemed to her that her mind was against her. While she'd watched him cooking from where she sat smoking at the kitchen table she'd felt hungry, anticipating the food to come. Yet once she raised the fork to her mouth all she could think of was having to put that bastard's penis in her mouth. The food sat heavy in her mouth, her saliva unresponsive. She'd felt the bile rise up against it to her throat and, rushing to the bathroom, was sick.

Here was different; the conversation was constant as they had decided, without saying so, not to mention anything that could upset Anne. They tried to have as normal an evening as possible, having pizza and a couple of glasses of wine. They sat in the far corner of the restaurant, Stella letting Anne choose where to sit. She sat with her back to the wall. Once placed with the wall behind her, the table in front and beyond that Stella, she relaxed. The complete fear that the streets outside had brought receded. The sky was still bright; it had been another beautiful day but, as Anne looked at the outside through the wall of window beyond Stella, it was horrifyingly large, a vast open space of danger. Now it seemed to contain a previously unthought of number of variables: anyone under this sky could charge for her, hurt her, punch her, rape her or kill her. All possibilities existed and she felt herself unable to offer any resistance.

The noise of the bottles of lager and glasses being put in front of them brought Anne's attention back. She looked at Stella, "I feel much better now I've managed to get here; that's something!"

They both laughed easily, Stella smiling in understanding and relief.

*

Stella left the following morning with assurances that, should Anne want to move completely away, she would have a home with Stella, Pete and the girls, any time.

Anne's love for her sister welled up inside her as she watched her drive away from the sitting room window. Stella's bare arm, waving up to the third floor of the house where Anne stood, looked pathetically small and childlike as she manoeuvred her way out of the driveway in her large saloon car. Just before the car gathered speed, she leaned her head, covered in its mass of red-brown curls, out of the window, casting a last smile back to Anne.

Anne turned back into the room, tears gathering in her eyes. Back alone in my goldfish bowl, she thought, as she walked over to the phone. Neil had finally gone back to work that morning, under protest.

"How can I just carry on as normal after what has happened to you? I don't think I can do it."

Anne had pleaded with him, Stella had reasoned. There had to be some continuity in life, not to mention money, Anne had said. But they both knew that the chances of Neil staying at work in this confused state of mind were slim. If only I could think of him at work, doing what he has to do, getting on with it, and worry only about myself, I could cope a lot better, she thought. She dialled the number of the station and asked for Detective Constable Rook.

Shadowy bruises had come out on the calf and ankle of her legs – she'd noticed them the previous evening. This morning she'd examined them again and seen the definite shape of finger prints, two impressions on one leg, three on the other. Stella had made Anne promise to phone Jackie before she left, saying that they'd probably want to photograph her again and that if she left it they could be faded by the next day.

Throughout the days the phone often rang; Neil's mother and sister, Valerie and the two or three of Anne's friends who knew. She'd come to dread the urgent sound of its ring. She rarely spoke to anyone herself; Neil was her buffer in that respect, it was he who gave the update on how Anne was feeling and what the police had said. Ringing the station now, it felt like the last time she'd dialled a number to have a conversation was in another lifetime, years ago. Now that Stella had gone, she wanted to make the connection again with Jackie, she wanted to talk about it, because there was nothing else to talk about. She needed to talk about her feelings, about what happened, almost continually, but she had begun to realise that she couldn't trust people's reactions. One thoughtless comment ("Was he really horrible looking?") from Neil's brother's wife, Yvonne, ("Why, does it make any difference?") and Anne found herself disproportionately brooding over it for hours afterwards. "I wouldn't have said that; she doesn't know what that does to me," she'd cried into Neil's chest as he rocked her slowly backwards and forwards, to calm and console her.

The photographs were taken, and then Jackie told her that she'd got everything she needed at the moment, but, as Anne wanted it, she'd stay in close touch over the next months until the trial; she'd phone and call round, whenever Anne wanted. She left Anne with the numbers of the victim support group and rape crisis for her to contact. Did she want Jackie to arrange for them to call round? No, not at the minute, maybe later. Anne shied from any kind of therapy, as her nature was not to overtly ask for help, and she felt her pride prickled by opening her heart to someone and assuming they could help. She'd always backed away from any group activity and the idea of group therapy made her shudder. "Us all sitting around telling horror stories of what has happened; 'Oh yes, well mine's even worse than that!' No thanks."

Jackie had assured her that they weren't all like that. "They could help, you know. Anyway, I'll leave it with you for a few days."

Neil returned in the early evening, his eyes wide, his walk deliberate. Anne had been sitting watching television (she hated it, now all she seemed to do when she was alone was watch it, hoping it would numb her). She'd turned over from the news, normally one of the few things she did watch, to an imported American comedy, listening to each clichéd sentence, often repeating what had been said in her head, to prevent any other thoughts from stealing into her mind.

She looked at Neil as he came through the living room door, and suddenly her lethargy left her. She jumped up and screamed at him, "What are you doing? What the hell are you trying to do to me?"

She tapped her finger against her temple.

"You'll drive me mad, I'm telling you. I need you, you don't seem to notice that. I've watched you over the last few days; a sip here and there, that's bad enough. But look at you now! You can't control it like you seem to think you can. You'll have to stop completely, otherwise I can't stay with you, I'll have to go to Stella's or Valerie's, to someone who can help me."

She shouted all this at him while he stood, breathing heavily, eyes down, head drooped, allowing the barrage of her ranting to rain down on him.

"And you standing there accepting all this like it's some kind of penance doesn't excuse you. Nothing excuses you unless you stop it, stop doing it now."

Wearily he walked past her, into the bedroom and sat down on the edge of the bed.

"I'm sorry," he said, lowering his head into his hands, elbows propped on knees. She relented immediately at that tone of his. Sitting down next to him, she draped her arm across his shoulders, putting her face close to his.

"I know you are," she said sadly.

It was always like this; the drinking would slowly escalate over a week or two weeks as he gradually lost the battle to control it. Then would come the binge that would take him over the edge. Experience had taught her that this was now imminent. The binge could last one day or one week, and then he would pull himself together, dry out, take interest in himself and his surroundings (her, the cleanliness of the flat) and return to himself at his best; caring, loving, the model boyfriend who cooked every meal, did the shopping and even bought the tampons.

Most of the evening was passed in nervous companionship. Anne knew he was struggling with himself to control the urge to go out and drink. She carried on watching television as her normal pastime of reading was now impossible for her. The book she had been reading had not now been touched since the previous Monday night and, as it now served as another unwelcome reminder, she'd returned it to the bookcase.

Having contacted Alcoholics Anonymous, reluctantly, on a couple of occasions, she knew that the absolutely worst thing she could do was to confiscate drink or pour it down the sink and try to prevent him getting access to money. 'They will always be able to get money or drink from somewhere if they need it badly enough' echoed in her head. Now, though she felt that these rules were not as crucial, the perspective on everything had changed with what had happened to her. Something in her cried out that now her needs were as important, more important, than his. Now she needed his support, his presence, so much that she no longer felt she had to subjugate everything to his needs: so she took the cashpoint card, cheque book and the cash from her purse and hid them, under the bedroom carpet, where a floorboard was loose and tipped downwards like a diving board, in the corner next to the wardrobe.

After nine o'clock, Neil became increasingly fidgety, moving round the room, then in and out of rooms, for no apparent reason. He kept looking at the clock. She knew that he was starting to panic because after ten o'clock the off-licence would be shut and after eleven o'clock he wouldn't be able to get any drink at all. She was now certain that there was no drink hidden anywhere in the house.

It wasn't long until he burst out, "I need a drink. I'll just go out and buy some then bring it home."

(As if he's doing me a favour!)

"Just give me the money to get some, will you? I haven't got any left."

The way he'd blurted it out – a statement of fact, then his demands – angered her, although she hadn't expected any different.

"No," she replied calmly. "You can't have any more money. I'm supposed to go back to work in a few days' time. Do you think I can do it? I don't. So what are we going to do for money? For Christ's sake, stop being so selfish. I can't walk out the door on my own like you can; I've only been outside a few times with you and Stella. I'm stuck, completely and utterly. You can go out, lucky you! And you'd bloody well go out and leave me alone. I'm scared, scared; do you understand that? You've got to stop and if you don't you can go and live somewhere else and drink someone else's money."

She stopped and leaned back for a second. Although her voice had become raised as she spoke, she'd managed to calm it down towards the end, trying to inflect some finality into what she said, although she knew that this was just the beginning of the scene.

Neil said nothing. He went into the bedroom and emptied her bag on to the bed. She sat where she was, waiting for the outburst. He came back into the room and stood in the doorway.

"Where's the card?"

"You can't have it, so forget it."

He walked over to her and knelt at her feet, placing both palms over her knees to balance himself.

"Give me the card. I mean it."

His eyes were blackened, his expression threatening, and he had now completely changed from the man she knew.

"Or else what? Are you going to hit me?" she taunted, knowing she was pushing him further, fearing for herself but still wanting to go on, on and on, making him see. The next second her emotions completely took control.

She jumped up.

"Don't you think I've been through enough? Stop it, please stop it."

He straightened and held her firmly by both shoulders. She moved one way, then pulled the other, but couldn't get out of his grip.

"Give me the money. You can't tell me what I can and can't do. I earn it too."

She started to cry, not hysterical tears, nor even frightened tears, just sad, tired tears. He relaxed his hold and walked purposely over to the window. She turned half-round and watched his back, uncomprehendingly. She had expected him to shout or plead, not walk away.

The window was open, the nights were still warm. He took the bracket from its fixture and swung the window open wide. Then, in one leap, he had perched himself on the edge of the sill. He sat there, still, like a bird. She was horrified, still not comprehending, but frightened again now, really frightened. He held on to either side of the window frame to steady the rocking motion of his body and turned his face to her.

"I'll jump. I'm not joking you, I'll jump if you don't give me some fucking money, I'll jump because I can't do without a drink. Give me it now."

His voice had risen, his pitch so high that it sounded as if he were about to cry, his voice about to break. Anne stood rooted to the spot and completely silent for a second. She couldn't believe it; he was threatening her with jumping from the window to force her hand. He could not have done anything worse. How could he use that against her? She felt worse than if he'd hit her: she had almost expected that, in any case she was prepared for it, but not this. From everything being in slow motion, as she'd stood there transfixed, she suddenly screamed and ran, ran into the bedroom, the tears blinding her as she knelt at the edge of the carpet and tipped the floorboard, taking out the notes and coins that lay below. Sobbing, she ran back into the living room, slipping where the carpet finished and the floorboards were exposed as she rounded the corner of the room.

Neil stood, coat on, stock-still, next to the other living room door, his hand on the handle, his face a mask.

"There you are, you bastard, go and rot in it."

She flung the money out in front of her, the notes fluttering, not going far before they fell around her feet, the coins flying out from her hands in all directions.

She turned and ran from him into the bathroom, knowing she could lock the door behind her, and, sitting down on the edge of the bath, lowered her head into her hands. She heard the front door slam.

*

For three days, Anne stayed with Liz and her husband Steve. For the first time she had escaped Neil's binge. She didn't feel the pain of it because she didn't see it and, although she was conscious of him being on his own somewhere, either in the flat or in a pub, she didn't actually think of him, or worry about him, as she normally did: he was somewhere getting wrecked and that was the end of it – she didn't want to know any more. While she had been with him both horrors fought for dominance, but now she was away from him, and in some way able to disassociate herself from him, the other took over entirely.

She still fought to control herself and keep on the rails. The next night, on Liz's settee in a sleeping bag, sleep itself impossible, she thought how people kept telling her how well she was coping. How else was she supposed to act? Did people expect her to lie down and beat her fists on the floor? She knew she had a good network of support in her few but reliable friends and in her sisters. She was conscious of the fact that people only like a trier and she wanted desperately to be liked and for those who liked her to be proud of her. She had always had a reputation for being a 'strong character'; people would say, 'Oh yes, but then you're such a strong character,' and she would find herself nodding because she'd heard it said so many times, without really knowing what people imagined they saw in her that reflected this. She supposed it was because she was never afraid to tell people what she thought of them if they annoyed or insulted her. She'd discovered that by being brutally blunt with people you often deflected any attention from your own failings and weaknesses. In the women she liked she often inspired loyalty, men in general were either attracted to her or she evoked feelings of fear, resentment and dislike. Now she knew she would have to call upon all of her resilience in order to live up to the reputation she had earned for herself and to keep the respect of those who were important to her.

Liz had driven Anne over to Valerie's the first day she'd stayed at her flat. They didn't say that Anne was staying at Liz's, answering Valerie's few questions about home briefly, saying that Neil was at work and Liz had called for her earlier that day.

It was the first time Anne had seen her sister since it had happened. Valerie had wanted to come over before as she lived only a few miles away in an affluent suburban town that epitomised the part of the country and the time they lived in. Anne had felt that she needed to assemble her own thoughts and attitude before seeing Valerie for, although she knew her sister's intentions were good, she feared being organised and monopolised by her. Her 'little sister' syndrome, she called it. Anne didn't know how much Valerie knew about Neil's condition, but it was unspoken between them that Valerie didn't like him, didn't think that he was good enough for her sister and it was also known, but unspoken, that Anne had her secrets and would cover up for him when challenged.

Valerie had made lunch for them in the garden and they ate, lulled in the afternoon sun. When Liz went to the bathroom, leaving them alone, she had leaned over and hugged her, holding her tightly.

"You poor, poor thing I don't know how you are carrying on. I'm sure I couldn't cope with what you've been through."

Anne felt tears rising with the dryness at the back of her throat, Valerie was traditionally the harder sister to get close to, the least emotional of the sisters, the toughest in her opinions on others, often appearing cold or unsympathetic. Now, out of character, she was showing her feelings and building Anne up, complimenting her in the way she was acting. She couldn't believe it. Through the tears in Valerie's own eyes, she looked at Anne, saying, "You know, this is the prettiest you've ever looked, Anne. I know that sounds strange, but your face looks so serene. You must be in shock, because all your normal expressions have gone." Here she pulled a variety of rather ugly faces for Anne's benefit. "You're normally so over-animated that your face is all over the place, but now you look simply," she paused, thinking, "well, simply a pretty face." She lightly slapped Anne's rounded cheek and Anne, half-turning away to light another cigarette, smiled to herself, thank God some things don't change, she can still give a wonderful back-handed compliment.

Andy, Valerie's husband, came home from work while Anne and Liz were still there, their children, Trevor and Fiona, having been sent to a friend's for the afternoon. When he came out of the back door towards the garden, Anne's heart started to pound. She felt embarrassed and did not know quite how to act with him. She'd heard his reaction to the news from Valerie, who'd said she found it very difficult to tell him, feeling in herself a resentment towards men in general through what had happened to her sister and wondering, hoping that he would understand the utter terror and disgust she felt, needing him to feel it too. When she'd got the basic words out, which she'd said was more difficult than she'd imagined after ten years of marriage, he'd smashed his fist on the kitchen table, which stood between them, and shouted, "The bastard!" When Anne had heard this, she felt that he had understood, for she'd never heard him swear like that. Valerie said that their relations with each other were strained for a while afterwards; he was unable to meet her eyes ('male guilt,' she concluded) and she found it difficult, though she knew it was wrong, to separate him from the rest of the male population who, at this moment, she hated and feared, feeling that there was a universal responsibility to be borne for what had happened to Anne. Anne understood this feeling completely; though they were different in many ways, both she and Valerie tended to blame the man closest to them for the crimes of their entire sex.

Anne had known Andy for some twelve years, and he was in many ways the brother she'd missed, but combined with this had been an awareness of his sexuality, since her initial schoolgirl crush, which now made this meeting even more difficult. Valerie suggested Liz help her bring in the dishes and Andy sat down in the vacated chair.

"Hello, Anne," he paused, she looked at him and made what she thought was a grimace at the awkwardness of the situation; it reflected in Andy's face as a flash of pain. He leaned forward, "I'm so, so sorry. If I, we, can do anything to help you, I don't know what to suggest but if we can do anything, please, just ask."

"Thanks Andy," was all she trusted herself to say in reply. She sighed her relief, it was okay, he'd said enough. The air was clear between them.

They had to leave to collect Steve from work. They stopped outside his office. He was already waiting outside the pale-bricked building; they were late. Anne got out of the front seat of the mini and climbed into the back as he strode over to the car, long-limbed, bobbing towards them, his jacket off and tie loosened. Anne counted the seconds until he got in; she was feeling the strain of these first meetings, the awkwardness of what was to be said.

"Hi darling. Hi." He glanced back towards Anne and she stared at him, retaining the image of his face in profile long after he turned to face the front.

"What a bloody day for the air-conditioning to break down in the office. My God, we were dripping by the· end of the afternoon. You would think they might let us all go home; apparently that temperature is against the law! But of course they don't."

Neither answered him. Anne had said nothing bar hello, and Liz had not even said that. The silence was broken by Liz swearing at a driver who pulled away from where he was parked on the kerb directly in front of her. Anne knew it was meant for Steve. Did Steve know?

Anne and Steve had never got on well together, as they were jealous of one another's influence over Liz. Steve, because he saw Anne's feminist beliefs turning Liz against him. To Anne, Steve was the kind of limited man, undereducated and unaware, on whom someone like Liz just wasted herself. Unfortunately for Steve, Liz was, abetted by Anne, coming to realise this, which caused arguments in their young marriage that tended to end in Steve's affirmation, "You would never have said that before you met Anne."

Lately, they had called a kind of truce, although Anne suspected that her being raped was seen by Steve only in terms of one more intrusion into their lives that would take up Liz's time even more and deflect attention from himself.

While they watched the news that evening, Anne felt her head pounding with the stress of not being able to communicate with Steve properly: still nothing about the attack had been mentioned between them. She felt anger and dislike mount, throbbing at her temples, as he spoke, talking loudly over the sound of the television, telling Liz about his boss's announcement at a meeting that day that he was to take over the responsibility of another section, which would mean he would be handling a budget of over £1 million. She felt embarrassed and outraged by the pathetic sound of the boast in his voice. Liz made noncommittal rejoinders, then left the room to make dinner for them both. Anne knew she wouldn't be able to eat, so declined the offer, smoking instead.

Steve made trite remarks about each news item that came on partly, she knew, to cover his own embarrassment and partly, Anne suspected, because when faced with a situation that demanded maturity and character he had neither the resources nor intelligence to cope with it. He was what she saw as the classic 'man at the pub'; at thirty-two he still joked about 'the boozer' on a Friday night and how many pints he could down (even though he knew someone who was going under from drink, to whom it was no longer a joke). He was a man's man and, as such, Anne and he were always at loggerheads; she couldn't stand his complacency – the world was okay, why shouldn't it be? Why look too closely or deeply at anything; I'm all right, so why change anything?

When the next news item came on about a middle-aged woman, raped in mid-afternoon in the West End of London, after being bundled into a car and taken to a nearby flat, Anne could take no more. She knew she couldn't bear any comment that Steve might make, and silence, after the previous barrage of banalities, would be even worse. She left the room quickly and went to the bathroom, thinking that she seemed to escape to that room to hide in a lot, being the one room with a lock on the door. She said to herself wryly, looking at her face in the mirror, safety: what a joke.

When she returned to the living room, Liz had come in with their dinner on trays. A cup of coffee sat on the table next to where Anne had been sitting. *Top of the Pops* was on the television, an inane, smiling, dimpled presenter introducing the next act. When the music started, Anne felt her defences instantly rising, recognising the sinister, threatening beat. The Alice Cooper song had been around for weeks now and from the first time Anne heard it she'd hated it. This was the first time she'd seen the video. He moved slowly across the screen, ugly in his sadistic make-up, with handcuffs and a torture rack behind him, visible through the screen of dry ice. Anne stiffened, Liz looked embarrassed, Steve looked on. While women in black and red corsets leaned and flailed around the set, their backsides pushed out and the cameras nosing down their cleavages, they struck the poses of the porn mag, their eyes narrowed, mouths open and pointed tongues protruding.

"Christ, do we have to watch this shit?" Anne burst out.

Liz, waiting only for something to happen in the room that would release her, shot up and turned the television off.

"It's only music, Anne."

Steve's voice was patronisingly paternal and long-suffering, his superiority unmasked. "And anyway, that's life. Just because you don't like it, it doesn't mean it'll go away. It sells."

*

Anne went back. She'd known that she would. Anyway, she hadn't made a decision to leave Neil permanently. She didn't feel up to that: she was just moving through the days, as they unfolded; she wasn't capable of making big decisions, of making things bend to her will. She told herself all this, just as she told herself that she wasn't trying to threaten Neil either. She knew that wouldn't work as she'd tried that before. She just didn't want to see the mess he'd got himself into, the horrible state and stages he'd go through. Simple. She went back the morning after he called at about midnight on the third night she'd stayed away. When the phone had rung she'd known it was him; all three of them knew it was him. Steve had answered the phone, passing it to Anne almost immediately, with an air of superiority that made her smart. To her surprise, Neil was sober. He said he was sober, hadn't drunk since the previous day, had spent all day drying out, said he hadn't wanted to contact her when he was in that state, didn't want to put her through that. Anne, with relief, knew that it was true. She knew from his voice, his breathing, his choice of words, she knew from every little thing that made his assurances superfluous.

She'd wanted to go home. She wanted her own things around her, to be in her own bedroom, with her own possessions. When at Liz's, she knew her own life was on hold, she felt as if a pause button had been pressed, which allowed her a reprieve, but that was all it was. She wanted to go back so that she could try to start to change things. She needed to move. What was she going to do about work?

When she saw Neil, the reunion was sweet. He had tidied everything up in the flat, and all the windows were open. He'd bought flowers which he'd placed in a vase in the middle of the

long oak dining table. She knew what a transformation this must
have been from the state it was in during his binge. He'd had a
haircut, his thick, dark hair was cut close around the sides and
back, swept to the side on top, very short, the way he knew she
liked it. His skin looked soft, newly shaven and dark, clean and
innocent-looking. She wondered again at how he managed to look
so attractive sometimes, after what he put his body through. How
much longer could he bounce back like this? He begged her to
believe him, that he would be her strength now. He said that
from the night she'd been raped he'd been slipping, and once he
was already on the road it was impossible to get off. He told her
that he'd been drinking a bit for a few days before it happened,
that he'd hidden bottles of lager underneath the massive horse
chestnut tree that grew at the front of the house, hidden a bag in
the foliage there, having some before he went to work and again
before he came back into the house. So it was inevitable, he said,
that once that happened and their life had stopped, been ripped
apart; however you wanted to put it, it had been inevitable that the
crash would come. She sat listening, part of her knowing that it
was true, knowing that nothing he did to hurt her had been
intentional, and the other part of her wondered what extremes
would have to happen to her to put anything before his spiral of
descent when drinking. She knew the answer. But she also knew
the truth of his commitment to change.

"Anne, you've got to believe me. I want to be here for you,
always. I want to change. For God's sake, I've got to change. If
I thought that I was going to be like this forever I'd kill myself
now."

So they agreed to try again, as they'd tried before: everything
hinging on Neil and his will power, his need to succeed. They
could do it, they loved each other and God knows they needed
each other now.

"Could you ever let another man touch you after what's
happened? I don't think you could, do you?"

She thought her answer through and answered honestly that no
she couldn't ever imagine even looking at another man sexually
now. How could she? It hadn't made her fear Neil in that way,

he hadn't turned into a predator overnight in her imagination. Because she knew him, he hadn't altered in any way. That had nothing to do with their sex; they were totally separate from that disgusting act. But how would she know that anyone else could be trusted? She couldn't know. Only the men she knew now – Neil, her brothers-in-law, her friends' boyfriends or husbands, and a couple of Neil's old friends from home – could be trusted in any way; either to talk to or be alone with. When her mind tried to go further than that she stopped. She knew that she and Neil wouldn't have too many problems, as the night after had proved. But she wondered just how much of that night had been her trying to prove something both to herself and to Neil: that nothing would change. That night, and since, she hadn't touched him anywhere other than his face, touching his cheeks and stroking his head, his neck, as he'd made love to her. She hadn't even looked at him anywhere else since then, averting her eyes when he walked from the bathroom to the bedroom, naked. She didn't want to see his innocent, loving body spoilt by that dark, messy area that didn't vary enough from one man to the next, not enough not to remind her of her torturer, just as that night she'd thought of Neil when she'd pleaded with that pervert, touching and forcing her to stroke that horrible thing, she'd thought, 'If Neil could see me now, if he could see what this man's making me do.'

These feelings, which she was gradually unravelling in her own mind, she explained to the Victim Support volunteers when they arrived. Jackie had called again to emphasise that the support was there, if she wanted help. Anne agreed to see them, more as a way of keeping the link with Jackie alive than through any real belief that they could help her.

When they arrived at the flat, Anne immediately felt the incongruity of the situation. It was as if any two people had walked off the street to come and hear her story. It wasn't in her nature to confide in people, and although she was very open with her friends she had always felt that authority figures, superiors of any kind, had to earn their respect and not just be automatically entitled to it by virtue of a position or title.

This is what she felt now, as she offered her hand to the middle-aged woman and young man who came into the room, having been led up the stairs by Neil. All four sat down. The woman was in her late forties, Anne thought, her light brown hair was short and softly permed, her face attractive though her features were sharp and slightly pinched, her large dark eyes sympathetic. She was very thin and looked slightly nervous. The man was probably in his mid to late twenties, Anne thought. He had fair hair, cut quite long, but still passable in a suit, which was, Anne imagined, what he wore to work. He was quite a large build and looked fit. He appeared the more confident of the two, but when he spoke sounded apprehensive. They'd introduced themselves as Kevin and Gloria.

"If you would prefer I will go into another room and just talk to your boyfriend."

Anne answered that it was quite all right, she didn't have a problem with him being there, fearing more any cosy 'girl talk' the woman might try to lead her into if they were left alone. A silence followed, when Neil went out to make coffee and Anne lit another cigarette. Gloria asked how Anne was coping.

"It's nearly a fortnight now; I know I've just got to sit it out and let the feelings pass over me, I know I won't feel this awful for ever."

Did she know this? She hadn't thought it until she'd said it. Did she believe it?

As she spoke, she heard the defensiveness in her own voice, but she didn't want to sit and listen to them recounting the standard phrases that would be said in these circumstances, she wanted to pre-empt them; saying it first. She knew she wasn't being fair, but she instinctively knew that these were lay people, people who knew nothing of what had happened to her; she wouldn't have chosen to confide in them in any other situation and therefore they were of no use to her.

The man, Kevin, leaned forward eagerly as Neil placed mugs on the table in front of them.

"That's a great attitude, very positive, especially so soon afterwards."

Anne immediately asked a question, needing to put the onus back on them. "Have you ever dealt with this kind of situation before?"

No, Kevin was a computer programmer, had only just joined the Victim Support group as a volunteer, and this was his first assignment. Anne smiled at him and turned to Gloria. She felt a need to have control of the situation and, as such, felt more inclined to ask questions than answer them. Gloria, sipping her coffee, spoke in a friendly tone, easy now.

"Well, I've been a volunteer for seven years now, but this is my first case of this kind. Mostly I visit people who've been burgled or mugged, usually old people. Some of them are very lonely and I'll keep in touch with them for ages, visiting them or giving them a call. It helps build their confidence back up. Some people find it very hard to accept the fact that someone's gone through all their possessions."

Anne said nothing, lit another cigarette and occupied herself with placing her coffee cup back very carefully on the low table in front of them. She began to regret having agreed to see these people. She knew that they would do her no good, although she recognised the closed door within herself that refused to let them in in the first place. The problem was her pigheadedness, she knew, and arrogance was one of her defences. She saw nothing in these two to earn her respect or deserve her trust. They were ordinary people with ordinary jobs, she a part-time teacher, he a computer programmer. She knew that she was probably capable of analysing her own feelings well enough, so what she needed was someone to look up to, an omnipotent being, she thought to herself, smiling inwardly. Someone who was more intelligent than she was, or someone with a greater knowledge to confide in, and she'd met that person already in Jackie. These people were no substitute.

When Gloria asked her to tell them what had happened, Anne refused. Before Gloria could come back with any answer to her point blank refusal, Anne carried on, "It's not that I can't, or that I'm bottling it up; it isn't that. It's just that I've told it all so many times before, I've gone over and over it with the police and

I've told my friend and my sisters and, of course, Neil, so I could do without saying it all again."

After the bluntness with which she said this and their polite, rebuffed reactions, she then felt it was up to her to tell them something to make amends, however much they were irritating her. She even found herself thinking wildly that if she shared something with them then she might be able to get rid of them, she'd have paid her dues.

She found herself telling them, without actually wanting to, that she and Neil had made love twice. She'd started to say it as proof that she was all right, then found herself saying that she was beginning to think that she was having a problem coming to terms with his body. That she only wanted his face and clothed body. That she couldn't bear to think of male genitalia at all. As she announced this, she realised that this was the first time she was telling Neil this as well. She wasn't sure how much he already knew.

Once she made this confidence she asked them to leave. She knew she hadn't come across well to them and she also knew that it wasn't their fault. She tried to make amends for her dismissal of them at the door, "It's just I've got a good network of support, I've got friends and family who are very good to me. I admire the work you do but I'm sure you give lots more to people who haven't got anyone or," she made a grimace, "or maybe people who are easier to get on with." The woman smiled, laughed a little in her denial, though her eyes still looked disappointed. The man shook Anne's hand warmly, then Neil's.

"She's a real intellectual! She's sorted it all out for herself. You've got a great girl there."

When Anne had shut the door behind them she turned, laughing, towards Neil. "Now I know they would've been no use to me. If he rates me that highly he mustn't have a clue. Easily fooled!"

*

Stella had asked Anne to come and live with her when she'd come down to stay. She offered to help Neil too. She knew that Anne wouldn't leave him and so she said that she would put them up until they found a place to live and Neil had found a job, to give Anne breathing space before she tried to find work again. She'd said that she understood that Anne didn't want to leave him and that although Stella felt that the best thing would be a complete break with him, she was prepared to help her sister on any terms.

Anne told Neil that that was what she wanted to do; that she'd had enough of this dreadful area that they lived in, she wanted to go north again and she wanted to be with her sister. Their flat was rented from a middle-aged couple who spent half of their lives in Mrs Lord's native country, France, and half in Vancouver where Mr Lord taught in the university. They came back twice a year to check over the house and renew the contracts. The six month one Anne and Neil had originally signed was up for renewal in two weeks' time. Now that a possible future had been mapped out for Anne that was what she wanted to do. To get out of Croydon, out of the whole overpopulated, intimidating area was what she wanted. She'd never been happy here and now she couldn't wait to leave. Her future would be with Stella, and with her help she could pull herself together again. Yes, now it had been suggested, it all seemed simple and the best thing to do.

Neil got Anne's manager's telephone number from the phone book and rang him the night before Anne was due to go back to work. Neil asked if Anne could have a meeting with him first thing in the morning, at eight thirty, yes, it was very important. Anne sat listening to the conversation, her heart sinking, the gulf between herself and her manager, or anyone she'd worked with, seemed wider than ever. A different world.

The next morning, Neil and Anne walked to her office, to the ugly hexagonal building, set incongruously in the middle of a roundabout at the fulcrum for roads going north, south, east and west. They came up to the front of the building through the subway and then went up the steps. Neil would have to wait here as you couldn't go further into the building without a pass. Anne had dreaded this morning, she'd dreaded the walk and, now that was over, dreaded even more what she was about to do. The mile walk in had been bad enough, and she'd felt Neil's tension too; it was the furthest from home he'd managed to go, without a drink, in a long time. Over the last year, perhaps more, their lives had increasingly narrowed, their horizons getting closer, until their flat and the five minute walk to Neil's work (and the pubs he passed en route) were all that was left for him. She wondered if the will to stop he'd shown for the last four days would collapse this morning, as he was faced with having to do something: to walk with her to work. It was always in situations like this, she'd thought as they walked, nervously, hand in hand, that his courage left him: the times when he was forced into doing something, where he had to be at a certain place and had to get there by walking far or, worse still, by taking the train or bus. That was when this strange phobia took hold of him.

This morning Anne had not mentioned it, had just been glad that in the end he'd come with her, without making a scene or having a drink. She didn't know how long it would be before she would really believe that he had cracked it, she didn't know how long until she could breathe out again and relax. But she hoped.

She stood close to him on the top step, the glass doors and the twelve floors to the offices where she worked in front of her were a mountain to be climbed. She felt small; this was the corporate world that meant nothing to her, that had ceased to have any meaning for her in the last fortnight. She had only been working for two years and had not found a place where she fitted in well or felt comfortable. The office politics, the game they all played, cutely if they wanted to succeed, she had never fathomed. She had so little in common with the people she'd worked with, and Liz was the only real friend she'd made. She knew that she was in the wrong job, but a mounting lethargy and a fear of failing prevented her from trying to change the way she was going. Her life had seemed to be too full of pressing needs, all bound up and connected with Neil, for her ever to be able to stand back and view her life and her work. She'd been fortunate to do well at interviews and be generally held as an intelligent young woman who was on the brink of proving herself and going somewhere, if she applied her mind.

Neil had told her to think carefully about what she was going to say and do. After calling Don Smith the previous night, he'd confused her by urging her to think it all through again. But Anne had remained convinced. How could she carry on working? She couldn't go out of the house alone. She was scared of everyone, except the handful of people she surrounded herself with. She tried to explain exactly how she felt – it was so important for him to understand.

"I feel raw, I have no protection. Everything jars on me. If some fool in the office touched me, or came up to me from behind, I'd leap into the air."

Neil nodded desperately, anxious for her to finish. "I know, I'm not questioning that. It's just such a big step, to actually hand your notice in. That's all."

"And I need to take it, because it's the only thing that ties me to this godforsaken hole. We can hand the flat back to the Lords, you can give a week's notice and then we can go."

Now she stood, more scared of having to walk, isolated and alone, into the building, than of resigning, of giving it all up and cutting her connections. She contemplated what was in front of her, walking past the security guards, the old boys who always nodded and smiled, who knew everyone by sight. Would they see the difference in her? Could she walk past them this morning as she had done for the previous eight months and look the same, speak the same way, hurry past them in the same way? She knew she couldn't.

"Good luck. Stay calm."

Neil kissed her and she walked through the revolving doors. The security man, grey and round, with his military moustache, beamed at her, "Been off on holiday?"

"Yes," she answered, trying her best to make that one word sound friendly, hoping she'd smiled, but not sure, as she hurried past him. She got out of the lift at her floor and walked into the office, weaving her way round, through the carrels, to where her desk was. How alien it all seemed. Only a fortnight had passed yet her desk seemed unfamiliar. Her own handwriting on the charts on the wall, highlighting important shows and conferences in the year, caught her eye and held her attention like an old toy from childhood, totally forgotten yet glaringly familiar, when you saw it again. The tray marked 'in' had a number of sheets of typed paper, stacked at angles, as they'd periodically been deposited by various people, piling up since she'd left. Internal memos mostly, she thought, as she lifted the edges and then let them fall gradually back. And what was I doing on the days these were written, she thought.

She stood in front of her desk, not knowing what to do. She could hear voices, early though it was. A man and a woman, she recognised them, but couldn't figure out to whom they belonged. Should she walk round to Don's desk? She felt like an impostor: she didn't belong. Or rather she felt as if she'd already left – the job, the building, everything to do with work – as if she were remembering, recounting this scene. Listening again, she made out the two voices; Don and the PR assistant, Sue. She could hear Sue's emphatic, raised voice, spilling out the details of a story about how the planned orchestral evening for the following Friday now had a major problem. Anne stood, not knowing what to do, only knowing that she had to speak to Don and get out before the office filled and the day began, when the people around her would expect her to be a part of it.

Sue's voice seemed to go on and on, "You know it'll turn out to be the same shambles that it was last year, Don, unless we sort it out now. I can't go to her, it will have to come from you."

Christ, thought Anne, who cares? Sue, that self-important idiot! Then she heard a movement behind her and turned to see Amanda, a graphic designer from the art studio, further round the circular floor.

"Hi! Had a good break?"

"Yes, sort of, er... thanks," Anne mumbled as she started to walk quickly passed the girl, who looked after her confused. She stopped short at Don's desk, not having thought through what she was doing, she had arrived there without realising it. Don and Sue looked up immediately, Sue stopping in mid-sentence. Don looked annoyed, whether with Sue's complaints or Anne's interruption, Anne couldn't tell. She stood there, still, saying nothing, then nodded in reply to Sue's question about whether she'd had a good holiday. She then turned to Don and said rapidly, "Please Don, I've got to see you now."

She stressed the 'now' and felt torn between the need to stay calm and the urge to yell at him. "Now, please."

"You can see I'm with Sue, I'll be with you in a minute."

She was dismissed. She hesitated, then hearing the hubbub of voices rising in the office realised she had nowhere to go: she couldn't go back to her desk.

"I'm sorry, I don't mean to be rude but as my boyfriend told you on the phone last night, this is very important, it can't wait." She apologised again and then stood still, waiting. Don excused himself to Sue in a way that showed he saw no reason for this immediacy and, rising, said, "Come on then," to Anne, striding off in front of her to one of the three meeting rooms behind his desk. Anne followed him in and felt that she could breathe again once she'd closed the door behind them.

"Okay Anne, what's the problem?" Now she had secured her sanctuary Anne realised the enormity of what was in front of her. Don pulled out a chair, sat on it, defiantly, and motioned for her to sit on the one next to him. There were about ten chairs around the oval table that filled the room, but she still stood at the door and then walked slowly towards him.

Don was a tall man, good-looking in what Anne always thought of as an American kind of way, with even white teeth and a broad smile. Anne knew that he was thought of as very attractive by most of the women in the office and, although she could see why, neither his looks nor personality attracted her personally. He was about thirty and always appropriated the latest buzz word as if it were his own. She liked him, he was said to be a great family man underneath all the good looks and charm. She liked him, but had nothing in common with him.

"It's difficult to know how I should put this but, as I can see you're annoyed with me, I'll get straight to the point. On the first day I had off I went out, late at night, on my own and I was," she hesitated and decided on the word, "attacked." She stopped.

Don's face looked momentarily confused. "Have you told anyone? You really ought to go to the police."

Anne wondered at his naivety, was amazed that he should think she hadn't been to the police.

"I've been with the police, off and on, the whole time I've been away," she explained carefully. "They caught him. I'll have to go to court." She added this to try and impress the enormity of what had happened on him.

"Where was this, Anne?"

"Where I live." She shrugged, "A mile away, I suppose."

She didn't know what reaction she'd expected, but it wasn't this. Although Don seemed nonplussed by what she'd said he didn't seemed horrified or shocked. Perhaps she hadn't explained it enough. As she thought this, Don spoke again.

"He didn't thump you or anything, did he? Did you have any money on you?"

Anne looked at him. There seemed to be a great abyss between them. This was the hardest part.

"Don, it was much worse than being hit or mugged. This was an evil bastard." She stopped, her lips tightening as she steeled herself. "I was raped."

She thought for the umpteenth time how unrelated that word was to what she'd been through. One word, one syllable, quickly said. It was nasty-sounding, but not excessively so; it sounded like 'ripped', which gave the impression of destruction, the negative, but it was a completely inadequate description of the horror she'd been through, the disgust she felt, the fear of dying, oh, more than anything it was the knowledge that this person controlled her fate, she would die at his hand, when and how he wanted. And she was only twenty-four. 'I haven't lived yet, I haven't even been happy yet, and now I'm going to die,' she'd thought over and over again.

Now she sat opposite this man, these thoughts going round and round in her head, while she struggled to make him understand through this one word. He looked down at the table in front of him.

"I'm so sorry. I don't really know what to say."

"Don't worry about it. There's nothing to say. It's just that I need to tell you because I'd like you to let me go. I can't carry on working here, I can't go out of the house alone. Neil is waiting for me downstairs. I want to get away from here, get away from London. I'm going to go to my sister's, in Chester. So, can you take this as my notice and let me leave please?"

"I understand what you're saying, Anne, but don't you think you should take it more slowly than this? It's a big decision, giving up your job. Why don't you take time off and think about it? I should be able to work something out with Personnel."

Anne knew that he was trying to do the best thing, but her need to get away entirely as well as to get out of the room and back to the safety of the flat, was mounting.

"I've had two weeks to think about it. I can't carry on living here. I can't walk down the road, for God's sake. I need to leave quickly."

"Why can't you walk down the road if he's been caught? Is he out on bail or something?"

Anne could feel her exasperation increasing as the conversation went on. She wanted to shout out, "Do you know what he made me do? And he was planning on making me act out a porn video, and I was so shit scared that I jumped out a third floor window. Have you any idea what that was like?" But she couldn't. She couldn't cross that barrier of what was acceptable to say and what wasn't.

She realised that she was going to have to censor the truth to make it palatable enough for her to say and for people to listen to. Yet she knew this was wrong. If more people were faced with the stark truth, raw, disgusting and unsanitised, there would be fewer versions of glamorised misogyny on television, at the cinema, in advertisements and pictures. She knew this, hadn't she always known it? She didn't need to be tortured to have it pointed out to her.

She spoke slowly to Don.

"No. He hasn't been let out on bail." Adding, to emphasise her point, hating herself for doing it, "The police wouldn't let him out; he's too dangerous. He's done it before and was put away for seven years. He served four, apparently, and then was released. Six months later: me. The police had been watching him in that time, but of course they can't do anything until he acts first."

She knew she had said too much, she knew Jackie had trusted her, had given the information in confidence, but she needed some way of getting across to him how serious it was, how close she'd been to being murdered and how she was with the police, so that she stamped out any thought he might have that it mightn't be as she said it was.

"He would've killed me only I got away. Please let me go." She finished quietly.

"Yes, of course," Don said quickly. He seemed anxious now to finish this interview. "Naturally I'll have to speak to Personnel, but I shouldn't think there'll be any problem there. They will write to you."

Anne stood up. "Thanks."

"If I can help, let me know."

"Yes, okay, thanks."

The classic exit line, the expected rejoinder. Anne stopped, "Oh, I don't really want anyone else in the department to know. Just say I wanted to move back up north or something, if you don't mind."

"Yes, of course. I won't say anything to anyone else."

He held the door open for her, standing politely to the side, for her to walk past.

"Did you know him then?"

Anne stopped and looked at him, knowing her expression was frozen.

He carried on, "It's just you know that he's been in prison before and was released early and everything. I just wondered how you knew so much, that's all."

"The police told me," Anne answered, flatly, bluntly. Defensively, she knew. "I don't know people like that, as I'm

sure you don't either." She then said goodbye and he responded
with the same and a, "Good luck. I mean it."

As she walked straight to the office doors and the lift, looking
at no one, she felt cross, cross with his inability to take it in and
hers to express herself. She knew that he was a good enough man
really, quite soft compared to some of them. But he had been
searching for a reason in order to make sense of it, some reason
why it should've happened, and to her. Did she know him? Yes,
that would explain it. Because it just didn't happen to anyone, did
it? Not to people you know, who then actually tell you about it.
It couldn't be that bad if they can then sit there and tell you about
it.

As Anne went down in the lift, she knew he wouldn't have
believed her if she'd told him the whole truth, what actually
happened; he wouldn't have believed she could be sitting there so
normally, hair brushed, lipstick on, in clean and pressed clothes,
hands lying folded in her lap. He wouldn't have believed it
because she looked so normal.

*

Released from work, Anne saw the future only in vague terms.
She saw life in the village just outside Chester with Stella and her
husband Peter, with whom she had never got on well, but who
would accept her now because of what had happened and because
Stella wanted to look after her. This was what Anne craved. She
wanted the responsibility of her life taken away from her. She'd
hovered on the brink for so long now, losing weight, living her
life in a state of apprehension, fearful of Neil's health and deeply
afraid of the weakness in him that made it seem like they were in
some triangle, where her rival and enemy was alcohol. Now she
felt she couldn't cope with any more, and the promise of care,
security and a release from decision-making was just what she
wanted.

She'd known from the start that Neil didn't see it the same
way she did. Although he often talked nostalgically of Wales and

home, he feared any return there, any return to his overpowering and authoritative mother and his five brothers and sisters, who had all stayed in the same community, all but one, ten years his junior, grown up now. Two of them were married and all of them were close-knit and reliant on their mother. The understanding of his relationship with this woman, whom he by turns loved, feared and hated, Anne suspected, was fundamental in any attempt to unravel his confused subconscious. She'd once heard it said that any man who had a problem with his mother would always have paradoxical feelings towards all women to whom he was close. The idea occurred to her often.

"But Stella said that you could stay with her as well, until you get a live-in job at a hotel. For God's sake, the place is teeming with hotels, you'll get set up quickly." Neil had just openly admitted what Anne knew he'd been brooding on over the last few days: he didn't want to go. They were due to leave in three days' time, the date arranged with Mr and Mrs Lord (Anne had told her the reason she was leaving, why they had been unable to give notice. She'd understood. Her husband, when Anne saw him later that day, was unable to meet her eyes). Stella was to come down with Peter, in a van they'd arranged to borrow from a friend.

The last couple of days had seen an increased anxiousness in Neil's manner, although she knew he wasn't drinking. Now he blurted out that they were making a mistake. Yes, he wanted to move, but he didn't want to go 'home' and he particularly didn't want to move within Stella's sphere of influence: he knew she would try gradually to separate him from Anne. He said he saw through Stella's idea of Anne living with them and him living in a hotel ten, maybe twenty, miles away.

Anne sat, listening to him. She had known something would stop this plan going smoothly. If she was honest with herself, she told him, she'd known that he didn't want to go.

"Why did you just go along with it? Why didn't you say so at the start, come up with another plan, take the initiative?"

"Because it was what you wanted. But honestly Anne, I've been thinking about it a lot over the last few days and I don't think it's the right thing to do. For a start, you'll never get a decent job up there, that is if you get a job at all. There's nothing for us there; I know, I used to live there. You'll regret it, we'll both regret it."

"I don't give a damn about career opportunities," Anne said scathingly. "I just want a chance to be happy and I want to be away from this bloody place."

"The other thing is that you'll lose your connection with Jackie and Adam if you go a few hundred miles up the country. At the minute you see Jackie every few days, she's there for you to talk to, she's good for you and she keeps your spirits up. If the trial isn't going to be for at least six months, maybe a lot longer, you need to keep in touch with them, you don't want to risk losing the venom you've got towards putting him away."

"Come on, I'm not likely to lose that, am I? I'm not likely to 'forget' what happened either, even if the court case is a year away. Don't try and find other reasons for it, and make out it's all for my good – be honest. If you don't want to go, then you don't want to go."

They'd found out that morning – Jackie had phoned – that the trial was going to be a long time away. This had been mentioned to Anne before, but she hadn't really taken it in. Now she knew that it would be at the Old Bailey and that it could take up to a year to come about. The idea that it would be at that famous court made her heart race. She imagined the pomp surrounding it. She had had an immediate image of the scales of justice on top of the domed roof. Another image too occurred to her, that of many inset windows and a revolving door: the news shot of the court; camera men showing people running in, faces covered by the lapels of coats or with files held up to obscure them. She'd been told that the Crown Prosecution Service had accepted the case immediately, something it had not even occurred to her to doubt.

In her day to day life she found it impossible to envisage a year ahead, imagine her life a year on. She still moved in a daze from day to day and had a dreamless sleep when she was able to lose consciousness, but that wasn't until it was nearly light at around four in the morning. Getting through each day was what she concentrated on; life with Stella and an eventual court case were hard to imagine.

So when Neil raised these points and became more emphatically against moving up to Stella's when faced with her apathy, she did not feel inclined to fight for what she wanted. For what did she want? She wasn't sure. Neil suggested taking Valerie up on her offer: to stay with them. Valerie, in her affluent Surrey suburb, just outside the bustling town. Was this what Anne wanted? Away from Croydon, but not far away. Valerie had certainly offered to look after Anne during the day, to be with her and take her out, while Neil went out and looked for a new flat for them to rent and a new job closer to their new home. Neither of them worked now, as Neil had done his last shift the previous day at Miguel's, in anticipation of packing and moving.

At first Valerie's suggestion had seemed impossible to Anne because it required Neil to do all the work, getting trains and organising everything. Now he was saying he could do it and it would work. Looking at him now, his face animated, full of resolve, Anne was tempted to start believing that perhaps he had changed, perhaps he had found the strength he needed to beat drink through the purpose of piecing together their lives again.

As Anne sat listening to him put forward all the reasons to stay in the South-East of England – jobs, independence – she knew one thing for certain; there was a chance he might succeed if she gave him all the responsibility and power to find them a new life in the way he wanted to, but that he would definitely fail and lapse back into alcoholism if she and her sister tried to coerce him into doing what he didn't want to do.

*

They moved into Valerie's and Andy's a couple of days later. Stella had been disappointed by this but, as she told Peter, she'd rather expected it. When it came down to it, Anne would always let Neil's stubbornness dictate, she explained to him. Neil wouldn't have wanted to come to Stella's, she knew, because the first thing she'd planned to do was to loosen his hold over her little sister.

Andy, Neil and Anne packed all their belongings into the transit van, while Valerie stayed in the house, getting the spare room ready and making space in the garage for the boxes of their kitchen utensils and bedlinen, records and books. Fiona and Trevor ran around her, helping and getting in the way, by turns.

As the loaded van, driven by Andy, with Neil and Anne next to him on the long front seat, passed under the bridge to head out towards the heart of Surrey, Anne closed her eyes for the few seconds, leaning her head tiredly against the cabin window as she thought, I never have to see that bridge again. I never have to come back to this place. I can shut the door on all this now and look ahead. Ahead? To what, the voice in her head demanded? Hopefully to a new flat in a quiet road, she answered, trying to convince herself of the existence of a future. A road with no pubs and shops, no litter, no takeaways, no hard people pushing and threatening her. She told herself she needed peace and quiet, so that she could learn to breathe in and out normally again and gradually relax.

They stayed a month at Valerie's. The kids were pleased with the novelty of having permanent visitors. Anne spent the last of the summer days with Valerie and the children in their back garden. Trevor was seven, Fiona five. Bright, attractive children. Trevor was blond and blue-eyed, his shorts slipped constantly down the back of his legs, seemingly unnoticed by him and though they impeded his running and constant charging around, were pulled up only when he was commanded. Fiona was dark-haired and dark-skinned like her father. Her manner was knowingly engaging, half flirtatious, half childishly open and giving. Anne felt she was being allowed to look in on normality. Valerie was understanding with her: concerned and careful not to be overpowering. Anne suspected that Andy had advised her not to dictate too much to Anne and thankfully all the criticism and digs about Neil had stopped.

Valerie tried to encourage Anne, in the freedom of hot summer days, to push herself a bit. She suggested Anne take Trev and Fiona through the buzzing centre of Epsom, unchaperoned. "Don't worry. Men don't take any notice of you when you have a child. You're automatically considered to be beyond the age when you are interesting!" she'd joked. As Anne walked with them towards the shopping centre, down the private road, past well-kept lawns and rigidly demarcated boundaries, she felt as if she was beginning to regain a better understanding of how the world really was. Normality was all around her, even in this suffocating suburbia. Though she didn't like the area, or what it stood for, she thought thankfully how removed it was from Croydon, with its endless rows of pubs, newsagents and video rental shops and torn, ragged layers of bill posters. Now she'd got out she hoped she wouldn't have to go back, realising now, from even this slight distance, that she would always associate Croydon with the depravity of what finally happened to her there. She now wanted to get happy quickly and stay that way. Enough misery. She knew she'd been in a spiral descent, even before that happened to her, and feared that if she went any further on, the way back would be blocked.

Valerie introduced her to some of her friends who, like herself, looked after their children, supported their professional husbands and socialised with one another. They were in their mid to late thirties, well-groomed, attractive women, university graduates with lots of stimulating hobbies; golf, ceramics, interior decorating. Anne relaxed, temporarily cosseted in this life, soaking up the polite, easy life, not really knowing if she wanted it for herself, but enjoying the difference from her own fraught past, feeling that she was charging herself up to resume her own life at some future date. Valerie took Anne and the children on day trips to Hampton Court and Kew, hoping to make her more balanced in her attitude to life, knowing she had seen only the shabby side of life for so long. She had not been surprised that Anne got plucked from the street by a rapist in a place like Croydon. Anne knew this, though it was never actually said, but she also knew that the rapists in the town where Valerie lived would only be dressed better and perhaps even harder to spot, for underneath the veneer of class and money the men would be the same – corrupt and depraved.

Within a week, Neil had got a job, at the general hospital only four miles away. He started immediately, in the much sought-after straight shifts from six in the morning to four in the afternoon. The evening and night work that most chefs' jobs entailed had always been a grievance, but now it was even more important to him to have a daytime job; for how could he leave Anne alone at night now?

He cycled to and from the hospital every day and, knowing he was being watched, he strove to pass the test that he felt he was being forced to sit: working during the day and looking at flats up for rent in the evenings. He knew that Valerie's approval was a barometer of public acceptance and he desperately wanted to be accepted and exonerated by Anne's family especially, and their friends and the police. He needed to be seen to be helping her.

After searching the papers and looking round a few places on his own, he came back one day and said he'd found somewhere. It was close to the hospital, about five or ten minutes on the bike. It was a fifties semi, similar to the type Anne had been brought up in. It had a long back garden and the flat comprised the ground storey of the house. They went to see it together, only a couple of stops on the train line. Anne watched Neil's profile in the train carriage: train journeys were the most daunting of all for him. She asked him how he was coping, seeing his eyes blinking rapidly, his fists clenched. He assured her he would get through it, telling her that the last couple of weeks had been easier: the longer he stayed off it the easier it got. As long as there was an escape route, he said, he could cope all right. If he were unable to get off the train should he need to, that's when he'd crack. Anne thought back to when she'd given up smoking for a year, about four years ago now: as long as she had the unopened twenty pack with her, in her bag, in her pocket, she was okay: she had the choice.

Anne linked her arm through his, "We'll be all right, won't we?"

"Of course, we'll always be together. I don't think anyone can be as close as we are now. I can't wait till we've got our own place again and we can relax. Just us two."

He slipped his arm around her and kissed the side of her face. Please God, she said inside her head, let it be all right. Let all our troubles be behind us now, surely we've had enough.

The brief passing countryside changed quickly back to houses and walls and gardens separated by conifers and fences, as the train pulled up to the station.

"This is it," Neil said and rose.

The living room of the flat overlooked the well-kept back garden, separated by wide french windows. The front reception room was converted to a bedroom. It had large bay windows and looked slightly incongruous as a bedroom, but Anne didn't mind. The kitchen was clean and modern, a good size, with the back door leading into the garden as well. The shower room had been extended on to the side of the house and there was a shed in the garden where Neil could store his bike. The house was at the top of a steep road that ran from across the station bridge down to the main road to Sutton, the nearest town. It was only two minutes' walk from the station, at the most, past a cluster of shops, a bakery, post office and a hairdressers.

The rent was four hundred pounds a month, one hundred pounds more than the flat in South Croydon. They told the property agent they'd take it, arranging to pay the deposit and one month's rent in advance, planning to move in the next week

"There's no getting away from train stations or railway lines around here, is there?" Anne announced as they walked back to the station.

"Not if you don't have a car, there isn't."

As soon as Anne moved into the flat she felt that now, hopefully, life could begin again. This restart of her own life was at once a relief to her and also very frightening, because she knew that it was now that she would have to prove to herself that she could actually cope and go forward.

She understood herself and her situation well enough to realise that her reaction to everything: to every event, TV programme and newspaper article would be affected by her memory. What she knew and what she had suffered would dictate how she saw and interpreted everything.

Alone in her new flat, Neil having set off for work on his bike at six in the morning, Anne sat on the cheap, coffee-coloured sofa and stared straight in front of her, out through the french windows into the garden. She debated whether or not to open the windows a fraction, as the sun was shining and the sky was unclouded, although the temperature had dropped from a few weeks earlier. She opened a small side window, looking out to the driveway and side of the house next door, instead. A woman, at the back of the house, on the newly made patio, was walking slowly indoors, leaving a small boy pedalling round and round the paving stones on a toy police car.

Anne sat down again. She had a cup of coffee and a piece of toast on a tray on her lap. She saw months stretching out in front of her, unchanged. The only event she could see with any certainty was the trial, and even this was at some unspecified time in the future, perhaps as long as ten months away.

She knew that gradually people would phone less and be rather less concerned about her, about whether she had any company that day, or whether they could take her anywhere, to get her out of the house. She knew that was bound to, and rightly should, happen, but what should she fill her life with now? It was as if what had happened to her had not only stripped her of her former life, but that the very business of giving statements, of talking to the police, the doctor, her friends and sisters, had given her something to replace the void with. Now though, she had the rest of her 'normal' life in front of her and had no idea what to do with it, how to act in it or how to carry on.

She knew she had acted sensibly, had won the respect of the people around her. She felt, however, that none of her reactions had been spontaneous, and that she had 'chosen' a way to act (the right way, as it happened), but she felt that had she not chosen that way she would have chosen another, any other, and adopted that guise instead, as nothing seemed to come naturally to her any more.

Now she felt her resolve begin to slip away from her: lethargy descended on her. Her life narrowed further over the next few weeks as she sat inside her flat, alone, looking out of the window, losing weight, smoking heavily, clicking the remote control for the television from one channel to the next, hating herself for doing it.

She stared out of the windows: a long, narrow, well-kept garden to the back and out to a residential road at the front. She sat in the chair next to her bed, looking at the row of identical houses sweeping downhill towards the traffic lights and the main road. There was a whole world of life and events out there, and it frightened her. She was scared of ever getting a job again, scared of going to the shops, scared of walking casually down the road on a sunny day. She could not imagine walking past men in the street if she were alone without having every nerve alert, ready to spring, to run.

She was also scared of the inside – the two types of inside. Inside the house she couldn't have her back towards doors or windows that might open, and Neil knew never to stand behind her, ever since the episode with the spoon he'd rubbed down her back from the nape of her neck downwards. She'd swung round on him and he'd immediately seen what he'd done. "Never, never do anything behind me when I don't expect it. Actually just don't do anything behind me at all, I want to see everything that happens, I need to know what to expect." She was afraid too of unlocked doors, and would try the handle of the back door when she went into the kitchen and the front inside door, that led into the communal hall, when she went past it into the bedroom. In the evening, as soon as night fell, she would turn on the bathroom light. It would stay on until the morning. She never wanted to see a bathroom unlit, where she would fear what was hidden in its corners, when she would, of course, be reminded of that other bathroom, the light which had gone on and off so many times. The bedroom light stayed on too, so that if she awoke in the middle of the night, or in the early mornings, before the light filled the room, she would immediately know where she was. She wanted no couple of seconds of confusion as her mind struggled out of its subconscious into the everyday world.

Then she was scared of the inside of her mind. As the weeks, then months, passed, she began to realise that in no way would any of what had happened to her ever leave her. She would never escape from that knowledge. She knew that she might gradually learn to think of what had happened to her without feeling as if she had been struck a blow: time might distance these feelings, and put a bolster between images and her reception of them. But that which she feared would remain, which was worse: the fear of what the knowledge, the memories would do to her life, colouring everything, every event, every conversation, every meeting with someone new. All would be coloured by the fact that she knew what had happened and therefore knew it could happen again.

Anne's views, attitudes, her interpretation of news items, other people's views, the papers they read, what they liked, had usually been thought of as extreme by most people she knew. Her close friends saw it differently, in the main. Like-minded people, they admired her unflinching moral stance. Now though, she feared the bitterness that might set in. The bitter expressions she had seen reflected in tired, worn women's faces on the bus, or walking round shopping centres, she now feared would gradually become a part of her own appearance. She'd overheard Neil, a few days after the event, talking to her friend Jeanette on the phone. "God knows how she'll get over it. Why her for Christ's sake? She's obsessed enough as it is, so I can't imagine what she'll be like when this sinks in. Why couldn't it have happened to some dim-witted little scrubber who didn't think so much about it in the first place? ...Yes, yes... I know, I know, you're right, but you can see what I mean, can't you?"

Jeanette, Anne's longest-standing friend, lived in the north-east of London. She'd come down a few years before Anne, to go to poly there. She was a strong-minded, serious-looking woman, statuesque and commanding, who showed people exactly how she wanted to be treated by the way she acted, not one who ever resorted to preaching to them, like Anne, in order to coerce them. Although their fundamental views were the same, Jeanette was much more *laissez-faire*, for she at least had learned to exist in a world where not everyone shared her views. She worked very much in a male atmosphere, in the management ranks above the factory floor, where she chose to ignore the lurid pictures above their work areas and next to their lockers and then stared pointedly at them when taunted, only to reduce the men to embarrassed confusion when the expected outrage and humiliation didn't happen. She won by calling their bluff and beat them at their own game. She fought the world on its own level while Anne demanded that people see things only as she saw them in order to prove to herself that her views were right, knowing she could cope with living in such a horrible, warped world if only some other people were, or could be made, like her.

What Anne saw in almost every programme, film and advertisement made her heart thump in anger. She saw it everywhere and had always been amazed by how most women failed to notice the misogyny with which they were surrounded. When in a video store she would watch the women, in ones or twos, walk around the shelves slowly, looking over the video covers, high and low, that showed semi-clothed or contorted women's bodies, or women prostrate with fully-clothed knife-holding or gun-brandishing men close by. How could they look at it all so unquestioningly?

Now Anne's mind was stuck on the wheel of man's ultimate threat; how clearer could the statement have been made to her than 'I have the power to subdue, enslave, rape, do what I want to you'? As she sat in the same seat day after day, her mind frustratingly went round the same thoughts until, heart pounding, she had to do something, phone someone – Stella, Liz, Valerie – Jackie, and talk, say what was on her mind, as if by getting it out it would leave her. Most days it seemed to her that she could only get off her particular wheel for that day by swapping it for another. So waking up in the night from her broken sleep, she would hear the voice saying, 'Okay, now it's time for the video, the worst form of propaganda I know but it has to be done,' in an almost comical, ordering command as he propelled her, sobbing, from the bathroom into the littered, dirty, bedsitting room. Then this scene, that voice, would go round and round in her head until displaced by some other scene or vehement feeling, of, perhaps, all the filth available in all the shops, supposedly for normal life: women's genitalia, open for universal viewing, for everyone in the shops to see, the child in the newsagents, the woman in the video shop to the filthy men who supply and buy the magazines, the books, the films. Then, then she could cry, in fear and desperation.

At these times, throughout the day she could think of nothing else, had nothing else to fill her housebound world with, so the thoughts circled in her head until Neil came home and she spilled it all out to him, her language becoming more crude. He listened, tired and concerned; suffering himself and sick of it all, struggling against his own nature as he got through each day, cycling past the off-licence and refusing to go for a drink after work with the other chefs.

Anne became preoccupied with what she described as the universality of what had happened to her. The lead up to that night recurred to her constantly and made her want to stand up and shout to the world, for recognition of her state and agreement with her. The need to make people see the corrupt world for what it was became paramount; encouraging and selling corruption, tut-tutting on the one hand when things like rapes happened, while, on the other hand, enjoying reading about it.

On that night, bored, restless, at about eleven o'clock, Anne had turned on the television and flicked from one channel to another. Worried about Neil, knowing that if he were not back home soon he would be drinking, she had finally put down her book, unable to concentrate. *Come Dancing* was on one side, a dated American sitcom on the other, golf on the third and a film, just starting, on Channel Four. She hoped it could keep her attention as the effortless, one-way nature of TV watching would pass the time more quickly than anxiously pacing the room.

The Last Movie started as a slow-moving, moody western with the usual leather-clad, laconic, silent cowboy. This, she thought, was watchable, if boring. After about three quarters of an hour, the tedium began to change to the infinitely more predictable tedium of a woman taking off all her clothes and moving around the room, everything in full view as she bent over and crawled over the man's body without, Anne noted cynically, the camera showing any more than the naked shoulders and self-satisfied smile of the man. The next scene came as a shock to Anne and changed the nature of the film dramatically. The pair, with another couple, were watching a sex show between, of course, two women. Angry and incensed, she got up and switched the television off just as the entire screen was filled with a woman's single breast and the other woman's mouth, licking and sucking. "Christ," Anne exclaimed aloud, "why do I always see the most offensive crap on the screen?" She looked at the clock on the video recorder: 12.11, and, her heart beating rapidly, she decided to go and meet Neil. Having finished her packet of cigarettes an hour ago, she was dying for one now. Her temper rising, through her anxiety and fear over Neil and compounded by the film, she shrugged off her dressing gown and pulled on pants, jeans and a T-shirt. Slipping her feet into the sandals by the door and grabbing her bag, she slammed the door behind her. She immediately felt apprehensive as she realised that the light bulb on the staircase between the first and ground floor still hadn't been replaced. Still she walked on, cautiously.

After he'd got her and pushed her in front of him through the doorway of the flat, the first thing she'd taken in was, with relief, that there wasn't a group of men waiting for the 'catch' to be brought in. That, as she'd grappled with the key in the lock, had been her greatest fear, when the possibility had occurred to her. Each fear at that time came to her as more horrific than the last, they vied for prominence in her adrenaline-filled, almost hysterical, mind. Simultaneously she saw the television, facing the door, and her mind registered the picture: a woman facing the camera, in black suspenders and stockings, nothing else, her legs spread wide open as she gyrated on a table top. The same film. Even in her sharpened state of panic, Anne registered this. Then in the bathroom, facing the open window, the television sounds in the background, him walking in and out of the room several times, the light going first on, then off, she thought, he's been looking out of the window to see if a woman, alone, gets off the last trains, while watching that vulgar, degrading rubbish, which gets him going, more and more.

Now, alone in the prison of her new flat, she wondered if those disgusting actors and treacherous actresses would ever know what had happened to a woman, in real life, after someone got off on them in (she often thought of the title, spitting the words out in her own mind) *The Last Movie.* Even then it hadn't been enough to satisfy him. Still he'd needed more, as he led her through the room. 'It's the worst form of propaganda I know, but it has to be done.' How that phrase haunted her. Searching, from left to right amongst the mess and rubbish covering the floor, for a film that would remove reality still further from life, so that all that would be left of 'women' were the genitals and breasts that bastards like this wanted to believe was all that there was, in order to carry out their gross, depraved violations.

Anne had told the police all this: first Jackie, then Jackie and Adam together. Jackie, agreeing with all she said, told her it would be very hard to get any of it to stick, that everything she'd said was interpretation and not fact.

"But," Anne had interrupted, "the facts are that it was a sexist, anti-women film and I'd turned it off; then when I was forced into his flat, it was on there. Those are facts, aren't they?" She'd listened, increasingly disillusioned as Adam Small had told her that it was on TV, on Channel Four, starting well past the watershed, therefore it couldn't be that bad. He'd stressed that they needed facts at court, that it was only facts that could put this man away not, he implied, Anne's half-baked feminist interpretations. "There's no proof that films lead to any act like rape and until there is there's no point in bringing it up in court, because it only obscures the real facts and would be thrown out immediately anyway."

Anne had replied, her voice becoming confrontational, that it sounded like the police were selective about what they wanted to come out at trials, though for the best reasons. "This is why it never becomes accepted that pornography incites rape, why there are no statistics supporting it: because it is left out of the story."

Adam watched her calmly, unblinking, as she'd blurted all this out, and ended by saying quietly that she should just concentrate on putting this one particular bad bastard away and not on saving the world, because that she could never do. "That doesn't mean that none of us should even try," she'd said to him, her voice become tearful.

Jackie broke into the conversation, her tones rational, down-to-earth. "Listen, Anne, you can say whatever you like. You've already mentioned the film in your statement, and that's fine, you can say it in court. All Adam is saying is that there's no point in the police pushing it too much because it's impossible to prove and we're not here to see what caused it to happen, we're here to prove that it did happen. The most important thing is to get him off the streets, right?"

Adam, fidgeting in his seat, his thin, wiry body always on the move, moved his gaze from Jackie to Anne. "Now come on, Anne, you're not trying to tell me that any bloke who watches soft porn is a potential rapist, are you? That would wipe out about 99% of the male population."

"Then that would just leave us with the 1% that are normal. Suits me fine," she replied, smiling slightly to alleviate the tension in the atmosphere, though her eyes were shining brightly and her chin still quivering with emotion.

Anne didn't go out. For the first weeks in Sans Souci Road she didn't set foot outside the front door and ventured out of the back door only to hang washing on the line or to empty the bins. Then she would close the back door behind her, knowing that if someone opened it to go in she would hear it creak loudly.

Neil encouraged her to stay in. He brought her two packets of cigarettes home from work every evening. His set daytime hours gave them some stability, encouraging him to come home and not stay out longer. In their own way, they were happy with each other now. She asked only that he stay sober so that their lives could follow some kind of regular pattern, and that left her with only the problems of getting herself capable of going out and to a state where she could think about getting another job.

Neil knew that this was his one big chance. When he had the most to lose, he normally crashed down the hardest. Now, slowly, he was inching his way forward, each day being built on the strength and growing optimism of the last. He felt the admiration of Anne and her friends, as he continued to earn the money they needed to survive. Now, for the first time, he was the one they both depended upon. He liked her dependence on him, and he was happy for her to stay indoors for the time being. They both knew this, though nothing was said. Anne didn't know whether he felt like this because he wanted to support her totally, in the way that she had him in the past, to make it impossible for her to leave him should he fall short and start drinking again, or whether it was because he too was frightened of what would happen to her were she to be out, alone, on a street again. Anne supposed it was a mixture of the two, shrugging off its importance.

When Anne tried to pull herself together and face the fact that she must go out again soon, her logic defied her. She relived over and over again her reaction when she'd first heard, then, a split second later, seen the man across the road, that night. She'd seen him hesitate for a second, then she saw the expression on his face: an animal with its prey. She'd stopped dead, watching him charge from the other side of the street, thinking, 'Oh God... here it comes... I'm going to die... this is it...' The shroud of civilisation was stripped away from the night, disclosing the ugly hatred underneath. Now she had the time to see him not as a one-off freak, a maladjustment, but as the extension of the intimidation and assertion of power that can be seen every day, in man's relations to woman, but taken to the extreme.

So even when she tried to see the situation objectively, she could only see that going into the outside world again, on her own, was taking her life in her hands again, trusting to luck. That one rapist had been caught, that he was on remand, meant nothing. There were any number of the same out there, free, and they all wore the same clothes, so how could she tell?

After about three weeks, Anne decided that today she was going to do it – she would go out. She had decided the previous night in bed, but she didn't tell Neil. She knew he'd try to dissuade her. From first getting up to being completely ready, with nothing to delay her any more, took nearly two hours, for she deliberated over everything. Getting showered and dressed took so long, much longer than it used to. Every stage of preparation was punctuated by a cigarette. She needed something to reassure her, something to replace a person by her side, something to put between herself and the outside world, to cover her nakedness. She took a knife from the kitchen: a sharp, professional chef's knife. She clasped it in her hand and then sank it deep inside her long trench coat, keeping her grip on it tight. The coat was too heavy for the light, crisp autumnal day, but covered and with protection she felt that she would be almost secure. She walked out. Out of the front door. She didn't want to use the back door, with its narrow path leading round the house to the front, hemmed in by two walls: an alleyway. She had only used it a few times before, with Neil. Normally, on the infrequent occasions they went out on a Saturday or Sunday afternoon, they used the back door, that gave direct access to their flat. Now she found herself in the hallway and saw mail on the door for the couple who lived upstairs. She saw their name: Andrews. Who were they, she wondered. She'd heard them walk across the floor, but had never met them. She pulled the door to behind her, facing forwards, towards the street. It was brighter, warmer than she'd thought, with the quietude of a weekday mid-morning around her. Walking down the driveway and out on to the road was a strange sensation. She was reminded of two girls she'd been friendly with when she was a kid: they lived a few doors away and were forbidden to go beyond their garden gates at any time. Their father was strict and frightening, and he had scared Anne and the other children. He was tall, very dark and swarthy and had a totally immobile face when he spoke. Anne saw his face now. Because the children had never been allowed out it was not questioned, just accepted. If you wanted to play with them, you went into their garden. They would see you off when you left, both waving to you, standing together, their straight, black hair shining, but always from just inside their gates, never beyond. Anne thought how she was probably feeling something similar to how they must've felt on their first trip abroad, unchaperoned by their parents, stepping into the public highway.

She felt insubstantial, as if she might fall over. She felt isolated and on show: highly visible and vulnerable as she walked along the footpath. Each step she took seemed to be in slow motion. She went past the high wall of the timber yard next to the house which formed the corner of Sans Souci Road. The open yard gates, with men's voices beyond, seemed like a gaping hole, from which anyone could reach out and pull her in as she passed. She clutched the knife in her pocket, her hands sweating. Her mind was racing. Her heart was pounding with fear and apprehension, yet on another level she knew she wasn't seeing the world as it really was: rather it was as if she were looking at it through a distorting mirror, or as if everything were slightly off centre, or at a slant. The world looked similar to the way it had done, but was bordering on a difference so small, yet entire, that it defied definition. She knew that she walked down the same kind of roads, in the same residential kind of area which she had known most of her life, with the same shops, yet everything looked slightly different, as if seen for the first time. She drank in the images before her differently, taking it all in: aware as she'd never been before. She walked round the corner and then saw the row of small shops in front of her, five in all. Immediately she took in every person coming out of the shops, the small transit van just pulling away from the kerb, a few people getting off the bus which, engine starting up, sounded so loud that it seemed to Anne the volume on the whole world had been turned up. She walked across the road, feeling tall and exposed, and went into the first shop: an off-licence, and bought two packets of cigarettes. The woman serving was talking to a man leaning over the edge of the counter, chatting easily, passing the time. No more than a minute's walk from where she sat all day this life went on: people talked and gossiped, asked for directions or shopped, the off-licence opened and closed for the day: day in and out, life went on. Without Anne. She smiled at the woman before she turned to leave the shop.

The calm that had descended once she was in the shop, after hearing the door click to behind her, left her as she opened the door and went into the street again. Passing the timber yard she felt the same intimidation. She glanced behind her, but no one was around. As she more hurriedly walked on she heard steps, somewhere behind her, quickly, almost running. She panicked, and instantly the rapid thudding of her heart filled her ears. Why was there a man running towards her? Oh no, no. She whirled round completely, to face whatever was coming. She saw a man sprinting across the main road that she'd just left, diagonally, away from her, towards the shops. She expelled the air trapped in her lungs. It came out in a gasp. She thought how before, when she was someone different, she would not automatically have assumed the worst if, in broad daylight, she'd heard running footsteps. She might not even have heard or registered them at all. Now the worst reason seemed the only possibility.

She made it back to the door of the house quickly, not caring if anyone saw her frantically rushing, her hand clutching the knife in her pocket. She hesitated before putting the door key in the lock, looked around her, to the right, then to the left, then stopped again to look right behind her. As she opened the door she feared someone rushing up behind her who would push her in, in front of him, then close the door behind them both, where no one could see or help. Only when she'd got through the next door and was back inside her own flat did she feel, to a certain extent, safe.

*

Anne's friends still supported her greatly; Liz, who called over a couple of nights a week, after work, with the grudging acceptance of Steve, and once, maybe twice, at the weekend, when she and Anne would either go to a pub for a drink or Liz would drive her over to her own house. It suited them, when they went out at all, to go out alone, without Neil or Steve. Valerie called also, either with or without the children. She provided the family support that she knew was crucial to Anne. She'd helped them both financially with the flat move and now produced the forms she'd collected from the DSS in order for Anne to get sickness benefit. Valerie went with Anne and sat with her while she stammered out her reasons for leaving her last job. It didn't seem to make much sense, even to her now, as she sat in the shabby government offices, trying to explain that she'd left the merchant bank because she'd not been able to envisage ever going to work again, after being 'attacked' one night and, at the time, it had been important to her to sever all links with Croydon and everything that kept her there. It would have made sense if she'd actually gone to the Welsh border to live with Stella but, as she hadn't, well, she merely shrugged her shoulders in answer to the clerk's questioning. She'd changed her mind, that was all. The young woman looked slightly aggrieved and continued to form her rounded letters on the sheet in front of her: uncomprehending, totally uncomprehending. Anne felt too weary to be bothered to try and explain it to her.

A week later she got a letter to say she wasn't entitled to any sickness benefit, although her doctor in Croydon, after being contacted by the police, had forwarded her a note to run for two months, describing her as mentally exhausted. She arranged another appointment at the DSS and Valerie took her again. "As you were a student until two years ago you haven't paid enough national insurance to be eligible," a diffident clerk explained to her, embarrassed at her situation and at the bureaucracy. She would be entitled to £27 a week, and that was only because she'd lied and said she lived alone.

Jeanette and her boyfriend, Gordon, came over from East London more often than before. Gordon and Neil had never got on well: their backgrounds and attitudes were totally different. Gordon wanted to succeed and Neil's inverted snobbery made it impossible for him to even try. Gordon, working in advertising since he'd graduated, was motivated by work and sport. Neil saw him as a type, he saw Neil as a waster – no ambition, no pride in himself – and what he had glimpsed of Neil's underlying intelligence only made it worse. Neil hated Gordon's clothes and the way he spoke, compared him to the Next models, assuring Anne he had as much originality. Anne had laughed, saw his point, knowing there was more to it than that. She knew where all this came from: he always felt resentment towards middle-class men, yet rarely women. Anne sometimes wondered at the selectiveness of his bad attitude. Subversion? Perhaps.

Gordon had known Anne for about six years and never could he comprehend why she put up with a man like Neil, because of his drunkenness and the chip on his shoulder which made it impossible for him to follow her when she mixed with her old friends or went to work parties. They generally got on together much better when Neil wasn't there: Anne relaxed and was less defensive and Gordon was less patronising. In private, both Gordon and Jeanette had commented that Neil's resentment was ultimately directed towards Anne herself, but now that he had been sober for coming up to three months and the situation made the usual animosities insignificant, they'd visited each other a few evenings, at the weekend, with no drinking and no embarrassment.

The similarities between Gordon and Anne also made their relationship strained. Their egoism, their need for others to be coerced into seeing that they were right, continually made them both surprised when the other stood up to them. Now their relationship changed. Anne put so much stock by people's first reactions to what had happened to her that it was the deciding factor as to whether she could bear to have them around her. With Jeanette it had been easy, as it had been with her sisters, for the two of them had helped each other out with so much in the past, with both Anne's parents and Jeanette's father dead, they'd dealt with one another's grief before and this was not much different. Gordon she had worried about, and she was apprehensive about how he would react with her and her him. Her heart had jumped when the door bell rang in Cadogan Road, the first time Jeanette had come to see Anne, on her own. Gordon arrived, hours later, to collect her. She wouldn't forget his reaction, he'd walked straight past Jeanette, who'd opened the door, to Anne, standing some little way back, and held her in both hands by the shoulders, pulling her towards him, saying simply, "I'm so very sorry for you." That was all: that was enough.

Once the subject of what had happened to her was broached and then overcome, discussed and aired with people, she was okay, she could relax. She could then talk openly, be herself, about what happened or anything else, it didn't matter, but that initial conversation about what had happened had to be got through. The right reaction was vital, then she could feel safe with them. But she needed that initial discussion, they needed to be receptive, able to listen, not say the wrong thing. She rationalised it to herself by saying that she had been through it and so, if they cared about her, then they should be able to listen to the story, able to talk about it, want to understand her.

One friend failed the test. On the same course at the polytechnic, Denise had always given the impression of 'being there' for her friends. She was good-natured and happy during the three years Anne had known her well. Coming from a secure and rather privileged background, she was able to see the world in terms of how much fun she could get out of it. Neil had told her what happened on the phone. Anne saw her once afterwards. She now worked in Leeds and arranged to call and see Anne when she was down visiting her family who lived in Kent. From when she first arrived Anne knew she didn't want to talk about it. She was friendly in a rather forced way, and Anne wondered if, through the distance of the year's lapse since they'd last seen each other, she had always appeared so superficial and lightweight, even in the old days. She knew she was probably being unfair. She was probably nervous. Anne tried to refer to what had happened obliquely, and made comments, "Of course, it's no wonder really that I've lost weight," in answer to Denise's exclamation, "but it seems pretty drastic lengths to go to though, wouldn't you say?" she'd grimaced, trying to lead Denise into asking her how she really was, how she coped, what had actually happened; tell me, tell me, I'll understand. The response though was only the briefest recognition of what she referred to, Anne later thought, reflecting back on the day: an expression and nod of the head which said, yes, yes, I already know. But she didn't know, she knew nothing and, amazingly, Anne realised, didn't want to know anything.

The tension inside Anne's head mounted, the division between what she was saying to Denise and what she wanted to say widening, until she wanted to scream at her, understand, ask me please, listen, help me.

It was a Saturday so Neil was with them. The day was bright and cold. They had coffee, numerous cigarettes and then Neil made lunch. Afterwards, Anne suggested they go out, though she could think of nowhere she particularly wanted to go and found herself even more fraught than normal. Denise suggested they go for a drive and maybe stop off somewhere for a walk, if Anne knew somewhere to go. She didn't, but didn't say so. They set off, leaving Neil behind as rugby had just started on the TV and he'd settled down to watch it. As they walked to Denise's car, Anne thought with amazement that one thing she was starting to relax about was Neil. Here she was, in one small way at least, just like a part of any normal couple, setting off with a friend for a couple of hours, leaving her boyfriend to do his own thing and not worrying, well not worrying too much.

In the car Anne started to talk, to talk about what had happened, not naturally, but because she felt she ought to, thought she could get through this invisible wall that made everything they said to each other just miss the mark. She knew as she started to speak that she was making a mistake.

"I want to tell you, I need to, do you understand that?"

Denise looked ill at ease as she consulted the rear-view mirror before turning a corner, her gestures exaggerated as she looked right and left, not answering but physically saying 'the whole of my mind is on what I'm doing'. Anne's words hung awkwardly in the air, echoing in her mind.

"What he made me do has made me a totally different person. I need to tell you."

"Anne, don't tell me if you don't want to; if it's easier don't say anything at all."

Her words sounded hollow, the trite cliché rolled off her tongue dismissively. Anne said nothing then, and if only to break the awkward silence, pointed to a coffee shop amongst a group of shops in a lay-by off the side road they were now on.

"We could pop in here if you like, any further down this road and I don't have a clue where I am."

Denise seemed relieved and when they were no longer in the close surroundings of the car the air seemed more relaxed. They ordered coffee and scones with cream, their childish excitement over the food bringing back some of their old innocent camaraderie. For Anne it was an act, and probably was for Denise too, she thought. Suddenly the idea of telling Denise what had happened seemed impossible – their friendship couldn't take it. She thought back to all the conversations of old, about sex, about what they'd done and hadn't done, she remembered the old AIDS awareness programmes of which there'd been such a spate in their first year at poly, their hilarity when they'd heard discussed, in all seriousness, what some people got up to, and suddenly she saw that this was the only way she'd ever talked to Denise. If she told her now what he'd made her do, how he'd spoken to her, what treadmills her mind now paced, it would sound cheap and hollow. Their friendship couldn't make the leap to the other side of Anne's mind.

She stirred her coffee, wishing the day was over and Denise gone. Her appetite had left her, and she pushed the scone around the plate, trying to disguise it. Denise was talking, telling Anne about a work dinner she'd been to a few weeks earlier, in London. How a group of them had gone on to a wine bar, and she'd got completely drunk, had it off with a guy at the back of Oxford Circus, with whom she'd worked on a project for a couple of months, and ended up going back to her sister's flat in Acton, alone, without being able to remember how she got there. This was her amusing anecdote, told to help release the tensions of that day. To Anne it was the final slap in the face. She couldn't believe Denise could take so little care of herself and trust to luck so much, knowing what had happened to her. She sat there stonily while Denise recounted the story, not even pretending to find it amusing as Denise came to the lame end, retreating into herself.

In the months that followed, Denise telephoned a couple of times, but Anne wouldn't speak to her. Neil said she was out at Liz's house or over at Valerie's and filled her in on the details of the looming trial. Anne couldn't forgive her. She realised she was probably being unfair, but her frustrations found an outlet in lambasting Denise. A bouquet of flowers was outside the door of their flat one evening during the trial. She hadn't phoned for almost two months. Too late, Anne said and after much persuasion got Jackie to agree to take them home.

This evening, after Denise had left, Anne let go, all the tensions of the day coming out.

"Doesn't she realise? What a bloody insult. It's as if she thinks what happened to me was in some kind of vacuum. That it only involved two people in the whole of the world: me and him."

Anne never said the name, could not speak it, didn't want to invest him with humanity, denote him as she would do anyone else by the use of a name.

"What I went through, as well as not actually wanting to know, she just discounts it as a one-off. Perhaps she thinks it could only happen to me. Maybe she thinks it would be worth it if she had a good enough night beforehand," she added bitterly.

With Jeanette she could talk it through, could try to untangle her feelings as they both went through exactly what Anne felt, how she was pushing herself to go out, if only to the shop, not a minute's walk away, once a day, knife in pocket, her hand clutching it.

"Jackie says it could actually be worse for me, carrying a knife. Someone could easily get it off me and then turn it round on me, with twice as much force. That's justice for you, isn't it?"

She went over with Jeanette what she felt in the few seconds when she'd lost it completely.

"Why, when he was charging for me, did I drop my bag and hold my arms out from my sides, Jeanette? My God, that's some defence mechanism, isn't it? Really, I was making myself more vulnerable than I already was because I was thinking, 'Do it, but don't hurt me, see I'm putting up no challenge.' If, in those couple of seconds, I'd acted differently, what then?"

With Neil, she went over and over it all, trying to rationalise it, make sense of what had happened and how she'd changed. What she wanted, needed, to do was to come up with an attitude that would enable her to carry on with life, to go forward, different from how she was, but still herself. One day, walking back from Carshalton, where they'd walked down to the ponds and got some shopping, Neil looked at her quickly, his face showing first pain, then breaking into a smile.

"That's better. You know I think that's the first real smile I've seen from you. Keep it up, Anne, please. And another thing, you're looking at people you walk past again now. I noticed that the other day, no more of that looking down stuff. You're coming back, I can see it."

It was changing; slowly, slowly, she was coming back to life. The problems they'd both feared over sex didn't materialise. She was coping with that too, though nothing was spontaneous, everything deliberate. Her real fear of having a disgusting image, a horrible memory, flash before her as she was making love with Neil never happened. She played a game with her mind and made sure that she didn't try to blank off her mind completely, deliberately, to the whole subject. She knew that what was in her mind every waking moment could not be banished completely at an emotional time. She let it wash over her at these times and told Neil nothing of it. She glimpsed it all at the side of her mind or passing over her, but never looked at it head on. She let the thoughts intrude if they tried and coped with them as they happened. And she did. Those thoughts never spoilt it all for her, though she knew if she blanked them out and they came at her with full force they would. Only general thoughts, half-formed, occurred to her, not specific scenes or memories. The only time she was reminded of it all forcefully was when she looked at him in that one place and felt nothing but revulsion. She tried not to look. She never touched. Neil understood.

A part of them seemed to carry on with sex to show that they could, that they were still a normal couple. The touching, the surprising one another, at any time, in any room, that had once set off their love-making, was gone. Now in bed, it was always Anne who initiated it, who set the parameters, as much as she could cope with, but it didn't matter too much that their relationship had become, to a certain extent, perfunctory.

*

Jackie came to see Anne every couple of weeks. She'd sent a card from all the CID officers on the case when Anne and Neil moved into the flat, delivered with a bouquet of flowers. She and another DC, John Fleming, whom Anne hadn't met before, came round after she'd been in the new flat a month, to help her fill in the criminal injuries compensation form. This had been mentioned before by both Jackie and the victim support people on their single visit, but it had been too early. Too early for Anne to think of the question of money in relation to what had happened to her and too early for Jackie to hope to assess how much money she was likely to have lost through it.

Now she felt better able to cope with something like this, over which she had such ambiguous feelings. To her cynical comments and jibes, Jackie stressed that she was not being 'paid' for anything, it was solely a way of compensating her for what she'd lost, through giving up her job, having to move (Anne wondered, would anyone naturally think there would be any financial losses through rape – she didn't think so). Also, Jackie went on, it was a way of cushioning her for the immediate future. She dutifully filled out the form; it filled up her day and the formality of it, the presence of the police again, made her feel that she was doing something worthwhile, adding another piece to the jigsaw that would eventually be completed by the picture of the trial. DC Fleming went through each question with her, reminding her to claim for the jeans, T-shirt and shoes that she would never see again. He stressed that it was worthwhile to do all this now, even though it was unlikely she would hear anything for months yet, due to the backlog of cases and, she suspected, though they both denied it, not until the court case had come and gone and a guilty verdict were returned would the government admit that it actually had a case to pay out on.

As the doctor's certificate had run out, Anne needed to find a doctor to register with in the area. She looked up the doctors in the phone book and saw that there was one in Park Street with almost the same postcode as her own. It must be close by. When Neil came home that evening he said it was the next road but one. Would she be all right to go on her own? He was working a six day week, and had been since they moved, to give them enough money to live on, though food and cigarettes were all they seemed to spend money on, except the cost of a couple of drinks, or some petrol money, when Anne went out with Liz. Even then she mostly drank mineral water, as she didn't know if she could cope with alcohol again; she never had been able to particularly well, as it had always made her unsure of herself and consequently too assertive or argumentative. They'd also decided that, if Neil was going to stop entirely, it required a complete change of habits for both of them. The question was: what were they going to fill their lives with to replace it? The only life he'd ever known was where he drank and went to pubs a lot and she was now so constricted that the idea of going out unaccompanied further than the corner shop was unimaginable.

She made an appointment at the doctor's for the next afternoon. From the time she awoke heavily the next morning and raised herself to kiss Neil goodbye, she worried about what was in front of her. The whole day was building up towards the point where she would have to go out and walk to a street she'd never seen before, though only a few minutes away.

"I've only gone as far as the off-licence before," she'd protested the night before to Neil.

"It's not much further than that, honestly. I've told you exactly where it is, you'll be okay," he reassured her, "and when you get back you know you'll have achieved something."

"You're right, I will, if I get back in one piece, that is."

"You know I don't mean it like that. Take the knife with you, hold on to it and you'll feel reassured."

She was walking rigidly now, past the row of shops on the other side of the road that marked the furthest she'd been on her own. Every step she took now was a step further than she'd been capable of before, she told herself as she walked on. Her heart pounded and she felt self-conscious as she passed by builders renovating a house on the first corner of a side road she had to cross. Halfway there, she told herself, to keep her mind off them. Her stride seemed to slow as she approached them, her legs felt heavy and her head sat awkwardly on her shoulders, it felt as if her head were twitching, although she supposed it was not as obvious as she imagined it to be. They became silent as she came towards them, stopping to stare openly as they watched her walk the gauntlet of the footpath, from right to left of where they worked. Don't let them say anything, please don't.

She came to Park Street running downhill parallel to Sans Souci Road, much more quickly than she'd imagined she would. It was almost an anticlimax when she sat down on the old leather chair in the surgery waiting room. She was here in, what, two minutes? There were two other women in the room, one with a child, a little blonde pony-tailed girl. Again, like in the off-licence, she realised that when the world was broken down into small palatable amounts, she could cope better with it. When all the generalisations of the outside world became the actual specifics, they were not as intimidating. Rather she could see the ordinary people and the ordinary lives that went on, irrelevant of her interaction with them. She felt separated from these people through her experience, as if she were inside a glass case, where she could see all around her and be seen, but was isolated and forever removed from them all.

After a short wait she was called into the surgery. She had specifically requested a female doctor when she'd phoned the day before, and now walked silently into the room and closed the door, taking up her place opposite the stern, attractive, middle-aged woman, who reminded her of her periodic visits to the head's study at school.

"You've just joined the practice," the doctor announced.

"Yes," Anne replied, not sure whether she was expected to reply.

"So," the woman folded her hands in front of her on the desk, intertwining her fingers, "what can I do for you?"

"I need a sick note for the DSS. My last doctor gave me one before and that expired yesterday, so—"

The doctor interrupted, "And what exactly is wrong with you?"

Anne's hand went to her throat protectively, surprised by the challenging, authoritative note in the woman's voice. Resentment rose in her in the couple of seconds' silence that passed. Just say it, she thought, get it over and done with quickly.

"I was raped, you see. That's why I've moved here, from Croydon. I can't go out really, I came here now, I know, but I only live two roads away and it took everything I could muster to get me here." She paused. "It's the furthest I've been." She was conscious of a substantiating tone in her voice, but felt relief now she'd said it.

"Where were you raped?" The doctor showed no emotion or feeling, just a glimmer of interest.

"South Croydon. Next to the train station."

"Whereabouts exactly? I live there myself, you see."

"In a flat, just next to the train station. Right next to it in fact."

"Why on earth did you go into a flat with a man like that?" She paused, her voice now scathing. "Or was he a friend?"

All the statements and questions, in her hard, flat tones, with rapid-fire delivery shocked and now angered Anne, as she realised exactly what this doctor's attitude to her was.

"No, he wasn't actually," Anne blurted out. "I don't have friends like that – do you? I went into the flat with him because he had a pair of scissors rammed into my throat, so I didn't have much choice."

She leaned towards the doctor, from her seat at right angles to the other woman, motioning, with force, the action of something being thrust into the side of her throat.

"All right, er, Miss Elliot, calm down please, I only ask because I live close to there myself." She looked at Anne as if expecting a reaction, an admission of coincidence. Anne wanted to say that she couldn't give a toss where the doctor lived, but said nothing, just looked away from the woman's gaze, lowering her head to look at her fingers, twisting, in her lap.

"Your records will have to be sent for from the South Croydon surgery," she continued, adopting her officious, brisk voice. "In the meantime I will have to phone your doctor there and ask for details, so if you come back tomorrow or Friday, I should have everything I need by then."

"You mean you can't give me the sick note now?"

"Miss Elliot, you have just walked off the street into this surgery, having lived in this area a very short time, saying you have the symptoms of agoraphobia. I have no way of knowing whether this is true."

Anne hated her: her self-satisfied security, her sensationalist, gossipy attitude to what she had told her, relating it only to herself and where she lived, hated her derision and her disbelief.

"I have not got agoraphobia, don't you listen? I'm scared of everything because I was raped and I cannot see any reason to believe that it will not happen to me again. I'm hardly likely to make that story up, am I?"

The doctor's look became long-suffering. "I am not accusing you of making anything up. But," she spoke very clearly, spacing every word carefully, "I have to check it with your previous doctor. I need to know what treatment you're receiving and what diagnosis there has been."

"I'm not taking anything, because I don't want to take any drugs. I can pull myself out of this. I just need time," she stood up, "and a sick note, so that I can get some money to live on," she ended, hoping that it sounded rude. She was at the door; the doctor's voice became dismissive and long-suffering now.

"Ring the surgery tomorrow and speak to the receptionist, who'll tell you whether there is a sick note ready for you."

Anne walked out, her eyes filling, from hatred and anger. The journey back to the flat seemed quicker than the walk to the surgery. Though she kept a firm grip on the knife in her pocket she was not as scared and tense: she was too angry and upset. She wanted only to be at home, the doors closed, to phone Neil and tell him and then to cry.

She phoned the hospital as soon as she got in, before she took her coat off and told him, her voice rising, getting out of control, that the doctor hadn't believed her, had only been interested because she lived there herself, selfish bitch! Anne exclaimed.

Neil came home early and immediately got the Yellow Pages, looking down the doctors' surgeries, searching for another one in a road name he recognised.

"You're not going back there, that's one thing for sure." Sitting at the kitchen table, opposite him, smoking, Anne almost smiled. He always seemed as if he was acting when he took this incensed, protective attitude. Perhaps he was but it didn't matter, she didn't mind. He was taking control at last, everyone had noticed it with a sense of relief; for once he was looking after her.

He rang another surgery and, sensing he would do better without an audience, she left him to it and went into the living room and switched the afternoon news on. He came in after a few minutes.

"I've spoken to the doctor at Chamberlain Street."

Anne pulled a face, recognising the name and knowing that it was a good twenty minutes' walk away. Neil spread out his hands in front of him.

"It's the closest there is, after that old bitch-face you saw this afternoon."

She smiled at his outrage, his annoyance on her behalf, and she felt suddenly more relaxed but tired, as though she wanted just to go to bed and forget all about it.

"I spoke to a Doctor Ahmed there and she sounds really understanding. I explained the situation to the receptionist and she spoke to this doctor and then put me through to her. She said that normally you couldn't register with a surgery and then immediately change, but that she'd find a way around it. You're to go tomorrow at three and she'll give you a sick note," he ended triumphantly.

The next afternoon she set off on the long walk. It was probably just over a mile away, but it was all new ground. She knew that it was along the tree-lined main road, in the opposite direction from the other doctor's, and then at some point a turn left on to another main road. There wasn't a bus route, as Neil had checked from work that morning. The health centre was in a cul-de-sac off Chamberlain Road. Anne cut her leg walking there. She could feel the blood ooze out and stick to her trousers, as the knife broke through the lining in her coat, because of the weight and pressure she put on it. She wondered vaguely how long the mark on her leg would take to heal, as it felt like quite a long surface cut. She still had the dark marks on her neck from the scissors and blemishes on her back and legs from the scrapes she got from the wall. She didn't seem to heal quickly.

The people she passed on the long walk seemed to be mainly middle-aged men on their own, scruffily dressed, hair long at the back, some with a newspaper tucked under one arm. This may be better than South Croydon, she thought, but it's still too rough, too overpopulated. She started to sweat round her hairline as she turned into the cul-de-sac, her legs feeling heavy. The strain of having almost got there was starting to tell on her. She wanted to run the last bit. She speeded up and, with a backward glance to the right and left, pushed open the swing doors of the old, shabby health centre. The waiting room was large and cold, the people around her looked poor and downcast, the children's drawings that decorated the walls were curled at the corners and faded.

She'd arrived; she breathed a sigh of relief, confident that she would soon see a doctor who could be of help to her. She wanted help now. Now she needed someone to tell her she wasn't mad and that she would get better. Valerie had been encouraging her to register with a new doctor for weeks, concerned at the endless days she passed on her own, imprisoned in the flat. She lifted a magazine to glance through while she waited, an expensive women's magazine with a striking, raven-haired, red-lipped model on the cover. She flicked idly through the pages and started, lethargically, to pass the time, to read through a predictable article, a rehash of the same worn-out old views, about the modern woman, who knows what she wants and asks for it, demanding more from her lovers, her career and so on. She was skimming down the column, only half-reading it.

Then the statement hit her like a punch: 'Modern women often indulge in rape fantasies, where a man they don't know (or sometimes a friend, or someone they do know) comes upon them unawares and forces them to have sex with them, ignoring protests. This is quite common; the emancipated woman who still harbours dreams of subjugation.'

Shaking with anger, Anne flung the magazine down on the table in front of her. Her unsteady hand shot to her throat, surrounding the front of her neck entirely. She tightened and loosened her grip several times, trying to calm herself. The receptionist called her name and she walked down the short corridor to the doctor's room, silently screaming at the people who wrote the article and hating them and the people who would read it, interested, fascinated by these masochistic tales. She wished it would happen to them, then they would know that it was not a fantasy, not a sexual adventure, but a hideous, revolting nightmare. She felt ready to scream out loud when she thought of how frightened she had been, getting herself to the surgery today: knife in pocket, her leg getting cut, her heart pounding every time she passed someone, until she was reassured by the sound of their continuing footsteps behind her, only to be faced with that insult, from and to her own sex. She pushed open the door of the doctor's room and went in.

Doctor Ahmed was a slight, youngish Indian woman, sincere and concerned, who won Anne's confidence immediately. When they'd finished and Anne walked to the door, putting the sick note deep in her pocket, she followed her.

"Don't worry, we won't let you just carry on trying to cope, we'll get you back on your feet; going out and getting back to work as well. Okay?"

The journey back was easier than the walk there. Something had been achieved today: here was someone she could put her trust in. She knew Doctor Ahmed would try to help her.

*

Anne was referred to a psychiatrist at the local hospital. When her appointment card arrived it was a month later. In the time between she'd gone out more with other people, up to London twice on the train with Valerie, to the offices where she worked on accounts a couple of times a month. When on her own she stayed in mostly, just going out for a few minutes to the off-licence or post office next door to it, or the grocer's shop across the street and, as the evenings drew in earlier, never in the late afternoon.

Neil arranged to have the day off work for her appointment. The hospital was a good half-hour's walk away. They had only seen the building from the road before, when they'd passed it once in Liz's car, but it seemed to be a sprawling mass of old and new buildings, set in a few acres of well-kept gardens and paths. Neil, always apprehensive when walking on unknown roads, was even more nervous than Anne, who feared what was in front of her in a vague, mounting way, as they walked along together, hand in hand. Anne, recognising his anxiety and fearing where it would lead, thought sadly how much they propped each other up, knowing deep down that this was the main thing that held them together now. Their relationship was unrecognisable from the early days of pubs and bands, friends and love, through the double blow of Neil's addiction and Anne's trauma. As they walked through the fallen, vividly coloured leaves into the grounds, Anne realised with surprise that she was now doing what she'd always told Neil he needed to do – get help – but he wouldn't agree to go to a doctor, let alone anyone more specialised. She wondered idly, as if in a dream, who actually needed this therapy more; him or her.

The waiting room was open and airy, populated with plants and chairs all arranged so that little groups of people could form and talk, separated from those around them, unlike most other waiting rooms with their rows of chairs against the walls around the room, waiting as if expecting a game of musical chairs to begin.

She didn't wait long. They were alone in the room, with only the receptionist in the room beyond, typing. A nurse came over and spoke quietly, saying Anne's name enquiringly, and led her away. Anne looked back over her shoulder at Neil, pulling a face, trying to lighten her uncertainty. She followed the nurse upstairs and along the gallery she'd seen from the waiting room and stopped at the last door in the row. The name on the door was Doctor Rye: the name on her appointment card. Man or woman, she wondered. The nurse walked in without knocking and after a second's hesitation, Anne followed her. The room was small, with one picture window that overlooked the gardens and a lily-covered pond. The doctor walked around his desk, a small, thin man, with a long, slightly hooked nose and sideburns, that gave him the look of an undernourished bird. Anne guessed his age to be around thirty-three, perhaps a little older. The nurse, having introduced him to Anne, left. He extended his hand to Anne and she went to shake it, then noticed, with a slight, involuntary shudder, that, as soon as she touched him, his hand went limp and he withdrew it, leaving her clutching air. As he motioned towards the chair on the other side of his desk, she thought of how you were supposed to be able to tell a lot about a man by his handshake. Not doing well so far. She sat down. She thought of the mileage she would get out of this later; this man, the epitome of what you imagine shrinks to be like, weak handshake and, yes, she could see now that he would have trouble meeting her gaze as well! Still, she didn't mind at all, it put her more at her ease, at least he wasn't burly, large and intimidating, and he wouldn't scare or alienate her, that she knew.

He started hesitantly, "I understand from Doctor Ahmed that you are suffering from post-traumatic stress disorder and possibly depression after your ordeal."

Anne went to nod at this pause, just to prompt him that she'd heard and he could carry on, like at a job interview, when she stopped, not sure what she was agreeing to.

"Well I don't know about either of those terms, I don't think of myself like that," she stopped then carried on, "but I am frightened of being on my own and I can't really see a future because it feels like I've got sand underneath my feet, not solid ground."

"That's interesting, yes," he nodded and again, she noticed, did not meet her eyes. He probably thinks he's done a great job, making me come out of myself and express myself, she thought cynically, feeling the boredom of her own story settling on her. She thought that he probably wouldn't appreciate that she'd never had any problem expressing herself, though she knew that was arrogant.

"Can you take me through exactly what happened to you last July?"

She was shaken out of her reverie. She groaned inwardly. "Do I have to? Do you know how many times I've told this story? I could really do without saying it all again."

He had a loose elastic band in his hands and pulled it taut between the fingers of both hands, leaning right back in his seat and spoke, "You need to really. I need to know and you, of course, need to open up and say it all."

She felt so much frustration mount up inside her at this that she wanted to bang the table and shout, "Look at me, look at me here, the individual, don't just apply a set of rules, reactions, that rape 'victims' have." How she hated that word 'victim', and wound herself up more even thinking in those terms. It all welled up inside her and she knew he could see it in her eyes as she answered, keeping her voice level, "Look, I have no problem in expressing myself, no problem at all. I never have had over this or anything else. I don't need to say it again, but if you need to hear it, I'll tell you."

Leaning forward to write on the pad quickly, he nodded, "Yes, please do."

She recounted the story in the pat manner she'd got accustomed to months earlier. It was already becoming like a story in her head, and she knew that if she'd left any detail out in the last couple of times she'd told the story, it would be lost forever now. This was the tale that ended with good winning over evil, the jump out of the window, the man being caught and returned to the scene of the crime and the police. It was starting to sound like a Dickensian cliffhanger even to her own ears, as if the question following it would be, 'and did she live?' to which she could reply, 'here I am: I lived to tell the tale.' While relating the events, this alternate conversation went on in Anne's head simultaneously, while she was partly amused and partly amazed at her own ability to remove herself.

When she finished, he carried on writing for a minute or so and then looked up, his expression kind, but impassive.

"Now I need to know about you in order to build up a picture of what you are like, what your make up and past are."

She then mechanically answered each question put to her. Parents: dead. Sisters: two. Sibling position: youngest. Birthplace: Manchester. Any lesbian affairs: no. Did the thought repulse her: no. (I'm not hung up about it, just straight). Many boyfriends since puberty: yes, fairly continuously. He dwelt on her parents, how she'd coped with their death, one when eight, one in late teens. Did she feel she'd changed, had to be strong? Did she think she'd had to compensate a lot for the fact she'd not had a mother from such an early age? No.

"I know that I'm quite tough really. I know that because my father was hard and so are my sisters, in a different way to me though. I'm... um..." She hesitated, groping for how to put this, not really knowing if it were the truth or merely what she wanted this doctor to believe of her. "Opinionated, not very sympathetic and, I think, resilient. I can put up with things. This, for instance."

He struggled to write everything down, but whether it was all she said or what he interpreted from what she'd said, she didn't know.

She went on, "Really I know that it's only time that will get me out again. When I start to forget how easy it would be to happen again. I came here really because my sister encouraged me to and because I'm frustrated that I don't seem to be getting anywhere and hoped that, in some way, the whole process could be speeded up." She smiled depreciatingly, at her own hopefulness.

She could've guessed his answers. The mind needs time to digest what has happened and a long recovery period, which would be slow, but there were ways to help; various options. He needed to know more about her, to help.

He went back over her family and her current situation. She told him about Neil, his alcoholism, finding that this was one area she could see the point of going over, of talking about in depth.

"He really needs help, you know; I first told him that he should go to the doctor over two years ago, but he's scared, I think. His father was an alcoholic."

"What's happened to me is his big chance, you see, but I'm scared he's going to blow it. I'm so scared that I can't see any kind of future for us and I can't try to plan one because he's let me down so many times, I feel I can't get up again."

This, she told him, was just as significant in making her feel that the ground could turn to quicksand under her at any time. As she talked she felt that it was becoming clear to her that one of the reasons she could see no future to her life was because the responsibility for it was more in Neil's hands than her own, because he could dash it to the ground at any time.

Doctor Rye, however, kept taking her back to her family, her parents' deaths.

"I think you have a lot of baggage, of stored up emotions. You don't want to let go, to actually lie down and say, 'I'm sick, I need help.'"

"What good would that do, Doctor Rye? I have family and friends and even my boyfriend, who all give me help without me being self-pitying and demanding it. I wouldn't have them for very much longer if I did that, would I?"

"That's not the point," he said emphatically. "You are scared to actually admit depression, scared of giving in to it. So you resist it all the time and push it back. But in order for you to feel this lethargy lift and for these fears to leave you, you will have to give in to it and then sit it out."

Anne could see that there was an element of logic in what he said, but she had always had a deep fear of giving in to any morose feelings, fearing a downward spiral which she could not then escape. She'd seen it in others, women she'd worked with, whose illness then became their hobby and finally their whole personality. No, no she wouldn't do that, no pills, no self-pity. She said as much to the doctor.

"A negative way to look at the problem, which you do because you are afraid of yourself, your own mind."

He went on, "I suggest you come into the hospital as a patient for a week, maybe two, under my supervision. There are what you'd know as anti-depressant tablets, a short course of which would help you break down these barriers. I am sure..."

He was interrupted by a noise, at once so loud and unknown that it seemed to surround Anne totally: it was so completely unknown that she could not recognise it at all. It happened again, as Doctor Rye opened his mouth as if to continue his sentence, Anne felt confused and disorientated – the only thing she could think that the noise resembled was a ship in deep fog. Then she remembered the pond outside the window. She spoke just as the doctor was about to resume his diagnosis.

"Is that one of the ducks?" she asked hopefully.

"No," he answered, seemingly irritated by her interruption, "it's Brenda."

Anne laughed, she'd heard enough, "I tell you what, Doctor, I think you should stick with Brenda, she needs you more than me."

"There are different kinds of mental illness, you know," he answered, obviously put out.

Anne told Neil all she could remember of the conversation on the way home. It was the week before Christmas, at the beautiful time when, on a mild day, in the hours between daylight and darkness, the light becomes sharper, images more defined, in the cold, crisp air.

Anne felt elated, full of purpose and, for the first time in months, energetic.

"The last thing I need is to go inside a place like that. I'm not depressed, I know that now. I didn't sit with my chin lowered to my chest accepting everything dished out to me. Do you know what I think?" She demanded, her voice becoming more animated, her pace quickening. "I think that he decided that I ought to be depressed. Poor orphan child, boyfriend with a problem, and now this. Who wouldn't be!" She felt her confidence soar, at this realisation that they were all wrong and she was okay after all. She turned to Neil, laughing. He was blinking quickly, squeezing her hand tightly, trying to smile, but instead pulling a kind of grimace.

"I'm sorry," she said, realising her tactlessness. "I didn't mean that in any way against you. But you know what I mean, don't you? It's just given me the kick up the arse to get better, without going on pills that'll make me into a zombie and without committing myself into God knows what."

She danced in front of him, suddenly remembering something that had slipped her mind, "You'll never guess what! I almost forgot. While I was with him, right at the end, I heard this awful noise, and I couldn't work out what the hell it was, a big whopping noise or some damn thing." She threw her head back and imitated the noise, but at a lower volume, laughing as she made it. "He just ignored it. I thought I was hearing things, then it went again and I thought it might be ducks on one of those ponds outside, but he said, totally deadpan, 'It's Brenda.' Like 'who else would it be?' That's when I thought, God, what am I doing in this place?"

*

Neil had most of Christmas off work and, for the most part, they had a happy time. One day, the day before Christmas Eve, he'd threatened to drink. They'd been out shopping, the air was cold, the lights in the shops hot, the shopping centre heaving with people. Neil had started to get angry, with people squeezing past them all the time. Groups of people passed them, from offices and shops, high with drink and in good spirits. Pubs beckoned to all who walked past them. He'd burst out, "I need a drink."

Anne, out shopping in crowds for the first time in almost six months, acting like a normal person out Christmas shopping, felt betrayed. Once he'd said that, she felt as if it was only in the last few hours that she'd come to believe that he was off drink for good, that they could be normal, that they might, eventually, be happy. At that moment she felt that she'd dropped her guard for only a short time and that had been enough. She even felt, in the blow of that moment, that the evil force of drink had been able to get to him because she hadn't been standing guard, protecting him against it. She'd stopped dead and turned to face him, "You can't! You just can't wreck it all. Don't do it. It's Christmas, don't, please don't do this to me."

He looked hard, uncaring, his eyes focused at some point above her head, his jaw twitching, as they stood, the glass-windowed shop behind her back, the crowds rushing past, unseeing.

"I need one. I just can't cope with this."

He sounded determined, stubborn. Hope left her, her head felt light, the pain in front of her unfaceable. One last shot.

"Then let's just go home. Let's just stop now, walk straight out and go home, until this passes. I can come out tomorrow with Liz and get what I need."

She clutched at this idea with renewed hope and pulled at his sleeve urgently. She had wanted to be out with him, Christmas shopping, a normal couple. But she knew the next few minutes were crucial and wanted to give him every escape route possible. They'd bought one present out of the eight they were supposed to and they still had all the food to buy.

"Okay let's go now," he said abruptly, then propelled her out of the shopping centre, against the crowds, and then they jostled their way out, towards the flyover, towards home.

*

After Christmas, Anne returned to Doctor Ahmed, and said she didn't want to go into the hospital and didn't want pills, that in her opinion she wasn't depressed and that with the New Year and no sign of the trial dates yet, she was going to register with the employment agency that had got her the last job and try to get some temporary, clerical work.

"That way if I can't handle it I won't feel too bad as, with temping, it's only for a week or two anyway. You don't actually owe them anything and then I won't be letting anyone down."

Doctor Ahmed nodded her agreement. "Good idea; perhaps Doctor Rye did you more good than you think as you've now motivated yourself to change things. Just don't put too much pressure on yourself, take one step at a time, and don't expect miracles. As you've rejected the psychiatrist's advice, it might be a good idea if you got in touch with a group: self-help may be more suitable to you. I've got some numbers here."

Anne told her of the abortive meeting with Victim Support. "Well Rape Crisis is rather more specialised than that, like you say Victim Support deals with the whole spectrum: this is women, many with similar experiences, trying to help other women."

Anne took the number but, once again, had a vision of women sitting in a circle exchanging horror stories. She knew this was probably unfair, but she didn't feel there was much hope there. Anyway, she thought, as she walked home, it's getting easier. She was on her own, it was midday, her hand was in her pocket on the knife, but she wasn't as scared as the last time. Gradually, inch by inch, she was regaining her confidence. Whereas, a month earlier, she had held her breath when she'd walked past men, watching them from lowered eyes, looking for any sudden move, startled when perhaps they took their hand out of their pockets when they passed her; now she met their eyes, when they looked at her, even started to offer her old confrontational stare when they appreciatively eyed her up and down. I can look back, she told herself, I'm not just here to be seen. I can see too, I can stare at you, she told herself as she walked back.

She phoned the recruitment agency she'd got her last two jobs through. She got on well with Diane Campbell, who'd started the company single-handed, ten years before. It meant returning to Croydon, if she got work through DC Recruitment, but now she'd chosen to stay in the area, it meant a choice of travelling either to London or Croydon. Sutton, which was only two miles away, held little hope for office employment, so she'd just have to accept going back there if she wanted to try to get back to work. She made an appointment with the secretary to see Diane the following Wednesday, Neil's day off, so that they could go together. She relaxed about it as soon as she came off the phone: it was a week away and Neil would be with her, so she didn't have to get worked up about it in the time between. She'd made a positive move, she told herself, that was easy to do – perhaps life would start to move for her again.

On an impulse she went to her coat and took from the pocket the slip of paper Doctor Ahmed had given her. She felt now that she'd made one move she could make another: this was the day where she'd initiate all the forward moves she wanted to make.

She dialled the number almost immediately, having no clear idea to whom she would be speaking, nor what she herself would say. A polite, reedy woman's voice spoke after two rings, with a simple "Hello". Anne immediately had an impression of a well-dressed middle-aged lady, speaking from her own hall or living room.

Anne hesitated; had she dialled the right number? How did she start, what did she say?

"Er... hello, um... is this the right number for..." she faltered, blushing, embarrassed.

"For Rape Crisis, yes, my name is Emily."

Anne felt immediate relief that the woman had cut through all the things Anne might have had to say. Simultaneously she thought, Emily, yes, that figures.

"Hello, my doctor gave me your number saying that you might be able to help me. I was raped, you see, months ago, but I still can't go outside the front door without being scared and even when I do go out, which I have been trying to make myself do, it's not far." In her head Anne amazed herself by carrying on speaking without realising what she was about to say. "I have to get a job again and I'm not sure that I can do it. I don't know what I expect you to be able to do really, and I think I am getting a bit better, slowly that is, anyway. It's just that I can't believe that every man I pass in the street isn't about to attack me."

"The most important thing is not to feel guilty," came the incongruous response. "Don't feel guilty about what happened to you and about the way you feel now," the voice carried on.

Anne listened to the thin, yet authoritative voice at the other end of the line, sounding so sure of herself, of her words. It sounded as if she might be reading the words from a book in front of her. Anne had a momentary mental image of this and felt her brow furrow in confusion.

"What do you mean, 'don't feel guilty about it'? I didn't say anything about guilt. I said that, bar the men I know, I am frightened of every man in the world."

"Everyone feels guilt," the voice answered quietly, "and you need to admit it and then discard it, throw it away."

"I'm sorry," (why had she said that, she thought angrily) "but I can assure you I don't feel any guilt. I know what I feel, and I don't feel that. Why on earth should you assume that you know how I feel? Anyway," she carried on, her mind becoming clearer, her temper rising, "why should that be the first thing you say to me? You're implying that it's natural for me to feel guilt, so in other words, if I'm not, you're planting the idea in my head that I should be. Do you see that?"

Anne's voice had risen during this speech, sounding increasingly forceful and annoyed. From the table in the kitchen where she sat she could see her reflection in the mirror opposite, her palm flattened against her forehead, her eyes opened wide in amazement.

The voice answered slowly, evidently to calm Anne down and, ignoring Anne's question, resumed, "We have a women's centre on Beech Road, in Thorton Heath. We run therapy sessions every Wednesday and Sunday evenings to help you cope with what has happened to you, or may still be happening to you. There are usually six or so women at any one session, and no men are allowed in the centre, I can assure you."

"Well, that might be reassuring on the one hand, but as I can't go out alone on a journey of any length in the day time, night time is obviously pretty much out of the question." Anne knew her voice sounded supercilious and some awkwardness made her think only of Neil as a possible companion for her trip there. "Anyway, just to set the picture straight," Anne continued, wondering whether the woman had listened to anything she'd said, "it isn't 'still happening' to me. I was attacked by a man who raped me in his flat and then I got away. He was caught," she finished curtly.

"You knew him."

Anne could not work out whether this was a question or a statement but, once again, as with Doctor Rye, she felt she was talking to someone with a preconditioned attitude towards her. Without knowing her, or anything about her situation, this woman, who was really only a voice, had decided what her reactions were going to be and believed she knew how she felt. After she'd held a match to a cigarette in her mouth, cradling the receiver between shoulder and chin, she lashed out angrily, "I don't know why you should assume that. No I did not 'know him'. He was a bastard who plucked me from the street. I don't know men like that. The men I know aren't rapists."

"Most women who are victims of rape are so at the hands of their brothers, uncles, fathers, husbands or boyfriends. Despite what the newspapers say with their sensationalist reporting, the idea that rape is by a stranger is a myth. Ninety-nine per cent of rapists know their victims."

Anne could hardly wait for the woman to finish her sentence, "How dare you tell me that being raped by a stranger is a myth! It happened to me, okay, do you understand that? And guilt has not happened to me, so don't try to tell me what happened and what I think. I don't care a damn for your statistics and as it did happen to me 'myth' is totally the wrong word to use." Her voice was getting louder, her speech getting faster, but her mind was clear. "I know that women are raped by their relatives and that's bloody disgusting, but don't try comparing the two or saying which is worse, and if you only know about one type then don't try to preach about the other!" She stopped, surprised at her ferocity.

Before the woman could answer, she spoke again, "Look I'm sorry, I shouldn't lose my temper with you, I'm sure you do some great work, but you obviously just don't suit my case. Thank you for your time. Cheerio." She was going to replace the receiver without waiting for a reply, not trusting herself not to argue again then, thinking that might be construed as the final act of rudeness, instead waited and listened,

"Er... yes, goodbye," the voice at the other end said. She replaced the handset.

*

By the time Wednesday had arrived, Anne, forcing herself to be determined and resolute, got the train into Croydon to meet Diane Campbell alone. She had to decided to go on her own and stressed to Neil the importance of doing so. She knew that, for a complicated mixture of reasons, he preferred her to stay at home and go out only with someone else – it lessened his worry, she knew that – but she also knew that if he didn't start to encourage her to go out into the world again, she would resent him.

He wanted to come too, but she knew that in order to feel confident when telling Diane that she wanted temporary work, and to believe that she could do it, she would need to know that she could get there on her own. Neil went across to the station earlier that day to find out about the train times. When she set off it was as though she were embarking on a journey that crossed countries and took years, such was their farewell. Neil had wanted to come to the train station with her at the least, so they stood on the platform together, frightened, holding hands. When the train came Neil looked anxiously at her; it was an old-fashioned, closed carriage train. His eyes widened anxiously. "Let me come with you."

"No, please, it's okay, look there are lots of women in that carriage, I'll get in there." They kissed, he held on to her hand for a few seconds, then she got in and slammed the heavy, dirty door behind her.

Reassured by holding the knife in her right hand, deep inside her pocket, she sat down, diagonally opposite a young woman in a suit and overcoat, open briefcase on her knee, reading her way through a sheaf of papers.

Anne thought how distant she was from the world of all the people around her, of going to work, dealing with its problems, juggling work and home life. Never totally at one with working life anyway, she now felt that she operated on a completely different level, as if public life ran alongside her own world, but she was totally cut off from it, as if a barely visible, but impenetrable, sheet of glass divided it from her forever. Yet who would know, she thought, looking out of the window as the train passed the backs of dull, suburban homes: she looked the same as she always did.

At the next station a man got on and, despite Anne's inward, repetitive chant, 'Please God, don't let him sit here,' he sat in the outside seat of the two-seater across the aisle from her. So close he could lean over and touch me, she thought shuddering. He was wearing jeans and a denim jacket, a scruffy man in his early thirties, with a droopy moustache and straggling fair hair. She glanced over at him, conscious of him looking at her, and saw that he was staring and had a faint smile around his mouth. She averted her face and stared straight ahead, rigid with anger and fear. Suddenly the train pulled up at the next station and hurriedly, a last minute decision, she stood up and rushed off the train and, walking quickly, rushed to get into the next carriage. Once in there, the train started to move again. She walked unsteadily down the carriage, passing row after row of seats before she found one she was comfortable with, opposite an old couple. He was in a Tattersall's shirt and tie, she had on what must have been her 'good' hat. They smiled as Anne, with relief, sat opposite. She smiled back and then leaned back in the seat, closing her eyes for a couple of seconds, her head pounding. The next stop was Croydon. As she walked up the sloping gangway, with only a couple of people around her, she prayed that the man in the first carriage was still on the train. She shuddered, imagining his eyes boring into her back, wondering if he was behind her. Should she look round? She hurried through the foyer of the station and out into the street.

The shops around the station were cheap and shabby. She crossed quickly at the traffic lights, intensely aware of the people to her right and left, those she'd just passed and those she was about to. She was so aware she believed that if someone she'd just passed were to turn round and stare at her back, she would see them. On the other side of the street, sandwiched between two department stores, was DC Recruitment. She walked in through the door only a couple of minutes after leaving the station. Once in the familiar corridor, its staircase leading up to the office where, door ajar, she could see the uniformed receptionist, she felt a surge of relief. She forced herself to slow down while walking up the stairs, realising she had a film of sweat over her face.

When she walked into the office Diane, from the back of the office, looked up and signalled to her to come over. Anne walked past well-groomed women sitting to the right and left, some on the phone, others talking to prospective employees, who, in their outdoor, winter clothes, were sitting opposite. Diane stood up and came round her desk as Anne approached and took one of her hands between her two.

"It's so good to see you, it must be about a year now. Have a seat, Anne. Would you like a coffee?"

Anne, relaxing by the second, accepted. She hadn't been forgotten: she found herself thinking how amazing it was that she was still able to be seen and talked to by people from before. They still spoke the same language. She decided to get the difficult part over with immediately.

"I'm not with the bank any more, Diane. I haven't been for months now. I was attacked last summer and, well, went to pieces for a while. I'm okay now and just want to get back to work." (Was this true? She had no idea whether she really wanted to go back to work or not.) "I've moved house too, I had to get away from South Croydon."

Diane nodded energetically, her sharp intelligent eyes taking it all in; she knew not to ask Anne for any details, not here.

"I did wonder about you, because of course the advertising assistant job came up again; Helen, in the personnel department, asked me to advertise it and when I asked about you, she just said you had left for personal reasons. I thought perhaps it had something to do with your boyfriend, he wasn't well last year, was he? Wasn't he off work for months?"

"Yes, yes he was. No, he's all right, thank God. They never did work out what that was, thought it might have been colitis at one stage. Anyway, he seems to be over that now. He's been very good to me actually."

Anne needed to say this. It was true anyway, wasn't it? There were so many versions of the truth – he was by turns the hero and the villain. One thing was for certain, he loved her, had earned the money they needed and hadn't drunk for months and had not once come out with any of the classic male responses to what had happened to her. He didn't regard her as his property that someone else had touched. There wasn't a proprietorial bone in his body.

Diane took her out for lunch. The normality of it all lifted Anne up: here she was in busy Croydon, walking along a street, towards a restaurant with a sympathetic woman, who would hopefully get her a job. She began to believe that it could all slot into place, if she let it, if she made it. They went to an Italian restaurant where she ate more than she normally did and even relaxed enough to have two glasses of wine. She told Diane more detail now. She listened intently, nodding her head emphatically at Anne's explanations of how she'd felt and reacted. She was obviously horrified by the sketchy account of events Anne gave, yet, Anne suspected, was intrigued and deeply interested in the story. As Anne recognised this, she told herself to keep calm and not dislike her for it. She knew that Diane led a protected, affluent life and was probably intrigued by the 'human interest' angle of the story. She could imagine Diane recounting it to her husband in the evening, praising Anne's strength.

"Of course, it wouldn't have happened to you if you weren't so pretty," Diane declared as they pushed their chairs back, rising, as the waiter came towards them with their coats.

I must be mellowing, Anne thought on the train home, because although she had corrected her – "Diane, he didn't have enough time to see whether I was young or old, fat or thin, all that he registered was that I was female, before he ran at me," – while seeing him run, feeling the fear, as she said it; she didn't show her annoyance at all.

"She was probably only trying to flatter me," she told Neil later, "and maybe she thought that having looks compensates for what happened to me or something. She certainly told me how well I looked lots of times; I don't think she could quite believe how normal I looked. Although she did say that I looked a bit skinny."

Anne looked at her own reflection, in the mirror above the bookcase, as she said this, not displeased by what she saw. She had on a navy suit, which she hadn't worn since her early days at the bank and had had her hair cut a few days earlier, so it fell to her chin in curls. Contrary to what Neil had said, as they went to the salon in the row of shops at the top of the street, the scissors used by the chattering hairdresser didn't bother her at all. "I've had my hair cut with those scissors stacks of times, for years, and only been raped once, so why would it bother me?" she'd laughed. Neil had looked confused and hurt. "It's okay Neil, come on, don't be so serious, it helps to laugh sometimes!" It was true, it made it easier sometimes, buoyed her up, made her feel as if he hadn't won; although she had to be careful about whom she acted like this with. She could not cope with being misunderstood at the best of times, but over this it would be unbearable. She knew if anyone then assumed she was taking it all lightly and thrown a joke back, she would've cracked and turned on them: I can laugh at it, not you.

Now looking at herself and seeing Neil's face beyond her own reflection, smiling at her vanity, she appreciated that she was still attractive, perhaps more so, with the weight she knew she'd lost. She could still laugh and smile, no one would know.

"Finished admiring yourself yet?" Neil joked.

"Yes thanks." Anne smiled, turning towards him and walked proudly from the room, into the bedroom, to change out of her suit.

*

It was three weeks before Diane found Anne temporary work. She'd understood her need to work somewhere near one of the train stations between Carshalton and Croydon. The booking she got her was one stop in. It was in a credit checking company, a completely undemanding job, which suited Anne. She sat in a computer mainframe room, chilled to the right temperature, on her own, the buzz of electricity in her ears, and, every fifteen minutes, went into a programme, accessed the thirty companies on screen and recorded whether they had the numbers ninety or ninety-five next to their names. Some were always the same number, others changed during the day, some were blank. No one told her what it meant and she didn't ask: it was unimportant, no matter what the explanation had been it would still be unimportant. What was important was that she was getting up every morning, putting on work clothes, looking better turned out than was actually called for and that she went to work on her own, one stop down the line, with all the other people going to work in the mornings. The job finished at five thirty, so she waited in the foyer of the building, sitting on the chrome and cushion sofa and looking out of the darkened glass window for Neil, who came for her at six. He cycled from his work in a few minutes and then they both got the train home, Neil hoisting the bike in to the carriage.

On Saturday, after the first week's work, she felt pleased with her own normality and though she'd felt like she was acting a part all week in the credit company, she realised that if she kept acting she would probably become deadened enough to believe that this really was life. For what other option did she have? She seemed to be striving towards the mediocrity she'd had before, because it was preferable to the hell she'd been in, but it still wasn't the life she wanted.

She'd invited Liz and Steve for dinner on the Saturday night, though knowing it would more than likely be just Liz. Neil was going to cook a curry and Anne suggested buying a couple of bottles of wine. "Only if you don't mind."

Neil had said he didn't. "Just don't get drunk and obnoxious, that's all."

Late that Saturday afternoon the phone rang; it was Jackie.

"Yes, I'm on my own, Neil works until six on Saturdays now."

"How's it been going then, has any work come through from that agency yet?"

"Yes, actually, I know you won't believe this but I've just done a week's work. Managed to get two whole miles down the road on my own, every day, would you believe?" she continued lightly, sarcastically.

"What were you doing?"

"Oh, mind-numbingly boring! Sitting in a computer room on my own seven hours a day, still, preferable to being stuck with other people I don't know though. I only talked to three or four people all week but, you know, I feel better for it."

"Well done! I'm glad to hear it. Any work for next week?"

"Yes, they've got me a sales ledger job at Brooks, which is likely to go on for months. It means going back to Croydon to work, but I don't see that I've got any choice."

"Will you be okay about going back there?"

"Oh, I expect so. I'd rather not set foot in the place again, but that's the way it goes."

"It'll probably help you get over your hatred of it anyway. It's not that much worse than a lot of places really." Her tone changed slightly, "Listen, Anne, we've got the court dates. Now it could change, right up to the last minute, but it's booked in for May the tenth."

Anne's heart, having skipped a beat at the words, now thumped loudly and painfully. This is what she had been waiting for, this is what she had been willing to happen since last summer, wanting it to come quickly. While the hatred and fear were always at the front of her mind, she'd thought that if too much time had passed she wouldn't be as incensed as she needed to be. She saw it as her exorcism, her entitlement. She regarded it as her chance to speak, her opportunity to exercise power over him, making him obey her. Her life was on hold until the trial was finished, and she'd willed it to come quickly and now it was only, her mind raced, six, no seven, weeks away.

"Oh God, I've been dying to hear that date for so long now. I don't know how to think about it; I can't believe I'll be counting down the weeks now. I feel scared, God yes, but I can't wait Jackie. Let me at him, we'll bang him up won't we?"

"Yes, I think it's safe to say he picked on the wrong girl in you. I have faith in you, we all do. No one on the squad has any doubts that his unhappiest moment yet will be when he hears what you have to say."

After the call, Anne sat down and opened one of the bottles of red wine. She lit a cigarette and looked out from where she sat on the settee into the back garden. She thought again that this seat, facing as it did the big windows that stretched from floor to ceiling and wall to wall, reminded her of sitting in the front row of the cinema: the window was the big screen, her view of life for so many months. She sipped the wine and savoured the luxury of it: enjoyment like this not having been hers for so long, in the recent past especially, but it went much further back. She hadn't experienced the innocent enjoyment of alcohol for a long time, not since she was at poly really, when it had all been good fun. It had become spoiled for her after that. Suddenly she saw a movement outside the window. She jumped up. She couldn't have said exactly what it was, but off to the right of her vision someone, something had definitely moved. She stood now at the end of the settee, also to the right of the room, next to the living room door, so she would be hidden from view, but still see outside. Her fear was tremendous and instant, her hand holding the cigarette shook, she felt sick. Her heart beat so painfully it felt as if it were in her throat. The wine was on the floor where she'd placed it before seeing the movement. She dragged heavily on the cigarette, her other hand clutched and pulled at her neck. Then she saw him. At the bottom of the garden he walked into her field of vision, but she was still out of his. She recognised him after one terrible moment where all she registered was that it was a man and all she thought of was that it could be nothing or no one except a rapist. He was the man from upstairs; she'd caught sight of him a couple of times over the months, from her bedroom at the front of the house, when he'd been walking into the driveway, after work. Now, on a Saturday afternoon, he was stalking around the garden. Why? Oh God, oh God, I'll die, I can't take it again, I can't. This chant went through her mind, over and over again, as she watched him, from the crouching position she'd now taken behind the door of the living room. He was walking up the garden, through the centre of the lawn, towards the french windows. The last she saw of him was him staring towards the house as, realising that she had trapped herself behind the door, she jumped up and ran quickly round the door, catching her right shoulder on the door handle on the way. She stood hopelessly in the small L-shaped hallway, her back to the wall, the kitchen behind her, realising that this was the only place in the flat where she could not be seen from outside, as all the interior doors were open. She faced the makeshift, internal door of their flat that led to the communal hallway, and she thought of unlocking that door and then running outside, but realised she could meet him at the front door if he came round from the back, and push her back inside, in front of him. She became conscious of a dim, far-off whimpering noise, then realised that it came from her. As tears streamed down her soaking cheeks, she heard the unmistakable sound of the front door opening and slamming then, expecting thudding on her own door in front of her, heard instead heaving footfalls bounding up the stairs, two at a time. She sank down on the floor, her knees drawn up to her chin, and sat there staring ahead for a long time.

Eventually she got up and returned to the living room, to the glass of wine she'd left. Her earlier idea of sitting and relaxing and mulling over the news of the looming court case and thinking through her reaction to it, was now gone. She went into the bedroom then, with glass and cigarettes and drew the curtains. She put a CD on, Lou Reed, sad and moody, and sat on the bed, thinking over what had just happened. What had happened? She didn't know. Perhaps he was just walking around the garden, with as much right as she or Neil had. What she did know was that she should never look proudly or arrogantly into the future again because when she did somebody, something, always taught her a lesson and made her see that, do what she would, things would always come, out of the blue, to knock her right down.

*

The next week, Anne started the temporary job at Brooks Distribution. Always a reader, losing herself in the pages of novels, living the lives of the Virago and Minerva protagonists – the lost, confused, trapped, so often propelling themselves towards final liberation – she now read every word with a new hunger, on the train each morning, offering as they did a release and separation from the world and the people she despised and feared by which she was now surrounded.

She'd been reading a Doris Lessing book when it happened to her: a story that throbbed with the heat of Africa, about the lethargy of the woman, her attraction to and fear of the man, of another race, until the finale that neither of them could escape, the determinism that enclosed both their lives, dictated their actions and drove them irrevocably to certain death. After it happened, she'd been unable to finish reading it herself. Unable to follow the words and dismiss the real world she was in to become involved in the story again, she'd almost given it up. Then, not wanting to never finish it and have it remind her of the night she'd stopped reading it, she asked Neil to read it to her. He'd read that book, and two subsequently, at night, in bed, while she lay back, eyes shut, picturing it all, blocking everything else out. There was only this character, this scene, existing, so far away from her own life.

Neil had carried on reading other books to her, because she'd wanted him to.   After he stopped, she'd tried to read herself again, but had been unable to leave her own world enough to concentrate and follow the meaning, and had given up on a couple of books, partially read, to either switch on the television and numbly watch it, or to stare into space and light another cigarette.

Now she felt herself enter her life and books again.   She was forcing herself to get on the train, to go to work.   She found the work dull and monotonous, the journey tense, but she knew that it would get easier, and each day she hoped she'd feel less isolated, less alien to the ordinary world of nine to five, of lunch breaks and gossip.   She read from the moment she sat down on the full, filthy train and closed the book after she stood up, ready to get off when the doors opened.

She made her way to the office herself and walked back in the evenings, in the half-darkness at five fifteen, to the train station with all the other office workers heading the same way.   This station, she would think as she descended the stairs, is where he followed the other woman from.   He'd followed her, after getting a late train from London, up the gangway and to her home, only a few streets away, where he'd pushed her in the front door.   This was all Anne knew, except for the fact that he had been sentenced for seven years and served less than four; let out apparently because his mother had cancer.   Poor man!   She'd asked and questioned Jackie for more information, but sensed that Jackie already thought she knew too much.   Every time that Anne had asked more questions, Jackie stressed that, at the trial, Anne could say nothing about what she knew of his past.

"Even if you're under pressure and they're getting at you, say nothing.   If you say anything, there'll be a mistrial.   The whole thing will be stopped and it'll be months before it comes around again.   The jury can't be told anything about him, nothing that could prejudice them against him."

"So everyone in the whole court will know the truth about him, except the jury, the ones who decide if I'm a bloody liar. Great!"

"That's about it, I'm afraid," she answered. "Crap system, but it's all we've got to work with."

It was six weeks to the trial. She'd told Diane, who said she could work on the assignment up until the last minute if she wanted, or she could finish a week or two before if she needed the time or couldn't handle it.

"Don't make the decision right away," Diane had said. "Wait and see how you feel at the time."

As Anne walked towards Albert House, the twenty-storey building where she sat at an anonymous desk on the south side of the tenth floor, she thought, well it's a month's work, and a month's pay, anyway. Although she thought about the trial, looming now, all the time at work, only a part of her mind on the job, she knew that it would be a lot worse at home, with nothing else to divert her and make the time pass.

It was Thursday of the first week. For three days she'd walked with the rest of the marching crowd towards the train station and she knew she'd come on. She'd crossed over some invisible line, and she was learning to cope. She was still scared but the protective layer that covered her, that made her face impassive when inside she was frightened and bitter, was getting thicker, more impervious. As she sat with a few women in the canteen at lunchtime she felt she was gradually becoming less of a stranger to conversation about what had been on the television the previous night, or what a rat their supervisor was. The others regarded her with slight bewilderment, could not understand why she, young and educated, was working in the sales ledger and archive department. She was unwilling to lie to their questions and didn't want to think that what had happened to her was some murky secret that had to be hidden, but hadn't yet worked out what she was going to reply to questions that she couldn't give a simple answer to, nor how much she was going to say.

From the start, alone in the seclusion of her own flat, she had refused to believe that she was going to hide it all away, pretending nothing had happened, but she felt too raw to open up to these women, whom she had nothing in common with. Logic told her that she hadn't gone around telling everyone her life story before, her hang-ups or her hardships, so why should she now? However, by saying nothing of the truth, by saying merely that she'd given up her last job because she'd been ill for months, and not expanding further, she felt uneasy. It was like the responsibility for what had happened to her became hers, through silence: like it was her big, black, dirty secret, because she told no one.

She was thinking this as she sat, alone for the first time, at lunchtime, in the canteen. She felt self-conscious and isolated. As a girl sat down opposite her, she thought that if the girl were to look out of the window opposite her, behind Anne's back, she would see, above the uniformity of all the roof tops, the spire of St John's, pointing confidently skyward, as if nothing could displace it, alter its existence nor its right to be there. She had deliberately sat with her back to this view, always averted her eyes from it and wondered now how this girl would react if she knew that she'd looked at that spire, months ago, from a rooftop close to it, naked, hysterical, and had wanted, with all the will left in her body, to climb up to the top of the spire and perch there so that she could be as far away as possible from the man and the world that had betrayed her? Would she wonder, Anne mused, how I can sit here and eat this salad at a table in a building not a quarter of a mile away? She was brought back to reality by the girl smiling at her as she realised, embarrassed, that she'd been staring at her.

"You were miles away, weren't you?"

Anne nodded. "Sorry, yes, I suppose I was staring at you like a lunatic and didn't realise it."

They both laughed.

"I'm Lesley. Have you just joined the company?"

Anne explained her situation temping, sensing that she had something in common with this girl, who rolled her eyes sympathetically when she said which department she was working in.

"They're pretty dreadful in there, aren't they?"

"Just a little bit."

Lesley was about the same age as Anne, maybe slightly older, she thought. Later she found out that she was actually younger, twenty-two. Her attitude was confident, her face serious and rather sad-looking with her large doe eyes that turned down slightly at the outer edges and thin, clearly pencilled lips. She was quite tall and broad, her movements slow and deliberate. Anne had seen her in the lift the previous day, and she'd guessed from her casual clothes that she worked in the art studio on the nineteenth floor.

"Do you know anyone who works in Brooks?" Lesley asked.

"God no, not a soul. I'll be here about a month probably. I'll be glad to finish, I'm sure. I'd really like something closer to where I live, for the next temp job anyway."

"Where's that?"

"Carshalton."

"Really? Same here."

They talked for the rest of Anne's lunch hour. She explained that she'd only lived there a few months when Lesley said she'd never seen her around there. Anne didn't know much about the places Lesley spoke of but then Lesley explained that she lived the other side of the ponds from the Carshalton Beeches side where Anne lived. Anne nodded, not totally sure where she meant, but not wishing to close the conversation up by showing herself to be even more ignorant. Lesley was local, but had been to poly in the north of England and knew Manchester city quite well. They talked easily, knowing that they understood each other's language. They had a similar background and, Anne suspected, a similar cynicism.

They met for lunch the next day and went to have a sandwich and a beer at the pub opposite, which was only five minutes' walk away from Miguel's. I've come right back to where I was, Anne thought sadly, as she negotiated crossing the busy road quickly, to get out of the rain. Anne wanted to really talk to Lesley – she wasn't sure why, but she wanted a bond with her. She sensed her underlying confidence in herself, in life, her security stemming from an uncomplicated life and loving parents probably, Anne thought. Now, for some reason Anne wanted her approval.

Lesley, it turned out, lived five miles from her parents and a couple of miles away from her boyfriend (Michael, she'd been with him since she was sixteen) and owned her own house; was surrounded by her friends; was closest to Sue ("absolutely my best friend since I was five"); lamented she was still skint as, though she was properly qualified in her field, she wasn't properly paid for it. Anne guessed her biggest problem was the overdraft at the end of the month. How Anne wanted to be her: she felt a mixture of admiration and envy. She was candid and friendly, saying to Anne, as they left the pub, that she already felt as if she'd known her for years.

"It's just so rare that you meet someone at work that you can instantly identify with, the way we all did when we were students."

"Yeah, I don't suppose you come across many kindred spirits in somewhere like Brooks!"

Anne told her the following Monday. There was something motherly and organisational about Lesley. She listened and nodded as Anne told her, briefly, the outline of what had happened to her. She didn't seem to be very shocked.

"I guessed that there was something, though I didn't think it was so recent, or so serious. I don't know why I thought that; I suppose it's because I've always been astute."

Anne smiled to herself; Lesley certainly didn't lack self-esteem. Anne was less open about Neil. She knew her reasons for this weren't admirable. Lesley was, in a way, like Valerie, contained and limited by a mixture of their upbringing and their attitudes, formed by what they'd exposed themselves to in life. It made people like them generally unsympathetic, Anne knew, to cases like Neil's. Unlike Anne, they believed that people mostly made their own luck: that free will was a natural state of being. Anne knew that only the very fortunate could still believe that by the time they were adult. She saw a hardness in Lesley, like those who believed that the homeless don't deserve sympathy, but cancer patients do (except those who get it through smoking). The deserving and the undeserving. She knew that she would fall into the first category, Neil into the second.

That Friday night, Lesley and Michael called round. They brought a Chinese takeaway with them and some bottles of imported lager. Anne liked Michael, and he was just what she'd expected: tall with regular features, an open expression inspiring adjectives like dependable, reliable. Lesley made an effort with Neil, asked him about his work, looked interested, wanted to like him Anne felt, but he was withdrawn and distant. Neither of them seemed surprised when Neil shook his head and held up a hand when they offered him a beer. Anne had one but refused a second. She didn't want to push it with Neil. The conversation was mostly between Lesley and Anne; she knew the gulf between Neil and Lesley or Michael required more effort to cross than Neil would be prepared to make.

"She's smug, Anne," was Neil's immediate verdict. "There's no other word for it. He's okay I suppose, but a bit stiff, really. Anyway, I prefer him to her, she's a bit like someone's mother."

Anne laughed, "Oh come on, she's not that bad. I knew you wouldn't like her much. Too privileged for your liking, isn't she?"

She was teasing him but he didn't mind. He'd often mocked her for her friends, mainly Denise, who swore constantly and loudly in her upper-middle-class accent in order to prove her ordinariness. Anne could agree with him, knowing he had a point, but she also saw that everyone was contained by their upbringing and while she felt a mixture of admiration and jealousy for those with an abundance of love, money and security, Neil felt only bitterness and resentment.

A few nights later, Lesley called for Anne and drove her over to her house. It was the first time that Anne had been past the pubs and shops that formed the centre of Carshalton. She loved Lesley's house. It was warm and untidy with an old sofa with an expensive woven rug thrown over it, dimmed wall lighting and an old bookcase, weighed down with books and ornaments.

They had a good evening, talking about lots of things unconnected with Anne's unhappiness: Lesley's possible engagement, which she thought "would shortly be announced", making Anne smile inwardly, and about her happy childhood which, she said, she appreciated even now and was still thankful for. Later Lesley said that she wanted Anne to know that she would be there for her during the trial and that if she needed lifts anywhere, or company at any time, she'd be there. Anne was grateful and felt protected by her assurances. She was amazed, as she hardly knew Lesley, and dismissed the uncharitable thought that perhaps her new friend was enjoying the drama too much by acknowledging that even the best people enjoyed being good: she knew her Camus and, as always, Anne needed to gain the respect of the respectable – she wanted them to think well of her.

She told Lesley about Neil, his fight, his problem. Lesley was surprised, "He seems like an absolute bedrock of support for you. I said to Michael, after we left you that night, that it's a pity every woman whom this sort of thing happens to hasn't got that kind of support. It was as if nothing in the world mattered but you and you know what toss pots most men can be about that kind of thing. I'm shocked, but you say he's stopped now?"

Anne felt weary, and in a way she wished she'd said nothing at all as she couldn't explain it properly.

"Stopped for the minute doesn't mean stopped forever, I think it just means stopped until the next time."

She needed to try to explain it, knowing that as the trial came closer both she and Neil were getting more tense, both sleeping badly. He was getting irritable, criticising the people he worked with, and she was seeing quick flashes of temper and frustration that she hadn't seen for months. She could explain all this to Lesley, go over and over it, but she didn't think she could ever show the full story, nor would Lesley ever be able to see it because she didn't know Neil at all, nor did she understand Anne completely.

"He's stopped for seven months now, but that doesn't mean that he won't crack tomorrow. It's just something that's there all the time; it's either in my face when he's drinking and my life's wrecked or it's bubbling under the surface when he's not, waiting to happen. Does that make sense?"

*

Anne worked until the week before the trial. One week two days to go, she thought on her last Friday. She now couldn't believe how quickly the time was moving on. The abyss between the banality of her job: counting, stamping, and inputting invoices on an old-fashioned, computerised system and the enormity of the unknown in front of her, and its removal from everyday life, was becoming too much. The step from this plodding, limited life she was leading and she knew not what both frightened her and filled her with adrenaline. She hadn't slept more than six hours in the whole of the previous three nights, when she left work that Friday. Over the last few weeks her whole sleeping pattern had changed. The death-like sleep she'd fallen into, trance-like, for so long, had gone. She dreamt vividly now, it seemed before she even got to sleep, after hours of turning and moving restlessly.

Her dreams were often the same: walking along a street, being followed, with the house she had to get to to be safe, only a few doors away. But her legs and feet were heavy and couldn't move quickly and, as her fear mounted, they moved more and more slowly. If she could only hurry up, run, while still making it look like she were walking, she might make it, might reach the house in time. Then the moment's hesitation, on the pathway towards the house, the person, never completely seen, still behind her. Can I make it? Quickly, quickly I'm losing time, then hesitation, fatal, the door of the house opening when she turns the handle, but he's close behind her now, he pushes her in front of him, no, no, please God, no. Then she awoke. Wet, along her breastbone, a pool of water. Always she woke up as it was about to happen. It never did happen, always just stopped short. "A bit like falling and waking up before you reach the ground and go splat," she told Neil. "I suppose I couldn't cope with any dreaming at first, but now that the initial shock has worn off, my head's decided to try to work it all out. It'll just be a stage, I'm sure."

Sometimes now, she had other vicious, sick dreams. The man figure, whose face she could never see, would turn into a large, lean dog, an Alsatian. She'd never liked dogs, hated the smell of them, the way they always sniffed around her, found them vaguely disgusting and totally alien to her. Now her unconscious seemed to be blending the two images of man and dog together – she hated and feared both. In one dream, a man pursuing her down a street changed into a dog after she bent down to change the wheel of a bicycle that had suddenly appeared, leaning against a high wall. As she straightened herself upwards, the dog facing her did the same, rising on its hind legs and, with its forepaws, pinned her against the wall. Her eyes moved from where they had been fixed, on his groin, up to where the animal widened, in a V-shape, to its broad shoulders. She'd grabbed it by the throat with her right hand, averting her face from the beast, tears soaking her face. Her grip tightened around the animal's throat, as though of its own accord, totally separate from her will: she knew what the hand was doing, but it was independent from her. She knew she was killing the animal, she didn't want to but knew she had to, for if she let go now it would kill her, she had to carry on to the end. She woke up, heart pounding, her face covered in tears.

In other dreams she was being forced to look at pornographic magazines and films, her head in some kind of vice that would not let her look to either the left or the right, only straight ahead, so she was not allowed to escape from seeing what was in front of her. When she woke up she felt mentally worn out, and often the muscles in her legs felt sore, as it she'd tried to kick herself free from the filthy mire of perversion she'd been soaked in.

She went back to Doctor Ahmed and was given two weeks' worth of sleeping pills, to get her through the countdown to the trial.

"If the case carries on longer than that then come back to me, but afterwards you'll have to come off them. They won't help you in the long run. You've coped so far and I'm sure you'll carry on getting better afterwards. Come and see me again when the case is over. Good luck. You'll be okay, I'm sure. It won't be as bad as you imagine."

Anne left the surgery with Neil. He'd taken a week's holiday to be with her. "Not much of a holiday," Anne had said when he told her. "You should've waited to see if you are called. Jackie says that the prosecution aren't going to call you, so it could be a waste of time."

But he'd said that there was no way he could cope with going to work, "As if that's important, compared with what we're going through next week."

She stopped herself from saying that it was her, not him, who was going to be going through it. She knew that was unfair and in a way it was both of them, but it all hinged on her, hers was all the responsibility, it was only she who could put him away. She had sensed over the last few weeks, as the phone calls from Jackie, Liz, Stella and Valerie stepped up, that he was feeling pushed to the side. She hooked her hand through his arm as they walked back from the surgery, thinking, I hope he's strong enough, please God, let him be strong enough to get through the next week or two and then we can start to get on with life again and see what's left for us, or even between us. If he can get through this, she thought superstitiously, then the worst will definitely be over and we'll be all right, I know it. Jackie had told her that she'd been chasing the Criminal Injuries Board for her, and it looked as if she would get some money from them within a month or two of the trial.

"Are they waiting to find out first whether I've made it all up or not?" she'd asked her wryly.

"Something like that, yes," Jackie had answered.

She'd suggested to Neil that they could put down a deposit on a flat, using the money to get them a place of their own. Some security, some permanence. She didn't know whether she wanted to settle down here, knew she didn't really, but she could only take small steps. She still felt too bound up to make big decisions, too scared of making the wrong ones and had no confidence in herself, and so couldn't imagine moving somewhere else now (where, anyway?). Stepping back and looking objectively at her own life was beyond her. She felt as if she had blinkers on and they would only allow her to see the trial at the Old Bailey, no further. In her mind, beyond that was only the vague and comforting idea of having something of her own, which would offer her protection and could not be snatched away by anyone.

Part Three

The clock ticked by, time speeding up, and every evening after darkness fell she sat and thought: one day less, only eight days to go, only seven days to go. The idea of the trial was so unimaginable, so unreal, part of another world that existed without and independent of her, that she found it impossible to believe it would actually take place. She remembered the night before her first day at grammar school, looking at the new, lovely-smelling uniform hanging up on the outside of the wardrobe, knowing that the next day she would be queuing with the grown-up girls who wore these clothes. She couldn't imagine it, had thought she was bound to die in the night so that it would never come. No precedent had been set by which she could judge this newness, this brink. This was how she felt again. School was now a memory, poly becoming just a memory and she realised that at some future time, this trial would be just a memory, something that had happened, that had a start, middle and end, that she would develop a way of looking at it, that some overriding feelings would outshine all others until that was all which would remain. Would what had happened to her ever feel like that?

They sat up late each night, until two or three in the morning, as if she and Neil were putting in the time of a prison sentence. They played cards endlessly: a game Neil had played with the others in the quiet times at work. A simple, compulsive game, it dismissed everything else from their minds. There was only the papery snap as both of them, with increasing speed, slapped down the cards, turn about, on the floor between them. It had occurred to Neil one afternoon, when thinking about the yawning evening in front of them. He brought the cards home the next evening and Anne, to pacify him, had reluctantly joined in. It passed the time; they could play, minds closed to all else, for, sometimes, two or three hours before one of them would look up at the clock on the dresser and Anne would think: another evening filled in, more time killed. It's closer now, sleep, then day six, or day five, tomorrow. She would take the two sleeping tablets at eleven and by four in the morning would be able to sleep.

In the mornings, she felt drugged and heavy. She decided she wouldn't take the tablets on the Sunday night before the trial started. She probably wouldn't sleep, but then she probably wouldn't anyway, even with the tablets. She needed to feel alive and alert on that morning, not heavy and sluggish the way she felt now.

Jackie cancelled the leave she'd booked the week before the trial started. It had been booked for months, and she had planned to visit her mother in Scotland.

"It doesn't matter, it's my own fault really; I should've cancelled it when we first got the court dates through. I can't leave you now, not in this state."

They'd just read over the three statements Anne had made, back in that hot, oppressive July. They sat at the kitchen table and, as Anne read, her hands shook as she couldn't cope with the intensity of the violence and the hatred coming from those pages. She'd forgotten how much of the language of woman-hatred he'd used – "you fucking cunt" over and over again – and it shocked and sickened her. When raping her alone wasn't enough: "Talk dirty to me, you fucking bitch. Come on, tight cunt."

The bile rose in her throat. She put the papers down; her eyes had filled minutes earlier and now they overflowed. For a few seconds she fought to stop them, then she let go; she reached the breaking point, the shock of what she'd just read showed her how far she'd come in these months, but now she was thrown back into that time, that night. She sobbed, the constriction in her throat loosened as she cried out loud, "Oh Christ, how can I say all this, how can I? The bastard, the bloody bastard."

When she'd first started to read over the statement she'd frantically skimmed over the words and lines.

"There's so much I've forgotten. I'd even forgotten that the first glimpse I'd had of him was on the other side of the road. I don't know how I'd forgotten that, but I had. I can't remember this detail, you know, like when he was on my left and when he was on my right." She'd read on frantically. "And here, my God, then the scissors were in my right side, here they were stuck into my throat. I won't get it right, I can't possibly remember all this."

Jackie had calmed down her hysteria – there was still a while to go yet, she could re-read this as many times as she liked. Anne had carried on, but it had got more difficult. She couldn't cope with the stark nauseating truth, the description, unsanitised unlike when she told others the story. She realised that in the months in between she'd formed an abridged version of what had happened, the worst parts left unsaid or described in one brief sentence that did not convey the full fear, the full disgusting horror.

Jackie was with her for a part of every day after that. Anne realised that perhaps Jackie had thought she was stronger than she was, hadn't expected her bottle to go right at the end. She had kept her head up through all this time and now told herself that she had to carry on, that this was the most important part coming up, the time when she could have her say. She feared losing Jackie's respect too, and she so desperately wanted to make her and Adam proud of her.

They bought a suit one day, as Anne had insisted that she buy new clothes; Jackie had advised against it. "You don't want to waste your money, and you've got things to wear anyway and you probably won't want to look at it again, after it's all over."

Anne had been adamant: she had to feel confident, know that she looked good. After they bought it they went for a coffee, and Anne laughed, "Even if I do want to wear it again I probably won't be able to. I haven't been a size eight since I was about fifteen. I'll probably go straight back to a ten or a twelve after all this is over."

"What weight are you now?" Jackie asked, serious now.

"Seven stone. I can't believe it, I still do eat you know, well, not for the last couple of days now, but in general I do."

"What were you before, eight or so, you lucky cow?" Jackie laughed.

"No. More than that actually, about eight and a half I think. I'd been around that for years."

"That all helps you know. I'll make a note of that when we get back to yours. It won't do any harm to come out in court that you've lost that much weight. That, and not being able to sleep, and what you said," Jackie pulled an exaggerated face, "about not being able to look at or touch Neil, down there. It'll all be part of Adam's statement to the court."

Anne asked how much of the trial would appear in the papers.

"That's a difficult one to answer really. It all depends on what else is in the news that week. Rape itself and rape trials are so commonplace that they often get only a few lines. Although the rubbish papers obviously love all those stories, so it'll probably get more coverage in *The Sun* than *The Guardian*. Not everyone's ideals are as high as yours!" Jackie smiled sadly.

"I tell you what, I'd like to make them all go through it, anyone who reads those reports and enjoys them."

She felt ambivalent towards any newspaper coverage. She couldn't bear it to be one or two lines or not to appear at all, as if to say that what had happened to her was nothing much or not shocking. She believed that people should know about it, but only if it were told in the right way.

To make herself feel in control, to give herself the impression that she could have some effect on any reportage she wrote to a Labour MP, one in whom Anne had a certain trust, having heard her speak often about women's rights and against pornography. Anne had watched, impressed and with some amusement, as the MP had marched through a large newsagent, lifting off the porn and placing it down in front of the shop assistant and hovering manager, demanding to know if they were happy to sell that trash, with cameras present. Anne wrote to her on the Monday, one week before the case was due to start. Once the idea occurred to her, she wrote the letter immediately. Not pausing to write a rough draft, she addressed it to the House of Commons and started it by saying that she would like the MP to follow the trial, which would start the following week, at the Old Bailey. She then described the events that had happened that night. In the final paragraph she said that she'd always believed pornography promoted and excused misogyny, and encouraged society to tolerate and accept it. She said that she believed there was a system of cause and effect linking that to which humans were exposed with their actions, and that her case showed that the link existed between pornography and rape. She underlined how *The Last Movie* was on the television, the bathroom window open and then it looked as if he'd gone out to 'find' a woman for himself after watching for anyone coming out of the train station. Also, she said, the whole story he told while he had her trapped was reminiscent of a bad drama and, she ended, she wouldn't be surprised if some porn film existed that mapped the same scene he'd made her act out. Finally, Anne wrote quickly, excitedly, knowing the truth of what she said, hadn't he been leading her through the room to try and find a porn video amongst the rubbish on the floor when she'd jumped out of the window? Hadn't he cried, "Now, video time, the worst form of propaganda I know, but it has to be done." The truth of this was fact, not opinion nor interpretation. She told how the police had explained that none of this would be commented on in court, the trial would be confined to the rape itself and nothing else. She finished by saying she hoped the MP would take up her case and use it to further her campaign.

She posted it immediately and got a reply by the end of the week. In it the MP said she would follow the trial, wished Anne strength during it and said she would always relentlessly fight the cause for women to live free from the degradation of pornography. The House of Commons seal, the friendly letter which started 'Dear Anne' and was signed with her Christian name, fired Anne up. She felt that now she was going into the trial for all women, not just to get justice for herself personally. With this letter and the confidence-building by Jackie and Adam's constant reassurance that she would damn him completely by what she would say, her faith in herself grew, as did her determination that she wouldn't let him ever do to anyone else what he'd done to her.

Adam had suggested going to a court case to see exactly how they operated. Anne told Jackie and Adam about the letter she'd got later that Friday morning, in the car on the way to Croydon Court. Jackie was pleased that Anne had got an answer so quickly, and said she hoped it would do good, raise awareness. Adam was cynical. He'd laughed, good-humouredly, but patronisingly, at Anne's politics and feminism, from the start. He thought men were men and there was nothing anyone could do to change that.

The courtroom was small, modern and panelled in light wood. The only colour was the shield behind the judge, made up of bright green and reds. The three of them slipped into the public gallery, which faced the jury, separated by desks at right angles, in rows like at school, on which sat various robed and suited men, facing the judge's bench. Two young men were on trial, surly in their ill-fitting suits, concentrating hard on not looking intimidated when the prosecution cross-examined them. Adam sat on one side of Anne, Jackie on the other. They whispered to her when the defence stood up and spoke, then when the prosecution did. They pointed out the various parts of the courtroom to her. Anne nodded, looking straight ahead at the jury: a large woman, fortyish, with purple-tinted glasses beneath her heavy, sandy hair, looked at her. She looked back, trying to think where she knew her from.

"I can hear her voice, but I can't think who she is," she whispered to Jackie. She couldn't stop thinking about it as the court case continued, and knew the woman recognised her too. The actual court didn't intimidate her at all, as it reminded her of *Crown Court* that used to be on TV when she was a kid, she told Jackie afterwards.

"I used to think it was bad acting that made them talk like that, but obviously it was true to life!"

As the court cleared after the session finished, Anne remembered where she knew the woman from.

"You won't believe this, but you know the garage next to the bridge where he got me, well, she worked there. It changed hands a week or two before that happened; the shop shut then. It sold cars after that, I think. Anyway, she used to serve in the shop there."

"It wouldn't have been open at that time of night anyway, would it?" Adam asked. "I'm sure it wasn't twenty-four hours."

"No, it shut at ten, so she couldn't have helped me, even if she'd still worked there. It's just weird to see her, out of context, as it were."

Adam now walked her around the empty courtroom. He led her to the witness box, asked her to go into it and, from his position below, handed her a card.

"The court usher will show you the witness box, when you're led into court. It always faces the jury. So remember; look at the barrister when they ask you questions and then answer the jury. Normally you stand in the box, but the judge might ask you if you want to sit down – some of them do." Anne, watching Adam intently, not wanting to miss anything, looked behind her now and saw the upright seat, flipped against the back of the box, like in a London taxi.

"Now then, read the oath out to me. I'll stand at the back of the room to see if your voice carries."

"Never had any problem with that one," Anne replied.

"No, I should think you'll be okay there, never had much problem getting yourself heard, have you? Seriously though, I know you've heard this 'truth, the whole truth' bit hundreds of times, but don't think you know it: read each word. It's different wording from the films and if you get it wrong the judge will make you read it all over again, and that'll knock your confidence right from the start. Okay, go."

"I swear by Almighty God that the evidence I shall give, will be the truth, the whole truth, and nothing but the truth, so help me God."

*

As with everything one expects, constantly anticipates but thinks will never arrive, when the morning of the trial arrived Anne was amazed that, despite all the waiting, it seemed in retrospect to have come about quickly. She was amazed too that everything – herself, the flat (the radio station turned on), Jackie when she arrived to collect her – looked the same. The people they passed who were on their way to work at seven in the morning, at bus stops, coming out of the shops, in front of them at the traffic lights, impatient, already thinking of the day ahead, were all as they normally were.

Anne stood looking in the bedroom mirror, freshly showered, with her underwear on, a towel wrapped around her wet hair: watching her reflection, she lit a cigarette. Neil was in the kitchen making a cup of coffee, having given up trying to persuade her to eat something. Here goes, she thought, I've got to make myself look the part; respectable, ordinary: make-up, but not too much. Then the suit, black, well-cut, flattering, skirt not too long, not too short. In her mind she carried on a cynical commentary, criticising why she did all this.

Her heart leapt as she heard the rap at the back door that meant Jackie had arrived; they were almost on their way there. The ball was rolling now, slowly, cumulatively. She was ready. She had carefully dried her hair, and it hung around her face in curls. She had smoothed foundation on her face as her skin had become clouded in the last few months; too much smoking and coffee, she thought. She looked in the mirror again and saw her eyes were frightened and haunted-looking. "God help me please," she whispered quietly to her reflection. Taking a step back, she looked at the wider picture of herself, yes, she looked okay, unless you looked up close, she thought, no one would know. She was easily affected by her appearance, her confidence not hard to shatter; a word of criticism from Neil would floor it, a compliment make her elated. Today she needed to look a certain way to give her the confidence to go through what she had to and, looking at her reflection, she was satisfied, felt capable.

She kissed Neil at the doorway as Jackie walked on, down the alleyway, to the car.

"The next time I see you, I'll have said it all. I can't believe it. I'll either have done a good job or I'll have blown it completely."

"You'll do brilliantly, I know you will." She felt an instant's irritation at how easily Neil could say this, which was quickly replaced by panic when she saw him bite his lower lip and look down. Please don't let him cry, she screamed inside her head.

"Don't brood all day," she said instead. "I'll be all right."

She kissed him briefly again and felt an emptiness as the gesture marked a separation from him. She let go of his shoulders and walked away. As she walked along the alleyway towards Jackie's car, all else slipped away, she cut free from Neil and thought only of what was ahead. He would stay at home, and she couldn't help him: she was going to the Old Bailey and nothing other than that mattered.

Jackie drove them to Croydon Police Station. There they picked up DI Munro and Adam. Anne waited with Jackie in the empty car park, until the other two drove up in a large Granada, a uniformed policewoman driving. Jackie and Anne got in the back with Adam and, as the car swung out through the open steel gates, Anne realised that the policewoman was the one who had been in the station on the night it happened, who had gone through the 'there, there, it's all over now' routine. She didn't acknowledge Anne at all, so Anne didn't show that she remembered either. That'll show you, Anne thought. You thought I was just some silly, hysterical girl, who'd probably had too much to drink and had a row with her boyfriend. Now you know.

Ian Munro started to tell Anne about the Old Bailey itself, who'd set foot in it, who'd been tried in it, leaning around in the seat to see her. She liked him; he was a kind man, very polite and softly spoken for a policeman, Anne thought, and he had a fatherly way about him. Unlike the way she was with Jackie and Adam, she felt embarrassed about how much he knew about her, about what had happened to her. Jackie had told her he was one of those rare things in a policeman: a family man, who adored the kids he and his wife had had late in life. Anne could imagine that and was glad of it, wouldn't have liked to think about him either on his own or divorced, as he was too nice for that. Though she knew that with twenty-odd years in the police he was hardly likely to be as nice or as innocent as he seemed, he came across as a gentleman.

He obviously knew that Anne couldn't be drawn away from the subject completely. She would've always brought the subject back to what she was about to go through, asking ever more questions. So he talked instead about Oscar Wilde's infamous trial in the court and *The Ballad of Reading Gaol*. Anne smiled at the incongruity of it all. The five of them in the car, thrown together for a short space of time: the silent driver, the literary police inspector, Adam and Jackie, on either side of her, making facetious remarks to make her laugh and show they made no pretence of knowing anything about Wilde or anyone like him. Anne saw Adam look at his watch; they were practically at a standstill in the traffic. Adam leaned forward and waited for a break in the conversation, then told the driver to go up the hard shoulder, time was getting on.

The atmosphere changed, the joviality left them, they were close now, in the centre of London, time itself was speeding up. Anne looked at her watch: it was five past nine. The trial opened at ten, Adam explained, anticipating her question, but the court had to be addressed and the jury sworn in before she, as the first witness, would be called.

"That'll probably be at about eleven or so. Now don't worry about it." Anne felt as if she was going to pee herself; this constant need to go to the loo had been with her all morning. Adam went on, "Just do as we've told you, speak up and speak clearly, not too fast now. Answer only what you're asked, don't offer any more information than what you're asked to, otherwise you can give them the rope they can tie you up with. These are smart guys and they're very good at getting people in a tangle, it's their job to try to trip you up, remember. The first one will be our man, Prendergast, anyway, so that'll be all right."

Jackie carried on, "Now I'm here for you, I'll be with you all the time. Our barrister will speak to Adam or Inspector Munro, but not you or I. We aren't allowed to speak to either him, or the defence, out of court."

"Why? When he's supposedly fighting my case for me? That doesn't make any sense does it?"

"Well, it's the police that are bringing this charge, you see, not you exactly. We call you as a witness in our case and it's policy not to allow the witnesses to be spoken to by either the prosecution or the defence in case they lead them in a certain direction. It won't matter anyway as anything that needs to be said will be said to Adam, who'll then pass it on to us. All right?"

Anne nodded. Looking out through the car window she saw the long, well-known, grey arches of the famous court. Well-known to all who'd seen it on TV, at the trials of murderers, IRA bombers and the rapists the media courted and gave such incongruous pet names as 'The Fox', 'The Beast', that made them as familiar to Joe Public as the actors in the coffee adverts.

The car stopped outside the front doors and they all got out except the silent driver. Adam went to the back of the car and Anne followed, but Jackie led her away, towards the revolving, darkened-glass doors.

"We'll go in now, they'll follow us in a minute," she said.

Anne looked back over her shoulder and saw Adam lift out a large, transparent, plastic bag from the back of the car. "What's that they're getting out?"

"Evidence, you know, article one et cetera," Jackie said quickly, obviously not wanting Anne to dwell on it.

"I never thought about that, you know. It makes me feel funny. What've they got in there, my clothes or what?"

"Yes, I suppose so. I'm not sure what all the articles are, really."

"Isn't it funny how I put on those clothes that night and they end up being taken out of a police car in a see-through plastic bag, months later?"

Suddenly she felt like crying, as she realised with horror that they might have been taking a dead person's clothes out of the back of the car. This is what it all came down to – evidence. To divert her mind and stop her heart racing, she asked, "How many articles do they have then?"

"I don't know, forty maybe."

"That many?"

"You ask so many questions, Anne, I can't keep up!"

They were queuing behind a group of people waiting to go past the electric tunnel that all the bags went through, past the cameras and out the other side. The same as when you're at the airport, going on holiday, Anne thought.

She was thinking that maybe the scissors were in that horrible plastic bag, maybe some of his stuff too, the crucifix, his clothes, the thought made her feel sick and she passed through the security check in a daze. She became conscious of eyes on her as she lifted her arms from her sides, as she'd seen the people in front of her doing. She looked beyond the woman searching her to a security man who was staring at her. He winked. "Just making sure that you haven't got a gun tucked into your suspender belt."

"Ha, ha!" retorted Anne, as sarcastically as she could manage, looking him straight in the eye, as she lowered her arms and walked on.

"Christ, even here!" she exclaimed. "I'd like to tell him what I'm here for and wipe that leer off his face. How can he act like that? He doesn't know who's who."

"Probably thinks you're one of the jurors. Not that that excuses it, the arsehole. Come on, do you want a cup of coffee?"

"Might as well, I can't feel that I'm going to wet myself any more than I do already."

They were in a large marbled foyer; people walked past, all smartly dressed, mostly wearing black, both men and women, carrying folders or files. Anne looked up to the arched windows high up on the walls, above the staircase, also marbled. They stood at the bottom of the stairs.

"Pretty impressive, isn't it? Have you been here before?" Anne asked.

"Only once. I remember the layout, there's a coffee shop and loos upstairs."

"Ah yes, toilet first please."

*

When Anne was to look back on this day later, the thing she was most amazed by was the way she and this unknown man, this rapist, were constantly pitched against each other, like two fighters in a ring, equal weight given to both, or two friends who were now enemies: always as if there were some link between them.

"You say he forced you to have oral sex with him, yet he says that he performed oral sex on you and then changed his mind about having intercourse with you."

Always what Anne said, then what he said, everything she said was qualified by what he said happened. It was as if they were two halves of a whole, the black and the white, the husband and wife in a nasty divorce suit. Both sides were given equal emphasis, Anne felt, and as the day went on both 'stories' were given equal emphasis, made out to be equally plausible. Whom do you believe? The way that the trial was conducted took time to register with her, she knew the truth, they all knew the truth, it was he who was on trial, not she. How could what she said be set next to his lies? It disgusted her. They all knew the truth surely, all, she remembered, knew the whole story, were merely acting out this farce – except the jury.

Jackie and Anne sat outside the double oak doors, waiting, hearing the noises of scraping chairs and occasionally a murmur from behind those doors, from within the courtroom. They waited over half an hour. Anne stared at the doors, feeling that the whole of the unknown lay behind them. The tension mounted with the wait and she began to feel that, having got so close, the shock of seeing what was behind those doors would kill her when she eventually walked in. She felt that brick wall again rise in front of her, the one she was always travelling towards, but had never reached, in the months up to the end of the last year. It was in front of her again now, she was moving towards it. She heard a deep, loud click and before her the handle moved downwards slowly, heavily the door opened. A pretty, young, black woman in a long black gown with, Anne registered with relief, an open and sympathetic face, said, "Come in now please, Miss Elliot."

Anne stood up, felt the rush towards her bladder, and ignored it. She tried to smile at Jackie, who'd stood up with her, but wasn't sure whether she managed it or not. Her knees felt weakened, like they could buckle under her.

She followed the woman inside. The room was very large and high-ceilinged, with old wood panelling all around. It was deathly quiet, though the room contained a lot of people, seated and immobile, singly or in groups. She knew that somewhere, wherever the public gallery was, Liz and her mother would be seated, perhaps with others, who, his family? She thought this only fleetingly as she took in the image of the two bewigged men in front of her. Everything seemed regimented. Behind these men were two other suited men. She knew, from Adam's detailing of the court, that these were the solicitors, the men in front barristers, though whose was whose, which was the good side and which the bastard's side, she couldn't tell. They were interchangeable. As she rose unsteadily into the witness box, she realised that the whole of the system faced her and before it she was small and naïve; but this was her chance. She would speak and they would all have to sit there and listen. I wasn't given a chance at the time, but now, now I can speak. Jackie and Adam had built her up so well, she stood in the box confident despite it all; though all around her was foreign, alien, she knew she was going to crush this bastard. She had the truth on her side, she was strong.

She heard the sound of a chair scraping, or creaking, and was aware of a movement off to her left, as the woman who'd shown her into the box closed the low door after her. It was the only movement in the room. She saw a man shifting in his seat at the back of the court and knew it was him. It was only an outline to her, from the side of her eye, but she knew. For a split second she saw herself through his eyes and thought, he doesn't recognise me, he's thinking, 'they've got the wrong one'. For how different she looked, in a suit where she'd been in jeans, face calm and made-up, where it had been clean of make-up and contorted, hair full, long and curly, where it had been scraped back, and a stone in weight lighter. Later, after the day was over, when she dissected it, she thought that in reality he'd probably been trying to unnerve her, by a movement in the silent court, letting her know that he was there. Would he have known her again anyway? She didn't know. Just don't look at him, she thought to herself, her hand on the upheld Bible and, as she started to read, she put him out of her mind. This is it, say the oath right, don't make any mistakes, he isn't important, pretend he isn't there. She heard a voice ring out, breaking the silence, filling the room. It was hers.

One of the wigged men stood up, older, thinner than the other one. She answered the questions he put to her gently, with her name, age, place of birth. Did she have a boyfriend?

"Yes."

"His name?"

"Neil Turner."

"How long have you lived together, Miss Elliot?"

"Four years."

Easily, slowly, they slipped into talking about the night of the 24 July 1989. The judge had asked her if she wanted to sit down after she'd finished reading the oath. He's not against me, she'd thought as, gratefully, she'd sat down, after looking at his kindly old face, wrinkled and thin, with his half-glasses perched on the end of his long aquiline nose. She'd thought that it was the judge she had to convince of the truth of what she said, until Jackie had told her otherwise.

"He'll know the truth, he has it all written in front of him, what he's done before, the lot, so it's not him, it's the jury you need to convince. It's them you talk to."

But Anne had still been obsessed for a while about what the judge would be like. She'd read in the papers of a judge in the north of England who'd thought that a man who raped his twelve year old step-daughter could be excused as his wife was pregnant and 'off sex'. "We all know that ladies can sometimes go that way, in that condition."

"Ladies!" Anne had screamed at Neil. "Any old fart who thinks it's okay because 'ladies' are sometimes like that is obviously out of another century. He really thinks a lot of these 'ladies', doesn't he?"

Through his one gesture, inviting her to sit down, she now believed that this judge wasn't like that, he wasn't going to be that removed from the world, nor would his sympathies be that removed from her, she hoped.

As Anne went through the events, after being asked to do so, in her own time, recalling exactly what had happened after she left the house at 12.11 a.m., she could see the pages of the statements before her eyes.

"He had the scissors stuck into my throat, although I didn't know that they were scissors then, because I hadn't seen them. I assumed that it was a knife. He said, 'Bend down and pick up your bag, slowly and don't make a noise, otherwise I'll fucking kill you. I'm not kidding, I'll do it.'"

She could see, in her mind's eye, the next part of the statement, it was like doing an exam, in her finals, when she saw the notes from which she was quoting. Her voice grew stronger as time went on. She knew she wasn't leaving much out, could see the barrister whom she'd now identified as her own, the prosecution, following it on the statement in front of him, knew he would stop and prompt her if she left out anything important. She could also see the other barrister, sitting at an angle to the long desk in front of them all, looking up and then down, writing then, forefinger across his mouth, face upturned, staring at the ceiling again. He didn't look directly at Anne.

Anne tried to remember every 'right' from 'left,' where the scissors were, whether in the side of her throat, or at the front or back of her neck. Because she was concentrating so hard on getting it all right, because she had said it all so many times before, she could hear her own voice in her ears, sounding controlled, factual and slightly false. As she spoke an inner voice screamed at her, 'get it right, please God, get it right, you've only got this one chance, say it with feeling, make them feel the fear, the pain. You've got to make them know that you thought you were going to die.'

She knew to glance at the prosecution barrister when he asked the question and then to answer the jury. As she looked at the jury she counted six men and six women, three black, the rest white, mostly young, under thirty, except for one man who was about forty-five and a middle-aged, very overweight white woman. As Anne answered the questions and went through the details of that night, she tried to pick out a person, in particular, to answer the questions to. She looked at one girl with straight, blonde hair as a possibility. She was probably the same age as Anne, was wearing a suit but, as Anne looked at her, head bent, writing away on paper attached to a clipboard, she looked up, stonily, impersonally, gazing blankly at Anne, listening to her words, not seeing the person. As Anne was saying one thing her mind was thinking another: 'How can you look at me like that, this isn't a story, it happened – to me, it could've been you.' Her eyes moved along the row, past a dark-haired woman of whose head she could only see the top, to a man, in his mid-twenties also, who was looking straight into Anne's face, but when, while talking she hopefully returned his gaze, he couldn't meet her eyes and immediately dropped his. Why? she thought. Why? Help me, make it easier for me, please. They looked so detached, she couldn't believe that they understood the enormity of it. Keep trying, she told herself, keep trying, make them understand.

She felt her voice falter when, in the scene in the bathroom, relating the horrible things he'd made her do, the rape, she had to go over all the words he'd said, all the curses he'd used, bombarded her with, all those vile words. Prendergast, the barrister, helped her, leading her through this horrible, difficult part where, in front of twelve people 'good and true', in front of all these eminent men of their field, intelligent and cultured and the formidable face of the British judiciary, she had to recount each time he'd said, 'you fucking bitch' and called her 'cunt', with each thrust he'd made and each gag she'd made.

And she was leaving one piece out, so far left out now as to be almost part of a different story. She'd told no one, not even at the start: her response to his demand for her to 'talk dirty to me', because, of course, she had tried to, feeble, tearful attempt that it was, because she would've done anything, anything she could to try to stay alive longer. She'd never repeat that, what she'd said. Her voice faltered, the tears came. They didn't roll down her face or stop her speaking altogether, they just made her voice rise and fall uncontrollably as, stopping and starting now, she was prompted through the rest of the story.

As the barrister helped her through and the jury gave her no sympathy that she could see, she began to answer him, not them. She became aware of the movement behind him, right at the back of the court. All morning, since the time she'd said the oath, she had not noticed, nor been aware of the bastard at all. Now though, the story and the time were telling on her and she became increasingly agitated and nervous. She could see him all the time now behind Prendergast. She moved slightly to her left and leaned back to try and obscure him from her view. Then she realised that the barrister obviously knew what she was doing. He watched Anne's expression as he spoke very slowly and deliberately, and moved slightly to his right, watching Anne's reaction. She let him know that he'd done the right thing, stopped shifting uncomfortably from foot to foot herself and tried, through her expression, to thank him.

His actions made Anne feel that in some unspoken way, through this undercurrent, she had found an ally. She hadn't felt that from his questions, as it hadn't been evident from them whether he was with her or not, it all had been so ceremonious, clinical and pompous. Now she knew.

The judge came in with, "Let's leave it there please, for the lunch recess," as Anne described how she first saw the open window, as he led her, searching the messy floor, across the living room and she first glimpsed the darkness, air and night of the outside that meant freedom.

The girl sitting directly below her, with small headphones on, stopped typing. All through Anne's recitation she had seen the empathy on the girl's face; she looked very young and had enormous, dark, doe eyes that looked up often, probably to watch Anne's lips to catch everything she said, but seemed to be looking at her as a friend, as she typed with the rapidity of machine-gun fire.

The court cleared, firstly the judge, then the jury, after which Anne glanced round, not wanting to look, but not able to prevent herself and, with relief, saw that both he and the gaoler had gone, unannounced. Present then absent from the court, but never referred to.

She got down from the box and was met by Jackie who, with Adam, had been sitting to her left and slightly behind, in a low-ceilinged recess the top of which, she saw now, formed the floor of the public gallery. Together they went straight to the public toilets. Anne barely spoke until she was in the cubicle. Once in there, no longer in a rush, she spoke to Jackie, who was waiting for her next to the wash stands.

"Do you think they believed me, I can't tell? There doesn't seem to be any feeling at all coming out of the jury and I've said it all so many times before that it sounds false in my own ears. What do you think?"

There was no answer to her question, just the sound of another cubicle door opening and closing. She pulled the chain and walked out. Jackie was facing her, obviously trying to tell her something. Anne looked at the end wash basin; there was the dark-haired woman from the jury, the one who sat next to the hard-faced blonde one, who had her head down a lot. Anne suddenly realised that the last thing she had said in the court was to assure the judge that she would not speak of the case, to anyone in the room, during the lunch break.

"Oh, I'm sorry," she exclaimed, looking from Jackie to the woman.

Jackie stepped forward, "Don't say another word, Anne."

The girl was drying her hands hurriedly, her feelings hidden under the masklike expression of her face as, head down, she walked passed them both quickly, eyes averted and said, "I heard none of that."

The door slammed shut after her. "Be more careful, Anne. If she wanted to she could go for a mistrial on what she'd heard. It doesn't look like she's going to and that's good news for us because it means she's sympathetic, but still. I thought they would've had separate toilets really, seems ridiculous to have us all using the same ones. Anyway, let's forget about that." Jackie paused as she went to open the toilet door. "Just remember, this afternoon, when the defence cross-examine you, remember, even if they push you to the limit, say nothing of what you know about his past, or that really will be it. The trial would then definitely be disbanded and you'd have to go through the whole thing again in six months' time."

They met Liz and her mum in the corridor. Adam had met them and brought them to Jackie and Anne. He waited until they joined them then set off immediately, only smiling briefly at Anne.

"He's not supposed to see too much of us during the case either," Jackie said.

"God, I feel like I've got leprosy!" Anne exclaimed.

Liz's mum hugged Anne, and she could see from their faces that they'd been crying, but were trying to pretend they hadn't. She loved them both for it and for being there, with her. She had to act well, she had to cope with it all, because they were there supporting her.

"Shall we go to the pub for lunch then?" Jackie asked, already leading them off. "There's one just across the road, but there may be jurors there, so we'll just have to talk about other things, okay?"

They all went. Everyone ate, except Anne. She drank mineral water and tried to reassure herself that she was half-way there.

The time for the recess was over, bar five minutes, when the four of them came out of the pub. They crossed the road, Jackie leading the way. She walked to a large archway, to the right of the main doors of the courthouse. Anne wondered where they were heading, then she saw a small sign on the wall: Public Galleries, courts 1-6. Liz's mum looked at Anne through her soft, brown, misted eyes. They'd only met twice before today, yet Anne felt relaxed with her, unembarrassed by what she had heard Anne say in court; they were at ease with one another, Anne responding to the perennial mother, as Mrs Bell related to the universal daughter.

They all hugged one another. Anne and Jackie then left them and passed through security and up the marbled stairs again. Anne wanted desperately to get into court quickly, get what she knew was going to be the worst part over with and get out.

They opened the already familiar oak door, that resounded with the acoustics of the vast, high, empty room beyond. There were only a few official people in the room. With the heavy weight of officialdom not present, it was more relaxed, like a classroom before the teacher comes in.

Anne entered the witness stand again and sat down. Jackie gripped her hand and then joined Adam in the seats under the gallery, where he was talking quietly to an elegant woman in a suit, whom Anne didn't recognise. Now she had a chance to look around. Anne's eyes met those of the clerk of the court, and she smiled warmly at her. The defence's solicitor, who sat in the row behind the man who, that morning, had sat at an angle to her and not met her eye, looked up and smiled also, his glance patriarchal, an older man to a younger woman, kindly. They can all smile, she thought, because the jury weren't there to see. Then she heard the hollow click of a door, coming from the direction of the small, unobtrusive door which led to the seat where the bastard had sat, cordoned off by a banister of wood. The whole area seemed to be separate from the room, cordoned off so it could easily be overlooked entirely. The room that consisted of the judge in the middle, the jury and public gallery to either side and the officials of the court in front, did not seem to include the narrow corridor and small door to the gaoler and criminal's seat.

Anne realised with horror that the noise was probably him coming in. Her heart thumped, hurting her chest. 'Don't let it be, please God, not before the whole thing starts and everyone else is in here.' She wanted the protection of the whole charade, everyone needed to be present to keep the threat of him from her.

She looked over, fearing to look, but having to. She saw the gaoler walk to the end of the run of the raised corridor. When he reached the end he leaned over and slotted a bar into the door from the other side, similar to the one in the pulpit she sat in. He saw her watching and, she felt, sensed her trepidation. He winked over, gave her the thumbs-up sign and mouthed, "It will be all right," while nodding his head at her. Anne felt like shouting out thank you, but just smiled back, her face brightening in gratitude. Some do believe me, she thought, speaking in her head to the gaoler, the clerk, the bastard's solicitor, our prosecution.

This was the truth, they knew the truth, neutrality was only for the jury. What a system, Anne thought, as all in the court followed someone's lead and stood up. The only people who didn't know the truth, who hadn't the whole story in front of them, were the ones who could return a verdict of not guilty through their ignorance. Outrageous. The judge had come in and, as Anne sat down again, she saw out of the corner of her eye that he, flanked by the gaoler, had slipped in.

During that afternoon Anne realised that, although she didn't know what the rapist's story was to be, he had known her version completely. In the defence barrister's introduction, he mapped out a story that started with Anne being a well-known drug user in the area. ('I've only lived there a year, I don't know anyone round there!' she screamed in her head.)

"My client", he continued, "knew her by sight, if not by name, from seeing her hanging around Miguel's in the evening."

Where did he get that from, how would he know she had any connection with Miguel's, she thought, then realised that in Neil's statement he'd said where he worked and how he'd had to work late that night, and then had a drink with the rest of the staff afterwards. 'It's not fair,' she screamed inside her head. 'He knew nothing about me, I could've been anyone, but he's been allowed to find things out. It makes him seem more plausible,' she thought, 'even to me.' She could see that the outlines of the truth would blur in the jury's mind.

The defence barrister – she never could remember his name afterwards – was a large, imposing man, with an aquiline nose and upper-class accent, who addressed his questions to her with a cold glance in her direction, which then became glazed as he seemed to look through or beyond her, as she answered.

"If you wanted to get cigarettes, why didn't you stop at the garage, just before the bridge, to get them? I would suggest that you didn't want cigarettes, you carried on walking, because you were looking for drugs, or a man, or both."

"What woman in her right mind would walk the streets looking for a man?" she rejoined immediately, hardly waiting for him to finish. "Women aren't like that. And don't say that I take drugs, because I don't and you know I don't. There's evidence to say that I'm not a user. I was forced by him to smoke a few drags that night. And anyway," Anne carried on, gaining confidence, "that isn't a garage before the railway bridge, it's a car showroom. It changed hands only a few days before that night, when he got me."

"That may be the case, but is unproven at the moment." He looked to the judge. "It will be looked into and commented on tomorrow, Your Honour." He turned back, glassy-eyed, to face her. She felt she'd scored a point and, without knowing she was going to, turned round to look at Jackie and Adam. She thought that in Adam's movement from being perched on the edge of the chair to sitting further back in it, she saw him relax.

"Don't you think it was a rather stupid thing to do, Miss Elliot, to walk down a London street, after midnight, merely to meet your boyfriend, who may or may not be coming home, for the chance of getting a cigarette from him?" Scathing, superior.

"Yes, yes, it was stupid," she bit in. "We all do stupid things, sometimes. I was anxious about him, I couldn't relax."

"Anxious, yes," interrupted the barrister, with significance, Anne saw, but in relation to what she couldn't tell.

"Yes, I'm anxious, okay, but that, like doing something stupid, like going out on my own, late at night, isn't a crime. What he did to me was." Her voice was rising, her face contorting. "And I'm paying for it now, aren't I?" She tapped her temple with force, leaning forward. "Every day I'll pay for it, for the rest of my life and now you're trying to make me feel even worse about it."

Anne couldn't tell the difference between the rapist's barrister and the rapist himself: they were interchangeable. The judge broke in and Anne stopped; she knew she had been aggressive, thought she had gone too far, feared she was going to be told off now and further alienated from the jury. The judge leaned forward from his bench, towards her and spoke in a low, calm voice.

"I understand why you are getting irate, Miss Elliot. It's not your fault that you are doing so, rather the fault of the British justice system, for conducting these trials in such a way. Please be calm, try to remember that it is not my learned friend's opinion which is being suggested by him, solely the view of his client. The defendant, by law, is entitled to have his point of view put forward, and his counsel, in acting for him, is doing just this."

Anne nodded, "Yes, I know, I'm sorry, it's just so difficult to be challenged like this."

The judge nodded to her, then nodded almost imperceptibly to the barrister to carry on. Anne looked ahead of her once more, to the jury and there saw the heaving shoulders and bent head of the dark-haired woman she had seen in the toilets. She looked up and met Anne's gaze, eyes streaming, then lowered her head again. Thank you, Anne thought, oh thank you.

The words the judge had said echoed in Anne's head, 'the fault of the British justice system': he was on her side! He was telling the jury that too, asking them to excuse her raised voice and argumentative tone.

As soon as the large, intimidating barrister spoke again, in his mechanical, upper-class monotone, her faith disappeared immediately.

"I put it to you that you are lying, Madam."

"No, no, I'm not, don't call me a liar!" she burst out, almost before he had finished. Then silence, and slowly, menacingly, he spoke in tones so low as to underline her hysteria, her shouts.

"I, Madam, am speaking only on behalf of my client, this is not my personal opinion."

"Yes, yes, I'm sorry."

"Is it not the case," he began again, more theatrical now, his voice swelling, "that my client performed oral sex on you and then, noticing a discharge, suggested that you should have a bath?"

He stopped, she didn't know whether it was to take a breath or to wait for her response.

"No, that is a total lie, it isn't true," she answered, quieter now, embarrassed about what he said and uncomprehending as to why this rubbish story was being invented. She felt tears coming close again.

He started to speak again, as if having got a response, any response, he could carry on. "Was it not the case that you were upset by this, humiliated, in fact, by his suggestion that you were unclean, that you then decided to 'show him' and made for the open window which, having sat on the edge earlier, smoking dope, you knew was not three storeys up, but rather gave on to the neighbouring roof, a matter of some feet down."

"A matter of some feet!" she repeated. "I could've killed myself by that fall and you know it! I'm so lucky that I'm not in traction from here down," she tapped at her neck with the side of her hand, "for the rest of my life. And no, I did not know what the drop was, I didn't know and it didn't matter because anything, anything, death even, as long as it was quick and at my own hands, was better than what he was putting me through. He would've killed me, and you know that too, but only after he'd finished with me, and how he would've done it God only knows. I saw the outside world from that window, and I wanted it more than anything. I didn't care what was outside that room, out of that window, I only knew that it would be better than this torture."

She stopped, sobbing, but controlled herself quickly, her face still contorted and shaking, managing to silence herself. As she recovered she realised how long he'd let her speak for, uninterrupted.

He kept on saying that she had a venereal disease and that she was insulted by 'my client' finding her disgusting. At every lie she butted in on him again before he'd finished, crying, "No, that's a lie, it's not true, how dare you say that to me!" Anne couldn't address the jury at all during that afternoon, she could only answer, vehemently denying it all, the person who accused her: the barrister. Back and forward between them it went – accusation and denial – for three hours.

She realised with relief that it was nearing an end when he said, quietly with, she saw, a more humane expression, even a slightly tired look on his face, "Please bear with me, I will only be another ten minutes, no longer."

She knew then that he wasn't going to win, that perhaps he didn't actually want to. She saw that he'd been going through the motions. It was coming to the end and he, too, was relieved.

Thoughts bombarded her head; he didn't enjoy this either, she'd nearly finished, her part of the trial was nearly over and he hadn't confused her, made her double-back, contradict or doubt herself. She hadn't been broken. She'd cried, but in anger, not in fear or submission. She grew more confident. After answering what he proclaimed was his final question, she responded, "Everything I've said so far is fact, facts and the truth, what he's said is made-up rubbish. The truth makes sense, nothing he's said does. This, though, is my opinion and I want to say it: he's not sick, it isn't that he's mentally ill and couldn't help himself, I'm convinced of it. He's evil, that's all there is to it: he's calm, calculated and enjoys it. He's evil."

She stood down and walked from the witness box on unsteady legs, after the judge and jury had left the courtroom, feeling she'd damned him.

*

Anne sat next to Adam in his car, with the orange dual carriageway lights, switched on already though it was still daylight, swishing rhythmically past. Jackie had been going to leave with them, then said that she would have to stay on for a while, at the court, with Inspector Munro. Anne sat next to Adam elated, a hundred thoughts and questions in her head clamouring to be heard at once.

"You mean to say that there is nothing, only my evidence, to say that he raped me?" As she spoke she wondered at her own lack of embarrassment with this man, who was six years older than her, very much a ladies' man, yet she felt that he knew her like a father did, or a doctor, only better. There was no embarrassment left; they were part of the same whole, both existing, in Anne's mind, only in terms of this trial, working for the same end.

"Nothing, no forensic evidence at all, which is why he's stuck to this story of his over the last few months. He says that he didn't have intercourse with you because he knows that there's nothing to say otherwise."

"I can't believe that he is privy to all this before he has to come up with a story. He should have to say his version right at the start, then, if he changes anything, the jury should be told that."

"Ah-ha, but that's the right to silence for you, isn't it? If that's changed then the whole process would have to change. It isn't right, but it's the best we've got. His counsel tell him and we tell you what the results, findings, are. We chose not to tell you until after you gave evidence today. There was no point in heaping even more pressure on you as it would only have undermined your confidence if you'd known you were completely on your own. But," he turned round and smiled at her, "we all know how Anne must have the answers to all these questions, so that's why I've told you now. We have the doctor on in the morning, the one who examined you. She'll tell the court that just because there's no medical evidence, there's no reason to think that it didn't happen. That, consistent with your story, he didn't come, so often there'd be no forensic at all. There were slight abrasions on you, which she says could be consistent with your story. She's also going to spell out to the jury that a woman who has had sex frequently need not, as a matter of fact rarely has, any rips or bleeding there. Also, she's going to say that he's a drug user, they can tell that from the blood tests; and you're not. Nothing at all in your bloodstream, other than a few milligrams, that matches a few drags of a joint."

Anne was turned towards him in the car, nodding, taking it all in.

"You were an A1 witness, Anne. As good as I could've hoped for. He'll go down. You can never be sure how a trial will go but you've done well, right from the start with that car showroom stuff. Great, I was proud of you."

"Well, you and Jackie had me going in there with my head so big I could hardly get in the door!"

"That was the plan, you have to be confident."

"That barrister was awful. You know, until the last ten minutes or so, when he said he was nearly finished, well it wasn't until then that I realised he was actually quite good-looking; before that I thought he was a monster.

"Was he? Not something I'd notice, Anne."

"It was as if he was as ugly as sin when he spoke to me in that awful monotone, looking through me and just lying all the time."

"He was quite easy on you really. He was going through what he had to, he didn't want to do that to you. Our man spoke to him at lunchtime and he said to him that the last thing he wanted to do was to go through you that afternoon."

Anne was silent. The car had drawn up outside her house. She thought of Neil and realised, guiltily, that she'd only thought of him briefly, at lunch, throughout the entire day. They both got out of the car, now she was anxious to get in and see him.

They walked around the house down the passageway, in the fading light, to the back door. She went into the kitchen with a feeling of disappointment, noticing that it was clean and tidy and having smelt no food cooking. Neil obviously hadn't made the curry for their dinner as he'd said he would, as she'd told Adam he was going to. She hadn't eaten since the Sunday morning and now, with relief and the high she felt flowing through her, she knew she could eat. Neil appeared in the doorway of the kitchen before she and Adam came in, his expression concerned and apprehensive, his heavy, dark eyebrows drawn together. She dashed quickly towards him, smiling to convey that it was all right, it had gone well. She'd gone to the Old Bailey that morning and had come out the other side. Adam made his excuses and disappeared to the bathroom. They both stood in the kitchen holding each other tightly, asexually, yet desperately. Anne couldn't tell who was supporting and who was reassuring whom.

"It wasn't that bad really," Anne said, pulling her head back from where it had been rested, cheek pressed against his chest. "I didn't go to pieces and I didn't falter. I just said it all, I cried a bit, but not that much, only at the worst bits, at what I had to say, not because he'd broken me down or anything." She moved away from him totally, walking over to her handbag which she'd dumped down on the kitchen table when she first came in. She took out her cigarettes, lit one and passed it to Neil, but he shook his head so, shrugging, she dragged on it herself.

"I'm so relieved, I've said all my bit now. I'll go back because I want to see him go down, but I think that's me finished. He was there, you know."

Neil looked downwards, not meeting her intense gaze. "Don't please, don't tell me about that bit, I can't take it. It's been terrible, just waiting all day."

"God, Neil, his being there wasn't the worst of it, not by a long way. Don't you want to know how today went? You've got to know."

He walked the couple of steps towards her again and put his arms around her shoulders, pulling her towards him.

"It's over now, let's put this day behind us."

She wriggled out from the weight of his arms resting on her shoulders, managing to hide her vexation as she heard the bolt on the bathroom door slide back. They pulled apart.

"Has she been telling you how well she did then? My star pupil!" Adam announced jovially as he came back into the room.

Anne went over to fill the kettle, sensing, but not understanding, Neil's disappointment in her: that she'd coped so well independently of him.

"Yes, great. I knew she'd be fine. She kept saying that she'd forget what to say or tie herself up in knots, but I always knew she'd be great," he answered, enthusiastically, but hollowly.

As Anne switched the kettle on she felt herself tense in annoyance. You couldn't 'know' anything, she thought.

"Is it all right if I just take Neil off for a few minutes to have a chat with him?" Adam asked.

"Yeah, go ahead, I'll bring the coffee in a minute then."

Neil, his expression now starting to look guilty, his whole appearance somehow looking younger, more vulnerable, walked out of the room with Adam: the one in control. As she watched them leave the kitchen, Anne's heart ached for him. She turned and looked at her own reflection, just visible in the windowpane. It's over, she thought, the worst bit is over and I've got through it and I've done it well, I know I have. I can hold my head up, I haven't let anyone down, she thought proudly. She felt she could take on more, could carry on into the night, damning him, damning the bastard and giving evidence against him. About how he'd changed her entirely, how he was in her thoughts every minute of every day, how what he'd made her do would never leave her...

When she went into the living room she knew Adam had already told Neil that he was needed in court the next day.

"The defence are looking for the weak link in the chain and they think they've found it in Neil," he'd told her in the car, on the way back.

"I'll tell him though, if you don't mind, it'll be better coming from me and anyway he's too scared of you." He'd smiled round at her as he said that, to reassure her, she knew, put her at her ease.

"Do you think he is, really?"

"God, yes, he's frightened of you all right. He looks up to you, but as well as that I don't think he can believe his luck in having got you in the first place. No wonder, it's a mystery to me!"

"So the defence is wondering why a nice girl like me is wandering down the road after midnight and they're looking for some explanation, is that it?" she'd asked, relieved to be steering the conversation away from the subject that was at once too personal and too confusing to be faced now, on top of everything else, with Adam.

He'd told her that they suspected Neil of having an affair with some waitress or other at Miguel's, and that's why he was late and Anne's suspicion was aroused so she set off to check up on him.

"That, of course, would add weight to their intelligent argument about me wanting to fuck the first man I met on the street that night," Anne had commented, sarcastically.

"You've got it, so we've got to make sure that Neil doesn't let us down: that's what I'm worried about. He's too soft and I don't think he will be able to run the course the way you have today."

Anne sat down next to Neil on the sofa. She felt the strain in the atmosphere; knew that Neil would be worrying not so much about having to stand up and speak in court the next day but about actually getting there – getting up to London, by car or by train, would be an insurmountable fear, looming in front of him.

Adam left quickly after drinking his coffee and having a cigarette, saying he'd see them both the next morning. Neil was morose and downcast, Adam falsely positive and jovial. Anne, her elation subsiding, was beginning to feel resentful at the way Neil was turning into himself, thinking only of what was in front of him, not what she herself had overcome.

At the back door Adam said that Jackie would come for them both the next morning, as Anne had insisted she would go to the court each day of the trial, whether she were needed or not.

"How could I do anything else?" she asked and was surprised at how quickly Adam had agreed with her.

They were to get the train up to London and meet Adam and Inspector Munro at the Old Bailey. When she shut the door Anne turned to look at Neil as he stood in the kitchen doorway, his hair standing on end from the way he had been twisting it. She saw his fear. She knew, in a way that Adam could never know or understand, how much this journey would scare Neil: would scare him more than giving evidence, more than seeing the rapist in the courtroom. Being forced to travel, having to do it, with no way out and no choice was his greatest phobia. She didn't understand why this was, but she knew it was an immense problem. But another part of her cried, 'Damn your phobias and fears, this is bigger than that. This is more important than either you or I. See it, see it and be up to it.'

She told him about the day. It was vital to her that he knew what had been said and understood it as he hadn't been there with her. There had never been any question of that. He had not offered to go, Anne had not asked him to and Jackie, privately to Anne, had said it would be much better if he were kept out of the picture totally. Now this wasn't possible. So she told him excitedly what the defence said to her, how her confidence had mounted. How he'd told her she was lying, how she'd answered. As she went through the events her excitement came back.

"And then he said, as the photographs were being passed round the jury, 'You see, Miss Elliot, the "cuts" you describe are really only very slight.' There was this disparaging laugh in his voice, honestly. 'You say you thought he was going to kill you,' he then carried on, 'yet, as these photographs show, they were really only scratches on your neck that could have been made in any number of ways and not as you've described.'"

"So I answered him by saying that it was irrelevant how far he pushed the scissors into my neck or even if he touched me with them. The point was that he had scissors, which could kill me, and that he told me he was going to do it if I didn't go along with him. And then I said that I knew he would have to kill me anyway, after he finished with me, because I knew where he lived, so what else could he do with me?"

Anne stopped, waiting for praise from Neil, or for him to ask her a question, but he only grunted in recognition that he'd heard her, but as if his mind were on other, more important things and as if she were babbling trivialities. She didn't want to antagonise him, but she could feel her patience running out. She went into the bedroom, saying that she needed to sort out clothes for the next day. He followed her into the room shortly afterwards and said he was going out to buy cigarettes.

She hated her own lack of faith in him as she thought, hearing the door close behind him, 'Please God, don't let him mess it up now.' Eight months, she thought, eight months without a drink. She turned the television on to divert her mind as she waited for him to come back; 'Let him only be a couple of minutes, if he's only a couple of minutes then it'll all be okay, he won't have bought any.' She had retreated to her old childhood trick of, 'If this happens like this, then it'll be all right, if it happens like that, then it won't be.'

He wasn't long. She watched him take off his jacket and hang it in the wardrobe, pretending not to, but she couldn't see any bulge in the jacket pockets: there was no sign that he'd bought anything other than the cigarettes. She took the sleeping pills, having missed them out the previous night. The chances were she wouldn't have to speak again in court, so she felt able to take them, although her mind was buzzing so much that she didn't know whether they would have any effect. It reminded her of when she had finished her finals, her mind buzzing with information, combined with relief that she had done okay.

Neil got quieter and more removed from her as the evening wore on. He didn't offer to make any food and, as Anne gradually became aware that she was hungry, she got up and made cheese on toast for them both. She wanted to shake him and say, 'This is nothing, nothing compared to what I went through that night or today in court. Yours is a bit part, why can't you see that?' but she didn't, as she knew that was unfair to him and she didn't want any raised voices, didn't want to antagonise him, so she said nothing.

They went to bed early. As she undressed and took her make-up off in silence, she looked in the mirror towards him, already in bed, his arms crossed behind his head, staring fixedly at the ceiling. She turned round to him as she put the top back on her face cream, "Don't worry, Neil, it wasn't as bad as I thought it was going to be, you'll be all right. Honestly."

She saw him move under the covers, his eyes not meeting hers, saying nothing for a moment.

"You're the big brave girl, aren't you?" he finally responded, his tone low and angry. "You're so brave." She stared at him, incomprehension in her eyes, not being able immediately to take in what he was saying, as it didn't make any sense to her, it wasn't expected, and so just sounded like a string of words put together. As what he was saying sank in, he continued in this new calm, menacing voice, turning now to meet her gaze, "And I'm just the weak little chickenshit, aren't I?"

"You bastard," she said, her eyes filling with tears. "How dare you say that to me!" She tried to make her voice sound as calm as his had done, but she could hear the hysteria hovering, just behind the words. "I don't believe you just said that. I don't deserve it."

He didn't answer, but turned deliberately away from her, on to his side, his back to the middle of the bed. She got in to her side and, as always now, left the light on. Now it was she who stared at the ceiling. Under the covers his hand found hers and held it. She let hers remain there, limp; it was easier.

Somewhere inside her, not heatedly, or violently, but coldly, finally, she hated him for saying that. She felt removed and untouchable now, above him and out of his reach, as she felt some vital part of her love and respect for him had been numbed and then frozen out of existence.

*

Fighting to the surface, feeling herself coming up, struggling through the layers that, like gravity, pulled her back into the heavy sleep, she dreamt that she saw him, vividly, watching the scene as, in the living room, sitting side on to where she watched him from the door, she saw him unscrewing the top from a bottle of vodka and steadily raise it to his lips, looking beyond and over the rim of the bottle, his eyes unseeing.

She snapped awake, totally alert. Her eyes opened immediately, her heart pounding. She knew. She looked to her left side, knowing already that he was gone, the space beside her cold. 'Not today, please,' she begged silently, knowing the futility of saying that, now. 'Let him hold on for just a while longer. Not now, not now,' she repeated to herself as she stealthily swung her legs over the side of the bed and got out. It was six twenty-five. The house was totally quiet. She took the couple of steps from the bedroom door to the living room door on tiptoe. She looked round the doorway to see Neil raising a half-bottle of vodka to his lips, his throat opening as she watched the gulps of alcohol slide down his throat. The betrayer.

She felt sick, sick at the sight of what he was doing. Hearing her he started, then lowering the bottle slowly, he turned to face her. Neither of them moved nor spoke for a moment, then she cracked and screamed at him, "You bastard! How can you do this? Not today, how can you?" With these last words she raised her fists from her sides in a childlike gesture of annoyance and defiance, as she stamped the words out with her feet. Then she sobbed, heavily, with all the despondency that the knowledge that her life was completely out of her control brought.

Neil, in his usual balance to her outburst, was calm: calm and removed. She knew she couldn't reach him; he didn't want to be reached so he wouldn't let anything she said, any action of hers, penetrate him. She knew all this as if the whole episode were a *déjà vu*. She ran after him as, bottle in hand, he walked into the kitchen and sat at the bench of the table, as if to disassociate himself from her hysterics.

"I've just dreamt that this happened. Christ, do you know how much you crack me up, how much you've tortured me? I just dreamt that I watched you raise that bottle of filth to your lips and then I wake up and see you do it!" She tapped her temple emphatically. "YOU, you are cracking me up, not anyone else, but you!"

She stopped there, not knowing what else to say and, turning, saw the reflection of her own distorted features in the mirror, staring back at her. She stared into her own haunted and enraged eyes, looking at the dark shadows that surrounded them in full circles, controlling her urge to go on at him: for she wanted to hurt him, hurt him to his core. She wanted to humiliate him, hold him up as the support he should've been and then mock him for his failure. She wanted to hurt him as he was hurting her. But no, she knew she must try, try to salvage something and get through to him. If she insulted him, he would be completely lost to her, completely unreachable. She had to get through while he was sober enough to know what she meant, understand what she said.

"You are going to court Neil, aren't you?" she continued, her voice calm now. "You have to, it's more important than you, me or that." She pointed to the bottle in his hand as she sat down at the table, opposite him. "I'm not going to be angry any more, it won't do any good. I just want you to go to court and get through that bit. We can worry about everything else afterwards."

He watched her as she spoke, said nothing, then raised the bottle to his lips again, took another gulp, then put it on the table in front of him and let out an expellation of air in a sigh that seemed to contain all of his defeat. "Eight months I've stayed off this. Do you think I wanted to go on it again? But you knew it was coming, didn't you? When Small said that I had to go up to the Old Bailey, that was it. It isn't the court or speaking or anything, that doesn't scare me. It's getting to London. It's getting on that train that I can't cope with. There's no way out for me and that's what I can't handle. I have to go. Jackie is going to come here in an hour's time and then I have to go, I don't have a choice. That's what frightens me. It's so bloody easy for anyone else, it sounds stupid that I can't do it. You see, I have to have this, you understand don't you? I need it to get me through it." He took another glug and then put it back on the table, trusting Anne now not to make a swipe for it, to try to throw it down the sink. "Like you say, the most important thing is that I go there and do this, so let's leave it there, can we, and not go on about it?"

Anne stared at him, different feelings fighting for dominance within her. She had wanted to interrupt him while he tried to rationalise his actions, his deceit and betrayal, and say to him that getting on a train was not the most difficult thing in the world to do. Standing in court and having to go over everything that had happened to her, being challenged at every turn, being conscious of him being in the same room as she was, remembering whether his hand had been on her right or left breast, all that had been difficult too, much more difficult than he could understand. But she knew that her rage and self-pity would be futile, for he was in the enclosed world of his own misery, a world that saw nothing but itself, knew nothing of her suffering, indulged only in its own.

She got up, "Come on, let's get dressed." He followed her into the bedroom. She only had one purpose now: the sentence. How her life would continue afterwards, where her life would carry on, she had no idea.

*

Jackie called not long after Anne and Neil had got dressed, silently, each in their own enclosed world. Anne opened the door to her and tried to silently signal to her what had happened, but Jackie appeared not to notice and, as Anne led her into the living room, she felt the weight of responsibility fall from her shoulders.

She knew that somehow Jackie would get Neil to court. If Anne had been left on her own with him she knew that he wouldn't have gone. But despite himself she knew he was intimidated by, and in awe of, both Jackie and Adam.

Neil came into the room, shoulders bent, looking to the ground, a lit cigarette hanging from his mouth. Anne looked swiftly to Jackie to see her reaction. By even his entrance into the room, his stance and movements, Anne would have known that he'd been drinking; Jackie appeared not to, for she glanced at him and said hello, her mood preoccupied. Anne thought with detached amazement how what seemed to her so obvious in Neil's actions, any little change in his movements that signified so much, and caused so much pain, was not evident to anyone else. She lit a cigarette herself as Neil sat down on the seat opposite her.

Anne looked from Neil to Jackie, wondering how she should warn her, without alienating Neil completely. She looked at her watch. They were due to leave in ten minutes and Anne's mind jumped ahead – how much drink had he got, what had he done with the vodka bottle?

"Right, Anne, there's no easy way to say this I'm afraid," Jackie began. Anne tried to concentrate and pull her mind back to what Jackie was saying, but the rivalry in her mind, between what was being said and the undercurrent that existed and needed to be addressed made it difficult. Jackie moved from her seat to the settee next to Anne, sitting near the edge, her body turned round to face her.

"Last night the defence asked for you to be called again today. I wanted you to have as good a night's sleep as possible so Adam and I agreed not to tell you until this morning, as you were planning on coming to court with Neil anyway."

She paused and glanced round to Neil, who smiled openly and idiotically at her. Anne knew he'd had a lot more to drink before coming into the room after Jackie arrived, from his banal and simplistic grin, which veiled both challenge and malice. Jackie looked questioningly at him and then carried on.

"They thought you did too well yesterday and have decided to scrape the bottom of the barrel to try and crack you. They want you to go into the witness box and explain the stains, marks, whatever you want to call them, on your pants."

"What? I don't believe it. Christ, what are they trying to do to me?"

Jackie interrupted her, "None of us can believe it, Anne. I don't think they quite know what they are doing either, because it could put the jury even more on your side. They won't like the defence much if they see them trying to break you like that."

Anne, tears of outrage and panic welling up behind her eyes, looked to Neil, believing that now the protective wall of self-pity would be broken. He stared blankly ahead, at a point above Anne's head. Time seemed to stop for a few seconds as, his expression suspended, she knew that this moment would return to her again and again in the future, unrelated to her fear over what Jackie was saying now, but as a further sign of her love for him breaking up.

"God, how am I supposed to handle that?" she demanded, turning to Jackie. "What are they going to do – pass my knickers around the jury and ask them to examine them?"

"Something like that I'm afraid, yes."

"Shit, I don't believe it." The feeling that what was being discussed had nothing to do with her finally left Anne, and the reality, the dirty, base reality finally hit her as, getting up, she ran from the room. She went to the bathroom, the tears building up in her eyes and then, as had so often happened to her lately, instead of their coursing down her cheeks they dried in her eyes and her face returned to the composed mask it generally looked. She went into the bedroom and put on her shoes wearily then took her jacket from its hanger. She wondered absently if Jackie were right; after this trial were over would she never be able to wear the suit again, would it, like the smell of a hot July night, always remind her of rape and humiliation? She turned round to find Jackie coming into the room.

"What the hell is wrong with Neil? He's sitting there looking into space like he doesn't know what day it is."

"He was drinking this morning when I got up. He's frightened about the journey up to town and, God I don't know, everything. I'm past caring, Jackie; all that's important now is the verdict on this bastard. I'm just frightened Neil will mess it all up, I'm not even sure we'll get him there."

"Oh, don't worry about that; I'll get him there and we'll get him into court, Adam will get him through that all right, though God knows everyone will hate him for having done this to you. It's not as if he has to go through a lot. He's bloody lucky he isn't you."

They heard a movement in the next room, Jackie looked at her watch. "Come on, we'd better go to get the 8.10."

"I can't believe that they're going to put me through this."

"It all stems from the fact that the defence has come up with this bull that you were infected. Then the forensic has shown that there is some discharge in your pants. They're clutching at straws, Anne, because you did so well yesterday. Ask the

barrister if he can account for every mark in his drawers! You
can do it, you can carry it off."

"I'll bloody tell him he should be thankful that was all that was
in them. I'm surprised the contents of my bowels weren't there
too."

"Yeah, say that. You'll be all right. Like Adam said, you are
CID's star witness."

*

Anne looked around Lesley's comfortable, messy room. The
low table lights and shawls draped over chairs and sofas reminded
Anne of the easy, middle-class student life that Lesley still lived.
Enclosed, protected, only a couple of miles away from Mum and
Dad, she was independent yet sure of her footing and her future.

As Anne sips the hot coffee and lights yet another cigarette,
she feels the whole bitter well of her isolation build up in her.
Why can't she be like Lesley? With her steady, assured boyfriend
and her comfortable home, always looking the same on her return
from work each evening, she never doubted that she would return
to the same disorganised affluent home she left each morning.
Why do I move from one reliable friend to the next? Anne
thought hopelessly. Each one having what I want, the continuity,
the safety, the predictable lives that know no fear. She pulled
herself from what she knew to be a self-indulgent reverie as
Lesley came back into the room.

"Are you sure I can't get you any dinner? You should eat,
even toast or something."

Anne shook her head, wanting the conversation finished. She
could not cope with the day she had just been through, the
thoughts going round in her mind plus the idea of food.

"You can stay as long as you like, whether that is weeks or
even months, until you sort out what you are going to do. It is
not going to be a problem to me, if it were I wouldn't suggest it.
We'll discuss some kind of payment for you as a contribution to
the gas and electric, because I'm sure you would rather have it

that way too. But anyway," she continued, seeing the alarm in Anne's face, "we'll leave that until you definitely make up your mind that you're not going back to him."

Anne leaned back in the sofa and closed her eyes. She felt safe here. Here, with Lesley, was a retreat, temporary security, yet she was uncomfortably aware that she was being deftly organised by someone who, although kind and concerned, was also enjoying the drama that such a recent friend's misfortune could provide. She wondered again at Lesley who, although two years younger than herself, always reminded her of Valerie, with her belief in herself and her standing in the world.

"So what actually happened then? Did he run out of the old Bailey straight after he gave evidence?" Lesley sat opposite Anne on a large bean bag on the floor, her back against the living room wall, a newly lit cigarette in her hand.

"Well, when we got there the police separated us immediately. We went into the big gallery bit that all the courtrooms are off and Jackie left us alone for a minute. She came back with Adam and Ian Munro, and they both looked at Neil like he was a piece of crap, even as if it was him who was up for trial, and it was weird, Lesley, I tell you, I felt nothing. I didn't feel like standing up for him, I didn't even feel responsible and apologetic for him, like I normally do. Anyway, even while we were on our own we said nothing. We couldn't have been left together for more than two or three minutes, and he just looked at the floor in front of him and I just stared ahead. There didn't seem any point in saying anything. Well, Adam took him off and that was the last I saw him. Ian was really angry, he said he had never wanted to knock somebody's brains in so much. I just sat there; it was like it couldn't get any worse and that even if it did it wouldn't touch me."

"So when did you know that you wouldn't have to go into court again about the knickers bit?"

"I don't know really, it must have been a couple of hours later at least, maybe lunchtime even. Did I tell you that Jackie and I went to St Paul's?"

"Went where? The cathedral? Why?"

"Well, after Adam took Neil off to sober him up for court, that's when Ian told me that the bastard is going to stand up and give his evidence tomorrow, saying that old crap about me coming back to his flat for sex and then his seeing that I had some infection or discharge or some disgusting story like that, so he wouldn't screw me and that's when I got all insulted and threw a wobbly and chucked myself out of the window screaming rape, just to spite him."

"Well, no one's going to believe that, Anne, are they?" Lesley said scathingly.

Anne took a drag of her cigarette and looked down at her hands, breathing deeply, before she answered, trying to keep her irritation out of her voice. "The point is that there is no evidence, it is solely a case of his word against mine. I'm on trial, he's on trial and there's nothing to back it up because that bloody jury doesn't know that he's only been out six months, three years early, after doing the same thing!" She put her head back on the sofa and closed her eyes as tears pushed their way out between her lids. "Sorry, Lesley, I don't mean to sound snappy. It's just I didn't know so much of it would be up to me, and what the jury thought of me. Like I've said before, thank Christ I wasn't some half-wit or some poor sod who was crippled with shyness, otherwise I'd be done for and the country would have to wait until someone articulate, with a brain, had been raped by him, until they could all rest easy again."

"So that's why they wanted you to go into court and explain the marks on your pants then, to reinforce his story?"

"Presumably, yes. Anyway, they changed their minds during the morning. Ian said they might – he suspected that they just wanted to see if I would come back to court, prepared to do it – which is a bloody mean trick. But if I'd refused they would have asked for the case to be dropped as the main witness was refusing to give evidence. And that's another thing that completely confuses me: I thought that I'd be part of the prosecution, but in fact I'm just a witness. How the hell I can be a witness to something that happened to me I don't know, but there you are. Anyway, I must go to the loo."

She went to the bathroom, feeling weary and unreal. When she walked in she thought, for the thousandth time, of the memories that bathrooms, any bathroom, brought to her.

The toilet, the bath, the sink, every one of them brought back such a vivid image, memories of such strength that leapt into her mind.

This bathroom had a mirrored wall that ran above the bath. She looked into it, her expression blank and the images that jumped into her mind were those of the diverse, exhausting day she'd had, with the odd, surreal break of walking around St Paul's Cathedral.

Jackie had told her that she and Adam had decided that it was best if Adam take Neil off and keep them separated until he'd given evidence. Anne had wanted to be in court, but they'd thought it best to reassure Neil that Anne wouldn't be there and had, in fact, left the Old Bailey entirely. Adam felt he would be able to control Neil better if Anne were not there to distract him. Anne had heard later that the first thing Adam had done was frisk him, to see if he had drink hidden on him. He'd then plied him with cups of coffee and kept talking to him, not letting him out of his sight for an instant, until the time came for him to give evidence. He'd cried, she'd heard. The defence had tried to get him to admit to being with a waitress after he'd finished work that night. He denied it, Adam told her, in such a way that he was not even sure if Neil had known what they were trying to lead him into. Anne had heard all this after she'd returned in the middle of the afternoon with Jackie. She couldn't really imagine him giving evidence in that court, to the austere, superior barrister. As she hadn't seen it, it was as if it hadn't happened. She couldn't get away from the feeling that when she wasn't in court it didn't carry on. How could she imagine that a few streets away, in the enclosed, stifled atmosphere of pomp and ritual, people sat discussing and dissecting her, her relationship and the minute details of what had happened that stifling July night; while she, in the cool silence of the cathedral, walked around with Jackie, hearing the echoes on the cold stone floor, as they looked at one statue after another. She thought, if only I could believe that this could help me, but all I can see are the plaster images of lifeless personifications of a story that's been told; she couldn't relate it to her own life and her own needs.   They'd stopped in front of an image of Christ with Mary Magdalene in front of him at his feet, her long hair swept from the base of her neck, cascading over his feet while he looked straight ahead of him, accepting the adulation as his right.

"That's where it all began you know," Anne had said. "We've got that man-made story to thank for all the virgin/whore problems that we've got now.   Wiping his feet with her hair indeed! Sexy or what? That's where we've been told our correct place is – at their bloody feet! And that's where they've tried to force us to stay ever since."

Anne came back into the room, wearily looking at the television that Lesley had turned on while she was in the bathroom.   The Channel Four news quietly told its audience, in the deadpan voice of the disinterested newscaster, all of the information that had wrecked the lives of millions that day, but affected the audience in only a passing interest or exclamation; forgotten as soon as it was uttered.

"I just wanted to see if they'd mention the trial at all," Lesley said, almost guiltily.

"Probably not; it amazes me really.   If this doesn't get high profile it makes you wonder what people have to go through to get the number one slot on the news.   Oh, I know what I've just said is a load of garbage," she continued hurriedly, "it's got nothing to do with how awful the crime is, the only deciding factor is how much mileage the media can get out of it, how much of a novelty factor there is in it. Ridiculous, isn't it?"

"Yes, I looked in the papers today, in the newsagents.   I actually bought *The Daily Express* and *The Telegraph*, oh yes, and *The Evening Standard* as well, because they all mention it, but not as much as I thought they would." As she spoke, she leaned over and rummaged under the coffee table next to her and pulled out the papers, all open at different pages, and passed them to Anne. She silently read the one column mentions of the start of the trial. They all named the rapist and described her as, 'a twenty-four year old woman' who 'claims' that the defendant 'attacked her, allegedly in the defendant's South London flat.' *The Daily Express* mentioned the 'grossly indecent sex act' he is 'alleged' to have 'made her participate in'. Anne read over all the articles, not sure what her reaction was nor what it should be, taking in only the key words and phrases that were supposed to illustrate and describe what had happened to her and what she had gone through, but from which she seemed to be completely removed.

"God, how can what happened to me be described as 'a grossly indecent sex act', it had nothing to do with sex, and 'grossly indecent' is a bloody awful, prissy understatement if ever I heard one."

Though she hadn't wanted to see the papers, she understood why Lesley had bought them and shown them to her. Liz was in court with her, listening to it all, following it. But Lesley was in work each day, involved in the politics of the design studio, meeting the deadlines of the printers and the salesforce and trying to pretend it all mattered.

"Right, where was I? Yes, off we went trotting off around the cathedral with all the Japs and the Yanks and had a totally surreal experience!" Anne said flippantly, smiling. "It was a bit weird, but it helped me calm down a bit. Anyway, when we came back Adam was sitting on his own outside the courtroom door and he just told me that Neil had done a runner. He was pretty embarrassed about it really, you know, having let Neil get the better of him and give him the slip. The important thing, anyway, was that he said what he was supposed to say in court: he got through that bit okay. Afterwards, he apparently took Neil outside, into the corridor, then walked a few feet away to speak to a journalist, or someone from the press anyway, because they wanted a picture of the bastard – but that's another story – he turned round a couple of seconds later and he'd gone, disappeared."

"Where do you think he is then, if he's not at home? Has he got money?"

Anne felt completely removed from Neil now. The mood between them since the trial began, especially since his words the previous night, had made her feel increasingly that whatever linked them was being severed. She still couldn't imagine him in court, and there were no shared experiences now: he hadn't been there at the time for her and now what they'd both seen of the court case was from different perspectives, as neither had been there for the other. It had driven them apart, not brought them together.

"God knows, Lesley. He'll be so pissed by now that it doesn't matter whether he's in a pub near the Old Bailey or whether he's in The Windsor in Sutton."

The trial had gone on after the lunch recess to call some of the people who had seen Anne hanging out of the flat window and later witnessed her on the roof. Adam and Jackie convinced Liz and her mum to leave and take Anne home. They'd been there in the morning and heard Neil. Liz, pitying him, described how he'd struggled to speak, gulping tears down as his guilt was compounded by the whole pomp of the judge, barristers and jury.

In the car on the way home, Anne could tell that Liz was trying not to say too much about how Neil had been in the court. They were both emotional and Anne could see that while trying to disguise her pity for Neil, Liz didn't want to upset Anne more by making her see the pity of it too. Liz drove her mother home first, her dad coming to the window of the living room to wave to the car, his glasses catching the light as he held the curtain back, his hand held high.

Anne wondered aloud how Liz's mum, good-natured, kindly, protected woman that she was, rationalised these last few days. Did she go home and tell Liz's dad everything that happened? Liz thought not. "She's very protective with Dad really. She's stronger than he is and he'd be very upset. I think she'd spare him that."

The image of tranquil domesticity Anne glimpsed in what Liz said merged with the snapshot sight of her dad at the window, framed by the soft curtains around him, and stayed with her a long time. The unattainable: the stability of a home, the person you return to, the one Liz's mother had gone home to through all these years.

They'd gone back to the flat not knowing what to expect: Neil drunk and slumped asleep on the floor or face down on top of the bed? An empty house? What they'd found was the house Anne had left that morning with nothing changed, the three coffee cups where they'd left them, despite all the changes and emotions she'd been through that made her feel as though she'd been away for days. The court, Neil's flight, the cathedral, her not being called to give evidence again, one more drama by Neil, separating them further; all this had happened yet the flat was untouched, her lipstick was still on the kitchen table, where she'd left it to dash to the loo one last time before they'd left, and forgotten to pick it up again. From the moment she'd put the key in the door, she knew Neil had not been home: everything was too peaceful and undisturbed.

Anne had made coffee. Liz was quiet, nervous and emotionally worn out. How long the last two days seemed. The rapist was to give evidence the next day, that much Anne knew, but that was as far away as she could see. It was his choice to do so. He was able to sit through the whole proceedings and chose only to give evidence at the last minute, knowing he could tailor his story to suit what he'd heard from Anne's evidence, Neil's, the doctor's, and that of the people who lived in the road. Three of them had been called after Neil. The man from the house opposite: the first face Anne had seen, after thinking the last face she would ever see was her torturer's. Also called was the woman whose bedroom roof Anne's bouncing body had nearly caved in, whose dressing gown Anne had wrapped herself in, after sitting naked, perched and shaking, on the guttering. First to speak had been the man Anne now knew to be called Bob: the man who, taking up a kitchen knife, had run down the road towards the sound of screaming and collided with a running man.

Liz had heard the first man give evidence in court and, under Anne's urgent questioning, while they drank their coffee said, "The first thing he said to him when he accosted him was, 'It's got nothing to do with you, get your hands off me,' or something like that."

"Then what?" Anne returned, desperate for more information. Liz was her ears in court that morning.

"Then they just asked him to tell how he'd brought the bugger back to the scene, oh yes, and he said that he only knew where to take him from the sound of voices and then the police siren. Then he said that the guy got frightened and started whimpering as he'd frogmarched him along. Oh, I can't remember what he said next! Oh yes, that when he arrived at the scene you were still on the roof and a crowd had gathered around and as he got there the police car drew up."

"God, it's frightening, isn't it? If he'd not got him, if he'd been like the other blokes who couldn't decide whether to get involved or not, he might not have been caught at all."

"Mum and I saw him afterwards, this Bob guy," Liz explained. "We went to get a coffee in the recess, just before you and Jackie came back. Anyway, he came over to us. I think he thought I was you; he didn't say so but from the way he spoke to me I guessed so, so I put him out of his misery, because he was embarrassed and having trouble speaking. Anyway, I said I was your friend and that you weren't in court that morning. He asked me to pass on to you that he really felt for you and that you were very brave and he didn't know how a girl could get over it. Come to think of it that's what he kept saying in court, he said lots of times when he was giving evidence, 'I just feel so sorry for that poor girl, I don't know how she'll get over it,' when the prosecution was saying what a great citizen he was and all that stuff."

"It's weird that this man has had such an effect on everything and I've never even seen him properly. It was so confused that night I don't even know which one in the crowd he was. What did he look like?"

"He's really big. Very tall and, well, fat I suppose, but very broad as well." Liz raised her shoulders for emphasis. "A big man at any rate. He's a carpet fitter, I think they said."

Anne looked at Liz, tiredly and affectionately. She remembered Steve and thought how fed up he'd be getting with Liz spending every free minute with her. She knew he wouldn't be able to appreciate that going to court the last two days was any different for Liz than going off to work in the morning: you couldn't just automatically click off when you got home. As the pressure had been mounting over the last few weeks, Liz had talked to him less and less, amazed by his inability to understand or empathise with either herself or Anne.

Anne sighed and said that Liz ought really to go home and that she could go to Valerie's or Lesley's for the night. "You've done enough, you really should go home to old grumpy shouldn't you?" she said, rising, lifting both cups.

The phone rang. It was Lesley. Anne told her that she was fine, Liz was there, Neil wasn't. "Yes he's drinking again, couldn't cope with it."

"Come over here then, please. Stay as long as you like, until all this is over at least. And if you decide to leave Neil then you can use here as a base and sort it all out from here."

It was too much and Anne felt her head swim. "I certainly can't make any decisions now Lesley, that's for sure. I can't think about Neil or myself until this week – or however long it lasts – is over, and the verdict and sentencing are out of the way. But yes, thanks, thanks, I need help now. I can't wait here until he stumbles home, if he comes home, and in the meantime just wait and wait."

Her voice was rising and she could feel the bitterness and fear come back as she admitted to herself that he could do this to her again, especially now, when that waiting, months before, had been the beginning of the ruin of her life.

Now, in Lesley's house, she looked about her as Lesley turned the television and table lamps off, preparing to go to bed, and thought, safety for the night, peace and quiet, that's all I need for the minute. She looked at her watch, and saw it was a quarter to eleven; there would be no calls from Neil now. Too many hours had passed since he'd first had a drink, he would be unconscious – somewhere.

*

The next day enabled Anne to step outside her own life and see how good and how easy life could be if only she were someone else. It was as if her own awful mess of an existence were continuing without her, with a substitute in her place, as she stepped out of the picture entirely and had the reprieve which being somewhere else and doing something else gave her.

It was a lovely day, one of the days that occasionally comes in spring to let people know that the rain and cloud won't last for ever; soon it will look like this. Liz had come up with the idea of going to Downes for the day, to see Darwin's house, stopping for lunch in a country pub somewhere. They drove, then walked, around the wooded lanes, the trees hanging heavily, laden with the rain of the previous days, which still hung from the bushes and flowers.

They both thought and spoke of the trial and tried to imagine what was going on as they sat in the pub and ate lunch. They also laughed and made fun: of the situation, themselves, their relationships, each other – it was easy, they were so close to each other that no explanations were necessary. It was a day out of time, out of place.

They drove on, up and down hills, through villages, not looking out at the passing countryside for a few minutes at a time while they talked, animated and excited. Then everything passing was glimpsed, Anne turned sideways and looked out: the impressions were like snapshots, a view seen once, not repeated, the altering landscape, fields and sky changing each second. Anne glimpsed herself in the wing mirror, the window open, her curly hair flapping around her face. She watched her own expression; interested, detached. She looked at her lipsticked, full mouth and as she stared, her lips curved into a wry smile. Her eyes, even to herself, looked hollow and sad, the shadows underneath, invisible at some angles, were vivid at others. Though she'd shed any extra weight she may have carried when she was younger, and probably lost some she couldn't afford to, her face was still full. Only her neck looked thin and wiry.

She watched the even, neatly hedged fields, some empty, others full; cattle grazing as if statues rooted to their own particular part of the field. They looked like the plastic cows from the toy farm she had had twenty years before: black and white, some with their necks and heads extended to the ground, others upright, heads pointing skyward. She remembered how she used to carefully place them at angles to each other, not too close, not too far apart, careful not to knock any over – sometimes they went over like skittles. Like this overly neat and laid out countryside, she left fallow fields in between and then when it was all set up and ready, in emulation of real life, she'd sat back on her haunches and, the game ready to start, not known what to do. It was the getting there that was the interest; when she'd got there she was lost. Not much chance of that now, she thought to herself, as she wasn't getting anywhere. She brought her mind and her field of vision back to the interior of the car, wondering how she'd got on to that train of thought. She hungered for the boredom, the composure and repetition, the feeling of having arrived, but she feared that her whole life would be a struggle, though she knew it probably wouldn't always be the complete, immense struggle she was going through at the moment. Surely, she said to herself, surely not always this bad.

Liz drove on, tapping her index fingers against the wheel to the time of the tape playing on the stereo. Anne turned the volume up, for once happy to sit in silence – willing herself to relax. She thought of Liz, how supportive she was, how much she understood. Anne felt their closeness to be a mixture of the emotional, intellectual and physical, without actually being sexual. She sorted through her own mind for an explanation of their relationship as it was now. It was as if their understanding of each other was entire – she was naked, vulnerable, yet unembarrassed before her friend. She turned her mind to Denise; Denise to whom she could barely tell a few facts. They'd known each other well at one time, when their knowledge and interests had coincided, but now that had all changed, they hardly recognised one another. She thought that she and Lesley might end up the same way: having recognised each other at this intense time they might not understand each other when, and if, life ever reverted to the banal, the ordinary. She thought of the stages of her life, through the loss of her parents, that memory now dimmed, the pain and guilt diminished, of the people she'd known and now knew nothing of, to her earlier life of bedsits, dope, pubs, clubs and punk, through poly and studentdom, mingled with Neil, and then her recent life here in Croydon, this life she'd ended up with, without actually choosing, that had turned into this hell of anxiety, fear and suffering. As she'd evolved herself, or been changed by events, she'd recognised and been drawn to different people, had known their type and had the feelings reciprocated and then when she became someone different herself one year or five years later, she could still see them, understand and know them, but she herself seemed removed by her change, her different experiences. They could rarely see her properly, it always seemed, that real person remained gagged and dormant inside, unknown and unrecognised. Now it seemed that the real person who was herself was unknown by everyone except Liz and Jackie. Others knew parts of her and she wondered now if, when she changed from this trapped, frightened figure, Liz would still understand her completely?

They looked around the grounds of Darwin's house, saw the plaque announcing his residence, a line of his achievements and his dates of birth and death. They didn't go in. Neither had really wanted to, but neither had wanted to say so. As they stood there in front of the house Anne said, "Okay, enough of all this, lovely though it is. Let's go to the pub again. I can't distract my mind enough to look at drawings of apes!"

They went to a pub at the next road junction, set on the road's edge between two large houses, screened by the obligatory, uniform row of conifers, the grounds glimpsed behind them luxurious in their neatness, like spongy, green carpets.

They had a lager each. Anne chose her seat carefully, without actually considering what she was doing. She sat at the wall furthest from the door, but facing it, the bar in full view to her left. Behind her was panelled wood, above her a mirror. As she sat down she motioned Liz, by an inclination of her head, to the seat opposite her, as she realised how, unthinkingly, she'd picked the safest, most protected seat in the pub. "So that I can see what's coming next time it happens!" she said to Liz, looking towards the door.

"You've been out so little in the last ten months, haven't you? I hadn't thought about it until today. It's terrible really."

"I just feel that I go through the motions at times like this really." Anne answered. She explained, "I enjoy it, but I have to be flagged by you all the time and driven about by you. It's ridiculous, but if I found myself on my own for even a minute I'd go completely to pieces. You know I can't imagine ever walking into a pub alone again, or a shop for that matter. I mean, I know it sounds stupid, but how would I get there? In Carshalton I can go to the off-licence right across the road to buy cigarettes, but that's it. The idea of walking around a shopping centre in Croydon or Sutton or whatever, on my own, and casually looking at clothes, seems so bloody removed from anything I'm likely to do, it's like a joke!"

They talked on, reverting to the trial, to what had already been said, things that the defence barrister had said to Anne, how the prosecution barrister had moved until Anne felt happier and the man's face was totally obscured – all these anecdotes were now cameos, mini stories, events with beginnings and endings.

In the middle of Liz relating how hateful the defence barrister had seemed, Anne put down her glass forcefully, her hand going to her mouth as she struggled to gulp down the drink in order to speak, laughter threatening.

"Oh I know, I know what it is I've been meaning to say to you, I can't believe that I've forgotten this until now. Do you remember the big-nosed, pompous git of a defence barrister telling the jury that after 'his client' left that dump of a pub he'd been to with his scummy cousin he went for a meal with him?"

Liz nodded, not comprehending what Anne was finding hysterical.

"Yes, I remember him saying something like that, why, what's so funny?"

"Well, then he said, God I can hardly get this bit out, he said that 'they went for a meal together' and I got this vision of two men in DJs with a tablecloth on the table between them, with low lighting and a candle on the table, being served by smart waiters, and then he went on," she paused, her voice rising, gulping in air as she tried to get the words out coherently, "'at *The South London Kebab Shop*!' Can you believe it; that's hardly going out for a meal, is it?"

They both collapsed laughing, Anne's lungs finally filling with the air they needed. She slapped the table in front of her. "I mean to say, for Christ's sake, going for a meal is a bit of an exaggeration when the real picture was probably stumbling up the road, kebab in hand," she paused again, laughing, and sipped her drink.

Liz, wiping the corner of her eye with the side of her hand, carried on the imagery, "Crashing from lamp post into shop wall."

"With," Anne continued, "lettuce and tomatoes dropping out all over the place."

The barman paused to take away the empty glasses on their table.

"Share the joke then, girls, it sounds like a good one, eh?" He gave them an exaggerated wink as, faced with their silence, he started to walk off.

"Bugger off, idiot, it doesn't include you!" Anne whispered as his back retreated.

*

Neil hadn't rung. Lesley told her with some amazement; Anne wasn't amazed. He was still out of it then, simple as that. She was more concerned with speaking to Jackie, now she was back to reality. The court day would be over, it was five o'clock.

Jackie rang as the three sat talking, drinking coffee and smoking; Anne the only link between the other two as they'd only met once before. Lesley motioned to Anne to answer the phone when it rang.

"He didn't damn himself Anne, that's the bad news, he's a cool customer all right. But he is contradicting himself all over the place and the changes in his story stood out a mile. He didn't even try that hard to camouflage them, just stuck to the story the defence put out in the first place – that you came back to his flat, had a disagreement and then out of the window you went!"

"Screaming like mad from sixty foot off the ground, just to wind him up and teach him a lesson, surely to God they won't take that."

"Exactly, of course they won't! But I suppose he thought he might as well give it a shot, he'd got nothing to lose. Anyway, he's had his say now. They've finished with him and then the defence did his summing up too."

"I've missed that? Shit, I really wanted to be there for that."

"It wouldn't have done you any good, Anne, believe me. It was just a rehash of all the lies and rubbish that had just been said by the bastard himself, only by someone cleverer and with a posher accent, that's all, and you can do without hearing that. And then he just pointed out that the jury should be careful when passing judgement in sexual cases like these."

"What's sexual about it? That makes it sound like some boy meets girl crap! It had nothing to do with sex."

"I know, I know, Anne. Of course it's wrong, no one's disputing that. But you can't be surprised at that, that's what the defence goes for in all these cases. They reduce it, as much as they can, to a sexual conflict thing and then underline every grey area possible."

"Okay, I shouldn't expect any different. Anything else?"

"I can tell you it word for word if you like, but basically that's it. The prosecution's summing up is first thing tomorrow, then the judge does the final summing up, then that's it, the jury goes out."

"Right, well I'm going for that."

"It's probably better it you don't as there's nothing either of them will say that's any different from what you've already heard.

God knows how long the jury will be out. They may not return a verdict until Friday morning, you just can't tell. There's nothing to be gained by your going, honestly, Adam and I have talked about it because we knew you'd say this, but really..."

"Please Jackie. I can't not go. Today, well it was just unreal, to be doing something else while your fate is being decided between four walls, miles away, with everyone acting like they're in the presence of God, making up their mind about whether you're a liar or not – Jackie, I couldn't stick it again."

"I told Adam you wouldn't take no for an answer; I'd probably be the same myself. I don't know how we're going to work it, because they mightn't allow you in the court itself and there's no knowing who'll be in the public gallery. Anyway, we'll take it as it comes tomorrow. I'll pick you up at Lesley's then, shall I?"

"Yes. I'm staying here tonight and hopefully will have some normality and get some sleep. I haven't heard from Neil anyway, I've no idea where he is, but I can't deal with that now. That can wait until all this is over. All right, I'll see you in the morning then?"

"Yes, around eight, we'll get the train up to town and then get a taxi over to the court. We're on the home run now so why don't you go out for a drink or something tonight?"

"Oh, I don't know, I don't think I could handle it." She paused, then, "They couldn't find him not guilty, could they?"

"You never know with juries, Anne, and that's the truth. It depends on what they are like as individuals. You can get some people, and, no matter what evidence is staring them in the face, they just can't convict."

"I'd put them in a cell with him for an hour and see if they couldn't bring themselves to convict him then."

"Well, that's pretty much how we all see it too."

"Funnily enough, I never would have had that attitude before, but now I can't see it any other way."

"In our job we see it all the time and it frustrates the hell out of us. But there just isn't any point in dwelling on it. He'll get put away. Everyone in CID has been following this and you couldn't have done any better. He'll get what's coming to him. The judge will lead the jury in the right direction, I'm sure of it. He was good with you, wasn't he, and he's got the previous conviction written down in front of him."

"Yeah, you're right, it'll be okay. I can't consider any other possibility at the moment. Anyway, I'll let you go, and see you tomorrow morning."

"All right, take care and remember what I said, try and relax a bit."

Anne went back through the arched doorway that divided the living room from the dining room, to where Lesley and Liz sat. Liz offered her a cigarette. She'd just put one out, hesitated then accepted it. They'd heard the conversation; Anne assumed so anyway.

"Will you and your mum go, Liz?"

"Definitely, yes. I spoke to her this morning before I came over. She said she couldn't not go."

"Good, I'm glad about that."

"Do you think I should take the day off?" Lesley interjected. "I mentioned to Carol today that I might have to."

"No, really. I don't mean to seem funny about it, but I'd be thinking about you and what you're doing, you know, waiting around and whether there'll be room in the gallery for you. It'll do my head in, to be honest. Liz and her mum know the score because they've been there and sat for hours waiting before," she grimaced apologetically at Liz.

"Yes, I suppose so. It's just I feel involved one minute and then not the next."

"I know. It's not easy for any of us. Let's just hope it's all over tomorrow."

Anne leaned back on the sofa, putting her legs up under her and thinking over what was going to happen the next day, then she spotted a pile of fresh newspapers piled up on the edge of the dining table.

"Are those more papers?" she asked Lesley.

"Yes, it's the really trashy ones. I thought you'd want to see those too."

"Yeah, pass them over then," Anne said, not sure whether she was pleased or annoyed. Now they were here she had to look, but did she want to see them? *The Sun* and *The Star* had, in a small side column on the front pages, GIRL ON ACID SAYS 'RAPIST'. Her ears pounded as she read the words, the blood pumping in anger. The inverted comas around the word 'rapist' added to the lies. She passed on to the next paper, wanting quickly to see the worst that could be said, before she felt she could be calm enough to read any of the reports in full. Next she saw 12 FT DROP OF FRIGHTENED RAPE GIRL. She went back to read the articles, but the only interest in the story was the jump from the window, whether because the girl in the story was on acid or some other drug or because she'd been raped, and in either case there was always the interest because she was naked. Anne couldn't decide which papers offended her most: the broadsheets because of their small mention of the case, in the 'home news in brief' section, along with burglaries and pools winners, giving only the briefest outline of the case, the underlying message being 'no news, happens every day', or this excited interest which said, 'isn't it awful, if it really happened, but don't we love reading about it either way?' Each of the reports contained inaccuracies which increased in proportion to the length of the article. One said, 'while she waited for her boyfriend at South Croydon train station'; another said she was twenty-six years old. All the puns and misprints from satirical programmes on the press occurred to her. She sighed and folding the papers over, placed them back on the table. She didn't want a post mortem of them with Lesley and Liz; she'd had enough.

Liz left soon afterwards, saying she would arrive early with her mum the next morning and go straight to the public gallery. Shortly afterwards, Michael came round and she had a beer with him. She quickly recounted the events that she'd heard from Jackie on the phone and tried not to sound weary, weary of the story and the telling of it. She was beginning to realise bitterly that she was obliged to tell everyone even slightly associated with her all the news: it was expected. She immediately regretted thinking this; Michael was a good man, he cared and was concerned, it was just she didn't want to talk about it any more. She forced herself later, guiltily, to phone Stella and Valerie as they'd been waiting to hear from her. Everyone was waiting.

*

They sat in the public gallery like the audience of a play: a play with a very strict formation of actors and a definite structure, some brightly coloured, some animated, all waiting for the final act.

Anne sat next to Jackie, surrounded by strangers. Most of the rest of the gallery was made up of a school party of fifteen or sixteen year olds. A row of boys sat at the back, in the highest of the tiered seats, arms crossed, looking nonchalant and uninterested. Anne had wanted to scream at them as she walked past them, down the steps, 'Why are you here, what has this to do with you? If you don't feel it, get out.' From somewhere in her mind came the phrase, justice must be seen to be done. Who'd told her that, Jackie, Adam? The schoolchildren around them were shifting and unsettled in their seats, leaning past each other to whisper to their friends, leaning forward to talk to others in the row in front. Anne had been feeling her anger rise and, as Adam walked across the courtroom below to the witness stand, she turned to the girl sitting on her right. "If you can't shut up, get out," she hissed, hardly knowing what she'd been about to say. The girl looked at her challengingly, then changed her mind and looked away.

Jackie, on her left, rested her hand momentarily on her arm. "It's okay, calm down."

Adam was saying the oath. He seemed so far away that Anne leaned forward in her seat, making sure she missed nothing. She could only see the back of his head and a part of his profile. The gallery was so much higher than the rest of the court that it seemed totally separate. She'd felt exposed as she walked down the steps of the gallery, so high up and visible to the man whose presence below she tried desperately to ignore. She knew he'd be below her to the left, and made a conscious effort not to look in that direction at all. She hadn't looked straight at him ever, not at the time, not during these days of the trial and she still didn't think she would be able to point him out in a line up. She could see him from the corner of her eye and knew he was looking up at her often. 'You won't freak me out;' she said inwardly to him, 'you won't scare me now.' Just her being here, of her own accord that day, showed him that, she hoped. She'd never been able to say his name easily and now that she was within sight of him she couldn't think of him in terms of a name at all, for it made him too human, suggested that he had a personality, family, probably friends, and made any connection between them more personal. Anne called her friends by their names, so she would not name him.

Adam was starting to speak. He was being asked about the contents of the flat. People behind Anne continued to talk so she looked around and saw Liz and her mother, a couple of rows behind, and beside her, who? A man in his late thirties, who was he? What was his connection? Anne couldn't bear to think of Liz's mum sitting next to some relative of his. The cousin he'd been out drinking with, maybe? She felt nauseous. Why, why am I sitting here with everyone else? I am not everyone else, it happened to me, yet I'm just the first witness called who isn't even allowed to sit in the room below. She stared at Adam, then at the jury. The blonde girl whom she'd seen making notes on the first day looked more involved now, more concerned and affected, the expression on her face no longer superior and removed. The girl Anne had met in the toilets, who'd later cried, looked up to where Anne was sitting, then they both looked away. Jackie told Anne to try to avoid looking at the jury, otherwise the defence counsel might complain about her being in the public gallery. She looked back at Adam again.

The prosecution barrister was speaking, "Miss Elliot has said that there was a film on Channel Four, late at night on the evening of the twenty-fourth of July, that she'd apparently turned off in disgust, later to see it on in the defendant's flat – was this film called *The Last Marie*?

"Yes, I believe so."

Anne looked with exasperation at Jackie. "It was *The Last Movie,* for God's sake!" she whispered through clenched teeth. She'd already corrected them on the Monday when the defence barrister had mentioned it, calling it by the same wrong name. It was obviously transcribed wrongly, she thought, and no one cared or thought it was important enough to correct, except herself.

"Have you seen this film, Detective Sergeant, in which Miss Elliot says there were, and I quote, 'gross sex scenes exploiting women' and the scene of, and I quote again, 'a woman, naked except for stockings and a suspender belt, dancing, legs apart, on a saloon bar,' when she went into the defendant's flat and saw the television screen facing her?"

"No, I have not, sir."

Was it Anne's imagination or was Adam slightly dismissive? Was this the prosecution giving the police a chance to make the connection between what this bastard was watching and what he did? If it was, Adam let the opportunity go. The barrister put down one of the sheaves of paper in his hand and asked another question. They went through the formalities of when Adam had first spoken to Anne and when the woman detective constable had first met her and when he had interviewed the other witnesses.

Anne felt cheated. When Adam listed the contents of the defendant's flat he said twelve video tapes, but not what the videos were – only to say that there was nothing in them to make them illegal or unsaleable. Anne knew they were being selective, and that anything that might not be seen as hard objective evidence was being left out. Neither the courts nor the police had ever recognised the link between what people watched and what they did. It seemed to Anne that Adam was making sure that this court case would not be the one where any new ground was to be broken. She'd had this discussion with Adam before: 'every man watches porn films from time to time, there's nothing wrong with that in itself.' It looked to Anne now as if the men in this court, the ones who held the power, were closing ranks. She tried to put these thoughts to the back of her mind. She wanted to put these thoughts somewhere where she could take them out and look at it all again. Later, not now. She couldn't afford to get upset by it now.

To her right, she saw a boy pass a newspaper back a row to the girl two seats away from her, pointing to the bottom of the front page. RAPE GIRL PLUNGES she saw in the oversized, imbecilic writing which is the trademark of *The Sun*. She felt her heart thumping at the base of her throat.

"How dare they!" she said aloud. Jackie tightened her grip on Anne's arm and glanced back to the security guard who stood by the door, gesturing to her right with a swift incline of her head. The man walked down the steps, deliberately and slowly. At the end of the row where they sat he leaned forward, arm outstretched.

"Give me that paper please. That's not the way to act here. If there is not complete silence I'll clear the whole gallery."

As he turned to go, placing the paper under his arm, he glanced and nodded soberly to Anne. Thank God, she thought, thank God someone appreciates what hell this is.

The prosecution barrister then summed up, and Adam left the witness stand. He spoke sometimes dramatically and sometimes confidingly as he listed Anne's evidence first and then reinforced the truth of what she'd said by quoting the man who'd stopped the fleeing man in the street, the two police constables who arrived on the scene, Adam and finally the police doctor who'd examined Anne.

Anne listened disbelievingly as, in upper-class yet emotionless tones, the barrister quoted the doctor as having declared, "'The condition of Miss Elliot's vagina was consistent to having just had intercourse. There were no cuts or marks around the entrance to the vagina; however, this, in rape cases, is not in itself unusual, as any woman who has had regular sex would not necessitate a penis being forced on her.' Consider this in conjunction with the fact that Miss Elliot has often stated that she did not in any way resist the rape itself, but stood motionless. You will remember she described herself as 'standing there dead from the neck down.'"

He glanced down to the table in front of him and, hands loosely gripping the opening of his black gown, continued, "The doctor went on to say that she believed, and here we must defer to someone who knows and does not surmise, 'that the contested discharge in the underwear of Miss Elliot was because of her menstrual cycle which, under normal circumstances, would have meant her period would have occurred the following week.' Furthermore, when asked what the witness's mental state appeared to be when the doctor examined her, some two hours after the incident, the doctor replied, 'She appeared to be in a deep state of numbed shock, which would be a normal reaction to being raped.'"

Anne looked straight at the barrister, cheeks burning, not able to look at anyone else. To hear herself described clinically and dispassionately like this seemed so much worse, so much more humiliating than when she had said all the disgusting details she'd been obliged to go through herself. She could not look at the jury, the solicitors or the clerk of the court. They all knew who she was and she felt she had been paraded before them; prostrate and open to their gaping and staring. Nothing was private. And these people she was surrounded by, these restless schoolkids, what did they care? She felt her head start to spin and stole a look, a plea for help, at Jackie, who mouthed, "Nearly over now, you're almost there."

The judge was beginning to speak, as Jackie leaned towards her, "He's just going to sum up, then that's it."

Anne looked at her watch, twelve fifteen, how long would he take? Presumably the jury would come back after lunch with a verdict. It wouldn't go on another day then, thank God. Then the fear of it all nearly being over rose in her: it was nearly time for the jury to decide whether she were a liar or not. The time of reckoning was coming and she both longed for it and wished it away – it was too final, too quick, now, after all this waiting, when it was nearly here. Quickly now, after dragging on for so long, it was almost here, and with it a new fear and panic.

The judge spoke as if trying to keep two bad children happy, by always giving the alternative version to whichever person's story he was telling. Again, Anne felt the extreme discomfort and anger of being linked to the defendant in any way, as the judge wove his way through the story. It was all constructed as if they were linked up, tied together by their desperate stories – as if they could even be conspirators, with one same version, trying to confuse the court in their collusion. The elderly judge spoke of corroborative evidence and the three corroborative points that had arisen during the week. Anne felt lost in hearing what she supposed were the court's rules about how the truth of the trauma must be bracketed. She let the words go into her head and out again: there was too much information there already, and she couldn't take in what she didn't understand.

After what seemed like only a few minutes, the judge's tone changed, showing that he was coming to the end. Anne became transfixed by him, by what he was saying in what were going to be his final sentences. She'd been told that he would lead the jury to return either a guilty or not guilty verdict, but from what he'd said so far she couldn't tell which side he was on; everything he said seemed to be weighted and measured for fairness to both parties. She felt in her heart that he was on her side – after all he'd offered her the seat in the witness box when she first went up and he'd not been hard on her when she'd called the defence barrister a liar – but she wanted him to spell it out to the jury. She felt as if the whole court were a façade, that it was all a confidence trick, that everyone knew the truth, everyone except the jury knew of his past guilt, knew the whole story. The point of the whole trial began to look as if its main purpose were to try to keep the jury in the dark until the end.

"In the defence of the man who stands accused of such a hideous crime it must be pointed out that this kind of crime is the only one a man can stand trial for which may be a complete and utter fabrication by the woman concerned. By virtue of its sexual nature it is difficult to determine and members of the jury should be aware of this in the return of any verdict they may make."

Anne's rage was instant. She made as if to rise from her seat but Jackie's hand was on her arm immediately.

"He had to say that, by law," she whispered to her, understanding, sympathising, but definite. Anne was incredulous. How dare he say that? This man was not someone with whom she'd gone out and had an affair, an affair that then went bad so she got bitter and vindictive. She thought momentarily of the media's invented 'bitch' figures, scarlet women, adulterous women, catty girls, and marvelled that this stereotype could include her. She believed that no woman would put herself through all the dirty washing of this trial, have herself and her life taken apart and inspected, held up and examined for faults, publicly, for the outside chance of putting a man in prison for doing nothing wrong: just as she believed no innocent man would leave his decision to defend himself until halfway through the trial that could end his free life for years.

Anne longed to speak to Jackie to say what flashed through her mind in half-formed sentences, images and arguments that were halted by the judge's next sentence.

"One final point that has not been drawn attention to in the evidence we have heard in the last few days is something that became apparent to me in the first day of this trial, therefore I feel it my duty to point it out to the members of the jury. It is this – would a woman who was intent on accusing a man of rape, when they'd merely had a brief, abortive, sexual encounter, be likely to say, 'I don't know, you tell me?' when the man was pointed out to her, in the back of the police van, and she, standing in front of it, was asked, 'Is this him?' Does that make sense members of the jury? If she were intent on pointing the finger of accusation at him wrongly would it not be more likely that she would have recognised him and said, 'Yes, that's him,' even when the headlamps were dazzling her eyes. If you feel that this is the case then you must return a verdict of guilty of rape. These are the areas that you must decide upon. The court is adjourned until a verdict is reached."

"All stand," boomed the clerk of the court.

They all sat in the long canteen in the courthouse. The jurors, Jackie told Anne, were all taken to another part of the court where they remained together until they reached a decision. With Jackie, Liz and Liz's mum, Anne sat with a cup of coffee in front of her. The other three had pasty, plastic-looking sandwiches, but Anne had nothing to eat. The sunlight streamed in through the

high, long windows. Spring, Anne thought, soon summer again.
God, the summer; would she ever think of the throbbing heat
without remembering those days afterwards, without remembering
the smell of the attic flat after heat had beaten down on the roof
all day?

"You should eat something, even a biscuit," Liz's mum said.
"It lowers your resistance, you know, being so thin and not eating
all day long."

Anne smiled weakly, but shook her head. "I've got to go to
the loo again, sorry." She scraped her chair back and walked off.
She passed a young, gowned man in the corridor. Their eyes met
and he looked at her appraisingly and smiled. After holding his
look for a couple of seconds, determined not to let him think he
had the right to look, she looked away and cursed herself inwardly
for not meeting the challenge any more.

She came out of the cubicle wondering how many times she'd
been for a pee that day and having got there, had lost the need to
go. Fear, she supposed, as she washed her hands. Looking up at
her face she leaned forward, closer to the mirror, thinking that
her face seemed to have got thinner in the last few days. She
noticed that the tendons and muscles in her neck looked more
defined. She knew she looked older. Only her hair still looked
good, full and curly, a frame to what might have been a happy,
pretty face; only now a haunted expression in her eyes made them
look as if they'd grown in fear and stared back at her, protruding,
scared.

The hours passed slowly. Naively, Anne had thought that
after the lunch recess the jury would come back with their verdict.
She considered the possibility, at the very edges of her mind, that
they might not believe her; they might think she had lied. As the
time wore on the agitation grew for all of them. They discussed
that morning, what had been said, the ultimate siding of the judge,
but after these things had been talked about and exhausted, silence
kept falling. The only thing to distract them all seemed to be the
continual offering of cigarettes between the three smokers. Anne
felt in some way responsible for their waiting, for their wasted
time. They were all there because of her and while the feeling

that they ought to be enjoying themselves was so far-fetched as to be hilarious, she did feel that the conversation depended on her: if other topics were to be brought up to lighten the atmosphere and divert them, then it was up to her to introduce them.

Adam came towards them, visible to Liz and her mum first. Anne swung round to look at him as soon as she saw the expression of recognition on the other two's faces. He ambled along with his usual gait, but his expression was troubled. Her heart thumping, she stood up.

"What is it? What's been said?" she demanded, as he approached.

"Nothing, nothing yet. Come on, calm down." He placed both hands on her shoulders and looked into her face.

Once Anne was seated, he pulled over a chair from the next table and sat down next to her.

"The decision from the jury has just been announced. They can't come to a unanimous verdict. Hang on, hang on..." he spoke through Anne's interruptions. "The judge has sent them away again to reach a majority verdict. He says he'll accept eleven to one."

Anne's mind raced. She felt as if there were no one in the room except Adam and herself; she wanted to see inside his head and automatically know all that he knew. She also felt cheated, since she was supposed to have been there for the verdict; she wanted to be so why wasn't she called? These thoughts ran parallel with the stunned realisation that not everyone believed her – some of the jury, how many, actually believed she had made all this up. How could they?

"How many?" she demanded angrily of Adam, needing to know. "How many have said they think he's innocent?" she asked.

"We don't know," he admitted. "The first stage is to see if there can be a unanimous verdict and that's fallen through. It doesn't mean we're lost though, believe me." Adam's words seemed to articulate for the first time, for all five of them, that there was the possibility that he could be found not guilty. Adam's very assurance that it probably wouldn't happen seemed to admit the fear that it might. That nagging fear, at the very back of her mind, little seen and admitted to by herself, was growing and becoming a reality.

Adam looked at Jackie, "If you all go outside court six now and sit there, I'll be round and about and, when the time comes, I'll call you all in."

God, it sounded like an execution. Adam nodded briefly and walked quickly off. Jackie turned to Anne, "Come on, we'll wait outside like he said and it shouldn't be too long now."

They all stood up and moved off, Jackie and Anne in front. "Once Adam gives us the signal we'll slip into the back of the court." Anne looked at her uncomprehendingly. "To the seats where Adam and I sat on the first day when you gave evidence," she explained. "We just think it would be better if you weren't in court for the verdict. Just in case, the press are in there and everything, so it wouldn't be very pleasant for you. Then you can go straight in for the sentencing."

They were at the great marble staircase again. "Back we go again!" Jackie said, with jocularity, over her shoulder to the two behind. Anne walked tensely forward, her legs moving very slowly, one in front of the other, all the strength sapped out of her, as if she were wading through water.

They sat and waited on the row of wooden, schoolroom seats facing the number six court. Adam joined them, sitting on Jackie's seat next to Anne, as she got up and paced the floor in front of them.

Adam offered Anne a cigarette and lit one himself, and as she watched him hold the match to the end of the cigarette she saw that his hand was shaking and, watching him in profile while he was absorbed in what he was doing, she saw a muscle twitching next to his right eye. Anne's heart missed a beat as she realised that he was nervous, he was frightened now too. 'My God, it's all going wrong,' she thought, 'I don't believe it!' She felt she could scream. She looked desperately at Jackie in front of her who caught her eye and pulled a face and gestured over her shoulder at a passing, shuffling, gowned old man, white hair sticking straight up from the top of his head.

"That one must be our judge's dad, eh?" she whispered theatrically to the group.

Anne laughed immediately, relieved to be letting some of the hysteria out. Their laughs ended abruptly as, with a heavy wooden creak, the door to the courtroom opened and Adam immediately sprang up to meet the clerk of the court. Without a backward glance, he disappeared behind the half-open door and it closed behind them both.

"I can't stand this," Anne blurted out, all traces of her smile gone. "I can't believe it could be so drawn-out and painful. It's frightening that we could lose it now, and even Adam's scared."

"We are human, you know." Jackie looked at her appealingly, then pulled a face.

Anne looked at her, wonderingly, so well-dressed, her short hair cut in a sharp style, her large, intelligent doe eyes, looking half-mockingly into her own.

"How come you aren't freaked out like the rest of us then?" Anne asked, admiration in her voice.

"Who says I'm not?"

At that, the door of the court opened again and Adam half-stepped out.

Anne stared, transfixed, at his face, fearing what she would see there. What would he do, how would he tell her what had happened? He looked straight at Anne and raised his right hand in the thumbs-up sign, his face a mask, and beckoned them all quickly inside, holding the door open wider as first Jackie then Anne passed through, followed by Liz and then Mrs Bell.

"Majority verdict, eleven to one, guilty," Adam whispered to Anne as she passed him. Anne felt relief, immense relief, but she knew she wasn't even having time to take this in as she walked unsteadily to the chairs, her legs moving even more slowly now. It seemed to take her an age to get to the small front row of seats. She was seeing the court now from yet another angle, the corridor and the bastard were raised above where they sat, to the left. The jury was directly in front of them and a group of reporters in separate seats to the side, cameras over their shoulders. The judge started to speak as Adam sat down on the other side of Anne.

Anne looked at the jury, studying their faces: who thought she'd lied? It can't have been a woman, surely it can't.

The judge introduced DI Munro who, he said, was going to provide any other information about the defendant that needed to be known before sentencing. In order to ensure a fair trial this information had been withheld until now..

DI Munro, unseen by Anne until now, moved from a seat to her right into the witness stand. He started to speak, his voice, shaky to start with, levelled out as he continued, "There is one previous conviction that is relevant. In May 1986," Anne's head started to thump, "the defendant committed a crime of which this attack is a carbon copy."

He traced the story; the woman on the last train from London to West Croydon. Anne visualised the seediness of West Croydon train station: the litter on the ground and the dirt and filth proudly displayed from the magazine stands, so that you couldn't even buy an *Evening Standard* without coming face to face with it from the ceiling to the floor.

As the details of what happened that night unfolded, Anne watched the faces of the jury; she could do that openly now she couldn't sway their opinion, since their job was over. She saw who it was that hadn't believed her as the black woman and middle-aged white man in the front row looked back accusingly with 'I told you so' written on their faces as they met the eyes of the young, sandy-haired man in the second row. 'I met his eye, I stared at him,' Anne thought, 'and he didn't believe me. How could he think I lied?' She felt she could meet the eyes of all the other jurors now – they'd said he was guilty and now their belief had been validated irrevocably: he'd done it all before.

As Anne had already known he'd been inside for the same acts, she wasn't prepared for the effect it had on her. As the details unfolded, she wanted to put her fingers in her ears and shout, stop, enough. He'd followed the woman back to her house, run up behind her as she put the key in the door, saying he had a knife. He'd forced her into her bedroom and produced a knife. Anne's mind started to swim, no, I can't take any more of this, no, I don't want to hear, no, she repeated over and over to herself to keep the words out that she couldn't stop. Another noise in the court made her jump. She looked over to the jury, where the woman who'd cried as Anne gave her evidence was sobbing. She couldn't take any more either. Why isn't the world full of people like her, Anne thought, people who can't stomach it?

"She was raped, then buggered, twice, then he fell asleep on her bed and the victim was able to contact the police by telephone; he was still asleep when they arrived," DI Munro finished. Anne's eyes closed. Poor, poor woman, worse, that's so much worse, I escaped that, thank God. Anne thought Munro would stand down now, but he continued in a quieter voice, "The only other case that can be mentioned at this point is a rape charge of which the defendant was acquitted in 1984."

No! Anne screamed inside her mind. Another one, and he didn't pay for it, not at all. How does that woman feel? How did she carry on? Anne looked at her legs, they seemed to belong to someone else, both legs shaking, in rapidly quivering motions. As she watched her knees and thighs before her, they seemed to shake faster.

Adam turned sharply to look at her, his eyes searched her face; had she made a noise? She didn't know.

"I'm okay," she mouthed to him.

The judge was speaking again – "menace to women when free" – Anne's mind focused in again on what was being said. She knew she had to take in and retain all this, these last few minutes. The clerk of the court demanded that the defendant should stand. The judge started to speak as Anne heard, to her left, a slow and deliberate movement. She knew he was standing up; concentrate, she told herself.

"I have had no explanation offered to me, nor can I see any reason why you were released four years before your sentence was completed, after being in prison for only three years."

Then his voice, his voice unheard by Anne since the abuse of that night, blurted out, "It wasn't three years, it was four." A bald statement in the flat, toneless monotone of South London.

"It matters not now whether it was three years or four," the judge answered curtly, annoyed.

Anne felt Jackie's hand tighten its grip on her arm as Adam turned again in his seat, his face looking more anxious. Anne looked at them both, not knowing where else she could safely look and having no idea how she appeared to them. Could she look at this bastard now? Something in her wanted to, she and the whole room were against him now. He couldn't touch her or harm her now. She'd won, he'd lost. After this week, when she'd found to her surprise that she was pitched against him, she now thought like this herself and she wanted to look at him once, because she could look at him now. He couldn't stop her looking at him now, she thought, not knowing that she would regret it later, having his face etched in her mind.

"In view of your previous crime, which went for the most part unpunished, I feel you need a stiff sentence to pay for your crime while assuring this young woman that the pain she has gone through, both at the time and in this last week, has not been in vain. I sentence you to fourteen years' imprisonment."

At the beginning of this speech Anne raised her eyes slightly to see him, arrogantly, emotionlessly, stare straight ahead, hands folded in front of him. She looked at his person but couldn't bear to focus her gaze on his face until the judge said 'fourteen years', then she looked. All her rage and anger, all her resentment and hate in her eyes. Take that, you bastard! she screamed in her head. He looked ahead, unflinching, an unremarkable, hard-looking man but a human being.

Without her knowing it, her face had become wet and then she felt her mouth distort. She put her hand to her face to hide herself as she felt her strength dissolve.

She was being propelled from the court, flanked by Jackie and Adam.

*

Outside the Old Bailey, they stood grouped together. Awkwardly, they said goodbye to Liz's mum, as she walked off to her husband's offices. She'd been there through the whole week, through the description of all the curses that had been rained down on Anne, through all the descriptions of her body, her state of mind, so how was Anne to say goodbye to her? She might see her the next week or six months later, but never would it be as it was now, at that moment. Never would they recognise each other's strength and vulnerability, as they did now. The desire for maternal support that Anne had hidden so deeply, surfaced with this woman who, through her need to help her daughter and her motherless friend, had fought against her husband and her mild-mannered friends in order to sit through each day of this stomach-turning and upsetting trial.

Anne felt her throat contract as she said, "Thanks for your support, see you soon, bye." The goodbyes between the two women were kept on a level which they could both cope with in their overwrought state of frayed emotions, while their hands gripped together, the squeeze each impressed on the other conveyed all they were unable to say.

The group split, Anne walking in front with Adam. She felt as if she'd just left a school she'd belonged to for years, never to go back, a chapter closed. Nothing seemed real, and all she knew was that she'd left behind the place and circumstances that had, almost exclusively, absorbed all her thoughts for almost a year. With what was she to replace it now? Her mind went briefly to Neil, but she couldn't concentrate on him, she couldn't call him to mind completely. She didn't know where he was or what thoughts had been in his head while she had fought every inch of this battle. The man she'd just put in prison for fourteen years was more real to her at this moment. It was his face that was in front of her eyes now, it was his life she thought of in parallel to her own. Where was he now? On the way to the prison he'd come from the previous week, or to another one? Anne couldn't remember the name the judge had said. Suddenly it seemed important to her to know the name, to picture it and him in it, in order to bury him.

She asked Adam.

"Forget it, Anne, leave it. You want to cut off from it now. You can't go on asking and trying to find out more. He's gone, you're done, put him away, let's talk about what you're going to do now. Have you left Neil for good then?"

"Oh God, how can I answer that? I don't know, I don't even know where he is now." Glancing at Adam and seeing his eyebrows raised, she continued, "I could have a good guess at it, of course. But anyway, I can't see how, as a couple, we could get over him acting like this and not helping me through the last week, but at the minute I can't think about anything in definite terms."

They had been walking for quite a time, but Anne didn't know how far, or in what direction. They just walked. She passed people whom she glanced at or looked through, her mind retaining nothing of them. Her legs moved automatically. She knew they were walking to some place where Jackie had arranged for a police car to pick them up. They were to have a drink together first and then they would drop Liz home, before going back to Lesley's.

As Anne stepped across a side road she felt Adam's hand grip her upper arm and pull her sharply backwards. A car sped past, braking sharply at the junction on the main road.

"God, Anne, look where you're going, girl." He shook his head, then smiled as he manoeuvred her across the rest of the road, looking back at Jackie and Liz as he reached the other side. "Only Anne, eh?" he said disbelievingly as he shook his head in an exaggerated movement. Turning back to her, he said, "Only you could've gone through all that and fought for your life in there, then walk straight out into the middle of the road without even looking. Imagine what a waste it'd have been if you'd popped your clogs there, eh?"

Anne smiled and tried to shake herself out of the stupor she felt herself sinking into, but for some reason what he'd just said made her feel sadder, as her sense of futility and anticlimax increased.

Liz and Jackie joined up with them, and Jackie pointed to a pub across the road. "What about this one? I've been in there a couple of times and it's usually quite quiet."

"Yes, fine, let's go then." Adam agreed.

The bar was light and airy, the acoustics magnifying each sound, making the music playing more tinny, their voices louder, more shrill. Adam bought everyone a drink and they sat down at a free table together, suddenly unsure of what to say. Should they go over it all or talk of other things? What was there to talk about that wasn't to do with what they'd been through together? What else did they have in common? Anne felt strangely removed as if she were watching what was happening and remaining dissociated.

"You did well, bloody well," Adam said, putting his glass down with force, acting out the relief he felt, then his hands tapped the pockets of his coat, searching for cigarettes. "And from now on," he continued, "you've got to think ahead, and," he looked straight into her eyes, "let go."

She watched his face, concentrating on each word. Nodding dumbly, she took the offered cigarette.

They talked over the last day, compartmentalising the story, giving it a start, middle and end: the hero, the villain, the self-realisation of the juror who'd said 'not guilty'. They had a couple more drinks and Jackie asked Anne how long she thought she'd stay with Lesley. Before she answered, Adam broke in, "Tell me, what is it that holds you and Neil together? I can't fathom it at all."

The question surprised Anne. Unexpected as it was, it made her weary and sad.

"You know," he continued, "you're such a good-looking girl, you're smart too, you've got lots going for you and he's a no-good deadbeat with what to offer you? I just don't see it, what is it that makes you pair tick?"

"Please don't ask me, don't put me on the spot, I haven't got any answers." She paused, knowing her voice had sounded weak and pleading. Suddenly she wanted him to understand. She wanted him to know that the weak, drinking, self-pitying side wasn't all there was to Neil. She needed to substantiate him, give him credibility. She started again, "I love him, or I thought I did; I don't feel much like I do at the minute. But alone, you know just the two of us, when he doesn't feel intimidated or threatened by people, we get along really well. If he's sober, that is," she added, seeing the criticism in Adam's expression, the disbelief. "Look, I'm not as strong as you think and he probably isn't as weak." She felt her explanation had been lame and, sighing tiredly, looked at Adam.

She looked in his eyes which stared back openly into hers and felt the strength behind them. This, combined with her closeness to him over the last few days and her gratitude to him, made her confused. She looked at his face, familiar now to her as a brother's or boyfriend's would be: the crooked smile, wide eyes and thin face, his habit of flicking his hair back with an exaggerated toss of his head. She wondered if that was a nervous movement or whether it was a habit of old, from when he might have had long hair. Even his East London accent, so horrible in other people, was attractive and reassuring in him. She knew he wasn't good-looking really, it was just the way she was seeing him and she wondered how much of what she saw in him was really there and how much she was attributing him with the characteristics that she wanted someone to have; how much was down to the fact that he was the one strong man whom she could look to in her life at the moment? How much, she thought, do I crave the patriarchy that I was taught to respect?

"Don't ask me any more, Adam. I don't even know myself what I was trying to explain to you. I feel that if I try to explain too much I'll just crumple. No more, please."

He held her glance for a few seconds, then turned abruptly to the conversation that Jackie and Liz were having and, while Anne leaned back in her seat, inhaling her cigarette deeply, he seemed to be immersed immediately in their conversation, though what it was about Anne hadn't a clue.

*

Anne let herself and Jackie into Lesley's house. She was pleased Lesley wasn't home yet. She would be soon but Anne was glad of the time to come to terms with her own feelings of anticlimax before she tried to explain her day to someone else. She thought of whom she would have to phone that night, the people she owed the end of the story to – Stella and Valerie at the very least.

They'd taken the police car back to Croydon Police Station where Adam got out, and then on to Liz's, where she went back to the husband who didn't want to talk about what Liz would want to tell him. The gulf between their two languages and minds was getting wider as Liz became more focused on Anne's mind and life, and Steve, not understanding and frustrated with his own failure and inadequacy, became ever more the joker – full of anecdotes and funny stories that made any future marriage of their minds impossible. It seemed to Anne that only by returning to the day to day mechanics of her ordinary life with Steve would Liz be able to gauge the extent of the difference that Anne's experience and life had made to her own life, her marriage.

Anne made coffee for them both. "Shit, Jackie, I really don't know how I feel. I know everyone thinks that fourteen years is a victory, but in a way it seems such a waste of time. When'll he get out? Maybe after ten?"

Jackie shrugged. "Impossible to tell. Not before ten certainly, not after what the judge said today."

"Okay, so say ten years. Forty years old and he's out, with a bigger chip on his shoulder, or madder, or whatever it is that eats him; it'll be worse. So what'll he do? Well, obviously he'll do it again, only worse probably, because he'll be older, madder and hating the 'bitches' that sent him there even more."

"I know, I agree, but all you can do is think of yourself now. It's 1990, he'll be away until the year 2000, at least. Now that's a long time and God knows where you'll be or what you'll be doing, but that's what you've got to concentrate on now. Let go.

It'll take time, but you've got to start letting go. If I were you I'd work out first exactly what you're going to do about Neil and where you're going to live. That's the first thing. You're lucky you've got Lesley. She'll be happy enough to carry on letting you stay here for a while, won't she?"

"Oh yes, that's not a problem; it's just all temporary though, isn't it? I mean, I can't think past next week. I'll stay here for a little while and then I'll go back or I won't go back, but that next place, either way, is going to be temporary too, isn't it?"

She looked at Jackie, wanting a magic answer, a solution to her problem.

"You know," she went on, "what Adam was saying to me earlier, did you hear? All about what I saw in Neil?"

"Yes, I heard part of it, and you could've done without that, I know."

"Well yes, I know people think I'm a bloody fool to have put up with everything from him, but I just don't know what I want, or whether I want him or not, or whether I even care for him any more. I don't think I'll know until I see him again. It's like he hasn't existed at all in these last few days."

"I don't think Adam understands your relationship with Neil at all. He just sees black and white. But listen, Anne, don't do anything for anyone else, or because you think other people know better. Just go by your own feelings," she paused and looked straight at Anne. "I'll tell you something which may help. I told you that I'd been married before, didn't I? Well, he was an alcoholic. He was a different temperament totally from Neil though – he was a hard man, really hard. Well, we split up because of that and I was young and hadn't really known what I was doing anyway, so it felt like a lucky escape really. Then I met Martin and we got married after three years and I thought the world of him and then the same thing started to happen. He hit the bottle and then, well, he started hitting me."

There was silence then between them as Anne tried to take this in. Jackie hadn't mentioned Martin much. Anne had assumed it was one of those rare, stable marriages that didn't need much airing, much discussion. She tried to digest this new information about Jackie. She certainly couldn't imagine anyone hitting her, making her crouch and cry with fear and then it occurred to her with a fresh shock that Jackie had in some way accepted it: she was still with him.

"I can't imagine this – and you stayed with him? I mean I just can't see you being with anyone who would do that to you in the first place, but even more than that I can't imagine you putting up with it."

Jackie laughed, "Don't put me on a pedestal, Anne. I'm just as bloody soft as any other stupid woman who's in love. That was it really. I told no one he'd hit me; as a matter of fact you're the first person that I've told and the reason is to tell you that it's up to you, not anyone else, to make the decision about what's good for you. You've got to follow your own feelings."

"So what happened with Martin, how did he stop drinking?"

"Well, I don't suppose he was as far gone as Neil, although it's hard to judge really. But, anyway, he was very bad for a couple of years, though this is all a good while ago, maybe five years. I was forever making excuses for him, about why we couldn't go to things and see people, always cancelling at the last minute because he'd started throwing it down his neck. Then the times I'd get angry with him and call him a shit, he'd thump me. Well, I left too. I left him for, oh, it must've been five or six months altogether and during that time he begged me to come back, told me he was sorry and all the rest of it. I loved him so I went back."

"Had he changed?"

"Pretty much, yes. We still have bad patches. But he's never laid a finger on me since and I don't think he ever would again. I think that was one of the things that shocked him out of it: when he saw the bruises on me. He still goes a bit mad on the booze now and then, but not that often, every few months or so and then he'll stay off it totally for a few weeks and then he'll have only two or three pints at the most for ages, because he knows after that he can't stop. But I can cope with that, I've chosen him and on the whole we do work well together. So you've got to decide what you want and fight for it, because either way it'll be hard.

It'll be hard to start again or go back to him. Just don't let anyone else decide for you, that's all."

*

The smell of dinner cooking and the sound of the local news, background television noise, reminded Anne of being a child, the cosy, insulated family home and the home she and Neil had created for themselves before his drinking tore the invisible seams of their fragile world.

Lesley talked in a happy relaxed voice to Michael in the kitchen. They were the picture of happy domesticity as Lesley cooked the dinner and Michael stood beside her, coffee in hand, as she related the day's events at court. Anne sat in the living room listening to the intonation of her voice, a balance between interest, concern and excitement.

Anne had asked Lesley to tell Michael herself as, having related the story to Stella on the phone and knowing she owed it to Valerie to ring her as well, tell her where she was and that a guilty verdict had been returned, she didn't want to narrate it again.

The smell of food was awakening in Anne what seemed to be like the memory of an appetite. It was Thursday and she'd last eaten on Monday, she thought, except, she remembered, for the lunch she'd had out with Liz the day before. She'd said to Lesley that she'd eat and she hoped she could – if they didn't talk about anything to do with the trial she knew she could – gammon, sweetcorn and a baked potato, it was like coming home. Slowly, slowly, she felt she might be able to relax, then, like a slap across her face, she heard that name. Quickly, she leapt from the settee across the room to the television and turned the volume up.

"...sentenced to fourteen years' imprisonment after the judge described him as 'a menace to women'. He had been granted an early release from a previous conviction of rape early in 1989, after serving three years of a seven year sentence."

'It was four, not three' was the immediate association in Anne's mind, as she knelt in front of the television, wanting to grab every last word said about him and about the trial. The bland voice of the newsreader carried on to the next subject. Anne turned the volume down again and sat down. Michael was standing next to the settee.

"Thank God they didn't show the bastard's face. You can do without that, can't you?"

"Yes, to be honest I could've done without seeing his face in court too. But I was trying to prove to myself that I could do it or something, I don't know why."

"Yeah, Lesley told me. I think I can understand that, it's like a power thing, isn't it? I can look if I want to."

"Yes, actually that was it exactly," Anne answered, surprised, relieved.

Michael, relieved too and pleased that he'd read the situation correctly, sat down opposite her. Looking at him, Anne thought how lucky Lesley was: eight years of continuity, of a stable life with a reliable man; kind and concerned, always there.

"I'd like to kill him, does that sound a pathetic thing to say? I know you would, of course you would, but I just needed to say to you that I could as well."

"That's funny because I'd like him dead, but I couldn't kill him myself, I don't think I could watch him if he were hanged either, but I'd still like it done."

Michael jumped up from his seat, "Oh I could watch, no problem at all. I'd like to watch or do it myself; I suppose that's the horrible killer instinct that men have coming out. I think it's sad that even after what he did to you, you couldn't kill him, but any man could."

Anne smiled at him, grateful, thankful that he could say all that from his heart, unrehearsed, unplanned, just a straightforward reaction. It was true for him, but she wondered whether it were true for all men, like he said. Did it spark that protective rage in Neil? Did Neil want to kill him with his bare hands or did Neil see it only as a tightening of the vice around his own head?

The phone rang. She knew it would be him. Lesley shouted through from the kitchen; did Anne want to get it? Anne answered the phone and the split seconds of breathing before he spoke told her who it was and what state of contrition he was in.

"Anne? I'm sorry. Please, please come home."

"Neil, it's not as simple as that. For God's sake, it's Thursday night and I haven't seen you since Tuesday. Have you any idea what's happened and what I've been through since then?"

She heard the kitchen door click to as Michael went out to join Lesley and leave Anne on her own.

A sigh, a sad, long sigh, on the other end of the phone.

"I failed you, I know that, but it's over now and I want us to try again. Please." His voice was pleading.

She felt the rage in her come slowly to the surface, but she didn't want to crack as she still couldn't afford to let go.

"'It's over now.' Is that all you can say like it was a fucking foregone conclusion that he'd get put away and I'd come out the other side smelling of roses? Well, I can tell you something, you weren't there," she hissed at him. "You don't know what it was like, so don't give me this 'It's over now' crap."

Without knowing she was going to do it, she slammed down the receiver on the last word.

She opened the kitchen door. Both were standing talking at the other end of the kitchen. She walked over to them.

"I couldn't talk to him civilly. He's sober and repentant, asking me to come back, but God, too much has happened now."

Anne saw the flash of anger cross Lesley's face, and again thought that in some ways she was so like Valerie.

"Don't feel bad about not being civil to him, he doesn't deserve it. How can he just call you up like that and expect it all to be okay?"

"I don't suppose he does expect it to be all right, but he's sober, probably hasn't drunk since yesterday and now thinks he can safely speak to me. Anyway, I don't want to talk about him, I don't know what I'm going to do, but I know I can't face him at the moment."

"I suppose he heard it on the news, just now?"

"I expect so."

Anne walked back into the living room and watched the faces flicker on the silent screen. She saw a middle-aged couple in their suburban garden, annoying the young couple in the next garden by unwittingly letting the water from the sprinkler go over the fence. She felt the old hatred well up in her, for all these comfortable, limited, narrow-minded people and their petty lives and all their mirror images who sat and watched this rubbish.

She said as much to Michael when he walked back into the room, two bottled beers in his hands. He handed her one.

"This country's full of complacent sods, you're right there."

"Do you know what I was thinking just now, before Neil phoned? Well, a couple of weeks ago when I couldn't sleep one night I counted up just how many times I'd met perverts. You know what? Counting this rather colossal occasion," she smiled bitterly at her sarcasm, "well, counting the horrible men who pulled themselves off in front of me in Alexandra Park when I was a kid and counting the dirty old men down alleyways who clicked at me and then had their things out when I looked, well, counting every single tiny incident that I can remember, I counted nineteen times. That's roughly one a year since I was five."

She felt her eyes filling with bitterness, emotion and outrage, and as she looked at Michael she saw that he looked like a child, a little boy with his eyes brimming.

"Oh I'm sorry, Michael," she broke out, her voice changed, the bitterness gone. "Christ, you're one of the good ones! I have an awful habit of making the man I'm talking to pay for what all the other, horrible ones have done. Don't let me upset you, please."

Lesley was coming into the room with a tray for Anne, the steaming dinner plate on it.

"Oh thanks, Lesley, I really feel like eating this, but I think I might've put Michael off his."

"Why, what've you two been saying then?"

"I'll save it for when we've all eaten!"

*

Neil rang the door bell the next morning. Anne had only been alone a short time since Lesley set off to work. She'd been watching a morning chat show, feeling annoyed with herself for being so apathetic, but not knowing what to do with her day. She had cigarettes enough to last her through the day and knew that she could manage to go to the nearest shop at the end of the road, only a couple of minutes' walk away, if she really had to. What stretched before her was another day in someone else's house, using someone else's stuff, ticking the time away until she once again had company.

Neil rang the bell then, only a second or two later, bent down to open the letter box, "Anne, it's me."

She hadn't been scared, she realised, when going to the door, and she admitted to herself that she had more or less been waiting for him.

She opened the door. He was clean-shaven with bright, yet guilty, eyes. His hair washed and combed, he looked younger than twenty-seven and more attractive than she'd seen him look for a while. Only the deadened look behind his eyes showed the respectability for the charade it was.

"Can I come in?"

She knew all his ploys. He would not assume anything now, he would ask permission for every move and through that penance would, after a time, feel he had paid the price for his bad behaviour and assume that they were once again on an equal footing.

"Yes, if you want." She stood aside. He walked past her after hesitating a moment when he was level with her. Anne didn't want to be touched.

"Do you want coffee?" she asked as she closed the door behind her. He seemed surprised by her normality, but immediately fitted in to echo her stance, "Yes thanks, if you're making it."

Anne walked off to the kitchen, acting out this domestic role as if she were at home, knowing she was confusing him. He doesn't realise, she thought, that it's done now, I'm deadened to him, there's no point in getting annoyed. She didn't want any more screaming rows, with thudding heart, her adrenaline pumping. There was really nothing left to get excited about.

He followed her into the kitchen.

"I brought *The Guardian* with me, I thought you might want to read what the report says."

"Two lines on it, are there?"

"More than that, but not much really." His head sank down, as if he were responsible for how much media attention the case got.

"Show me then." Anne stretched out her hand. Neil reached in to the deep pocket inside his coat and drew the paper out. It was opened and folded on the second and facing page and he passed it to her, his forefinger showing the column to read.

'Fourteen years for double rapist.' How she hated that word. One column wide again and counting down, four, no five lines deep. The article told of his earlier release for a similar charge, like the news the previous evening, and that within six months he'd committed rape again, 'the Old Bailey jury heard yesterday.' She wondered at the players in this story, rapist, judge, jury – she didn't feature. She handed the paper back disparagingly to Neil.

"Thanks for that. Which is worse, 'Rape girl plunges' or that, like it isn't really important, like I wasn't even there? Mind you, you probably don't even know what I'm talking about, do you? You wouldn't have seen *The Sun* on Wednesday because you'd gone to some nicer place."

She looked at him and made a drinking gesture, lifting her right hand to her mouth, suddenly wanting to twist the knife. He put both hands up to cover his face, "Don't please, I'm so sorry, I couldn't handle it. I just couldn't."

"I know," she sighed her response, as she poured the coffee, "you're weak and you can't take it. I think I'm past blaming you, you are what you are."

When they'd sat down again he said, quietly and simply, "Please come home now, Anne, I've cleared everything up and got the place looking right again."

Fleetingly she imagined how bad it must've been and how it would now all have been put to rights. She was glad that, this time, she'd been spared seeing it and hadn't been the one who had to put everything back together again.

"There is no way I'm just going to go back home with you, just because you've decided to come back to the land of the living. Do you think it's that easy, to opt out when it's too difficult and then waltz back in again when it's all calm and sorted again? Christ, I don't want to have this conversation, I don't want to get annoyed with you. I just want a bit of peace and quiet."

He was watching her, silent, waiting for her to carry on raining criticism down on him, then he could feel better, feel he'd paid his due. Wearily, she saw it all clearly.

"We need each other, Anne. No one else understands that."

"Yes, I needed you and where the fuck were you?"

"I'm sorry, that's all I can say. I'm sick, Anne, please."

He got up from sitting opposite her and sat down beside her on the settee, "I won't do it again. I promise you that, I won't, not ever again."

"Not if I don't give you the chance, you won't. You can't say 'never again', you've said it over and over again and now it counts for nothing. It's meaningless, can't you understand that?"

With each rejoinder she made she felt herself start off flatly, worn out, not really caring, not wanting to have this conversation at all. Then her bitterness and anger started to come to the surface again and she wanted to lash out, to hurt him.

"Look, I don't want to carry on having the same conversation and winding myself up more and more. We've said all this before. I've always got up again after you knocked me down before and had some kind of faith in you again. But this time it's worse. Much worse. Do you understand that?"

His hands were gripped round his knees and his head hung down to his chest, repentant. She felt angry and this is what he wanted: a torrent of condemnation. He wanted to be told how bad he'd been and get his punishment so that he could be forgiven, forgive himself.

No, she cried out inside. No, I don't want to do that. She stood up, "Please go, I'm tired, I'm completely worn out. It isn't as easy as you seem to think it is."

"I don't think it's going to be easy," he interrupted. "I just think it's best for us both if we start again as soon as possible. We need each other, Anne, we do."

"Don't keep repeating that, it's meaningless, after what you've done to me."

They stood facing each other. "I want peace and quiet now, so that I can think about what I'm going to do. I'm scared, I can't go out, I've got nothing and I feel totally broken. I don't know what I feel about you, so don't ask me. All I know is that I want to spend time with the people who are close to me. Those people – Liz, Jackie, Lesley – they're the ones who've helped me, not you. You've made it worse."

She stopped, her voice nearly breaking. She looked at him. "Leave me alone for the minute. Just go away now," she said more quietly. She looked into his eyes and saw, for the first time in all their many scenes and arguments, a realisation that perhaps it wasn't going to be that easy.

"All right, I'll go. Can I ring you tonight?"

"Tomorrow, not tonight. Just give me some breathing space."

He lifted her hand, gripped it tightly, then walked towards the door. "I'll ring tomorrow then, goodbye."

She watched him open the door and walked up to close it behind him. Out of the window next to the door she watched his receding back, his coat flapping as, hands in pockets, he walked away, eyes downcast. Pity rose in her. She felt it move from her stomach up through her body, into her throat in long, heaving gasps. She sat down in the seat next to the doorway and, placing her hands over her face, was able to let out all her feelings of pity, for herself, for Neil, for her whole life that had left her now with nowhere to go, with no future – only a black darkness ahead.

*

Michael took Anne and Lesley to a French restaurant close to
Lesley's flat – he just arrived that evening, straight from work,
and announced he'd like to take them both out. Anne hadn't got
much with her to wear which was suitable for eating out in, but
she put on a long black skirt and a big, black T-shirt. They suited
her thinness, and then she'd run her fingers through her hair a few
times and looked at her reflection critically thinking, I don't look
too bad really, all things considered. She enjoyed getting ready,
the normality of it, CDs playing in the background, Lesley in the
next room getting dressed too. She thought of how often she'd
wanted all this, these surroundings and ambience, with Neil, and
wondered why he wouldn't, couldn't, let it happen – it wasn't
asking for too much, was it?

She couldn't see further than the next day – her life was still
on hold – but she tried to enjoy the evening for what it was, an
isolated place, where she could pretend her life was other than it
was. She told them both that she didn't want to talk about the
trial or anything associated with it: her appetite would completely
disappear if she did.

Neil turned out to be the main subject of the evening – would
he stop drinking? Did he mean to keep his promises? Was he
really ill or was it self-induced, a form of self-indulgence? Anne,
weary of the conversation and her own mixed up feelings, tried,
without much success, to steer the conversation away from this
detailed inspection of her life and relationship. She fought down
her feelings of ingratitude towards Lesley, knowing she'd been so
good to her, but the melodramatic side of Lesley's questioning and
deductions gradually got on her nerves. She saw her eyes widen
with excitement as she repeatedly examined what Neil's feelings
towards her must be, as she was in effect 'harbouring' Anne and
protecting her from him.

"And how must he feel when he compares how much stronger
I am than him and how much more of a help I've been to you, by
being there, listening and being the rock, so to speak, for you?"

Unflattering thoughts went through Anne's mind as she listened to this monologue of self-aggrandisement. She wondered how sensible she'd been in making a friend of Lesley, so quickly, so intensely. She fought down these thoughts and then caught Michael's eye and felt, for one split second, in their shared glance, that he was thinking along the same lines as she.

"Mum said that, having coped so well through this stress, I should think about doing something like counselling or the Samaritans."

With an embarrassed cough Michael changed the subject immediately to whether they should get another bottle of wine with their sweet. Anne felt sure then that she was not alone in her thoughts. Despite Lesley's appearance of maturity, Anne thought, she really is just a silly little girl. Anne's feeling of bitterness and age-old knowledge and cynicism welled up inside her.

She'd chosen steak in a red wine sauce. She'd felt starving when she smelt it as it was placed in front of her, but the sauce was too rich for her starved taste buds and by the time she had eaten half of the meal in front of her she felt her mouth tingle uncomfortably. She ran her tongue over the ridges behind her teeth and tasted blood from the tender skin. Unhappily she left the remainder and carried on drinking the wine, which travelled down to her fingertips and spread a warm glow through her body. Gradually she relaxed.

"What about having Tom, Alison and the crowd round tomorrow night, Les?" Michael suggested.

"Oh yes, what's this?" Anne broke in, seeing an opening for a lightening of the conversation.

"Well it's just an idea," Lesley answered "I was thinking of having all that crowd round. We'd arranged to go to The Five Bells with them anyway and I just had this thought the other day of having them round and ordering an Indian takeaway and playing that game I got for Christmas and we've never opened. What's it called Michael?"

"Oh, I can't remember. *On The Piss* or something like that. Only joking, I really can't remember now."

Seeing Anne's confused expression, Lesley carried on, "It's like Monopoly really, only everything is to do with drink, not money, like if you land on some square you've got to drink five different shorts in a row or whatever. Do you fancy it?"

The idea of this game, along with all Michael and Lesley's old schoolfriends, none of whom Anne knew, filled her with fear and anxiety.

"Well, actually Liz was going to call tomorrow night, both her and Jeanette called me at your house today and said they'd come over tomorrow, but I thought it was a bit far for Jeanette as she wouldn't be staying over or anything and anyway I haven't seen Liz since the last day of the trial, so I'm getting withdrawal symptoms!"

"Well, you're more than welcome to be there tomorrow night, and Liz too."

"No, but thanks anyway. You and Michael could do with some time with your other friends anyway, and I'm sure you've had enough of babysitting for me!"

"Will you get Liz to drop you back later on then?"

"No, I'll stay with her if that's all right. I'm sure Steve will be thrilled with that, but she wants me to. As you can imagine their relationship hasn't improved too much with her devoting so much time to me."

"Well, come back Sunday morning then. You know you're welcome to stay as long as you want. Do you think you'll live with Valerie eventually, until you get something sorted out for yourself?"

"Lesley, I just don't know. I don't particularly want to stay with Valerie, even though her heart's in the right place. She'd have me organised and be pushing me to do this and that, exactly how she thinks I ought to be doing things, before I know it. I can't be doing with that at the minute. I need time to put feelers out about what I want to do, and what I'm able to do. I just don't know what to do next, to be honest."

"Well, you know you've got me for as long as you need."

"Thanks."

248

*

"I'm glad to see you've started eating again anyway," Liz said as she placed stuffed mushrooms in front of Anne.

"Well, I don't think I could've gone on much longer like that, but all last week I couldn't think about eating. Now I'm feeding my face today, and Michael taking me out last night too. My mouth's still a bit tender, but all in all, I'm getting better I think. I feel like I'm coming up for air, from the bottom of a deep sea."

"I think you're doing really well. Just carrying on the way you are is amazing in itself."

"It still doesn't feel natural, you know. Everything is still on pause until I make up my mind whether I'm going back or not."

"Lesley's said you can stay with her for the time being though, hasn't she?"

"Well yes, but you know how awful it is when you're staying with someone and living out of a bag all the time, never having anywhere to put any of your stuff. I can't start getting my act together until I've got a home again."

"Do you think you'll go back to him?"

"Oh, I don't know. He phoned again this morning. I feel so sorry for him. He's sitting there at home all on his own. Everyone is my friend and he's got no one. He just keeps saying to me that that was the last time and he'll not drink again and that he needs me to do it. But how can I believe that? It was about nine months the last time and then he wrecked everything, worse than ever before."

"Yeah, but the circumstances were pretty extreme though. He was under so much pressure to live up to what was expected of him."

"Yes and look at what he did. I don't know what I feel for him, except pity. I feel like he's a lonely child who needs me, but I don't need that, do I?"

They carried on eating, a bottle of wine opened between them. Liz's kitchen, the evening light shining through the windows, gave Anne a feeling of transitory contentment. If I ever have this security, with the knowledge that it will go on and on, I'll appreciate it, I always will, I'll say thank you all the time for it, she told herself. She was glad to get a break from Lesley and, with Steve away, it felt like her and Liz were cocooned together: the atmosphere relaxed and close.

"He doesn't understand one bit you know, I can't believe how badly he's acted over this," Liz was saying. "I've always known that Steve either blanks out or can't understand anything of the deeper, darker side of life, or people, or however you want to put it, but he's just come across as a complete jerk with everything to do with you."

They had moved back to the living room now, with a fresh bottle of wine opened. Steve had gone out with a friend of his in Godstone and was staying the night there.

Either he hadn't wanted to be there when Anne was coming round, or Liz had really encouraged him to go and leave them alone together, Anne hadn't asked which.

When he'd come back from the residential course he'd been on from the Monday to the Thursday he had only wanted to talk about the 'workshops' he'd been involved in, Liz explained in amazement, relating anecdotes, describing the others in his team. He'd gone on about the dinners they'd had – "black tie, you know, and the divisional manager was sitting next to me at every meal" – Liz explained, imitating him.

"The meals were fantastic, apparently, better food than at any five star hotel!"

He'd listened on sufferance to her relating what had gone on at the trial, she said, wanting only to hear the outcome ("as if it were the score after a football match") so that he would be able to draw a line under the whole episode and place it in the past.

Liz's need to discuss it and tell him everything, so that the experience could be shared with him, he either ignored or was incapable of seeing.

*

The following lunchtime, Liz drove Anne back to Lesley's. Steve had arrived back at the flat quite early and the atmosphere between the three of them grew quite strained. Steve asked Anne nothing about the week that had passed and Anne, tempted to bring the subject up to make him feel bad, decided she could be even more effective by saying absolutely nothing about it.

She became increasingly wound up by him, so by the time she got to Lesley's she wanted more than anything to be in her own surroundings, her own company.

Lesley wasn't around when she first went in. Michael opened the door into a silent house. Anne sensed they had rowed as she followed him in. Liz hadn't come in, deciding the best thing was for her to go home and try and patch things up with Steve.

"Neil rang twice this morning. He asked if you'd call him when you got back. Oh yes, and Jeanette rang last night."

Anne immediately felt guilty on two counts: not having contacted Jeanette yesterday as she'd said she would, and Lesley and Michael being disturbed by lots of phone calls for her.

She sat down opposite Michael, not sure what to do, unable to tell if Michael's bad mood was because of her.

"Where's Lesley then?"

"She's upstairs, in bed."

Silence fell again. Anne didn't want to be there, knew she shouldn't be there.

Michael started to speak again, his tone different: confiding now.

"She got a bit out of order last night, to say the least. It was all pretty embarrassing." He paused and Anne said nothing.

"Tom, Vanessa et cetera were all here. Anyway, I don't know what happened. She didn't seem to be having more to drink than anyone else. We were all knocking it back a bit I suppose with this stupid game, then she just flipped out."

"God, I can't imagine Lesley getting out of order. What happened?"

"Yeah, nor could I and I don't want to see it again. She went to the loo, then wouldn't come out. Sue was talking through the door to her for ages, must've been for about an hour or so. I tried at first too then I just gave up and left her to it."

Anne didn't know whether to ask Michael more or just let him carry on, if he felt like saying anything more. She could tell that Lesley had certainly lost some credibility in his eyes. Anne had never heard him speak of her in a critical tone before, but what, after all, was the crime in getting really drunk and locking yourself in the toilet?

"I couldn't believe it," he carried on. "When she eventually came out of the loo she was crying her eyes out and shaking and then she started screaming at the top of her voice and didn't stop until Sue slapped her face."

Anne felt herself grow cold, she knew, though she couldn't exactly define why, that all this was going to be her fault. Attention-seeking dramatics? She didn't know, but she knew that it had been done to get some particular reaction from Michael and that it obviously hadn't worked.

They heard movement upstairs. Anne wanted out of it, wanted to be away from the whole situation.

"She reckons it's all to do with the strain she's been under lately," Michael said flatly. Anne felt her jaw harden and jut out as she kept her eyes looking downwards; she couldn't risk looking at Michael otherwise he'd read her expression.

They heard footsteps on the stairs. Lesley came into the room, her large brown eyes looking sad and slightly haunted. Her expression was both demanding sympathy and defensive.

"Hello Lesley, a bit too much last night?" Anne tried to sound light-hearted and friendly, but could hear the hollowness in her own voice. Oh God, this is so uncomfortable, she thought, and she guessed it was about to be blown out of all proportion. But she was determined not to give Lesley the attention she knew she wanted.

"Not exactly, no. As a matter of fact no, not at all," Lesley said coldly. She didn't look at Michael as, drawing her dressing gown more tightly around her, she sat down. Anne silently gestured a cigarette towards her. She shook her head, saying nothing, and momentarily closed her eyes. She then looked at Michael defiantly.

"I've just spoken to Mum and she says I was showing the classic, textbook symptoms of shock last night."

'No, you were just pissed,' thought Anne. I can't bear this, she said to herself. Stop it, you fool.

"Shock about what?" Michael rejoined curtly.

"Strangely enough, you generally have to be shocked by something in particular, to go into shock," Anne pointed out, her tone light and flippant. She knew she was being cruel and that it must sound like ganging up to Lesley, but she wanted to kill this conversation and if the only way to do it was to make a fool of Lesley and shame her into silence, she was going to do that.

"Of course I've been shocked. Constantly over the last few weeks," Lesley almost shouted, directing her anger now towards Anne. "It hasn't been easy, you know, I've felt a real strain with the court case going on and having to carry on working every day and then supporting you emotionally so much. Mum says it's just all too much for me and I'm going to have to start thinking about myself for a change."

Anne, staring ahead of her, did not know what the expression on her face was showing. But inside her head her anger pounded. Oh you poor, poor little thing, I can put up with all this crap, all this strain, month after month, a trial and everything and you, you poor sensitive little thing, crack because you've had to witness it for the last week. She said it all inside her head and said nothing outwardly. She wondered if Lesley imagined she was made from a much more refined substance than she, that she could put up with so little. Do you think that this last week or two is 'being through it' she wanted to ask her; no it's not, you've enjoyed it really. She knew she was being too hard on her: Lesley had been generous. But why did she have to throw it back in her face, Anne asked herself.

Lesley was still speaking, defending herself to Michael, "It had nothing, nothing to do with drink. I'd hardly had any anyway."

"Okay, okay, have it your own way, it doesn't matter much anyway. I've got to go now, I'm meeting Robert for golf at two, remember? I'll call in later." He stood up and went to the door. "See you both later."

Silence again.

"Mum says it was classic: a textbook case of shock and she should know, shouldn't she? She is a nurse."

*

She went home. She'd known she would.

She didn't examine her reasons for going back too closely, except that she knew she was too tired to do anything else. Tired of imposing herself on other people: tired of being surrounded by them. Tired of not having the small security of being surrounded by her own things.

She couldn't forgive him. Somewhere at the centre of herself she was cold: as removed and untouchable as she had been that Tuesday morning of the trial – when he had drunk the vodka and looked at her with disdain and dislike, prepared to throw it all away, everything that mattered to her, to them both, because at the bottom of it all he didn't care enough.

She listened to his apologies, noted how clean the flat was: the polishing and cleaning he'd done to cover the vomit, to clear the smashed plates and broken ashtrays. He'd opened all the windows and the back door to air the flat after its endless, cave-like days of having all the curtains drawn, light and life closed out, as he degenerated further – unseen by anyone – sinking deeper into the abyss of his self-hate.

For a week or more he was constantly apologetic, doing everything he imagined she might want him to do. He made lovely meals each evening and they sat outside in the garden together each day in the sun, on his days off. Amazingly he'd kept his job as his boss was not surprised that he'd needed a second week off with the trauma of the trial and knew nothing of what had really happened. She imagined the tale he had told, about not being able to leave Anne at any time during that week, work being the furthest thing from his mind, the story he could spin. She didn't ask him how he'd excused himself for not phoning in to tell them what was going on: she didn't want to hear. It was enough that he'd still got a job, that money was still coming in, not much but enough to pay the rent with.

When he occasionally had to work evenings, Liz, Jackie or Lesley often came round. After that Sunday morning in Lesley's flat the incident wasn't mentioned again, but both of them seemed to have come to a silent agreement to remain a little more detached from each other's lives. Lesley would call round once or twice a week, sometimes with Michael, mostly without. Anne was grateful that, although Lesley disagreed with her going back to Neil, she said nothing, made no judgement. Anne knew she did judge her, but she kept it to herself.

Valerie also called round, determined to keep Anne feeling that support was there if she needed it. Other than the occasional dig about Neil and the odd disparaging comment which Anne pretended she didn't catch on to, Valerie said nothing of the hatred she felt or her powerlessness to help if Anne didn't open up to her. She suspected what might have gone on during the trial, Anne knew, but Anne said only that she'd stayed with Lesley for a few days, as Neil was working evening shifts.

Valerie loved her sister, though she was impatient at her pigheadedness and insulted by the many lies she told to cover up for Neil and to disguise the life she was leading. A couple of weeks after the trial finished Valerie made one last effort to get Anne away from Neil. She arranged an interview for her at a friend's company. He wanted an administrator to "man the offices in Guildford", Valerie told her, "and help with their marketing ventures, that kind of thing, all the stuff you've done before."

Again, Anne felt that events were overtaking her, beyond her control. "Hang on a minute, Valerie, Guildford is miles away so I'd have to go into town or at least as far as Clapham to get a connecting train."

"Nonsense, there's a train from Epsom."

"Okay, so I'd have to go and change at Epsom every day. I'm not up to that, please. I don't know what I'm going to do but I'd rather temp again and take each step slowly. I don't want to commit myself to something and not even know whether I can get myself there without flipping out and then letting everyone down. Do you understand that?"

Valerie, without ever actually underlining Neil's exclusion, said she could come and live with her for the time being and she would take her to the station each morning and collect her in the evening. Then, when she felt up to it, she could buy herself a flat, "in Epsom or Guildford, somewhere nice and non-threatening. You don't have to live around Sutton, you know."

"Valerie, I don't know if anywhere is 'non-threatening'. At the minute the whole world looks threatening and scary to me. I'm frightened to make a move in any direction."

"I can see that," Valerie said, her eyes sweeping in the room, in one sarcastic glance. "All I ask is that you think about it. Think of your future. You're going to have a lot of money soon and you want to think about what you're going to do with it and protect yourself, for heaven's sake, make sure no one else can get their hands on it."

"I don't want to think about the compensation money Valerie, and I've no idea how much, or how little it's going to be, so let's just forget about it, please."

"All right, but I'm only trying to look out for you, someone needs to."

Anne did think about the job, and the more she thought about it the more frightening it became. She was scared of the thought of working in a place she'd never seen and couldn't envisage and she wasn't even sure how far away Guildford was. She was scared of leaving Neil, and scared of giving up what little freedom she had and becoming absorbed in Valerie's life.

The Thursday after Anne went back, the next issue of *The Croydon Advertiser* came out. Anne waited for it, not able to focus on anything else. She began to feel that the drive for action and change, the need to make a difference to life through what had happened to her, was running out. She'd thought the court case would produce some outcry, the fact that a man who should still be serving a sentence for rape got out and immediately did it again. She'd, naïvely now she realised, expected the newspapers to have it as front page news but, other than the tabloids and their interest in the fact that she'd been naked when she'd jumped from the window, she'd been disappointed by how little the case was taken up.

Neil was working a straight shift, from seven in the morning to five. She'd dreamt the night before about the walk to the shop to buy the *Advertiser* and sweated as, with each step, she hardly appeared to be moving at all; just remaining exposed and vulnerable, alone on the empty street. When she'd looked around her in the dream the road was flanked, not by houses and gardens, but by an airfield that seemed to go on forever, out to the horizon. She woke up, hot and perspiring, her hair sticking to her face. In his sleep Neil rolled over, his hands reaching out to find her body. She lifted them and put them back to his own sides, as his breathing became deeper and heavier. She didn't want him, she knew that now. But she didn't want to hurt him. He was on the rails now, looking after her, the only one bringing in money. He was needed and was doing well. She couldn't imagine what he'd be like without her. But she couldn't imagine getting over the next time either, and the time after that. How could she ever listen to his forgiveness pleas or his 'never again, believe me' speeches again? (How could she have listened to them so many times already?)

That morning she got up just after Neil left and got showered and dressed. She boiled the kettle, then left the house to go to the shop. It was still difficult, she was as if naked and exposed, but her mind didn't go as berserk as it had done before when she went out alone. She looked up and down the street as she walked out of the driveway. A woman with two children walking towards her in one direction, an old man shuffling away from her in the other. She felt a certain relief: she'd pass the woman in a moment or two on the way down the hill.

She walked into the shop not more than a minute later, her head pounding. She felt a little security when the door shut behind her. Keeping her eyes lowered from the top shelf of misogyny and sadism, she walked deliberately to the counter where she could see the heap of newly delivered papers. The emboldened, gigantic words of the headline didn't make sense to her, so much so that she couldn't read them properly, at first. 16 STONE CARPET LAYER – HAVE A GO HERO. Her eyes frantically searched the other minor headlines as she lifted a copy from the pile. No, nothing. Placing the paper on the counter she saw the photograph and the name below, Bob Hayman. It made sense now: the man who caught him.

She forced herself not to look at the paper at all, until she got home, then threw herself into the seat at the kitchen table and digested every word. Underneath the headline it read: 'Kind-hearted Bob who stopped a rapist in his tracks, was awarded £100 by judge.' She read through the half page article that mentioned her briefly as a 'twenty-four year old, five foot four woman.' "Wrong," she said aloud, "Five foot two, actually."

The article, written by a man, about a man, in order to appeal to men, incensed her totally. It was as it she hadn't existed or only in so far as to give this man a chance to prove himself to be so brave. She was horrified at her own uncharitable reaction towards the man who had caught the bastard trying to run away and made the case so airtight from the start. But it wasn't him she was annoyed at, she said to herself, it was the journalism. It reminded her of the selective evidence provided by the court which ruled that pornographic videos were not relevant, but dope was. Here it was again. Any objectivity of the case gone – 'local boy does good' was all that was important. She, a foreigner to the area, a woman, with no standing in financial or community terms, neither very young nor very old, was not important. How much less interesting she was than the sixteen stone man who obviously stood much more of a chance against another man than she did. How much more courageous was he?

She said as much when she rang the paper, demanding to be put through to the editor and then, on hearing a voice at the other end of the line, she announced that she was the woman who didn't feature in her own rape case. "I'm the one who jumped out of a sodding window to get away, but you obviously don't think that's important."

She was put through to a woman straight after this outburst, who said her name was Helen and told her calmly that the paper had been granted an interview with Bob Hayman after the trial, through the police, and that was how they got their angle on the case.

"Unfortunately, we weren't allowed to speak to the victim."

Anne seethed, hearing the inverted commas around that word, victim.

"In these cases it's difficult, unless the woman chooses to speak to us herself, as you're doing now."

"I'm not so much 'choosing to speak to you'," Anne said quickly, adding her own set of inverted commas, "it's just I'm pissed off with your 'boys in the pub' article. It was a bit more than just a 'have a go hero' night, you know."

"Yes, no one's denying that, but surely you do appreciate what he did for you, in capturing this man?"

"Yes, of course, of course I do. It's not him I'm criticising, it's you, or rather," she looked down to the paper, spread out in front of her, "Paul Woods."

"What I would like to suggest is that I call out and we have a chat about how you feel and then next week we'll print that. Have you, as a matter of interest, read the other article on that page? I've written that one and it's an interview with the first woman he was put in jail for raping."

"No. Good God, you got in touch with her?"

"No, she contacted me, rather in the same way that you've just done. Anyway, I'll tell you all that later and leave you to read it in the meantime. Will you be in later this afternoon?"

"Yes, yes all day. Come any time you like."

She arranged to call at three that afternoon. Anne rang off, feeling completely different from when she'd first made the call. So this other woman was still living in the area too. How had she found out that he had done the same thing again? Through the paper, the news, God, what an awful thought.

She found the article: WOMAN RAPED FIVE YEARS AGO SPEAKS OUT. It told how the woman heard that he'd raped again on the local news, the day the trial started, thinking him still to be in prison with another three years to serve for his attack on her. She'd realised that when he was first out of prison, six months or so before going inside again to await trial, she'd still been living in the same house he'd followed her to. She'd moved from east to north Croydon only a few weeks before hearing about the trial on the news. She said she was outraged that he'd been released so early and angry that she hadn't been informed he was out, especially considering that he came back to Croydon and he obviously knew where she lived.

The article ended by saying that the woman still suffered from flashbacks and still felt constricted and haunted by what had happened to her. The last statement of the article read, 'I really feel for this woman who has had to go through what I did. She should never have had to: he ought to have still been locked up in prison.'

Anne's heart was thumping by the time she'd finished reading. Perhaps this was the angle that she needed to concentrate on to get the whole country to sit up and take notice and realise the horror of what this man had been allowed out to do – again – and would be allowed out to do yet again. When he was forty, and free.

She decided to write to the MP, Joan Marshall, again. The idea just occurred to her, as soon as she finished reading. She thought she should write to someone who might be able to help, someone in a position to do something: to prevent the men who did it from ever being able to do it again.

Her hands shaking with emotion and purpose, she wrote the letter again and again, chain-smoking as she did so. She described the shortcomings of the trial, the pitching of the two sides against each other, the refusal to recognise the importance of *The Last Movie* and the porn films he was trying to find on the floor when she'd jumped. She ended by asking Ms Marshall to try to do something to rectify the insult to the first woman, who'd gone through everything at court to find out that, after three years, he was free. She demanded that something be done to prevent her, Anne, from sitting one evening, unaware, watching the news, and have his name or photograph thrust upon her and hearing that he'd done the same thing again or that perhaps the girl hadn't been able to get away this time because he'd killed her afterwards.

With a purpose she'd not felt since the trial ended, Anne went out to the post office at the end of the road and posted the letter. Walking back she passed a few women collecting their children from school. Her single-mindedness had reduced her fear, momentarily.

Helen Johnstone arrived just after three. She gave Anne her business card as soon as she came in. She was a couple of years older than Anne, not much though, thin and slightly old-fashioned. She seemed intelligent, but ultimately uncaring or uninterested. Anne couldn't tell which, but they didn't connect well with each other.

Anne told her of having written to Joan Marshall, asking that she do something to draw people's attention to the justice system that allows rapists to reoffend, on each occasion going further than the last, as their hatred and perversity increases and the need to get whatever sick buzz they get becomes more extreme. She told the calm journalist, who watched her and wrote constantly, that she was convinced the man would've killed her had she not managed to get away. She criticised the trial for not considering what would've happened if she had not escaped, as her torture didn't come to an end; she'd brought it to an end herself.

She asked Helen Johnstone if she could give her the other woman's name and telephone number as she wanted to speak to her, see if they could meet and together make people listen.

"I can't really do that as I don't have her permission. When she met me she wouldn't even come to the *Advertiser* offices. I interviewed her in my car in the car park of where she works. So I'd say she wants to keep a pretty low profile. After all, it was about five years ago she was attacked. What I'm trying to say is that she had pretty much tried to bury it all before this broke and she'll probably want to do so again. What I will do though is give your number to her and then she may get in touch with you. Is that all right?"

"Yes, fine, thanks. I hope she does phone me. I suppose what I'd really like is to hear that things do get better and that you stop feeling so scared all the time."

*

It was the beginning of July: warm and humid. Almost a year later, the seasons had ticked past, unstoppable. It seemed to Anne that her life was ticking past; while she still clung to the wreckage of a ruined relationship – moribund, in fetters.

She sat in the garden with Jeanette, the morning sun beating down on her half-closed eyelids, sipping her too hot coffee. She lit a cigarette, her chest hurting as she dragged deeply to light it. On the whole though she felt healthier now – she'd put on some weight again, ate regularly and didn't have such massive surges of adrenaline.

"Do you think he can keep it up?"

"Oh, I don't know," Anne answered, "I never thought he'd be capable of letting me down when he did." She paused and added, as if to justify him, "After so long; it was nearly nine months."

"But in the meantime you wait for the next time?"

"Pretty much."

After a few seconds' silence she carried on, "He couldn't do enough for me at first, eternally apologetic and everything, but I just felt nothing, except pity for both of us really. He's not bad, he really isn't. You know he once said to me, 'If I thought I'd be like this for the rest of my life I'd kill myself.' To me that's so bloody sad. I don't know how strong you have to be to kill this addiction, but I don't think he's strong enough."

"There's nothing you can do though, is there, other than stick it out and stay with him? You've done that for ages and he's still breaking down and giving in."

"Every time is the last time though and neither of us knows that it isn't until the worst happens."

Jeanette sighed, "I can't tell you what to do and I wouldn't want to, but to see you living like this, after everything that's happened to you, is really difficult. You should just think of yourself for once."

"Don't think that still being here is entirely selfless. I don't know what I'm doing to be perfectly honest. I wish to God I could ask some," she paused, searching for the right description, "I don't know, some parental figure or some God-like person, what the hell the right thing to do is. Then I could just follow orders and do it," she ended, laughing sadly.

"Well, ask Valerie, or Stella and they'll say the same as me, you've got to get away from him, from here, and get on with your own life. All those clichés! But it's true. Anyway, at least you've got some money now, to act with."

"Oh that," Anne exclaimed, "that seems to have caused more problems than it's solved."

"Why's that?"

"Well, it's ten thousand in advance, isn't it? God knows I was surprised, but then I didn't know what to expect – one pound or one million, neither seems right. Money doesn't seem right in the first place. Hush money or payment for services rendered or something like that."

"God, Anne, that's crap!"

"I know, I know it is really, but it's difficult to rationalise it to myself. Anyway, you can tell I've got problems with it in the first place and then it seems that anyone I discuss it with says the wrong thing and that makes it worse." Seeing the look on Jeanette's face, she added, "Not you though!"

Through the rest of the morning Anne told Jeanette everything, what she'd been doing and all she was feeling, hoping it would sort things out in her own mind. Until she started to talk she hadn't known how much there was to say, how many incidents, comments and looks she'd hidden in her mind, how much her fear was still with her and how she feared making any move to break away.

The notification of the money had arrived the day after she'd made up her mind to start temping again. She had contacted the recruitment company and Diane had offered her a temping position starting the following Monday. The job was at a big oil refineries' sales office in Croydon, a small office with three other women. She could see St John's church spire as she walked up to the offices from West Croydon train station, but she had trained herself not to look above eye level as she walked there over the last month's daily journeys.

She came and went each day by herself, forcing herself to do it, but she felt panic at certain recognisable points: when she walked over the bridge at Carshalton Station and passed the narrow alleyway on her right, and she felt her heart pounding every time she went through the underpass in Croydon, there being no other way to cross the six lane carriageway.

She was glad she'd got back to work, the job was simple, the atmosphere in work was tranquil and, most importantly of all, female. She'd told all three women, separately, in her first week there, that she'd been attacked and, forcing the word out, raped, the previous summer. No other details, but she felt she could breathe again and not feel like a criminal with a dirty secret, as she sat a mile from where she'd lived a year ago.

The money posed a problem in itself: how to view it. She couldn't jump up and down for joy, she obviously didn't want to, but it would undeniably make a difference to her life. In any other circumstances the ten thousand pounds would have been enough to make her feel like a millionaire. But this was different.

At first she felt it was like hush money. Her mood was predominantly one of deflation, but she'd forced herself to contact Diane Campbell for temporary work, because she'd seen it as a way to hang on to her sanity, give her life a routine. The buzz that had filled her when she'd written to Joan Marshall and spoken to the journalist left her gradually, over the next few weeks, with nothing to replace it but emptiness and the brick wall, beyond which she could see no future.

The report in the *Advertiser* the following week was a bland piece of self-promotion. The opening paragraph of the page five column was about how the *Advertiser* had put the two 'victims of the double rapist' in contact with one another. It went on to say that the woman, whose 'ordeal had resulted in the fourteen year sentence' was 'still angry' and felt that the prison term wasn't long enough. Anne read it through twice and then, without further comment, cut the report out and put it with the other newspaper cuttings she'd collected, wondering why she was doing it, feeling obscurely that if she didn't keep these the whole thing would cease to have happened in other people's minds.

She spoke to Sarah once. A difficult conversation. She sounded much older than Anne had expected. She said that the one positive thing she could tell her was that it got easier as time went on, not for a while yet, but she said that gradually she would realise with surprise that she hadn't thought about anything to do with it at all for maybe half an hour or half the day, or whatever.

"Are you still frightened, really frightened of everyone you don't know or pass in the street?"

"Not as much as I was, no. But it'll probably never leave you totally. I still get panic attacks when I hear footsteps behind me, but not as frequently as I used to. I think you just learn to adjust your life and then you'll find out how best you can cope, bit by bit."

She said that, after her initial shock and anger when she heard the report on TV, she'd managed to calm down. She said she was planning on writing to her MP about the fact that he'd served less than half the time he'd been sentenced to for his crime against her. Anne told her about having written to Joan Marshall. After that there was nothing much to say. Anne knew they would probably not speak again, for what really had they in common? Nothing other than what had happened to them. Sarah was forty, married, she said, to a very supportive and understanding man, who was frightened of what going through all this again would do to her. She hadn't told him she was ringing Anne as it was easier not to.

Anne asked her if she ever went out alone in the evenings. "Yes, I couldn't let one incident change my whole life. I forced myself out at first and now I do it naturally, not exactly without thinking about it, but it isn't so much of a trauma now, as it once was."

They rang off, Sarah saying she'd ring again if she got a positive result from writing to her MP. Anne felt a mixture of emotions: this woman had survived and she knew that she would too. But then she also knew that she could never go out on her own after dark again, she knew she couldn't cope with that fear, not ever. Who could say that it wouldn't happen again? Of course it could. Just because it had happened once the probability of it happening again wouldn't be reduced if she were in the wrong place at the wrong time again.

*

"At first it was, 'It's your money' all the time. It was difficult for him to know how to react to it as well. Anyway, I was saying, 'No, it's our money,' because I wanted him to feel secure about it and if he felt secure about it then I thought we might be able to use it more happily and feel better about it."

Anne looked at her watch, noting the time; he should be home in twenty minutes as he finished at one that day.

"Carry on, I can guess what's coming."

"Sorry, I was just thinking about when Neil gets home. Will you be okay with him?"

"Oh yes, I don't have a problem with him personally, don't worry about that. So what's the position about the money now?"

"Well, all of a sudden I knew what I wanted to do with that money. I wanted to buy a place of my own, or our own or whatever. I could use the money as the deposit. I just want somewhere that's mine, not a stinky capitalist landlord's."

She smiled at her own, self-parodying voice. "So I thought we could get a decent flat around here or even out towards Valerie's where it's a bit nicer. The best thing, I thought, would be to put six thousand down as a deposit and then spend the other four on the solicitor's fees and all that crap and then spend what's left on furniture. Well, at first, that seemed like a great idea as far as Neil was concerned until, after it bothered me for a few days, I said we'd have a sixty-forty split on the flat. Do you think that's so awful?"

Jeanette shook her head and, before she could answer, Anne went on, "He hit the roof. Said that it wasn't fair because if we split up he could walk away with nothing. Charming, eh?"

"Well, he wouldn't bloody well be in with a chance of getting the mortgage in the first place if you weren't prepared to put all that money up."

"Well, exactly. Then, to make it worse, he came out with all this rubbish about how I might get another fifteen thousand from the CICB and then I'd be well off and he'd have nothing, if I had that attitude."

"Christ, he takes some beating, Anne. I'd be bloody careful if I were you."

"Well I don't know what to do. I know that I want a place I own, and things are getting a bit better between us. We've even actually got it together properly a few times lately, which is the first time since before the trial. The thing is he was good to me, at first, and he has helped me in some ways."

"And he needs you, more than anything?"

"Well, yes, I suppose so. But that's not all of it. Perhaps he just needs a chance. Anyway, that's not the end of it. I let the subject drop for a few days and in the meantime we're getting all these details through about flats around here. Yesterday I mentioned it again and said that if we told anyone else about it, they'd say it was fair because if we do split up it'll only be for one reason: that he can't stop drinking. Do you think I went too far to actually say that?"

"No, not really. I mean it's fairly blunt, but then again it's pretty much true."

"Well, his retort to that was to kick the chair as he got up and then to kick the speaker of the stereo. You won't believe the next bit – he then said, 'Don't you think I've suffered too? I have and I deserve some of that money.'"

"Good God, I tell you, Anne, you need to be careful with him. That money is yours as a kind of cushion or whatever you want to call it. Anyway, he's got no right to speak to you like that."

Anne knew the unspoken part of what Jeanette said: astonishment that Anne could let him get away with speaking to her like that. Anne looked at Jeanette, envying her certainty, her sureness about herself and her feelings. Anne admired her and suddenly had a great need to tell her everything and have her absolve and reassure her.

"And he's not the only one who's said something you wouldn't believe. Valerie came over to see me last week. Well, her eyes positively sparkled when I told her about the money. She said, 'You're such a lucky girl' and hugged me!"

Jeanette laughed with a mixture of amusement and disbelief, "Only your sister!"

"It's all right to laugh, it does me good to take the piss out of everything. But wait, I've saved the best one till last."

Jeanette closed her eyes in mock incredulity, "Go on, Anne, shock me. Not Liz or someone like that?"

"No, not Liz, she understands. You know this monkey temp job I've got? Well, as I said to you, I told them in one sentence, with that magical, explanatory word in it that doesn't really explain anything," Jeanette nodded for her to carry on. "Well, obviously I never learn with people as it's always a case of too much too soon with people I let in and tell things to. Well, I told Donna, the supervisor, that I'd got that money and she actually looked jealous and then said, 'Tell me, if you'd known you were going to get that much would you change what happened now?' I could've killed her! I was so upset that another woman could've said that to me."

"You've got to watch whom you tell things to. Your problem is that you always tell everyone everything. But with things like this, people are saying awful things to you, whether it's because they don't realise the enormity of it, or because you're sitting there looking perfectly normal so they don't believe it was that bad, I don't know."

"You're exactly right, you know. People who don't know me very well don't quite believe it happened. Perhaps they think I'm a bullshitter or an attention-seeker or something. This same prat Donna then announced to me the next day that she'd had a dream the previous night about 'a serial killer'. What does she do, dream in American film plots? Anyway, she then said that this man chased her up the stairs and she had to, wait for it... jump out of the bedroom window to escape him. Can you believe she looked me in the eyes and said that?"

"Oh Anne, she's a complete idiot. It sounds to me like she finds it all exciting because she's seen too much TV and hasn't a clue what reality is. People just don't live in the real world, do they?"

"I know, I think I've learned my lesson now. All I told her was, that one word, 'rape' by some stranger in the street who grabbed me and that I'd got away by jumping out of the window of his flat, three storeys up." She paused then, lighting a cigarette, with her hand cupped round the flame, "I don't know, perhaps that does sound too farfetched, what do you think?"

She laughed with a smile that she knew hadn't reached her eyes. She looked at her watch, the hollow laughter disappearing as she realised that it was almost half past one.

"He should've been home by a quarter past, twenty past at the latest. Oh shit, I think he's doing it again: he's never late now."

"Why would he crack today Anne after... how many weeks of not touching it?"

"I don't know. But I feel it, I really feel it. I know as surely as if he were in front of me."

Despite what Anne had said to Jeanette that day, there was another strain of thought in her mind: a part of her wanted to trust him, wanted to believe that this time he could carry on. She wanted to love him and give them a secure life together, by having their own place. But she'd been let down too many times to voice her slight flicker of hope to herself, let alone anyone else. It was only as the minutes ticked by and he was almost an hour late that she saw for definite that slowly, slowly she'd been starting to believe in him again, just slightly, but the belief had been growing, without her even realising it.

It seemed to her as if the omnipotent being who was set against her had waited, waited until a tiny glimmer of hope appeared before, once again, it was stamped out – finally and irrevocably.

Jeanette took her to Valerie's house. She'd insisted, enraged when Neil had walked round the side of the house, fiddling clumsily and bad-temperedly with the latch of the gate. As he reached out like a blind man grasping for the back door handle, he turned his head around, jerkily, to look to where Anne and Jeanette sat, watching him silently. He shot them a look of venom, swung round and went in through the back door, slamming it behind him.

Neither spoke for a second, then Jeanette looked at Anne to see her eyes brimming with tears.

"Come on, I can't watch you putting up with this. It's a year later for Christ's sake and you're in exactly the same position. He's still walking all over you. He's selfish and childish and he's pulling you right down. I can see it each time I come here and your spirit's broken more. You deserve better than him and if you don't move now, it'll be too late. Please let me get you out of here, I can't go back to London and leave you with this. He's dangerous, he's full of hatred, for you, for everyone. I could see it in his eyes."

Anne agreed to go, thankful now to be able to obey someone else's command, after all these months of determinedly sticking with him despite what everyone around her had advised her to do. She saw that he'd done it today to teach her a lesson about the money and what he saw as her greed over it. He'd shown her he was still in control and he'd chosen to do it on a day when he could with a clear conscience hand the responsibility of looking after her, of being with her, over to someone else while he became oblivious of himself and life.

After hearing no sound from inside the house for a while, they both went in. Anne looked at Neil, face down and spreadeagled, fully clothed, on the bed. She packed. She packed the two cases they had, a vanity case and a holdall, more than she'd ever taken before. After her initial tears in the garden, which had barely spilled over, she felt calm and deadened again. She packed as much as she could, some small lacquered jewellery boxes; an ugly, discoloured, brown bear from her childhood that always lay, unnoticed, next to the bedhead. She also packed the building society book, holding it up for Jeanette to see, "Mustn't forget this bone of contention, must I?"

She knew it was different this time. She knew that now, only hours after planning to buy a flat with him, that she was leaving Neil for the last time. The cord that painfully linked them together had to be cut. Perhaps it took her to try to do something, to try to make a move to free herself from her bondage of pain, fear and inertia in order to see that first she must free herself from him.

Jeanette didn't go into Valerie's house, but sat in the car until Anne came back down the neat, well-cared for pathway to say that yes, it was okay, she could stay. They unloaded the cases and bags and both carried them to the open front door in the late afternoon sun. They set them down in the porchway and turned to face each other. Anne could see Fiona at the window, eating a bar of chocolate and looking out pensively at Anne, Jeanette and the cases before them. Anne waved to her, she immediately smiled and came away from the window to appear quickly at the door.

"I'll leave you to it then. It's the right thing to do, you know, the only thing you can do really."

"I know, thanks."

"Give me a ring sooner rather than later," Jeanette added, "and let me know what's going on."

"Yes I will, I promise. Thanks again."

She left, and Anne went inside with Fiona, who happily slipped her hand into Anne's as they went into the kitchen, where Valerie was waiting.

"I thought it would come to this, I've been expecting it for ages now."

The words were what Anne expected from Valerie, but the tone wasn't. She walked over to Anne and hugged her, then held her in her arms slightly away from her and looked into her face, saying, "You are my little sister, you know, no matter what happens, and I care about you. I wish you'd turned to me earlier, I've been waiting for you to."

The softness of Valerie's voice and her words almost broke Anne, then the sound of Fiona's voice behind her rang out, "Auntie Anne, Auntie Anne, are you staying to dinner?"

"Yes, she is, for lots of dinners probably," Valerie answered and moved away. The moment passed, Anne breathed deeply and swallowed her tears: she'd be all right.

Later, she told Valerie everything. She held no part of the story back to save Neil, or herself, embarrassment. She told of him threatening to jump out of the window, all those months ago, unless she gave him money. She told her that he'd probably been an alcoholic for two years, possibly more, it was difficult to place the time exactly. She related the three day binge during the trial and how, once more, he'd gone off the rails today. She tried to explain to her sister the self-abnegation and depravity he sank to and wallowed in and the self-hatred he felt afterwards. Valerie listened intently but her face was set. When Anne tried to explain what she knew of the vicious circle of destruction he was caught in, she dismissed it with a shake of her head, interrupting: saying everyone had freedom of choice and that it was only through his own selfishness that he carried on. Valerie said she'd seen for the last couple of years how Neil tried to pull Anne down with him, how he made her dependent on his weakness, until her world was narrowed down to include only himself.

Anne knew it was all true to a certain extent but she still pitied him – she knew that he didn't want to be as he was and that the bad, weak parts of him were as if exercised by a third force, not controlled or controllable by him: rather by a demon of determinism that had predisposed him to be as he was. She had people to turn to but he had only her.

"But why, Anne, ask yourself that. It's because his mother, his brothers and sisters, friends, whoever, have all had enough of him and his self-pity. He uses people until he can't get away with it any more. Don't worry too much, he's a survivor all right, Andy said that from the start about him. Just as soon as he realises he's had it with you and your sympathy has run out, he'll move straight on to someone else, you wait and see. In the meantime," she carried on, "if you show any weakness towards him he'll keep on chipping and chipping away at you to get you back."

Anne saw the truth in what she said, but she also knew her to be too black and white, too hard. Then again Valerie was saying all this for a purpose: now she had Anne in her house, away from him, and prepared to open her mind to the truth about Neil, she was prepared to do all she could to make sure Anne didn't go back. Anne, for her part, knew she was separating herself further from Neil by opening up so completely to Valerie: it was one more irrevocable step towards her freedom from him.

This at least gave her a purpose, the purpose she'd lost after the court case finished. She also wanted to do something definite, to campaign or write about the injustices of rape trials and reveal the truth about the nature of rape itself: the condoning by society of what fuels it – the videos, magazines, advertising, attitudes, everything. It was so obvious and so much part of life that no one seemed to see it at all. She knew she'd never be able to do anything truly constructive while she was with him. Her mind oscillated between her preoccupation with Neil and these other thoughts. At the minute, she was still too close to it all and too absorbed with the mess of her life to even unravel her thoughts properly, let alone act. These plans, aims, hopes, however she thought of them, were to be kept for another time when, she thought wistfully, her life would be stable and uniform within its secure, uninterrupted routine and she could then try, somehow, to make a difference to a world that didn't seem to recognise the war it waged against its womankind. But this, Anne knew, would never happen while she was with Neil.

Anne carried on going to work in Croydon, catching the train from Epsom Station each morning. On the Monday she walked purposely down the prestigious, private road where Valerie and Andy lived, through the town centre, to the station. She avoided the short cut through the park and, more surprisingly, said no to Valerie's offer to drive her to the station. She wanted to do it on her own. The different surroundings, her removal from Lesley and Liz, who'd helped her so many times before, helped her feel that this time was different.

That day at the office, she concentrated on trying not to think of how Neil was passing his day, in his parallel life. She'd gone to Valerie's on the Saturday afternoon and throughout that evening and Sunday had heard nothing from him. He was probably drying out and planning to contact her tonight, after a call to Jeanette to find out where she was. Then he would expect a couple of days' pleading before her return. She actually wanted him to start calling soon, so that these well-worn routines and stages could be passed through, to reach the point where he would believe that things were not going back to the way they were, not this time. Anne was going to go onwards, not back into the loop this time.

She didn't have to wait long, he'd rung by the time she got back to Valerie's that evening. She'd met Andy at the station, he'd arranged to be on the same train from London which stopped at Croydon, so that they could walk back to the house together. He was sympathetic, treating her gently. Anne knew he wouldn't be surprised if she went back.

He phoned again, while they ate their dinner. Anne answered.

"I'm sorry." He stopped after this sign of contrition. His breathing was heavy at the other end of the line as she listened, and she could sense the hysteria behind his words.

"She isn't going to let you come back, is she?" He carried on, his voice rising.

"Don't be so bloody stupid. It's you who's blown it, you can't blame it on someone else. I'll stay here as long as it takes me to get my act together and get my courage up to get somewhere of my own."

"So you're going to buy a flat on your own, are you?"

"That's pretty unimportant, isn't it? It doesn't matter to you whether I buy one or rent one, does it? The point is I've taken all I want from our place and I'm not coming back."

His mounting anger dropped immediately. "I'm in trouble, Anne, real trouble. I don't know what happened the other day. It's just, well, I've been fighting it for weeks now and I just couldn't do it any longer. I couldn't..." his voice became a squeal. "I tell you, I tried."

"Okay, calm down. I'm not going to argue about it, but you can't expect me to come back again, and I'm not going to, so that's it."

He started to cry, "I haven't drank all day, promise," he sobbed. "It didn't last long, I'd stopped by Sunday evening and as soon as I got straight I phoned you. Please."

"What about your job? Have you got another week's compassionate leave, like after the trial?" She knew she was making it worse, but she didn't stop herself.

"I think I've lost the job," he said in a quiet voice, "well, I will have by now because I haven't phoned them and I should've been in for two early shifts today and yesterday."

"Well, I suggest you phone them and see if you can hang on to your job, you idiot!"

Valerie had appeared in the hallway, hearing the last of the conversation. "Don't ask him anything, it's nothing to do with you now," she mouthed, whispering the words. She mimed the action of putting the receiver down and then went back to Andy, the children and the news.

"Please Anne, I need help. Come and help me and I'll go to the doctor's and see if I can get helped off this fucking drug."

"You go to the doctor, get sorted out. It's up to you, I've never been able to help you anyway, have I? I think I just make it worse. I have to go, so take my advice and go to the doctor tomorrow. For yourself, not for me." She clicked the receiver down.

The phone rang almost immediately, as she walked away from it.

"Pull it out of the socket," Valerie called from the other room. She did.

*

In less than a week's time it would be exactly a year. Anne began to realise that time would carry on, ticking by, on and on, putting first a year, then two, then maybe five or ten between her and what had happened to her. She couldn't affect it, couldn't speed it up, it happened ceaselessly, whether she did something to help herself or nothing at all. And it would get easier, she was beginning to see that.

For the last few days Neil had phoned continually in the evenings. He obviously hadn't been able to remember where she worked or he would have phoned her there too – or perhaps he was beyond that much logical thought, she didn't know.

After that first night when he'd phoned, he'd been drunk again. The next night he'd just said "hello" when Anne answered and then sighed deeply. Anne, with growing detachment, recognised this too. Instead of being good to get her back, he was trying to get attention by being bad. Again she'd pulled the plug of the phone out of the wall, after hanging up. He'd made no sense at all.

The next day she got a redirected letter which was crested the House of Commons: a thick manila envelope. Joan Marshall had answered her again. Neil's handwriting, shaky and slanted, had written Valerie's address on the front. The letter thanked her for hers and sympathised with her. She said she would always campaign both for women's rights and to make the law more lenient for women who had already suffered so much. She applauded Anne's belief in the damage of videos and magazines, especially on already unbalanced minds and said that cases like hers helped herself and other MPs in their efforts to get the law to recognise the damage they can do. She ended the letter by advising Anne to go to Rape Crisis to discuss her fears and thoughts and then said to write again if she needed to.

Anne went straight upstairs with the letter, read and reread it. She'd hoped for more. But what more could she say? What more could she do than acknowledge her state and agree with what she said? Maybe that was enough anyway. Maybe that was all she needed from a public figure like her. This woman had been campaigning; lifting down the magazines at WH Smith, asking, "Are you happy to sell these?" opening up the pages for all to see and be humiliated by, long before Anne had been raped. Anne knew that her beliefs were right, her connections of cause and effect hit the mark and that Joan Marshall shared them. That was enough: her actions, her rage and anger were endorsed.

She thought briefly about Rape Crisis again. Could it work? Then she imagined the horror of talking to a whole group of women with shared experiences, going away, filled with more hideous images, not less. Or talking though the whole episode of events again, step by step, as she had with Jackie, the psychiatrist, her sisters and friends – no. She'd been through that stage, she didn't ever want to have to say it all again, she didn't have to, she'd said it enough times now. If that meant that it would always be buried and unresolved then she'd just have to cope with that too – otherwise what resolution could there be?

*

A year to the day. Valerie and Anne, Fiona and Trevor went to Wisley Gardens, "Somewhere sane and tranquil for you," Valerie said. Anne had finished the temping job the previous Friday and said to the agency she wanted a week off for nothing could have induced her to go into Croydon that day of the year. The day was heavy and humid, the sun coming out from behind the clouds in great bursts of light, giving tremendous heat, and for the rest of the time the dull warmth was everywhere.

"I don't think I could've coped with this day if I hadn't left him, you know. It's as if this last year would've all been for nothing unless I was at least heading for something positive. For some reason it's as if it's all connected: what happened to me and my relationship with Neil. Strange, really."

"Well, not that strange, when you think that between the two of them they've almost cracked you up. What happened to you compounded the misery that Neil was already putting you through. Something had to give or change or you would've snapped eventually."

"Do you think he will get better?"

"I don't know, I don't even know how much he wants to get better. He's weak and I think he needs to start being strong for himself now, if he's to stamp it out. What he doesn't need is someone being strong for him. That's probably part of the reason he allowed himself to fall apart in the first place."

Anne hesitated. She had been going to question whether he actually 'allowed' himself to go under in the first place, but decided against it. She didn't want to disagree with Valerie now and she wasn't sure enough of what she thought about him in her own mind to actually reason it out.

He was in hospital, that much had been achieved. In the same psychiatric hospital that Anne had been to see Doctor Rye. Valerie and she walked on, and the children had run on ahead, dashing in and out of the rows of near perfect, symmetrical flowers and plants.

She'd seen him yesterday. Against Valerie and Andy's advice. But they took her there. She'd walked up the long avenue to the hospital alone as Valerie drove on. It was lunchtime, she'd only be an hour or so, she thought, so she could get herself back to Epsom on the train. Another test for her, pushing herself further, getting the train when it wasn't peak time, therefore not so many people around. She'd had to change carriages at Ewell East Station as it turned out, and the train had been an old one with closed carriages, and at the station the women to whom she'd sat close for security had got off and she could only see one other head, much further down the aisle, a man's. No one else had got on there so, blood pounding in her ears, she'd alighted and run down to the next carriage, able to check the people in it and get on just before the train pulled away.

Neil had met her before she reached the hospital building, as he'd been sitting next to the driveway, on the lawn, under an impressive plane tree, on a wrought iron seat. She'd first noticed him move out of the side of her eye because he sprang up when he saw her. He looked better than she'd feared, he was clean-shaven and in clean clothes, but his eyes were hollow and his face thin.

The last couple of days had been horrific. When he'd managed to get beyond Valerie or Andy to speak to Anne, he'd just demanded drunkenly that she come home, otherwise he'd kill himself. At first she'd been angry: how could he thrust that responsibility on her? Then she'd heard the urgency, the plea in his shrieking voice and known that he was desperate. She'd phoned their GP, Doctor Ahmed, against Valerie's advice, and, having got past the receptionist, told her what was happening. She took Anne's assertions that he would kill himself seriously, perhaps because she knew Anne quite well by now and, through her, had been aware of Neil's condition.

She'd gone to see him that day and got him to agree to go to the hospital. "He's only going because I told him, again and again, that you're not coming back," she told Anne later. "That's his obsession: getting you back."

Tears had coursed down Anne's face as she'd listened to her. She felt responsible for him, responsible and full of pity for him, as if he were a small dependent animal, or a child. That's not love, she'd told herself afterwards.

Sitting next to him now she knew it wasn't love. She'd agreed to see him because he'd begged her to on the phone, describing how awful it was, how he was on a course of beta blockers and had three counselling sessions a day, programmed for the next week. Now she was with him she just wanted to hear him out and then leave with a clear conscience: to hear that he was being helped, that he had a fighting chance if he wanted to beat drink. She wanted to find out that the responsibility for him had become someone else's. She didn't want to be dragged back to him and as he spoke her fear receded, it wasn't the same: she was free of him.

She saw Doctor Rye walk across the lawns opposite as she sat with him and the image of him playing with the elastic band came into her mind. How things changed.

"The doctor asked me to list, from one to ten, the most frightening things I could think of," Neil had been saying. "Number one was to be the most frightening thing I'd have to do that I could think of. Well, my number one was getting on a train to London and then being in the middle of that hellhole." His face had become contorted and ugly as he'd said this. Then looking round at her and meeting her gaze directly for the first time, he'd said, "So I can't be blamed for what happened at the Old Bailey, can I? It's my biggest fear in the world."

"I'm not blaming you any more," she answered in a resigned, quiet voice, thinking, we all have our own fears and have to live with them, not just you. She knew he needed her absolution, so she gave it.

"Stick at this treatment, Neil, for your own sake. I blame you for nothing now. We both need to take control of our own lives, separately. You're a good person and you tried your best, you're just sick and that's not your fault, so thank God you're getting help now."

"I love you Anne."

She'd known he would say it, as if it were an answer to everything. It wasn't, not for them.

She'd left him shortly afterwards, rejecting his attempts to kiss her. "No, I don't want that, and I won't, not ever again, Neil, we've got to get that straight."

"Will you come and see me again?"

This was the part she'd been bracing herself for. "I'm going to Rhodes for a fortnight with Liz." She'd added, "Next weekend." Her body had tensed, as if for attack.

"You bitch, you fucking bitch!" He'd spat the words at her.

"Don't please, don't speak to me like that." Her face was crumpling, but she'd not known whether from fear or pain.

She'd turned to walk away. After a dozen or so steps she'd heard him starting to run behind her. She'd swung round fully to face him, her heart pounding. "Don't run like that. Are you trying to frighten me to death?" Her voice had become raised now as she felt the whole situation slip out of her control.

"I'm stuck in here, in a bloody lunatic asylum, and you're going to Greece. You bitch." He'd turned and walked away and then marched back up to where she still stood, afraid to move. His voice had become quiet now. "Please don't go."

"I'm going. I need to get away. I only decided it yesterday. I asked Liz and she wants to go too. I deserve a break, surely you can see that?" He'd rolled his eyes theatrically and she'd known what he would say next. She'd anticipated him. "It isn't my fault you're here, just as it isn't your fault what happened to me. I'm not doing it to spite you, you know, I'm doing it because I'm about to snap."

"Yes, I see that, I'm sorry. Can I phone you when you get back?"

"Just get better. I'll have to go, Valerie's waiting," she'd lied and could see by Neil's face that he hadn't considered how she'd got to the hospital, or how she was getting home.

They'd separated, he became calmer about her going away but Anne knew that it was only a different tactic in order to spin out the hope that she might come back to him when she returned.

*

Valerie and Anne walked on.

"I'm glad we did this today," Anne said as she watched Fiona come towards them, hands cupped around a frog. Trevor was rushing up behind her with a butterfly in his, to rival his sister for their attention.

Anne began to feel a calmness spread over her. It were as if she were starting to pass through the sheet of glass that had separated her from the ordinary life around her. She'd seen it all go on around her, happily for her family and some of her friends, yet it had always excluded her. She had seen and been surrounded by these lives, but had not been able to join in.

Now, for the first time in a year, she felt she was doing something that might eventually result in her being able to join in with life. Step by step she would move towards the future: she knew with certainty now that she would take no more backward steps. Hope lay in front of her. Not a guaranteed happiness, but some hope at least, some belief that in this world, under the same sky as she moved now, people could be happy, could be autonomous and secure, could do what they wanted without being continually thwarted. And, more than any other hope, there was the hope that it would never happen again.